GOOD DEED
BAD DEED

A NOVEL MYSTERY

Marcia Morgan

TABLE OF CONTENTS

CHAPTER ONE

Ben had agreed to the location under protest, the dismal weather adding to his aggravation. Too much noise combined with the smell of beer and damp clothing made him wonder why his agent had picked this place for a meeting. A decent interview in this pub was an unrealistic expectation. The environment annoyed him, and given that the interview was to be conducted by a female, all he could seem to think about were the three things he disliked most about women in general. Number one would always be a woman who shows up late. Next is the woman who shows up right on time and turns out to be a terminal bore. Last, but not least, is the woman who seems afraid to eat anything that isn't green. Not to say that Ben disliked women, quite the contrary. His tastes had been formed through extensive experience with the fairer sex.

He sat at the cluttered bar, sipping at a pint of ale while mentally kicking himself for agreeing to the meeting. He scanned the crowd with a rather blank expression until his attention was drawn to a scruffy-looking man who approached and sidled up to the bar. He crowded another patron aside and stood next to Ben, who noticed the damp musty smell of the wool coat he was wearing. The man removed his cap, exposing a balding pate framed with a fringe of stringy brown hair. He turned toward Ben and raised his chin in a gesture of acknowledgement. The barman took his order and soon returned with a pint of stout. The man laid the book he had been holding on the bar then pulled a cell phone out of his pocket, asking the barman for a napkin to dry it off. Just then it rang. The man answered, listened, and hung up without saying another word. He managed one long gulp of his beer, paused before taking a final swig, paid and made a quick exit.

Ben's scrutiny of the man had helped pass the time, but for some reason, he found the man's actions and his demeanor rather sinister. He blamed the impression on his habit of looking for a story in the minutia of life. Ben noticed that the man had forgotten the soggy book, so he picked it up and saw that it was a London pub guide. He thumbed through it and began to read to himself: *The English pub has always been an institution, a gathering place— a group of second family.* He observed the crowd and concluded that it had evolved into a venue that provides opportunities to seek social interaction. *That's a polite way to put it,* he thought.

* * *

The patter of light rain on the taxi windows made Ana wish more for a novel and a glass of Cabernet by the fire than for an arranged meeting in a pub with a no-doubt egotistical author. There were three things she couldn't abide in men. A man who arrives too early topped her list. No matter how punctual she may be, she appears to be late. Second is the man who arrives late, leaving her to imagine she has been stood up. Running a close third would be a man who, less than halfway through the evening, makes it clear that he knows they've connected and would she like to go somewhere private. If Ana were to list her relationships, even the temporarily successful ones, there would be few entries. Months ago she had declared a moratorium on dating and taken refuge in her decision.

The taxi pulled up in front of her destination in Kings Cross. Ana was a bit anxious about the whole thing and hesitated before stepping out into the unseasonably drizzly night, leaving her borrowed umbrella behind. She looked down the dark and dingy cobbled alley in front of her and noticed lighted windows. Still confused, she turned back toward the taxi, shrugging in doubt and asking the driver whether that location could possibly house a trendy gastropub. He rolled down the window and confirmed he had delivered her to the right address, explaining that what was once a red-light district was now an upscale area. She thanked him and turned back toward her destination. As he sped away she remembered the umbrella and scolded herself for being so distracted. *Nothing to do about it now,* she thought, and then looked skyward, feeling the touch of light rain on her face.

Reassured by the appearance of a young couple walking toward her, Ana proceeded down the alley slowly, navigating through the puddles, trying to save the heels of her boots from the cobblestones, until she reached the lights and noise. She saw the establishment's sign and leaned forward to peer through the smudged glass windows at the animated faces of people enjoying each other. *What would they all be doing without alcohol to loosen the tongue,* she thought. Returning to the matter at hand, she took a minute to adopt her professional stance before walking toward the entrance.

* * *

Ben was bored with waiting and swiveled on his barstool to face the crowd. He was an inveterate people watcher, prone to zero in on a particular face and proceed to create their back-story. As he surveyed the crowd his eyes fixed on the doors. He half-wished that she would be late so he could just get out of there, grab a cab, and go home to his bed, book, and bottle of Scotch.

The rain had formed a puddle at the entrance, and as Ana pushed through the swinging door, one of her boot-clad feet slipped in the wetness. She stumbled in, barely staying upright. Several male patrons jumped up to catch her, but she managed to straighten up, pausing to adjust her raincoat before checking the crowd for the man she was supposed to meet. Instinctively Ben had jumped from his stool to assist, but was too far away to make contact. However, he was close enough to see her quite well. He focused first on her dark wavy hair, glistening from the mist and slightly askew over one of her eyes. The raincoat she wore was the color of a tropical sea and complimented her olive skin. Ben glanced at his watch and realized that the appointed time for the arranged meeting had come and passed. At first it didn't occur to him that this damp vision of beauty and clumsiness could be the person for whom he was waiting.

Ana walked further into the crowded room and continued to scan the crowd. Her expression was serious, her brow lightly furrowed in contemplation of an aborted opportunity to carry out the assignment. She was meant to interview Benedict Alexander McKinnon, the current rave author of travel fiction. Her eyes fixed on a tall man standing very still at the bar, looking her way with a rather sly smile on his face and a pint in one hand. He was wearing jeans, a deep blue turtleneck sweater, and a well-worn leather jacket. It didn't occur to her that this could be the man. She had expected him to be a professorial type: horn-rimmed glasses, an old tweed sport coat, and the look of being slightly underfed. This was definitely not the case. He was built for his height, with broad shoulders and what she could see of a trim waistline. His thick hair was dark auburn, slightly long and combed straight back from his handsome, angular face. She admonished herself when wishing he would turn around and lean on the bar, proving that he looked just as good from the back. She came closer, and when they made eye contact she could see that his eyes were blue, the color of his sweater making them all the more noticeable.

Ana's impulse was to engage him, and she went with it. She approached him slowly, and when they were face to face, she cocked her head slightly and said, "I'm not sure why, but I have a feeling you're the man I'm supposed to meet for an interview. If not, apologies."

Ben paused before answering, looking her up and down discreetly before their eyes met again. "I think I'm the right guy. And with the entrance you made, I sure couldn't miss you." Ana looked down, still feeling a little flustered by her entrance. "Glad you didn't hurt yourself. We would have missed our appointment," he said.

She looked up at him, trying to think of what to say next. His smile lit up his whole face, and having once again replayed her entrance in his mind, he was trying very hard not to chuckle. Ana sensed this, but still had difficulty looking away from him.

The din of the crowd enjoying their evening in the pub made conversation difficult. Ben disliked having to talk loud into a woman's face, so he suggested they look for a relatively quiet corner to conduct their business. The dread and annoyance he had felt while in limbo at the bar, waiting for whom he expected to be a brash journalist with a masculine edge, faded quickly when he caught sight of the mass of hair, the dark searching eyes and embarrassed expression of the woman who stumbled in from the rain.

Ben placed his hand lightly on the small of Ana's back as they jockeyed through the crowd. She became very aware of his touch, and liked it, but knew it was just what a gentleman does rather automatically when guiding a woman forward. They saw a small corner table being vacated and hurried to lay claim. Ben had noticed her walk and had always liked that certain natural sway some women have, usually when wearing high heels. He was very partial to women in heels.

Once at the table she began to remove her raincoat. Ben assisted and slid it from her arms, quickly noticing the way her waist tapered into very feminine hips. She was dressed in a red cashmere sweater and gray wool slacks. He could see they were slightly damp at the cuff, and that her boots had suffered from the puddles on the sidewalk. She unwrapped the printed silk scarf from her neck and tied it on the handle of her bag. Long gold hoops hung from her ears, and as she turned to sit, he caught a faint whiff of her very pleasant scent.

"Are you cold?" he asked. "I can see you've done battle with the weather tonight."

"I had to wait in front of my hotel for a cab, then ended up having to walk a bit before I could catch one. My hotel doesn't have enough stars to warrant a doorman to do that sort of thing for guests."

"I'm sorry this ended up being scheduled on such a nasty night. I don't want you to come down with something over this. If you feel chilled, you should get back to your hotel and change. We can reschedule. I'm anti-interview, but with what you went through to get your assignment done, I'm feeling more cooperative than usual."

"That's lucky for me then," Ana said, hoping she might be part of the reason for his cooperative mood.

"I really didn't think being published would have so much 'peripheral responsibility,'" he said, making air-quotes with his fingers.

"Being published is one thing, but when you have two best-sellers in a row, and rumors abound that a third book is in the works, the 'peripherals' escalate. But I promise to make this as painless as possible." Ana felt compelled to look deeper into his eyes, to be sucked into those whirlpools of ocean blue and learn instantly who this man was at his core. *Those eyes could get a girl into serious trouble,* she thought.

The desire astonished her, but it was quickly countered by the feeling that she was entering dangerous territory and should temper herself. "Don't worry about me being a little worse for wear due to the rain. I'm relatively dry, all but my boots." She leaned sideways, looked down at them and said, "They don't look too bad. And you've basically given me your evening. You could have been home, wherever that is, reading by the fire with your trusty retriever sleeping at your feet and a whiskey on your side table."

"Wait just a minute! Sounds like you're describing an old man's evening. How old do you think I am?" Ben sat back, put his hands on the edge of the table, and made a pretense of being annoyed.

"Oh gosh. Sorry. No, not old at all. It was just a picture that came into my head. Frankly, it looked like a scenario I would enjoy, especially on a night like this. I think your age is a matter of record, somewhere, but I didn't research that fact ahead of time because to me it isn't that relevant. It's the work that interests me."

"Well, since you covered yourself so well on that subject, I'll tell you. I'm thirty-nine for another two months. Then I plan to have the proverbial mid-life crisis, maybe a few years early, and move to an island where I'll live in seclusion and produce absolutely nothing."

"Wouldn't your scenario require a 'comely island girl' to keep you company?" As soon as the words were said, she realized it was flirting and ordered herself to rein it in.

"Hmmm. I hadn't considered that part of it." Ben paused for a moment, unable to avoid the picture in his mind of Ana filling the role of comely island girl. He sighed and continued. "Maybe I should rethink the seclusion part. Maybe a sportier car would do the trick." His thoughts seemed out of control. Now he envisioned Ana beside him in that sports car, her abundant hair blowing wildly, her laughter increasing in tandem with the car's speed. He quickly returned to the present and said, "I hope the last bit was off the record."

"Oh yes. We haven't even started yet and it's nice to keep it casual for a while. I won't quote you on anything until I tell you that I'm officially interviewing. And I'll be asking you if you mind my using a tape recorder … just for the purpose of complete accuracy."

"I understand that's the way it's done now. I'll just have to remember to 'edit' before the fact, not after. But I still don't see myself as interesting enough for a printed interview. It's my characters people must like … or a plot that takes them to places they may never see. I think it's wise to create a story line that appeals to a variety of people, and sometimes, to their fantasies of one kind or another."

"Well that sounded like a good quote, but since we're still in neutral mode here, do your best to remember it when the time comes. And before we become further acquainted, or whatever we're doing here, I would love a brandy to warm body and soul."

Ben leaned back against the leather booth, looked up at the ceiling and shook his head. "Apologies for the bad manners. I was caught up in our conversation once we sat down, and I didn't even think about it. We'll get you a brandy, but I think I'll just stick to beer."

He caught the waiter's eye and ordered warm brandy for Ana, and a sleeve of ale for himself. In spite of the pub being crowded, the service was fast, and soon the drinks were placed before them, along with a bowl of pretzels. Ana held the warm snifter with both palms and brought it to her mouth as if it were a bowl of café-au-lait. She let it barely touch her lips, enjoying the warmth and the brandy's rich aroma. Flickering light from the candle on the table reflected onto the brandy-kissed lips of her partially open mouth. Ben rather shocked himself with his sudden desire to lick the brandy from those perfect lips and transfer it to her mouth with his tongue. He also felt the need to shake such libidinous thoughts from his head and get a grip on reality. All he could do was to shut his eyes tightly for a minute and try to will away the images.

Unaware of his wishful thinking, Ana kept her mouth near the rim of the glass and looked squarely at him. She didn't know what the expression on his face or the tightly closed eyes were saying, but it seemed as though something had disturbed him. She was sure she had caused no offense during their conversation, so she let her curiosity slide and continued to sip the brandy. She would never have guessed that with each sip, Ben would be both plagued and pleasured by his vision of licking and sucking the brandy from her lips and letting his tongue dance with hers in passionate kisses. He couldn't remember if there had ever been a time when a woman had affected him so quickly, or had made him feel so strongly those sensual preludes to hot sex.

Then he was struck by the fact that he had forgotten her name, or maybe it had never been mentioned. But it was strange that she hadn't offered him her card. He could only assume that in terms of purpose, she was legitimate. The arrangements had been made weeks ago, and to tell the truth, his lack of enthusiasm had caused a lack of attention to what was being said. All he had managed to remember was time, date, location, and that a woman would conduct the interview. This additional lapse in manners disturbed him further. The last thing he wanted was to ask her to identify herself. It would be humiliating, and he was bound to lose status in her eyes. Any status he may have gained with her was an unknown, but he wanted to hold onto it and was sure this wouldn't help. He had to ask himself why he cared about her opinion and had to admit that he did care. That was another part to the mystery of why this woman had unknowingly cast a spell on him.

Ana reached across the table and touched Ben's arm lightly. "You seem to have gone to another planet. I could hear the wheels turning. I guess you didn't hear me."

"I'm sorry. I can be guilty of letting my mind wander at inopportune times. I really didn't mean to be rude." He ran his fingers through his hair self-consciously.

"Is that a common occurrence with writers? Do you 'go off' into a different realm where ideas form and stories are born?"

"Maybe sometimes. This time I think it was to escape the noise. My head is buzzing."

"Understandable. I've had enough too. Think I'll make a quick trip to the ladies' room before we decide when this interview will actually happen. Watch my coat please?"

Ana slid out of her seat and then moved gracefully between the tables until she was out of his sight. As Ben scanned the room he noticed that the scruffy man had returned to the pub. He was seated at a table with another man, and they were deep in what appeared to be a serious and very private conversation. The other man looked to be in his twenties and was dressed in a suit and tie, but in spite of such attire he did not look the part. The scruffy man leaned back in his chair as his companion leaned forward and pounded on the table several times. He rose quickly, grabbed his old wool coat and made another quick exit, this time heading for the men's room. The man in the suit waited for a short while, finishing his beer, then got up and left. By this time, Ben's curiosity was more than piqued, and his imagination had started to work overtime.

There was a long queue for the Ladies, but Ana joined it and waited. She tried to avoid eavesdropping on the friendly conversations of the women lined up against the wall. She noticed an elderly man come out of the men's room and tried to step aside for him as he squeezed by the line of women in the narrow hallway. Another man entered the hallway from the opposite direction, and as he strode by, he very nearly pushed the elderly man against the wall. As he passed Ana, she caught the scent of sweat and damp wool. He went into the Men's and came out rather quickly. He pulled a phone out of his coat pocket and dialed. When the party answered, he spoke in a hushed tone. Even though he was turned away from her, his proximity allowed her to hear his anxious words over the women's banter.

"He's still here. He's drinking at a table. Talking to some woman," he said, turning around to see who might be listening. He paused, waiting for the person on the other end to stop speaking. "Our unwilling associate Mr. Logan hasn't turned out to be very cooperative. I've been talking to him at a table and he got wound up, started banging on it and drawing attention. We need to change our plan. He won't like that, or what's going to happen to him if he causes trouble."

Before he had finished his call, it was finally Ana's turn to enter the restroom. She went in, freshened her hair and makeup, and tried to push what she had overheard out of her mind. After all, there was a handsome man waiting for her, and he probably wondered where she'd gotten to after all this time. Coming out of the restroom she noticed that the man had left the hallway. She didn't understand why his leaving made her feel relieved.

Ana returned to the table, and Ben stood to push in her chair as she sat. She had brushed her hair and applied lipstick. Her cheeks were still rosy from the cold, and Ben became even more taken with her. He pushed the two men from his mind and returned to the matter at hand. "I think we've squeezed all we can from this evening," he said. "Would it work for you if we set up another meeting, maybe tomorrow or the next day?"

"I'm sure we can work out something that's convenient for you. I must admit, my feet are really cold now. I think I'd be smart to get back to the hotel for a warm bath and some sleep."

Without being summoned, Ben's previous train of thought returned. But in this fantasy Ana was languishing in a perfumed bubble bath, surrounded by soft candlelight. Her hair was piled high on her head, and the soothing sounds of Debussy filled the air. Once again he shook himself back to the present, mystified by how she had become the main character in a variety of possible story lines going through his head. It was much simpler than that. He wanted her.

Ana stood and reached for the raincoat Ben had slung onto the back of a vacant chair. He got up quickly and helped her ease into it. She wound the silk scarf loosely around her neck and glanced up at Ben, wondering what would come next. He seemed to be hesitating, and Ana could tell he was thinking ahead, perhaps deciding how to play out the rest of their first meeting. When Ana picked up her handbag and tablet case, obviously anxious to leave, Ben knew he wanted to slow things down.

"We still haven't decided on a time for the 'real' interview. I'm only in London for another three days. Then I'm expected at my parent's country house for a scheduled period of questions and suggestions about my life."

"Well, your tone of voice didn't sound resentful, so I guess you don't mind, or else you're used to it."

"No, they're great. I don't mind their efforts to micro-manage my life. I listen politely and then do as I please. And though they wouldn't admit it, by now they know it goes in one ear and out the other. Actually, I think it's a case of needing a periodic catharsis for all of their secret worries about their children. These few days of 'advising' will last them for months."

Ben's expression softened as he spoke of his parents, and although he wouldn't have guessed, it gained him some points with Ana. As they headed for the door Ben stuffed a generous tip into the jar at the end of the bar, earning him a smile and a nod from the harried bartender. As they started through the doorway, Ben put his arm around Ana's waist. She turned to him with a devilish expression and said, "No worries. I plan to make an exit that's much more graceful than my entrance."

Once outside, they paused under the portico and noticed that the rain had stopped. A chilly breeze carried the scent of wet pavement and an eclectic assortment of aromas from nearby restaurants. The sky was cosmos-dark, and stars peeked through the wisps of gray clouds that remained after the all-day rain.

Ben turned to her and asked, "Are you still cold? I'll need to dash up to the street to get you a cab. Do you want to wait here or come with me?"

"I'm too cold to just stand here and wait. It'll save time if I come with you. Remember, I won't be able to keep up with your long legs. I have to tip toe around the puddles or these boots will be history." Ana looked down and sighed. "They may be already."

"Hold onto my arm for balance. And by the way, what possessed you to wear suede in this weather?" His laugh said that he was teasing, not criticizing.

"I travel light. It's the only pair I brought. Guess we Americans don't know English weather very well. Live and learn." She slid her arm through his and said, "Let's go."

When they had made their way up the alley and reached the street, Ben stepped out to the curb to see if he could spot a cab approaching. He looked both ways and saw that the street was devoid of vehicles. At the same moment, a dark sedan came around the corner, tires screeching, slammed on its brakes, and stopped directly where he stood. A man jumped out, ran around the back of the car and lunged for Ben, startling Ana and causing her to yell for help. The man had a shaved head and wore a frayed leather jacket. He kicked at Ben with muddy motorcycle boots, trying to knock him to the ground. Ben momentarily lost his balance and the man grabbed his arm and violently twisted it behind his back. Ben cried out with pain, but managed to spin around, only to meet his assailant's fist with his face. Ben fell backwards against the car, disoriented. As he rushed forward in another effort to fend off the attack, Ana once again screamed out for help.

In a brief moment of serendipity, a trio of robust-looking young men came lumbering up the alley from the pub. Seeing what was happening, and being full of beer and bravado, they willingly jumped into the fray. The driver of the sedan finally got out to assist in subduing Ben, leaving the engine running for a quick getaway. Ana felt helpless and terrified, but she immediately recognized the driver as the man whose conversation she observed while waiting in line for the restroom. The young men tackled the two assailants. The largest of the three pounced on the man with the shaved head, and the other two took on the other. Both men were pushed to their knees and then face down on the sidewalk, while their arms were held behind them, ready for handcuffs. Ben was still staggering from the blow to his face, but had tried to join the fight. They told him to stay back, and Ana ran to his side.

There wasn't a policeman in sight, so without handcuffs or weapons, they had only two choices: They could stay and continue struggling with their prisoners while a bystander called 999, but the two would continue trying to free themselves; the other choice was just to release them and send them on their way. Evidently, the young threesome felt they had given enough of their time, so they released the assailants, kicked each of them in the 'arse,' all yelling expletives, and watched them jump into their vehicle. As quickly as they had come, they were gone, the dark sedan screeching away on the wet street and disappearing into the night.

The huskiest of the three took Ben squarely by the shoulders and asked, "What in hell did you do to piss them off?" His buddies chuckled and slapped each other on the back. "Are you all right, mate," he asked, his tone now serious. "Do you need an ambulance?"

"Yeah, I'm fine. No ambulance needed," he said, showing a bit of bravado himself. He reached up to wipe the blood from his chin.

Ana wondered if the bravado was for her benefit or theirs. At that moment her only focus was the terror she felt when he was in danger. One of the other young men could see that she was shivering, obviously shaken by the experience. He took her aside and asked if she wanted him to call 999, in spite of what Ben had said. She shook her head no, but then countered with her concern for whether Ben had any significant injuries. The miscreant had hyper-extended his arm, kicked him, and punched him once, hard. Blood was trickling from his nose and the side of his mouth, and his bleeding lip was beginning to swell. The sight of his handsome face in that state brought a lump to Ana's throat. She revisited the need for medical assistance, but again Ben declined. The three men hung around for a short while, high on the excitement and mindful of the possibility of another try to abduct Ben. The resulting noise from the goings on had drawn a small group of curious minded pub-crawlers, and when they crowded in around Ben, Ana warned them off and asked them to disperse. Since there was no more excitement, they quickly lost interest and did as she had asked.

Within a few minutes a cab happened up the street, and in the hope of a fare, began to slow as it approached the group. The three men flagged it down and escorted Ben and Ana into the back seat. Ben asked for their names and addresses and couldn't thank them enough. They declined, and because of the trio's collective youth, tried to make light of what had happened, saying that it was all in a night's work.

As the cab pulled away, the good Samaritans continued their evening, loping down the street, punching each other in the arm, laughing, turning to look at a pair of young women who were passing them by as quickly as possible. Ben and Ana settled back in the seat, both incredulous about what had just happened. He informed the driver that her hotel would be the first stop. Ana replied that she was worried about leaving him on his own, but told the driver the name of her hotel.

"So you don't think I can take care of myself?" Ben sounded a bit offended, and Ana knew he was only half kidding. "You know, that guy took me by surprise. If it had been just one guy, he would be sporting more than fat lip and aching shoulder."

"What in the world would they want with you? It was obvious he wanted to get you into that car. Clearly, it was meant to be an abduction." She paused then added, "They didn't seem to have any use for me. It was definitely about you."

"Thank God for that!" he said, shaking his head and reaching for her hand. Other than the assistance of his arm as she navigated the puddles, this was their first real touch. In spite of the fear and violence of the last hour, his warm hand on hers, the feeling of his fingers closing around it, the squeeze that was just strong enough, all served to send a different kind of adrenaline rush throughout her body. During the quiet moments that followed, Ben's hand remained there, his touch easily taking away Ana's fear.

As the taxi continued to jockey in and out of traffic, they both looked out the windows into the night. The streets were still wet, and reflections from the street lamps and lighted signs sparkled on the pavement. Eventually, Ben spoke. "The whole thing is odd. I may have sold a few books, but I'm a very unlikely candidate to bring a decent ransom." He was quiet for a few minutes then continued to assess the incident. "But the strangest part of it is about the guy who was driving. It was that disheveled man in the wet wool coat. I couldn't forget that smell. He'd sidled up next to me at the bar while I was waiting for you."

"Oh my God... I saw him too, when I went to the restroom. I couldn't help but overhear him talking to someone on his mobile. He was almost mumbling, definitely didn't want to be heard, but I was in line rather close to where he stood, and I did hear part of the conversation. He said that some guy was at a table drinking with some woman. Could that man have been you?" Ben didn't respond, waiting for her to continue. "Then he pushed an older man who was leaving the men's restroom against the wall. Seems our smelly man was trying to get out of the hallway in a hurry. From his expression I thought the guy he pushed was going to go after him, in spite of his age."

"While I was waiting for you to come back, I watched him at a table with some young guy— rugged type. He had his back to me so I didn't see his face. I could tell they were arguing. I'm sure the young guy wasn't the one who grabbed me. But it happened so fast that I didn't see much before whoever it was punched me silly. All I remember is that he smelled of leather and fried fish."

"I got a look at him. His head was shaved, and it had a black tattoo across the top." Ana shuddered, made a sound of disgust, and added, "But it's still not much to go on, is it?"

She pulled a handkerchief out of her handbag and turned toward Ben. There was a fair amount of blood on his mouth and chin. A small amount had dripped onto the blue sweater, the whole scene making it look as though his injuries were more severe than they actually were. Ana dabbed at the blood on both his face and sweater, but it had dried. When Ben saw the nurturing look on her face it comforted him. He leaned his head back against the seat and whispered, "Fuck, my shoulder hurts."

CHAPTER TWO

The taxi driver had no choice but to join the heavier traffic flow on Regent Street, one of the main thoroughfares leading to Ana's hotel. Neither Ben nor Ana had made any effort to separate their hands. His grip had relaxed, and when glancing aside she saw that his eyes were closed; however, his forehead was creased and showed his level of discomfort. She noticed the driver glancing at them in his mirror several times, possibly curious about the blood on Ben's face.

At the next red signal, he turned to them and in an unrecognizable accent asked, "Might be he need doctor?"

Ben and Ana both started to talk at the same time. He said no and she said thanks anyway. The driver shook his head and turned back to face the road. Several minutes later the taxi turned a corner onto a quiet street, where about half way down there was a lighted hotel sign. Ana scooted forward preparing to get out. Ben turned slightly to reach for his wallet. He let out a stifled sound of pain as his left arm refused to reach back. Seeing the grimace on his face, she reached for his arm and gently rearranged it in his lap.

"I'll get this," she said, digging into her bag. She handed the pound notes forward and then hesitated. "Ben, you just can't go back to your hotel. You won't manage with so much pain and without the use of your arm. You really do need some attention. Besides, do you really want to walk through your posh hotel lobby with dried blood all over your face?"

"Who says I'm staying at a posh hotel," he said, trying to lighten things up a bit.

"One would assume that the digs of a successful author would have more stars than my humble lodgings."

Ben had a look of exasperation on his face and was shaking his head as he said, "I'm not staying at a hotel, posh or not. I keep a flat in Chelsea."

"I besiege you, Benedict McKinnon, quit trying to be clever and face the reality of the situation. Come in with me, at least long enough to get an icepack on your shoulder. We can reassess later, after we see what the ice does."

The driver revved the engine as a polite way of telling the couple to disembark and let him be on his way. With a sigh of agreement Ben pulled himself forward with his good arm, turned toward Ana and said, "I'm afraid you'll have to reach across me to open the door." Ana did as he asked and pushed it open as far as she could. Clearly aggravated, Ben added, "I should be going around to open your door and escort you to the entrance of your hotel. Instead, I'm being treated like a child."

"You know what our parents always said: If you don't want to be treated like a child, don't act like one." She looked at Ben impatiently. The driver got out and opened the door on Ana's side, and she quickly went around the vehicle to help Ben.

He was out and had slammed the taxi door before she got there. He had put his hand in the pocket of his jacket in a vain attempt to support the shoulder. He took her arm with his other hand and led her toward the entrance, pausing for a moment to make what Ana took as a revealing comment. "I've been asked up to the hotel room of a few women in my time, but never because I was in need of an icepack. I hope this is the one and only time for that."

Ana smiled and replied, "That's a bit too much bragging for a man in your condition."

He broke into the first smile she had seen since early in their conversation at the pub. Ana pushed open one of the double glass doors and held it aside for him to enter.

"I have to admit, most gals would be turned off by blood. But you're quite a trooper."

"You underestimate us. And besides, the boys in my neighborhood were always getting into fights. Your split lip and bloody nose aren't the first I've seen," she said, walking confidently into the lobby with Ben following close behind.

There were a few stares from guests who were still reading or socializing in the overstuffed chairs, and the concierge immediately set his eyes on them. He called out from behind the counter, "Is there anything you need, Ms. Doherty? Will your friend be staying?"

Ana knew that having guests in one's room was frowned upon in London hotels. Her face blushed red, and she made a mental note to leave a negative comment at checkout regarding the privacy of guests. She responded with surprising bravado. "Whether or not my friend stays is not your concern. Your main responsibility is the comfort of guests, and in aid of that, we will need ice, lots of it, as soon as possible."

The concierge seemed to shrink a few inches as a result of the reprimand, and injured or not, Ben could barely contain his laughter until they were on the lift. As the doors closed, he started to let it go, but the laugh quickly became a moan from the pain of jostling the shoulder. In spite of that, he couldn't resist teasing her. "So much for your reputation!"

"Who cares about what strangers think? ... Not me." She pushed the fourth floor button then neither said another word. Soon the lift jerked to a stop, the doors opened, and she led Ben down the hall to her room. She pulled the key card from her bag, and soon they were inside. Ana turned on all the lights, which Ben thought was an overstatement, and then she asked where he would be most comfortable. She immediately answered her own question and ordered him to the bed where she carefully helped him remove the heavy jacket. During the process he was vocal about the pain.

He climbed onto the bed, and after Ana arranged the pillows he leaned back, supporting his arm with another pillow. A rapid knock on the door announced that the ice had arrived. A staff member carried in a tray holding two ice buckets, filled to the point of spilling. She asked him to put them in the bathroom, shoved a tip in his hand when he came out, and sent him on his way. She went to get the ice, wrapped half of it in a towel, and then wet the towel slightly before cupping it around Ben's shoulder. When it first touched him he yelled a little at the shock, but settled back as the cold began to numb his pain.

Ana scolded herself for thoughts she could not seem to banish. Just the fact that he was on her bed aroused her. After all, it was the place where she had slept, the place where she had enjoyed slipping naked into the clean white sheets. She felt guilty for thinking of being in such a state, in that bed with Ben, especially considering his misery. However, remembering how long it had been since there had been a man in her bed, she understood the reason for such selfish thoughts.

After thirty minutes, she removed the ice and asked how he felt. He answered, "The numbness is wearing off and it still hurts like hell."

"Well, then it's decided. I'm either going to call the desk and have their on-call doctor contacted, or I'm going to call for a taxi and we're taking you to the hospital. No back-talk."

"I give up. I have to do something. This pain goes beyond a sprain. See if you can get the on-call doctor. But since I'm not a guest here, you'd better say it's for you."

"If the same guy is on duty, he's going to know it's not me. He had to have seen the blood on your face. But I think he may want to please me after the dressing down I gave him. Then I might forget my intention to leave that negative comment."

Ana contacted the desk and asked to have the doctor called due to her sudden attack of nausea, no doubt the result of a poor food choice. She commented to Ben in an aside that she was both surprised and glad that a hotel with so few stars even had a doctor on call. The concierge was cooperative and said that it would be at least an hour before he could get someone there. In spite of his conciliatory tone, Ana could tell he had his doubts.

In less than three-quarters of an hour, the doctor arrived, dressed in jeans and a sport jacket over pajama tops, and introduced himself as Doctor Jonathon Harrow. He was tall and thin, slightly bald, and had a face that Ana could only describe as kind. She managed the confusion about who had the nausea, that being no one, and explained what had really happened.

The doctor scrutinized them, his expression one of vague intolerance. He checked Ben's facial injuries first, as well as his eyes, for signs of concussion. Then he approached the shoulder, feeling around the joint and carefully trying to manipulate it. Ben cried out in pain and the doctor sat back and uttered a gruff, "Uh-huh! No wonder that hurt."

"What is it, doc?" Ben asked, a look of concern crossing his handsome, blood stained face. In her haste to treat his shoulder, she had forgotten to wipe away the blood, now completely dried.

"You have a subluxation— in laymen's terms, a partial dislocation," the doctor answered. "Quite simple to fix, if you know what you're doing. And I do." He stood and put his hands on his hips. "Get ready. I won't lie to you. This is going to hurt!"

Ben nodded his head that yes he was ready. The doctor went around to the other side of the bed and climbed up, steadying himself on both knees. He asked Ben to shift onto the opposite hip, and arranged himself into position for the manipulation, his body supported by the headboard. He straightened Ben's arm, producing a groan. He then steadied Ben's elbow and did a twist and pull motion so fast that Ana was startled. Ben yelled several expletives loudly enough to cause the guests in the next room to bang on the wall. She was sure they were wondering what was going on in the bed.

"I can't believe it," Ben said, gently rotating his arm. "It's a little sore, but the intense pain is gone. Good job, doc."

The doctor edged his way off the bed and stood up. He crossed his arms and looked down at Ben before saying, "You should have that arm in a sling. Use a towel for now, but keep it as immobile as you can for a few days. There's always some soft tissue injury when a joint is dislocated."

Ana said, "I'll sort out something for tonight and then do my best to see that he gets a proper sling tomorrow."

"Remember, Mr. McKinnon, if it doesn't heal properly, you may end up with scar tissue and surgery to repair that." His tone and expression were paternal. He picked up his medical bag and made his way toward the door, talking as he walked. "So, no one is nauseated? Are you through with me then?" The doctor gave them both a sideways glance and snickered. "Ice it for fifteen minutes every four hours until morning and the soreness should subside. I would give you a prescription for the pain, but you'd have trouble getting it filled at this hour. All I have is a morphine syringe, and that's more than you need."

"I have ibuprofen. That might help some," Ana said. The doctor concurred with a nod. She wasn't sure about the protocol of a nighttime call such as this. Was it appropriate to tip a well-respected professional? Would there be a significant charge on her bill? She opted out of a tip and decided not to worry about the charge. Her publisher was picking up the tab anyway, and she could explain that taking care of Ben was in aid of the interview. But that wasn't her motive. She cared, seemingly more than she could have expected.

Dr. Harrow said good night and to have the concierge call if there was any problem. As he opened the door to leave, he turned back and remarked, "I hope the other guy looked worse than you." They called out another thank you, and he closed the door behind him.

Ben immediately swung his legs to the floor and prepared to stand. He said, "Well, I'll get out of your way now." Ana saw a grimace of pain on his face as he slowly got to his feet. Once he had his balance he said, "I'll be able to get a taxi up the street, right?"

"You're not going anywhere yet. Remember, the doctor said to ice it again."

"Are you always this bossy?"

"Only when I confront disobedience." She tried not to smile and turned away, taking the ice pack into the bathroom to refresh it.

Ben settled back on the bed and kicked off his shoes, obviously too tired to argue. Ana fed him the ibuprofen and re-applied the ice, then sat on the edge of the bed next to him. Now that he wasn't in such pain, her thoughts drifted back to what it would be like to have him there under different circumstances. Her body was responding to these thoughts, and she hoped it didn't show in her expression. The blood on his face was disturbing, so she went to get a wet cloth and proceeded to dab gently at his lip and chin. Once again Ben saw the sweet expression that had comforted him in the taxi. There was no denying that now he wanted her even more. He also wanted to know who this woman was below the surface, what made her 'tick.' Considering his history with women, this was unprecedented.

Ana finished treating his lip and backed into a chair adjacent to the bed. She crossed her arms over her chest and began to stare at him. He was quite sure she was considering how he should be handled. Eventually she said, "So, can I get you to rest now? I think you need to be under my watchful eye for a while longer."

But knowing his intention to leave eventually, she needed a plan, and knew he would be better off with someone for the night. He agreed to rest, and with less discomfort he was able to recline slightly and lay his head back on the pillow, his arm resting across his body. With Ben settled, Ana excused herself and went into the bathroom. She had been chilled for hours and wanted to get out of her damp slacks and boots and slip into something cozy, like a robe and warm socks, but she was at a loss as to what would be appropriate. Somehow, changing into sleepwear didn't seem the thing to do, considering their short acquaintance. Then she returned to the consideration of how she could keep him from leaving, care for him properly in the short term. Ana was an independent no nonsense woman, and therefore, her concern for this man stymied her.

Quite a bit of time had passed since she closed the bathroom door, and she wondered what Ben was doing. It was quiet, although she had given him the television remote. She opened the door a crack and saw that he was asleep, head back, mouth slightly open, and looking quite peaceful. The scenario pleased her, but she then began to wonder what to do about a place to sleep. Ana was exhausted by the night's events. Without further contemplation she stripped down to her bra and panties and reached for the fluffy white robe on the hook behind the door. Wrapped in its warm comfort she tiptoed through the room to the bed. She carefully removed the ice pack from Ben's shoulder and then slipped under the comforter. Ben was on top of it, and she wondered if he would become cold enough to wake, yet she couldn't chance covering him or he would surely wake immediately. While pondering that situation, fatigue took charge and she was quickly asleep.

In the wee hours a howling wind accompanied by rain hitting the window startled Ana from sleep. She slid from beneath the comforter and went to the drapes, pulled one aside and stared out at the reflection of moving headlights on the wet street. A ceiling of charcoal gray clouds had formed, sporadic downpours obscuring the starlight. They roiled slowly through the night sky, allowing only faint glimpses of the waxing moon. Ben remained in the arms of Morpheus, no doubt in a very deep sleep due to the trauma of the night's events. Ana closed the drape quietly and returned to bed. She checked the clock and saw that it was after three. Ben would be there until morning, a fact she found both calming and strangely provocative.

She lay awake, listening to the rain and thinking about her life. In some ways it was empty, a fact that was all too evident as she glanced at the handsome, charming and injured man sleeping on her bed. There had been a few men, filling the role of lover more than potential mate. Her free-lance profession required great flexibility and few ties. Ana had said over and over again that it was just for now, that she would have plenty of time for a relationship later. But later hadn't come, and she often found the nomadic life of a journalist to be tedious and in many ways incomplete. She turned to face Ben and focused on his breathing, enjoying little snorts and gasps that made him seem vulnerable, real and approachable. Lying there, very still, her thoughts raced. Ben wasn't the only one with imagined scenarios, but in hers, he was the star.

* * *

Ben was the first to wake. The storm front had dissipated before dawn, and a beam of sunlight streaked through a gap in the drapery panels, creating a path across the carpet. He was disoriented and for a moment only half remembered what had transpired the previous evening. However, he did remember the vivid dream he was having as he awoke. He was an invisible observer of the two men who had attacked him. They were speaking in hushed tones to a woman whose face was turned away from him. The three seemed to be conspirators, and when the woman turned to face him, it was the kind and beautiful woman with whom he had just spent the night. The outlandish nature of the dream made him want to splash his face repeatedly with a good amount of cold water. He began to ease out of bed, but his first movement quickly reminded him of the injured shoulder. Having been still all night, it was stiff and sore, as was his body in general due to the beating. He turned slightly and saw Ana, still sleeping peacefully. He had no idea that she had been awake until just before dawn.

Wisps of dark hair were lying across her tranquil face, some remaining lipstick slightly smeared below her lip. Her breathing was deep and relaxed, and the lips he still desired were slightly parted. With the fluffy robe pulled up around her neck and every other bit of her drawn up under the comforter, Ben thought she looked as if nicely tucked into a comfy nest. He laughed to himself, surprised by the tenderness he felt as he watched her sleep. Not wanting to wake her, he gritted his teeth, managed to stand, and walked quietly to the bathroom. He didn't shut the door, only eased it closed for privacy.

As he came out, he noticed Ana's purse on the small table near the door. It had obviously been tossed aside with haste because the contents were strewn across the table, or half inside the purse. He noticed her press pass, displaying her name and photo, and it dawned on him that if the occasion had arisen, he couldn't have called her by name. Surely by now she had noticed his reticence at engaging her by name. He was thankful for two things: the opportunity to avoid embarrassment, and that she was legitimate. She was Ana C. Doherty and he knew he would never forget it, not only due to the close call, but because she had made an unforgettable impression on him in a little more than twelve hours. He returned to the bed, looked down at Ana, and tried to decide whether to slip out and grab a taxi home, or to wake her and say goodbye.

Perhaps sensing his eyes on her, Ana began to move. She rolled onto her back, drew her arms from under the comforter and stretched with feline grace. It took her a moment to register that Ben was standing by the bed. Watching her wake up, stretching and brushing the hair from her face, served to intensify the magnetic attraction he was experiencing. And as yet they had scarcely touched.

Ana glanced up and saw him staring down at her, smiling. His overnight growth of beard seemed to render him even more attractive. Both his expression and her reaction to the simple fact of some stubble made her self-conscious. "Was I drooling, snoring, or both?" she asked, trying to make light of what she hoped had not happened.

Ben laughed and said, "Neither. You looked so peaceful that I debated about whether or not to wake you before I left. I sure didn't want to slip out of here without a word and have you think I was ungrateful for your good deed. For everything you did last night." Ben paused, walked over to the opposite side of the bed and sat down to put on his shoes. Finding them slightly out of reach, he sat up and turned toward her. "You know I appreciate it, right?" Then he reached instead for the leather jacket that had been thrown hastily on the nearby chair the previous night. He ruffled around in the pockets to see if his phone was there, hoping it had survived the attack. On first look he didn't find it and turned his attention back to how Ana would answer his question.

"Of course I know you appreciate it. You'd do the same for me ... I think." She waited for a positive response then tested his indulgence with her persistence. "Right?"

His shoulder ached and patience for the subject had run out. "That question is too silly to answer, and you know what the answer would be anyway." He stood and dropped the jacket back onto the chair.

Ana had no idea why she had pushed him to answer a redundant question. She hurried the conversation in another direction. "Well, I hope never to get myself into a situation like the one last night. You really should take it seriously because I think it was an abduction gone wrong. I guess such a thing could even happen to me. Anyone can be abducted."

"But there has to be a reason to abduct someone. I still think they must have been given some faulty information. They'd have no reason to want me ... for anything. It was just a one-time thing, wrong time wrong place. Nothing to be worried about." Ben paused, then shook his head and continued. "I just wonder who the poor devil is who does have something to worry about."

"I don't think it's a smart idea just to forget about it. You should report it to the police and give them whatever information you have, what you remember, what I remember. It could even help the potential victim—the intended one."

"Well, there's a day at least half gone ... if I report it," he said. "Plus, that will delay the interview. I'm just saying ... I have to leave in 48 hours to visit my parents, and you have a deadline." Ben walked to the window and pulled one of the drapes aside, intending to let the morning sun warm the room.

"Forget the deadline. It's not imminent. Alerting the police to what happened is the only task that matters right now." Ana pondered his expression, wondering if she had reached his sense of conscience. After a short pause she asked, "How would you feel if someone else ended up hurt ... or even dead?"

"Like I said last night, you're a stubborn lady ... but the prettiest one who's ever tried to boss me around." There was a certain twinkle in Ben's eye and a restrained smile on his face that Ana found disarming. She looked down, not knowing why. He had meant to compliment, not embarrass her, so he added a footnote to his remark. "Well, to be honest, my mother is quite attractive."

There was an awkward moment before she rallied and said, "Don't try to distract me with compliments. I want to get up and dressed. You'll need to look out the window or something while I dash to the bathroom." After Ben obliged, Ana threw back the comforter and took hurried steps to reach the privacy of a closed door. She called out from inside, "I know you'll wait for me because you can't reach your shoes, let alone get them on."

Just loud enough for her to hear, he said, "You're pretty good at getting what you want, aren't you?" However, he was thinking that shoes or no, he would not have a problem waiting for her, any time, any place. He sensed it would be worth it.

Ana's answer was a purposely-loud laugh that came from behind the closed door. "Sure am," she said, and then he heard the shower running.

Ben sat in a chair listening to the sound of water for a few minutes then decided to check for his phone again. He took his jacket off the chair and saw the phone lodged at the back of the cushion. It had survived, but the battery was run down. He had wanted to call a taxi but would have to use the room phone. First, he had to settle with Ana about the interview, which now seemed even more shallow and unimportant after what had happened to them. But it was the best excuse to see her again. The pain in his shoulder made him angry, angry that he now had to deal with this complication in his well-planned life.

He looked around the room for the pain reliever, but couldn't find it.

He called out, "Ana, when you come out would you bring the ibuprofen, if you can find it in there?"

She answered that it was there and opened the door slightly to toss it onto the bed. With her towel wrapped head barely visible in the small opening, she said, "Your first stop has to be the druggist, or somewhere they have slings. If you don't, you'll pay for it later!"

Ben knew she was right, but what he failed to realize was that his resistance to her nurturing was just a way of hiding his fondness for the extra attention. He helped himself to the pills and washed them down with bottled water from the bedside table. He knew that he needed an ice pack, but was anxious to get out of the hotel room and away from the vague tension he was experiencing. He was locked in a private space with Ana, one with a bed. Even if she were interested, the timing was wrong. He fully intended to get closer to her, but preferred to have two good arms with which to do it.

He made his way back to the window and checked below for taxi stands, but soon realized that the room was located at the back of the building. Surely he would have no difficulty finding one nearby, once he could get things settled with Ana. He noticed that the pain in his shoulder was settling down a bit, but his body felt stiff and sore from the assault. The pills hadn't helped that. Ben realized that he hadn't checked himself out and was sure there must be some bruising on his ribcage. He also noticed that his right knee was reluctant to bend. Whether or not he should see a doctor was the last thing he wanted to consider. He would go home and see if some ice would put him right.

While deep in thought, he heard Ana come out of the bathroom. He turned to see her wrapped in a towel and rummaging through her suitcase. "I really won't be a minute once I find something to wear," she said, and then pulled out a pair of jeans, holding them high as if she had found a prize. She dug for a sweater and dashed back into the bathroom. Shortly she emerged looking fresh and well put together, other than her bare feet. From another bag she pulled out a pair of designer sneakers and quickly put them on.

Ben liked the casual-looking Ana. Her jeans were slim cut and fit her perfectly. He noticed immediately that the pink sweater was short enough to allow a complete view of her shapely derrière. The cause of the vague tension he had been experiencing was becoming clear, and he realized that he really had to get out of the room before he did something stupid and premature. He found himself moving toward the door, preparing to escape the environment, as well as his feelings. He wasn't used to pacing himself when it came to women. His philosophy had always been one of seizing an opportunity, and he had the looks and charm that brought about such opportunities with regularity. But with Ana, something told him to take it slow and just let it unfold naturally. He had always made an assumption of success with women, and the air of self- assurance he presented had most always worked in his favor. It was different this time. Ben was forced to consider that Ana might not fancy him.

She noticed his movement and said, "You seem anxious to leave. Was it something I said?" He could tell she was joking, and just smiled due to lack of a response. She continued, "You know we haven't set up an appointment for tending to our business at hand. I don't think today would be a good idea. You need to rest a while longer."

Ben answered, "There isn't much I *can* do other than rest until I have full use of my arm. I could certainly talk to you, but I won't be able to drive until I can lose the sling." He tried to rotate his shoulder just a bit and uttered an expletive under his breath. "It's lucky I took a taxi to the pub last night," he said, reaching with his good arm for the leather jacket resting on the chair nearest him.

Ana could see that he was ready to go and quickly said, "How do I know that you'll go straight to the pharmacy for advice on a sling?"

He held the jacket up in the air and said, "All I can do is swear on this, my best and faithful friend."

Ana shook her head in mock-disapproval and asked, "Seriously? You must not make friends very easily if your jacket rates that high." She observed that it did appear to have had a lot of use. An unbidden scenario distracted her: Ben's arms around her, her cheek against the jacket, and the heady scent of leather complementing his very obvious masculinity. With an undetectable sigh she returned her attention to their conversation.

"The right leather jacket can be the link to a man's identity, his sense of who he is. Mine has been through a lot with me and hasn't let me down. You women feel naked without a purse, and some men feel that way without their leather jacket. At least for me it's just a jacket … not a flashy sports car or a flask of whiskey as my constant companion."

"Understood. No more comments … maybe. And I must admit, it definitely does suit you." A teasing little smile crossed her face. Ben saw the sexy glint in her dark, expressive eyes, and as he was enjoying her willingness to spar with him, a potent surge of desire ran straight through him. She would be a welcome challenge.

"Well then, let's ease you into that precious jacket so we can get on with day," Ana said, taking the jacket from him and gently slipping the sleeve onto the arm of his sore shoulder.

"So *we* can get on with it? I don't need a nanny to get me home," he said, grimacing as she finished getting him into the jacket.

Ana wondered if Ben was defending his independence or just being snarky. "I know you don't *need* my help. You could have conducted your day without wearing it. I'm sure you're a regular one-arm wonder." She stepped back, arms across her chest, looked him straight in the eye and said, "I'll give you your freedom just as soon as we get you into a sling. Deal with it." She paused and then added, "Just don't bite the hand that brings you ice and helps you put on your magic jacket."

"Sorry— I'm just not used to limitations or having people help me, especially a woman. I didn't intend to take it out on you. I don't know you well enough to be free to act like an ass." His attitude was compliant, but his eyes expressed the enjoyment he took in her talent for sparring with him. She didn't back down. He liked that as well.

Ana stuffed her belongings back into her purse, pulled the strap over her shoulder, and opened the door. "After you, sir, and no more snarky behavior," she said rather too brightly, and Ben shook his head in mock-frustration as he closed the door behind them.

* * *

Shifts at the hotel desk had changed, and the concierge on duty was a young woman, tall and slim, with a bleached blonde ponytail that was at odds with her business-like navy blazer and gray skirt. She was standing at attention behind the counter, having been engaged in conversation by a rather elderly guest. Ana commented that the concierge from the previous evening would have raised one eyebrow as they exited the elevator together, obviously having spent the night in her room. They left the hotel and looked up and down the street for signs of a taxi, and within a couple of minutes one appeared. Ana waved to lay claim to it, while out of necessity Ben stood idly by, hating his current status. After climbing inside, Ben asked the driver where they could find the closest pharmacy.

The hefty man behind the wheel asked, "You mean a chemist?"

Ben answered, "Yes, chemist … somewhere they have medical supplies."

The driver nodded and pulled away from the curb rather too quickly, his tires screeching as he entered the flow of traffic. The streets and sidewalks were all but clogged with cars and shoppers. This was normal for the day after a rainstorm, and everyone looked purposeful, or seemed to express an air of enjoyment at the morning's abundant sunshine. Soon the driver pulled to a halt and pointed to a shop on their left. Ben had put his wallet in his right pocket and managed to retrieve it, but handed it to Ana so she could pay the driver. They got out and reached the sidewalk as quickly as possible, just managing to avoid a careless lorry driver pulling out of a loading zone.

They entered the store, told the bright-faced young woman behind the counter what they needed, and soon Ben was wearing a proper sling. "It does feel a lot better supported like this," he said, and Ana smiled while she dug into his wallet again to pay the salesgirl.

Ana suddenly said, "Wait. There's something else you may need." She turned to the young woman and asked, "Would you please get us some ibuprofen? A small bottle should do."

"You assume I don't have something like that on hand?"

"You're a man, aren't you?"

Their eyes met. Neither looked away. Ben stepped closer to her and said, "I most certainly am."

Ana reacted to his seductive air of confidence by looking away demurely; however, what she was feeling was anything but demure. Again, there was the pleasant adrenaline rush as she thought of the ways she would like to help him confirm that particular fact.

CHAPTER THREE

Their business drawn to a close, Ben and Ana joined the flow of diligent shoppers scurrying up and down the street. They strolled for a block or so, enjoying the sun and the colorful offerings of a flower seller whose kiosk was set up on a busy corner. Ana noticed a quaint café whose entrance was graced on each side by wooden boxes filled to the brim with a variety of spring flowers. There were lace curtains on the paned windows, and as a customer opened the door to exit, the aroma of fresh baked goods served to lure them inside. Neither had eaten anything other than the pub's stale pretzels since lunch the previous day, so with just a mutual glance of approval they went in and took a table by the window. Both enjoyed a hearty breakfast accompanied by pleasant and diverse conversation that excluded any mention of the previous night's assault.

When they had finished, Ben asked, "Do you have an office here in London that requires you to appear in person on a daily basis?"

"No, thankfully. When I accept an assignment, I'm on my own until it's completed. Sometimes they check in— ask me to call with an update on how it's going. They like to make sure I'm not enjoying myself too much on their dime."

"Then they'd be pleased to know what a rotten day you had yesterday, at least the part after we met in the pub," Ben said, his tone almost questioning. Perhaps he had needed to confirm that meeting him had not been a completely negative experience.

"I wouldn't call it rotten. Some might call it exciting. But I'd call it frightening, other than the brief part where we were enjoying our informal meeting in the pub."

Ben couldn't resist that opening and chimed in, "That was the best part, even better than the invitation up to your hotel room." He winked at her and waited for a response that didn't come. "Forgive my 'cheek,' but I think we need to lighten up and try to make something good out of what happened."

Ana agreed with a nod before replying, "You should know that you are definitely the first man I've ever asked up to a hotel room, for any reason." She wondered if he believed her. The lull in their conversation made her uncomfortable, and she said, "I've always had a soft spot for lost or injured dogs, even cats." As soon as the words left her mouth, she regretted them, unsure of whether a comment labeling him 'lost' might incur a negative response.

Ben sat up straighter in his chair and she noticed he wasn't smiling. "Is that how you see me after less than twenty-four hours of acquaintance?"

"Of course not. I was just trying to keep it light... as you advised."

"I can assure you that I'm completely self-sufficient... in normal circumstances. I've never been one to let a woman baby me, nor have they wanted to, as far as I know." Ben leaned back in his chair and placed his used napkin on the table. "I tried to just go home, but you didn't give me much of a choice."

"You're right. I didn't give you much choice. I can be bossy, like you said, but my intentions were good. I admit I can have a tendency to 'take over' in certain situations. Boring stuff from childhood. I'm sorry if I came on too strong. But part of it was how scared the whole thing made me."

Ben's tone softened. "I understand that. A man isn't supposed to be weak or scared, or *appear* scared anyway. But I was, and I don't mind admitting it to you." He leaned forward and with his good arm, reached for Ana's hand. He closed his fingers around hers and said softly, "I'm glad we can talk to each other about this. And if I haven't said it enough times already, you were great. You *are* great, and I'm very glad to have met you, Ms. Ana Doherty."

Ana was affected by his words and looked down rather self-consciously. She felt that special little ache near the heart that told her she was starting to care for him beyond simple attraction. Clearly it was too soon, and she would probably be wise to avoid the complication all together. There had been only one man in her past that had caused the little ache, but she had been so young, fascinated by his interest in her and suffering from a fragile ego that was naïve to his intentions. Yet this time the response was not about her ego. It was about the way she had met him, the circumstances by which she was starting to know him. But mainly it was about how easily he could elicit a physical response in her at his slightest touch. Before, she had known that on some level her actions were wrong. With Ben, everything felt right.

Their waitperson disturbed the moment by asking if they would like anything else. Ben declined and requested the check. That settled, they were soon out the door and standing on the sidewalk. It seemed that once again each was waiting for the other to make the next move. Ben was the first to speak.

"Now that I've been fed, I really need to get home and clean up." He paused for a moment, expecting a response from Ana, but she was waiting for what might come next. Continuing, he said, "I'm sure you have some sort of work to attend to ... maybe report in, or do some shopping."

Ana realized that they were at the point of going their separate ways. The prospect bothered her even though she knew they would meet again for the interview. "As a matter of fact," she said a little too brightly, deflecting her disappointment, "I may as well do a little sightseeing ... maybe visit the Tower of London ... see where some of the historical horrors took place."

Ben let out a little laugh and said, "That should keep you busy for a while. You won't like the queues at the tourist sights." He shifted from one foot to the other, reluctant to leave her. Finally he said, "Let me get you a taxi. I'm going in the opposite direction, so I'll hail one for you then catch one for myself."

Ana nodded in agreement, and before she had a chance to make some sort of plan to accomplish her assignment, a taxi came their way and Ben waved it down with his good arm. As she climbed in she turned and called to him, "You have my card, right? We still need to schedule the interview."

Ben assured her that he would be in touch later in the day and would find time for them to meet just as soon as possible. He closed the taxi door and waved to her as the driver pulled out into traffic. He didn't like seeing Ana disappear from view. It caused him an unfamiliar discomfort, and as he walked briskly toward the next corner, he had to remind himself that he would see her again. Once he reached the busy intersection, taxis were plentiful. Soon he was on his way to Chelsea and thinking about a long hot shower followed by a nap.

* * *

On the ride through town to his flat, Ben fought to stay awake. When they had turned off King's Road onto Sloane, he caught sight of the familiar building and felt a sense of comfort. He had left his wallet in a front pocket so was able to pay the driver quickly. Soon he stood before the steps leading to the building's entrance. Glancing to the left he saw his neighbor, Mrs. Ward-Thomas, sitting in her usual place at the ground level window of her basement flat, watching life go by as she fussed with the flowers in her window box. None of the other neighbors knew how long she had lived there, and she kept to herself most of the time.

As Ben looked at her, the sun shining gently on her face, he thought she must have been quite beautiful in her youth. In spite of the wrinkles around her eyes and mouth, there remained a healthy blush in her complexion, and he was quite certain there had to be an interesting story behind those soft gray-blue eyes. Her white hair was confined in one thick braid that reached all the way to her waist, ending with a small satin ribbon. That small attention to detail made Ben smile. She was wearing a brightly flowered dress, or blouse, he couldn't tell which, topped with the ruffled white apron that was her signature. She was so often in that spot, and Ben had always intended to speak to her, but had procrastinated. There always seemed to be some kind of hurry to get up the stairs to his flat and shut out the rest of the world. As a consequence, he was only on nodding terms with most of the neighbors. He supposed that she had limited human contact. *A lonely life,* he thought.

"Mr. McKinnon," she shouted to him in a slightly wavering voice. "Can you stop a minute? I want to show you something."

"Yes, of course," Ben replied, turning to walk around the staircase to her window. "I'm not good at speaking to my neighbors, but I often notice you there at the window. It's always nice to see the flowers in your window box. It tells me I'm home."

"Thank you, dear. I've always believed that flowers soften the soul." She stopped picking at the dead blooms and said, "Maybe one day you'll have a 'cuppa' with me." She sat up a little straighter, squaring her shoulders, and continued, "I've read one of your books, you know. And please call me Lilith."

"Don't let me forget now, Lilith, because I'd be interested to hear what you think about the book, whichever one it was."

"Never mind about all that now," she said, and leaned further out the window, motioning him to come closer in order to speak more softly. "Don't be obvious, but turn around and look at that square black vehicle parked just there, up a bit from the entrance."

Ben turned carefully and glanced in that direction. "They call it an SUV. Why does it concern you?"

"Because it has been there too long and no one ever got out. I've lived long enough to know that whoever is inside is up to no good." She tossed her chin back and pursed her lips tightly. Then she furrowed her brow and shrugged her shoulders in disgust.

"I suppose there are hundreds of black SUV's around London. And I think most of them have innocent reasons for being parked on the street."

"Well I don't like it!" Her tone was at once authoritative and timid. "I'm going to call the police to come and see who's in there and why. I'm not climbing into my bed tonight until it's gone." She wrung her hands and peeked around him to peer at the vehicle again.

"I'm sure it's nothing," Ben said gently, "Try not to let your imagination run away with you." While speaking to her he had continued to sneak glances at the vehicle. "You'll have to excuse me, Missus... Lilith... but I need to get upstairs. If you really feel frightened later, don't hesitate to call 999." He reached through the open window and patted her hand.

"I will, dear, but I just hope they leave soon." She paused momentarily, and before Ben was half way up the stairs, she called him back. "Wait a minute. Come back and come to my door. I have a fresh-baked sweet for you to take upstairs."

Not wanting to offend her, Ben did as he was told, rounding the banister and taking the few stairs down to her door, which already stood open. He remained in the doorway, fully aware that going inside would mean at least an hour of conversation and that cup of tea she had mentioned. While he stood waiting for her to wrap the treat, Ben heard a horn honk and turned to see the said vehicle's door had been opened, causing an oncoming vehicle to swerve in order to avoid it. Less than an instant later he saw a familiar sight. The man from the night before, with his ratty leather jacket and bald tattooed head, was coming toward him at a fast pace. He stepped quickly inside Mrs. Ward-Thomas' flat and slammed the door shut, locking it. He then rushed to close and latch the window.

She came out of the kitchen, clutched her chest in shock, and asked, " What's wrong? Why did you come in and lock the door?"

"I can't explain everything right now," he said emphatically, speaking in haste. "Go to the back of the flat ... No! Go out in the garden and through the gate to the alleyway. Stay there until the police come. But don't come inside until someone you know comes to get you."

Lilith turned and took short quick steps through her kitchen to the garden door. She turned once, calling out to Ben, "What's happening? Why must I go outside?

"There's a man outside who I'm quite sure is trying to kidnap me. He already tried once, last night." He reached into his pocket for his phone and quickly dialed 999. Unable to think of a way to explain the danger they were in, he told the operator that someone was trying to break into his neighbor's basement flat, that she was elderly and very frightened. They assured that a car would be there shortly and not to engage the perpetrator. In a moment, Lilith came back into the sitting room. He told her again to go outside, and this time his tone was even more desperate. Then he noticed what she had in her hand. She extended to him her only means of defense, a golf club.

"Here, take this. It belonged to my husband. I've kept it around here on the odd chance I might have to defend myself."

Just then Ben saw the man's face at the window. A moment later he heard the man throw his weight against the door. It didn't give, and there was a pause before he tried again. After providing Ben with her weapon, Lilith had made what was a hasty exit for a woman her age, and he didn't have to worry about her at the moment. The door would surely come down with the next impact from the man's shoulder. Ben positioned himself just behind the door, readying for the confrontation. There was no one to intercede on his behalf this time, and he only had complete use of one arm. Fortunately, that was his dominant side, but he was forced to pull the other arm out of its sling and ignore what damage using it might cause.

As expected, the man rammed the door one last time and it gave way, opening, but not coming off its hinges. This allowed Ben to stay partially hidden. The man stepped over the threshold and began to scan the room. After his would-be attacker had taken a few more steps forward, Ben took his shot. He winced with pain as he used both arms to accomplish a swing that might have reached at least the ninth hole. However, he was aiming high, and he caught the man mid-torso, causing him to cry out and fall to his knees. Ben readied himself to take another swing, hoping to neutralize his enemy completely, even knock him unconscious. But the man was as tough as he looked, with his dirty black boots and tattoos, and he got to his feet before Ben could get off another blow.

He spun around and grabbed at the club. Ben could only grasp it strongly with one hand, and soon it had been taken from him. This time he saw the man's smile. He was missing two teeth, and the rest were the yellow-brown of a smoker. He was clean-shaven, but several small scars marred one side of his cheek. He came at Ben, who was backing toward the door, hoping to escape outside and call for help. *Where's that damn Panda full of cops,* he thought as his heel hit the threshold. Ben turned and tried to run up the few stairs to the street, but his attacker reached him and started up the stairs, grabbing for his pant leg. Ben tried to continue forward, but was pulled off balance and fell forward onto the stairs, wincing with pain as he failed to protect his shoulder.

Just then he heard noise from inside the flat. The heavy sound of men running became louder, as did their raised voices. Two strapping lads broke through the doorway and jumped on Ben's assailant, hoping to restrain him until the police arrived. Once again his brute strength secured his freedom. He dashed up the stairs and onto the sidewalk, signaling to his cohort to back up and get him. The SUV screeched backward and the door swung open. He looked fiercely at Ben one more time, shaking his fist as he jumped in. The vehicle door slammed shut, and the perpetrators sped into traffic and out of sight, once again managing to elude arrest.

The two young men helped Ben up and asked if he was all right. His shoulder was throbbing again, but nothing had been injured other than his ego, having once again failed to detain his attacker. The expressions on their faces were questioning, obviously waiting for some kind of explanation. "I'll tell you about it in a minute. But right now I need to attend to Lilith. She's probably still standing outside the gate, wondering what's happening."

They nodded in agreement, and just as Ben turned to go through the house and outside to fetch her, the Panda car pulled up the street and stopped in front of the building. Two officers jumped out, checked the address, and one spoke into his shoulder radio, most likely confirming their arrival at the scene. Ben asked the young men to talk to the officers long enough for him to bring Lilith back into the house. He hurried through the kitchen and down the steps to the garden, where he found himself surrounded by rows of vegetables growing in front of a backdrop of lanky sunflowers. The old wooden gate was almost hidden among their giant leaves. He pushed it open and began to call her name. She had made her way up the alley to the edge of the building and was standing in a tiny circle of shade provided by a neighbor's peach tree. He jogged to where she stood, took her gently by the arm, and guided her back toward the garden. All the while he was explaining what had transpired.

Lilith waved her arm to indicate she was out of breath, so they stopped. "I truly didn't know I could still move that fast," she said, bending to put her hands on her knees and take some deep breaths. Then she stood straight again and added, "I'm so relieved you're all right."

"Where did those two lads come from?" Ben asked. "They saved my bacon. No doubt about that."

"I've watched those boys grow up. They came up the alley just as I opened the gate. They're polite boys and spoke to me. Then they saw I was in a state and asked why, and if I needed help." Lilith walked over and leaned against a half-painted fence. "I was frantic. I told them there was a neighbor being attacked inside my flat. They didn't hesitate, just took off running toward my back door. Brave boys, eh?"

"I was a lucky bastard again. Last night, coming out of the pub, three men who looked like footballers drove off the same guy." Ben motioned her to come along back into the house. "We have to speak to the police.

They're here now," he said. As they walked through the garden he asked, "Do you know the boys' names? I have to find a way to thank them."

Lilith said she wasn't sure, but that they were brothers and lived in the next building over. Back in the flat, the two policemen and the two young men were standing in the middle of the sitting room, engaged in some sort of argument between them. As Lilith and Ben approached they heard enough to know that the officers had the wild idea that the two heroes were the thugs breaking into her house. Ben eased Lilith into her armchair and then interceded for the boys, making clear what had happened and how they may have saved his life. He then told the story of the previous night and asked to file a report on the attempted kidnappings. In order to do that, he was told that due to the nature of the purported crime, he must appear in person at Scotland Yard.

When the policemen had left, Ben asked Lilith if she felt all right. He said he would feel better if there was someone he could call to come and sit with her until she calmed down a bit more. He was able to reach her daughter's mobile and was assured that she would be there within fifteen minutes. In the meantime, he brewed Lilith a very welcome cup of tea.

She sipped her tea quietly, and then said, "After what happened to you, wouldn't you like something stronger than tea? I have some sherry in the cupboard."

"Thank you for offering, but what I need is to go upstairs and ice this shoulder. It's punishing me for taking off the sling." Ben found the sling on the floor near the threshold and slipped it back on. The door was hanging a bit off kilter and would not be secure when closed. A quick call to building maintenance took care of that problem. Within a few minutes the building 'super' appeared with tool belt at the ready. He told them that although he could make the door secure for the night, a piece of the frame was cracked and would have to be replaced. He made the temporary repair and promised to return before noon the next day. As he headed up the stairs Lilith's daughter passed him on her way down.

She ran to her mother, knelt down and took her hand before speaking. "Are you all right, Mum? What have you got yourself into?" Then she turned to Ben and said, "What happened? Did someone try to hurt my Mum?"

He explained that no, she wasn't in any danger, and that she had actually helped keep him from harm by coming back with the golf club. He could see that she was holding back her opinion about her mother's part in things, but wisely, she chose not to comment further. The cracked doorframe had been mentioned, and she insisted on spending the night and remaining there until it was repaired. Now certain that Lilith would be fine, Ben thanked her again and took his leave. He looked around carefully as he went up the few stairs to the street. Nothing seemed amiss, so he ran up to the entrance, punched in his security code, and hurried into the building.

The lift stopped at the third floor and Ben got out, fumbled for his keys, and was soon inside. His flat was cluttered with books, and yesterday's newspaper had been strewn all over the dark leather sofa. Dust motes floated freely in the rays of sunlight shining through the half open wooden shutters. The air was stale, and there was the faint odor of unwashed dishes. Ben looked around and shook his head. *I could never let Ana into this place,* he thought, removing his jacket and casting it onto a chair.

He made his way to the refrigerator and pulled out an ice tray before grabbing a kitchen towel and spreading it out on the counter. With a couple of hard bangs on the counter the ice came free. He bundled it up and headed for the sofa, where he flopped down, put the ice on his shoulder and closed his eyes. His thoughts raced, trying to sort through what had happened over the last twenty-four hours and why. The whole concept was inconceivable to him. He wasn't a rich man— comfortable perhaps, but not rich enough to be a target. His parents were doing well, but in no position to ransom their son. His head ached, but the ibuprofen was in the pocket of his jacket, too far away. He didn't want to move. Closing his eyes again, he drifted off.

Ben slept for an hour or so, and when he finally opened his eyes it was mid-afternoon. The melted ice had soaked his shirt and one of the sofa pillows. He swung his legs around and sat up, then put his head in his hands, beginning once again to sort through events. Getting nowhere, he headed for his bedroom and the long overdue shower. Later, feeling refreshed as well as ravenous, Ben thought about how good an Indian takeaway would taste.

Before he could get organized to leave, a voice in his head warned him what being out on the street at night could mean. Third time could well be the charm for his newfound enemies. He decided instead to scour his cupboards for sustenance. All he came up with was some dry pasta and a tin of sardines. He put on water for the pasta and opened the sardines. They were packed in tomato sauce and oil, so when the pasta was ready, he drained it and proceeded to toss it all together. There was just a tad of *parmigiano* left in the cardboard shaker, and he added it to his dish. He knew this would appall his mother, who insisted that the container version wasn't real food. The half-bottle of red wine he found displaced in the refrigerator served to cut the taste of his makeshift meal.

While eating he was struck by a disturbing thought. Ana had seen the bald man, had actually seen both of the men. There was a possibility they had been followed during the day. He couldn't understand how they could have known where she was staying, or how the two of them could have been tracked down the next day, but it had to be considered. Of course they could find his address, and did. An unlisted phone number was of little help in the current age of technology. But regardless of how they had found him, the fact was they could also find Ana, so she was in danger. He felt guilty that she had been drawn into whatever was happening, and he knew it was up to him to protect her. Ben concluded that just keeping her at a distance from him would be of little help. The best course would be to keep her with him, or better yet, to keep her in the country, far away from these men.

The challenge would be to coax Ana into accompanying him to his parents' home. He didn't want to frighten her with the truth of his motivation to get her out of London. Suddenly it came to him, and he felt quite clever for creating an appropriate ruse. *It's perfect,* Ben thought. He planned tell her she was needed because of his shoulder, that he couldn't begin to drive that far.

CHAPTER FOUR

The dismal sky and constant drizzle of the previous day had given way to sunshine and the bright colors of a landscape washed clean. Paris McKinnon walked briskly up the path leading to the museum's employee entrance, dodging the few puddles that remained. Before going in she brushed at the sides of her blonde hair, checking for any stragglers set free from her chignon by the pleasant morning breeze. She had met a friend for coffee and then had trouble hailing a taxi during the morning rush. These days she often thought that the commute to London three days a week was becoming too much for her sixty-two years. The timing had to be just right: Make the train to Paddington, catch the Tube, then a brisk walk or taxi—depending on the weather.

As she headed down the hall toward her office, a male colleague caught up with her, and without any preface of greeting, asked if she had received the paperwork on the exhibit scheduled for display at the start of the following month. Her office had been empty for a week due to the short trip she and Hugh had taken for their anniversary. Her colleague was a rather prissy man, crowded into his clothes as if they were keeping him upright. Perhaps the reference she once overheard about his being 'spineless' was the reason he wore such close-fitting attire. She smiled at the thought. Although he could appear quite affable when met head-on by proper etiquette, Paris was sure that he coveted her position and influence with the museum board. She could imagine that as a boy he had been the perfect type for class tattletale.

"Good morning to you, too, Mr. Brett," she said, making a point of his lack of civility. "I'm sure you're aware that I was out of the office last week. There's bound to be a stack of correspondence and forms piled on my desk. I assure you I will go through it first thing." She reached her door and turned to face him, putting on her best smile before turning back to unlock the door.

"Well, it's imperative that we're properly prepared to receive the containers," he said, his tone condescending. "The contents are more valuable than anything in this museum. They've hired several twenty-four-hour guards for that specific display case." Mr. Brett threw his shoulders back and pulled at the tie encircling his pencil-like neck. That adjustment made, he continued, "Please make this your top priority. If there's a glitch, there will be hell to pay."

Without further response Paris unlocked the door, making a quick escape inside. When he didn't follow, she sighed with relief and scanned her desk to assess the day's workload. *There's not enough money in the Bank of London to get me to stay late today,* she thought. Ben was coming, and she had preparations to make for his favorite foods ... and she must invite a few of his old school chums to dinner ... make it a festive visit. It had been too long since she had wrapped her arms around her son. She wondered if Olivia would give up a couple of days of her overly-active social life to come home—so they all could be together, just like it used to be. She shook her head away from reverie and began to sort the mess on her desk.

A couple of hours later she was still opening assorted envelopes and trying to put everything into piles based on subject. The next small padded envelope she picked up had something inside. She tore it open and found a cassette tape labeled with her name. *Rather old-fashioned,* she thought. Shoved into the back of her desk drawer was a small cassette player she sometimes used for meetings. She had learned from experience that it was the best way to avoid confusion about who said what.

The tape was blank at the beginning, but soon there was a heavily accented male voice telling her to pay close attention. "We have your son.

If you do not do exactly as you are told we *will* kill him. We do not want a ransom. Only you can save his life. You will be contacted about your task." Then there was no further sound other than the static whirring of the tape.

Paris rolled her chair backward, seemingly in an effort to distance herself from the threat within her cassette player. Besides the sudden and extreme tightness in the pit of her stomach, she was confused. She wondered what power she had to do anything significant, and what in the world they could want. Her first instinct was to call Hugh, but thought better of that choice and decided to call Ben first, to hear his voice and know he was safe. His phone went straight to voicemail, causing Paris to feel panic rising in her chest. She then called Olivia to see if she had been in contact with her brother during the last twenty-four hours. "What good are these damn things? No one ever answers!" she said aloud. Paris fetched her coat and purse, ran out of her office and went across the hall, where she knocked loudly on Lyle Brett's door.

"Enter!" he called out in his usual haughty tone.

Paris burst into his office, her words flying. "I still haven't come across the paperwork for the exhibit, but you know what's coming, don't you? What is it?"

"You seem in quite a tizzy," he said, clasping his hands in front of his chest and seeming determined to make her wait.

"Please just answer the question. You mentioned the exhibit's value, so you must know something about it."

Lyle leaned back in his chair, casually put his hands behind his head and said, "I can't be exact about the value until you unearth the paperwork on it. The rumor mill has it there's even concern for the transport from the exhibit's last location." His tone carried a tinge of excitement at the thought.

Paris said nothing while she considered what to do next. The exhibit was of no consequence to her in light of what she had just heard on tape. Eventually she said, "I have to leave for a while. When I get back I really need you to help me finish sorting documents. Between the two of us we'll find the paperwork faster." Lyle frowned, and Paris could see that he was curious as to why she would dare to ask him a favor. Sensing his need for further explanation, she said, "And please don't ask me a lot of questions right now. I know we aren't what you would call friends, only co-workers, but trust me when I tell you that this is important." Lyle paused and stared straight at her. She could see the wheels turning, could read his face as he mulled over what he could get out of helping her. *What a supercilious little prat,* she thought. But she needed his help, so said nothing.

He stood and leaned forward, hands now on his desk. "I'll help you ferret through the rest, but I may need a favor someday, and I'll expect you to reciprocate.

Paris wanted so badly to take that opportunity to tell him why he had no friends at the museum. She suspected the same of his outside life. What she really wanted was to be able to call him a supercilious prat out loud and then proceed to tell him that his suit was too tight. *Maybe someday,* she thought, and walked swiftly down the hall to the exit. She was thankful for having worn flat shoes and all but ran to the curb, where fortune smiled and a taxi appeared immediately. She got in and gave the driver Ben's address. The morning commuter traffic had thinned out, and although for her the time seemed to drag, they reached his building in quite good time.

Paris paused before the stairs leading to the entrance and thought about how she had promised both of her children that she would never just drop in unannounced. She wanted to give them the privacy due an adult, her promise based on the incident long ago when Hugh's mother had walked in on them at an intimate moment being taken on their living room sofa. The woman's expression had been burned into Paris' memory. But this was different. It could be a matter of life or death. She punched in the security code that Ben had given her some time back and heard the door click open. While in the elevator she was struck by a shot of adrenaline coursing through her chest. The doors creaked open and she stepped out into the hallway. It had been so long since visiting Ben's flat that she wasn't sure if it was located to the right or the left. The first guess was correct and soon she stood in front of his door, hesitating before she knocked.

Ben had been reading yesterday's newspaper when he heard the knock. A bolt of fear shot through him when he considered that it might be another attempt to abduct him. He got up slowly and placed the paper on the sofa before walking quietly to the door and looking through the peephole. He couldn't believe it was his mother standing there and opened the door immediately. She ran into his arms and began to sob.

"For God's sake, Mum, what's wrong? Is it Dad? Olivia?"

She continued to sob, but she shook her head no. He gently broke away from her embrace and led her to the sofa. Then he closed and locked the door before joining her. Words spilled from her mouth, rambling, with short pauses to regain her composure.

"Okay Mum. Calm down now and tell me what has you so upset," he said, taking his mother's hand in his.

She regained her focus and looked squarely at Ben, noticing as he lifted his left arm gently and placed it across his stomach. Then she saw the sling lying on the coffee table. "What's all this then?" she asked, gesturing toward the table. Without conscious thought Ben reached up to rub his shoulder. It was obvious that Paris was becoming agitated again. She began to shake her head and said, "This is all too much. I want an explanation. Did someone try to hurt you?"

"What would make you ask that? How do you know I didn't fall ... or get into it with some jerk in a pub?" He didn't want to upset his mother further, so tried to make light of the injury.

Paris would not be placated and informed him that she had good reason to think that someone might have tried to cause him harm. She launched into an account of what had happened in the office, the backlog of work, and about coming across the tape, almost by accident. "I panicked," she said. "It could have been lying there for over a week. I hadn't talked to you since before your father and I went away." She paused to take a breath, then continued, "You could easily have been held captive for almost that long. And I had no idea what it was that I was supposed to do to get you back. I had to rush over here to see if you were all right, that no one had taken you away."

"The fog is clearing on this thing," he said. "I know this will upset you, but you have to know. Last night, then again early this afternoon, two men made attempts to kidnap me. I can see now that I was being followed. Who knows for how long." Paris gasped and covered her face with both hands while Ben continued to explain. "It was a very close call both times, but I had luck on my side with the timing of the attacks. Both times some young men, different men, intervened and drove them off."

Paris wrapped her arms around herself and leaned back against the cushions. Her voice shook as she asked, "Ben, what are the police doing about this?"

He explained that he had yet to go to Scotland Yard to make a complaint, and that there was more to tell. The rest of the story, including the part Lilith Ward-Thomas had played, served to put even more worry on his mother's face. "Don't you see?" he said. "When they mailed the tape they figured that by the time you received it, they'd have me stashed away somewhere. It was probably sent just a few days ago at most, because last night was their first try."

"I'm so glad your elderly neighbor wasn't hurt. She was quite spunky to come back with the golf club." Her worried face took on a tender expression. "Bless her heart. I must meet her, thank her for helping my son."

"Sure, but not now. Her daughter is with her and she's very protective. I'll bet she's tried to put her to bed—without any luck." Ben's tone turned serious. "We have to figure out what they want from you. They'll probably try for me again, but we don't know if they're aware of Olivia.

She could be in danger too. They seem to have done their homework about our family."

"I tried Olivia, but with no joy. Of course, she rarely answers. I left a message asking if she'd talked to you in the last twenty-four hours." Paris reached for her purse and checked her phone, hoping for a message from Olivia. "She knows better than to just text me when it comes to family, and there's no voicemail." Her brow furrowed and she closed her eyes. Now she was in fear for her daughter as well.

It was time for Ben to tell her about Ana. She had been drawn into the drama unwillingly and also had need of protection. Ben took his mother's hands in his and fixed his eyes on hers. "There's someone else in this mess." He paused to be sure that Paris was focused on what he was saying, then continued, "The pub I was in last night … I was there to meet a journalist, Ana Doherty. She's a freelancer from America and is supposed to get an interview with me, because of the new book." His mother nodded in understanding. "She was with me on the street when the first attack happened. She screamed for help while a big tattooed bloke was trying to subdue me. He twisted my arm so hard that he dislocated my shoulder. That's the reason for the sling. Just then, three footballer-types, a bit in their cups, came up the alley from the pub and jumped on the first guy. Then they grabbed at his partner, who had gotten out of the old sedan to even up the fight. But he was no help… just got himself punched up. The young guys were too much for them and got in some good blows before pinning the big one on the ground.

"The lads made the point that it would take a while for the police to come, and they couldn't keep them face down on the pavement that long. If I'd known it wasn't just an isolated mugging, I'd have asked that they sit on the two of them and wait for the police. I had been punched in the face a couple of times, shoved hard against their car, and I could barely move my arm. I couldn't help them or myself."

Paris kept a stoic expression, but there were tears streaming down her face as she listened to what Ben had been through. Ben handed her the wet towel used to ice his shoulder and said, "It's okay, Mum. I'm fine now, thanks to Ana." When Paris had wiped her tears, he continued, "I think the lads had had enough and wanted to get on to the next pub. So they released the two of them and they made a quick getaway. I had seen the driver when I was in the pub. He had pushed his way in to stand next to me at the bar while I was waiting for the journalist to arrive. It was Ana. Then I saw him again, talking at a table to some man who seemed mad as hell."

"There are more details, especially about the rest of the night, but they aren't relevant right now. The point is, I have to do something about Ana. If they think we're a couple, they could resort to taking her. That would still be a way to apply pressure on you."

"This is beyond belief, Ben. Things like this don't happen to run-of-the-mill families like ours."

"Seems they do. So, we need a plan. Is Dad in the city today?"

"No, he stayed home … something to do with a carpenter coming."

"Then I think the best thing is for you to get on with your day as you normally would. You've been gone for over a week so there must be a lot to catch up on. Maybe you'll be lucky and come across something that sheds light on the situation."

Paris became agitated, and worry masked her attractive features as she considered her son's suggestion. "I agree that the key to this has to involve work, but I'm not comfortable with letting you out of my sight," she said, adopting a stern maternal expression.

Ben told her that she would be most useful trying to figure out, well in advance of the next contact, what it is they wanted from her. That would require time spent in the office. Ana was his immediate concern, and he explained to Paris that he had to find her quickly. He provided reassurance that he would be aware of his surroundings at all times and take every possible precaution. She reluctantly agreed to do as he asked and got up from the sofa. She put her arms around Ben again and held him as if a fierce wind were about to rip him away.

Then she let him go and walked toward the door. "Please, please, check in with me as much as you can this afternoon, while I'm in the office. I'll leave my mobile within reach. I won't accomplish anything unless I have hourly reassurance."

"Just take the train home on your regular schedule. Bring Dad into the loop and try to keep him from starting calls to all his contacts. It's not time for that."

He opened the door and Paris stepped out into the hallway. She turned back and pleaded, "Ben, I really think you should come home right away, not in a couple of days. Keeping an eye on you would be so much easier there, and when you find Ana, ask her to come too. Your father will keep you both safe."

"That's not Dad's job anymore. I feel more like I need to keep the two of you safe. I hate the unpredictability of this whole thing," Ben said, shaking his head in frustration. He walked Paris to the lift and pressed the call button. The doors opened and he reminded her to call immediately if she found something relevant. Then she was gone, and he hurried back to his flat to plan a way to find Ana. He threw a few things into a valise in preparation for escaping to the country house, figuring that he wouldn't have to come back to the flat and risk another encounter. His focus had to be on finding Ana and talking her into joining him in the country. The ruse of a shoulder too sore for driving was about to be tested, and he hoped he could pull it off.

Ben remembered that Ana was going to do some sightseeing, starting with the Tower of London. Surely she would have moved on from there by now. If she hadn't returned to the hotel already, she might be urged back by residual fatigue from the previous night's events. The best bet was to wait for her there. His car was parked at the end of the block. He all but ran up the street and then hurriedly tossed the valise in the back seat. It had been at least a week since he had driven the classic Jaguar, the purchase of which was his one indulgence after the success of his first book. The engine turned over and assumed a low growl that turned to a purr. After a short warm up he pulled into traffic and headed for Ana's hotel.

When Ben reached the location, he pulled into an underground garage and paid the attendant for the first few hours. He emerged into the light and shadows of the fading afternoon, walking quickly toward the hotel, with a brief stop to purchase a London Times. As soon as he walked through the entrance, he noticed the concierge following him with her eyes as he looked for a comfortable place to wait. He picked a chair with a clear view of the entrance.

The young woman approached him and asked, "Are you waiting for a guest, sir? I don't believe you're staying with us, are you?" She tossed her hair and smiled, clearly having looked for an excuse to talk to a man she found attractive, even to flirt a bit.

"Yes, I'm waiting for Ms. Doherty. She's expecting me, but I believe she's been held up. I'll just wait here and read the Times."

"But sir, I think I saw her come in a short while ago. We were just changing shifts and I only caught a glimpse, but I'm quite sure it was she. Let me see if her key has been picked up." She hurried back to her station and checked the numbered cubbyholes, running her finger along the row, stopping at number 438. It was empty.

Ben watched her turn and start back to where he was sitting. She spoke before she reached him. "I was right. Her key is gone, so she must be in her room. Would you like me to call up to announce you? It's protocol, really. I'm required … it's an extra protection for our guests."

Ben agreed that she should call, and he followed her to the desk. He could tell that the phone was continuing to ring without being answered, and he became disturbed. The concierge shrugged her shoulders, but kept the phone to her ear. After a few more seconds Ana answered. He was announced, approved, and the young woman hung up. Not having taken notice of the room number the night before, he inquired and was soon on the elevator. The doors opened at the fourth floor and he proceeded down the hall to number 438. He knocked somewhat softly and waited.

"Who is it?" she asked.

"It's Ben. And you were smart not to open the door, even if you did think it was me on the way up."

The door opened slowly, revealing only Ana's head, wrapped in a fluffy towel. She opened it just far enough for Ben to enter then explained that she had been in the shower. She felt quite unfit to be seen but hadn't wanted to leave him sitting in the lobby. He stepped sideways through the doorway, turned, and saw that the rest of her was also wrapped in a towel— only a towel. She clutched at it tightly and backed slightly away from him. This unexpected situation caused Ben to swallow hard, his intention to lure her to the country suddenly taking a back seat to an attack of desire. Her graceful neck, feminine shoulders and shapely legs were a feast for his eyes and he could feel his heart beat faster. He stepped back, putting her at more than arm's length while he tried to summon his self-control. *When is the time going to be right?* Ben thought.

Ana broke the brief period of uncomfortable silence. "I know you must have a reason for showing up here without calling. Not that I mind— I'm just curious." She waited for a response, but it seemed that Ben was weighing his words. While waiting for him to speak, she noticed how well he fit her idea of the handsome and casual Englishman. He was very appealing in his well-worn jeans, black tee shirt, and the famous leather jacket. It would have been easy to stare, but she turned away slightly, protecting herself from embarrassment.

Ben took a deep breath before beginning. "I have a proposition for you," he said, and then realized the inappropriate nature of his words, considering Ana's state of undress. As a distraction he walked to the window and turned his back to her before speaking. "What I meant to say is that I need to ask a favor."

"It's perfectly fine that you're here in person, but why didn't you just call?" Ben hesitated and Ana continued, "Could you please stay turned toward the window? I want to trade this towel for a robe."

"I'll stay turned around, scout's honor." Ben was becoming nervous, anxious to convince Ana of his story. He knew they should get on the road right away. The words he had planned to use escaped him, and he wondered how he would get her to drop everything and accompany him.

"Okay, I'm decent now. Turn around and tell me what kind of favor you need from me. I can't imagine." She crossed her arms and sat down on the edge of the bed.

"I'm needed at my parents' house a couple of days earlier than I had planned. I threw some things in a bag, jumped in my car and took off before remembering my promise to you ... about the interview. I remember telling you we'd have a couple of days to get it done." He waited to get a read on her response to his feigned forgetfulness. She just sat there, looking at him with a neutral expression and waiting for the rest of it. "I didn't have the hotel's number, so I decided to stop here and hoped you'd either be here, or I'd wait in the lobby and watch for you. I'm glad you were here."

"Well, obviously I'm not happy that you're leaving sooner than you had planned. I'll have trouble putting off my editor for another week or so and continuing to ask him to cover expenses." Ana got up and started to pace in front of the bed, then said, "But you still haven't asked for the favor. Is to forget about the interview what you're asking?"

"No worries about the interview, or your editor. That's why I wanted to catch you. My proposition is that you come with me to my parents' house. They love company. You'll like them, I promise." His expression was expectant.

"I couldn't just 'show up' and put them on the spot. I would be too uncomfortable."

"I promise you wouldn't. I used to bring a buddy with me sometimes. They are always very gracious. Besides, the interview isn't the only reason I asked you. Even on the drive over here my shoulder started to hurt. It's really in no condition for such a long drive. If you come with me, you can help with the driving. That way, everybody wins!"

"Are you kidding? I've never driven in England. I'll kill us both!" she said, covering her face and shaking her head back and forth. "Why can't we just take a train?"

"We'll need a car while we're there, and besides, everyone has a first time." Ana shot him a look he couldn't quite decipher. Continuing to plead his case he said, "So don't worry, you'll have me guiding you. I'll tell you which lane you should be in, how fast to go… you know … the basics. I promise to be patient." She searched Ben's face for a clue to his sincerity. He paused a moment before declaring, "If I'm not afraid, you shouldn't be either."

The period of silence continued, and Ben could almost see the wheels turning as Ana paced around the room, her expression a bit serious. Finally she spoke. "I guess that if I want to get my assignment done, I don't have much choice," she said, then added, "But you have to suffer through getting us out of the city. There's no way I'm driving in London."

Ben could tell by her tone that she was not looking forward to having another unexpected challenge foisted upon her by the man she just wanted to interview and be done with it. And as yet he hadn't told her that she would be driving a powerful sports car. "So, are we on?" Ben asked, breaking into the most charming smile he could muster.

Ana sighed and slumped her shoulders before answering. "You have me in a corner, Mr. McKinnon. I guess I'm going sightseeing in the country." She paused, obviously thinking of what should come next. "Now tell me, what kind of clothes are appropriate for being a guest at a country house?"

CHAPTER FIVE

Ben went down to the lobby while Ana busied herself making a few quick choices from her Spartan assortment of clothing. She had always prided herself on packing light, and lacking the drama and aftermath of an attempted kidnapping, most of her previous assignments had been completed in short order. As she piled things into her bag, she thought about what kind of impression she would make in general, appropriate clothing or not. Granted, the opinions of Ben's family would be out of her control, but driving on the wrong side of the road and arriving in one piece was of greater concern. She slipped into her one pair of jeans and the black tee she had been talked into while sightseeing at the Tower of London. Some might have called it tacky, but she liked the bright colors in the screen-printed crown imbedded with fake jewels. The bold design spoke to her, some sort of message about the monarchy. Whether it was good or bad remained an unknown. Best-case scenario, Ben's parents would see it as her *homage* to the queen, rather than an insult. She grabbed her own leather jacket out of the small closet then pulled the room's door shut as she wheeled the suitcase out into the hall.

An older couple was waiting in front of the elevator and stepped in quickly when the doors opened. Ana hurried down the hall and called after them, "Hold the elevator, please. I'm in a terrible hurry." The man managed to keep the doors open with his arm and nodded to her as she entered. The woman held her umbrella close to her body and stepped closer to her husband. She looked Ana up and down before turning away, nose in the air. *Uppity cow,* Ana thought.

The elevator stopped at the lobby, and before the doors had opened completely, she spotted Ben. He quickly subdued his laughter when he saw the tee shirt, causing her a moment of doubt that bordered on embarrassment. "Well, I thought the trip would be shorter than it's turned out, and what little I brought was for business." Continuing an unnecessary explanation regarding her wardrobe, Ana said, "The shirt is just a souvenir. Besides my raincoat and what I was wearing when we met, I'd only thrown in a pair of jeans, a jacket and a couple of sweaters. But I thought a sweater might be too hot for the drive. I run hot when I'm nervous," she said, rambling on in defense her choice.

"It suits you. I like it. On you it's more whimsical than tourist-y."

"Nice recovery. I really have no illusions about its tastefulness. I just liked the colors. And when you only have one tee, black is better for spills. This is a lot of talk about a tee shirt."

"That shirt is nothing compared to some of the wild outfits my sister puts together. She works hard at being unconventional. She would call it trendy." Ben's tone was disapproving, but with a tolerant edge.

"So, you have a sister. Will I get to meet her at your parents' house?"

"Her name is Olivia. I have no idea if she'll be there. She makes a project of keeping her activities to herself. Thinks it makes her look independent. But she still depends on my parents quite a bit. I guess she'll grow up in her own time, not ours."

" You're the big brother?"

" Yep… by about twelve years." Ben reached for Ana's suitcase and said, "Let's go. Nothing matters other than getting out of town. I think rush hour is winding down by now. Are you ready?"

Ana walked over to the desk and told the concierge that she would be away for a few days, but that she would keep the room, that some of her belongings remained there. Ben took charge of her suitcase and handed her the leather jacket. He jumped on the opportunity to ask if she'd had it long enough to consider it a dependable friend. Ana rolled her eyes and followed him out of the hotel into the fading afternoon. For reasons of safety Ben did not want to leave Ana standing on the street while he fetched the car, so he requested that she come with him. They walked a quick block to the garage entrance, Ana trying to match Ben's long stride.

They stopped at the kiosk and Ben gave the attendant his ticket. The young man matched it to the number on the key and jogged down the row to fetch the car. Ana's mouth dropped open when she saw the emerald green Jaguar approaching. The attendant stopped the car in front of them and got out. He opened the passenger door and waited for Ana to get in; however, she stood firm, her expression incredulous. Ben opened the trunk, tossed in her suitcase and closed the trunk with a flourish. He went 'round to the passenger door, and as he motioned Ana to get in, said cheerfully, "Climb aboard! We're chasing the light."

Ana's expression was still one of shock. "Seriously?" she exclaimed, "Surely you don't expect me to drive a sports car— and on the left side of the road! I can barely function with a standard three gear transmission, let alone what I imagine is four or maybe five in this four-wheeled museum piece."

Ben had to laugh at the brief diatribe, and then said, teasing, "Are you insulting my baby? You can be sure that it's up to snuff in every way." She hesitated a moment before speaking. "We need to get a few things straight. Should I get it in writing that I'll be relieved of any responsibility for damage while driving this car?"

"That won't be necessary. Like I said before, I have faith in your ability to rise to a challenge. I've seen you in action." Ben smiled, hoping to put her at ease. "For the record, you're not liable. Also for the record, this is a classic 1962 XKE 2+2, so I don't race around in it like an idiot. It's not that kind of sports car, at least not to me."

Ana sighed, seeming relieved, and then slid into the passenger seat. With his good arm Ben pulled up the seatbelt and handed it to her. He shut the door, then hurried around to the other side and climbed in beside her. She looked things over, first running her hand over the walnut instrument panel then the supple leather seat, its color reminiscent of warm caramel.

"Have you noticed yet?" Ben asked.

"Noticed what? I've noticed there's a back seat and that the whole interior seems to be top grade."

"Do you see a gear shift?"

It took Ana a moment before she realized what he was telling her. She looked more closely and noticed the leather encased gear knob extending from the console. A bit confused, she asked again what she was supposed to see. Ben had been playing with her and decided it was enough. They had a two-hour drive ahead, if traffic cooperated.

"It's an automatic transmission. I couldn't help but enjoy watching you stew about having to shift." Ana picked up on the playful glint in his eye before he continued. "This is definitely a classic car, but as I said, I don't drive like a racer. It's actually quite easy to maneuver."

"So you let my angst be your entertainment, Mr. McKinnon?" Her tone was accusatory, but unconvincing. Ben could see that besides being beautiful, she was a good sport. "I'm too relieved to give you a thrashing, but don't pull anymore stunts on me, or you'll be driving yourself, shoulder or no."

Ben agreed to be good, and then told Ana about the extensive work the previous owner had done on the Jaguar, which included rebuilding the engine and replacing the transmission. "I wondered why the man would consider selling it after spending so much to put it right. That might have been a red flag to some people. Fact is, I just wanted it, no questions asked. It ended up being a good deal." He reached up and patted the dashboard.

Ana thought about his attachment to the leather jacket, and now this elite automobile. She wondered if he could relate to people in the same way, especially to a woman. There were those who could only attach to inanimate objects, the predictability and ability to control being the key. If this were the case with Ben, she would be gravely disappointed. The

Jaguar's engine turned over with a powerful growl, bringing a startling end to her pondering. It settled easily into a satisfied purr before Ben pulled away from the kiosk, exiting the dark garage and embarking on what was expected to be a few relaxing days in the country.

The commuter traffic had not eased, and it was slow going across town, although it was good sightseeing for Ana. Reaching the M40 from Regent Street required passing through a tollbooth, around Trafalgar Square and then skirting Piccadilly Circus, where five main London roads converge. Ben pointed out the Shaftesbury Memorial Fountain and the only tall building left with a large neon display. After more signs and more streets, London began to thin out and they finally eased onto their route toward the countryside.

Modern buildings gave way to green fields and pockets of forest, all sliced clean through by divided highway. In spite of the slight variations in the road's direction, they were basically traveling due northwest. The sun was settling toward the horizon and glared through the windshield, making the view ahead indistinct. Gazing out the side window Ana could see clusters of rooftops nestled here and there among the rolling hills. She imagined each village to be like the charming backdrops created by Agatha Christie for her novels of murder and mayhem.

Ben angled off onto the M25 toward Oxford, then junction eight toward Cheltenham. Once settled on his route, he reached forward to turn on the CD player. His hands were settled back on the wheel before the soft and mournful sounds of a ballad by Johnny Cash filled the void. Ana listened quietly and after a moment or so she turned her body slightly to face him.

"Seriously? Country music? You're just one surprise after another."

"Don't you like classic country?" he asked. "Would either James Taylor or the MJQ be more to your liking?"

"No, it's not that, although the MJQ is definitely a favorite of mine. It's just not what I expected from a Brit with a literary education."

Conversation was suspended while they listened to lyrics of unrequited love and heartbreak. Ana had known another man who liked country music, but he was from the southern U.S. and it was to be expected. Her philosophy about men who like country lyrics was formed as a result of her experience with him. She concluded that some are either incapable of expressing deep feelings, or uncomfortable sharing emotion. They can find emotional solace in the lyrics, so often about lost love. Privately, she admitted that such an opinion was a rather harsh analysis, when based on only one romantic interlude. Yet she still fancied herself an armchair psychologist. It could come in handy for a journalist.

Ben broke the conversational silence. "I can't remember whether I told you this, but I was an 'American' until I was almost thirteen. Actually, I am an American. I was born in the U.S. ... San Francisco. Maybe I'm one of those people they call an expat."

"No, I don't think so, because you have two passports. Even though you've been here since you were just thirteen, you haven't picked up much UK English accent. You sound about sixty percent American, forty percent English—a nice mix."

"Yeah ... that's been brought to my attention more than once. My mother sounds very public school, as she should, since her education was tops." Ben smiled, then added, "I think my 'Americanization' has always disappointed her a bit."

"I guess you must actually *feel* more English though, since your parents both come from the UK."

Ben turned down the sound and continued, "While I was attending university here in England I did a year of study abroad. I was born in San Francisco, and attended school there, so I decided to go back. Those were good memories, my childhood, except that my father was gone a lot with work."

"SFSU or USF?"

"San Francisco State University. At that time their Humanities department was highly rated. So with my English major, it was a perfect choice."

"So I guess it's like they say … the guy's a little bit country, a little bit rock and roll."

"Guess so– but not so much the rock and roll. I generally like all music, some kinds more than others… except rap and hip hop."

Ana put her purse down by her feet, settled into her seat, and said, "That's a relief. I'd hate to be trapped in the car with either of those." She turned to him, conjuring up something else meant to impress, and said, "I remember being told by some guy about Kris Kristofferson doing country lyrics … said he was quite a poet. Or maybe the poetry was set to music. I don't remember exactly what he said"

Ben straightened up in his seat, stiffened his arms and tightened his grip on the wheel. Ignoring her reference to poetic country lyrics, he asked, "Just a guy, or a boyfriend?"

Ben's question was immediate, and she wondered why his tone had been curt and the question rather personal. But she had to admit to liking his interest, given that it could be interpreted as a bit of jealousy. "Just a guy at some party. Don't even know why I remembered." Her choice of a white lie was meant to diffuse any further questions about her past. She knew it didn't matter because she never wanted to see Luke again.

"Well, you're right about Kristofferson," Ben said, his voice subdued yet more relaxed.

He declined to comment further, and they settled into a slightly tense lapse in conversation during which Ben turned up the volume. Ana noticed that he was clenching his jaw and wondered if his shoulder was starting to hurt. Half way through an old standard by Patsy Kline, he lowered the sound again and asked, "Is that your phone I hear?" He took another opportunity to tease her and said, "Who has a song from The Wizard of Oz for a ringtone. Ding-Dong the Witch is Dead? Really?"

"That's no sillier than others I've heard. Besides, it's my favorite movie," she added, defending her choice as she fished through her purse, digging deep before bringing the sound to the surface. "It's my boss. Uh oh." Ben turned the music off and waited to see if she would answer. "He probably wants to know why I've gone 'off the grid' with this assignment. No way I can explain all of what's happened. I'll try to get away with just sending a text." Ana leaned her head back against the headrest and contemplated what might be a satisfactory answer to her boss's question. After a moment's pause she began to type her one-fingered response. Ben also wondered how she intended to justify her presence in the Cotswolds rather than in London, where she was expected to be knee deep in words and hovering diligently over her laptop.

He waited a few minutes and then asked, "What did you tell him? Any details?"

"Not specifically. I just said that I was pursuing a very interesting piece of back-story on you, and it required me to leave the city. I hope that keeps him at bay for a few days, but I can't stall longer than that."

"I'll do whatever I can to keep you employed," Ben said, trying to lighten the mood.

"There are worse things than losing an assignment," Ana countered, "But I'm in too deep with this one. I've convinced myself that I'm the only one who can do justice to an article about Benedict McKinnon … or maybe I should say I'm caught up in an adventure with Benedict McKinnon." She glanced at Ben, her comment having brought a smile to his face and a certain glint to his eyes. "In any case, I can't walk away … unless you send me."

He glanced at her quickly then returned his focus to the road ahead. "I hope I don't have to send you away. If I did, it would be for your safety." He realized that very soon he was going to have to explain to Ana the fact that he had whisked her away from London for just that reason, and under false, though innocent, pretenses. "I sincerely hope the adventure part is over—at least the dangerous part." Ben's gut told him not to believe his own words, and that the danger was likely far from over. He paused a moment before adding, "I'm sure there's a lot more to what's happened than we know right now."

"You're probably right. I don't think you should let your guard down."

"No worries about that. My eyes are open," said Ben, hoping to reassure her.

"Regardless of what's happened on this assignment— whether it turns into a full-fledged adventure or not— I'm pretty maxed out on moving around constantly. It's the curse of being a journalist." Ana turned her head to look out the window, her thoughts drifting. When she spoke her voice was so quiet that it seemed she was reluctant for Ben to hear. "I went into it assuming that being on the move all the time would be glamorous." She sighed a weary sigh, an unspoken lament that piqued his curiosity about her history.

After another half hour they exited the A40 and went through a series of roundabouts before finding the B4425. From that point the roads became increasingly narrow by the mile. Soon they were passing through a quintessential village called Bourton-on-the-Water. Ana thought the village names were often very strange. Ben mentioned in passing that the village was known as the Little Venice of the Cotswolds, due to its canals. She asked if they could come back another day to take a look, and he agreed. He noticed that she was trying to stretch in her seat, but was inhibited by the belt across her chest and thus settled for leaning her head against the window. Seeing that she was tired, he assured her that they hadn't much further to go before reaching his parents' home.

Ana's reluctance to drive the Jaguar had kept her quiet when Ben failed to ask that she take the wheel so he could rest his shoulder. He had been so adamant about his need for assistance with the driving and she couldn't figure out why he looked so comfortable and happy driving his 'baby.' She finally decided to ask. She turned down the music, now a medley by Norah Jones, and said, "I like this CD. It's mellow and relaxing. Is that why you look so relaxed at the wheel ... in spite of a sore shoulder that you thought wouldn't hold out for two plus hours on the road?"

Ben smiled—slyly, Ana thought—and kept his eyes on the curves ahead. "Busted! Stitched up! In the frame... and whatever other terms there are for being found out. I will confess… but not until we get to Mom and Dad's."

Something about his reaction made Ana laugh, her tolerance boosted by the fact that she really had not wanted to drive the car anyway. He seemed genuinely contrite as he tried to deflect her question with humor. Ben felt that her laughter was a reprieve, and his thoughts returned to their pub meeting and his unbidden vision of her beside him in the Jaguar, her hair swirling in the wind, the crescendo of her musical laugh as he increased speed.

Ben quickly returned to the present when he turned off of the village's high street onto a narrow road. In a few minutes the road split and the car bore left, although the directional sign had been turned cockeyed— no doubt a prank by some mischievous youth. The road narrowed even further and required his complete concentration. He reduced speed, and with the hedgerows that grew close to the pavement as his guide, he focused on the wide swath of brightness from the car's xenon headlights. Beyond the hedgerows on either side were small stands of trees— pocket forests as he had described them to Ana. There were no streetlamps on country roads, and the blackness was setting in quickly. They hadn't met another vehicle since leaving the village. She was careful not to distract Ben with conversation, having become edgy as soon as the light died and the road became one lane. Moving beyond the small forests, the landscape cleared to grassy fields that climbed gently toward the hills ahead. The last vestiges of the setting sun glowed gray lavender from behind the softly rolling silhouette of the Cotswolds.

Ben broke the silence. "The driveway is just ahead, beyond that long row of trees arched over the road."

Ana sat up straighter in her seat and became more alert to the surroundings. She rolled down the window and stuck her arm out into the cool air. It began to blow her hair, first across her face, and then as she brushed it away with her hand, it billowed out around her head. Ben was once again taken back to his fantasy of the laughing beauty riding beside him.

"I hope I remember the code," he said. "I've only been here once since they added the gate security. The gate's always been there, but it used to be secured with only a padlock. I can't tell you how many keys my sister and I lost."

"Maybe they added an intercom. Then it won't matter."

He slowed and turned the car left, coming to a stop in front of tall double gates. On either side limestone walls stood tall, covered in well-trimmed greenery now robbed of color by the moonless night. Stopping beside the lighted key code box, Ben lowered the window and punched in some numbers. His memory served him well. The gates opened slowly and he proceeded, looking back to see if they closed behind him. The gravel driveway was tree-lined and rather long, ending in a circular drive. Ana rolled her window down halfway, hoping to hear the yap of a fox or the song of a nightingale piercing the darkness. She could hear water and could just make out the colorless shapes of a hedged circular enclosure and what she imagined was a fountain. Ben pulled the Jaguar in close to the front walk and shut off the engine.

CHAPTER SIX

Valerie Amesworth McKinnon had spent the better part of the afternoon with her therapist. The aftermath of those sessions had always seemed to cause more conflict than resolution, and as a result she would feel at loose ends for the rest of the day. But on this particular day, it was more than that. She felt herself the victim of a personal attack and now wondered why she should even continue. Nothing had changed as a result of being in therapy. But she appeased her parents by assuring them that the process was helpful, and after all, they were footing the bill. So far she had refused to see that her willful nature stifled her progress. Valerie had seen each visit as a skirmish, and rather than change her own behavior she saw each verbal exchange with the therapist as a chance to gain what she thought was an upper hand. She had maintained the delusion that the doctor would eventually take her side.

She stopped for coffee at a corner kiosk, a quick espresso downed in two gulps. The final quarter hour of her appointment had left her slightly disoriented, so in order to clear her head she decided to walk part of the way back to her place of business, Boutique Le Bijou. Yet within a few blocks she became tired and hailed a taxi. Before reaching the boutique, she told the cabbie to pull over. She paid, quickly got out, and crossed the sidewalk to an open gate leading into the neighborhood park.

In this corner of London, spring had done its work, handing off its magic wand to summer. Color washed the flowerbeds and trees that had been laid-bare by winter's cold. A warm wind blew the trees, once again lush with green, their abundant leaves rustling in tandem with each playful gust. She meandered along the path, pausing to observe a bed of luxuriant yellow roses, and then stopped at a green iron bench directly across. Valerie settled there in the shade, her face to the sky, listening to the occasional birdsong and the buzz of an insect around her head. Soon her thoughts began to run deep.

Once again, as she had done countless times before, she returned to the beginning, to that first moment she believed her life was set plainly before her. When she had met Ben in a London pub on her spring break, she was a senior at Vassar, and he was in his first year of grad school. After they met, he pursued Valerie daily, feeding her fragile ego with his youthful eloquence. She was the girl with the flaxen hair— the color of her eyes lay somewhere between green and violet, like the sky or sea on a sunny day—she had the body of a goddess. Though she could see now how over the top his words had been, such poetic expression from a young man her age had been unknown to her. She had never before been romanced.

The two had become mutually besotted, and within weeks she was enchanted with the idea of being married to who she believed would be a famous author. She recognized that she was a rich girl, consistently indulged and used to getting her way. It suited her. An inbred talent for manipulation had always accomplished this result. In her girlish imagination of their life and Ben's success, she would be another version, a better version, of Hemingway's Martha Gelhorn.

Valerie came to resent her parents. She had replayed their part in the downturn of her life many times. When she announced that with only one semester lying between her and a degree she would not be returning to school, they had all but washed their hands of the daughter who had always been their princess. She remembered the day she told them all about Ben and his aspirations. Even more unacceptable to them was her intention to marry a graduate school student who aspired to be a writer. Her father's constant rant still rung in her ears: A world of poverty, my girl. That's what you're signing on for. Her mother would whine about the fact that she would never make any of the 'right' party lists being married to a virtual nobody, and an English fellow to boot. Of course the more they disapproved, the more strongly she set her course. The final disappointment was an elopement. Valerie could still picture their faces when she and Ben arrived at her home and announced their marriage.

Much later, after things fell apart, she had been sure that Ben always resented having excluded his parents, with whom he was extremely close. It was clear to her now: Pushing for the elopement had been her first mistake. Ben had seen, too late, that without a doubt she would require his complete and total allegiance in all things.

As memory carried her back through their relationship, she all but cursed her romantic imagination. The life of a writer's wife hadn't turned out to be the glamorous adventure she had envisioned. They struggled financially, and in spite of her pleas, Ben wouldn't take help from his parents. Nor would he have allowed interference from her family, if they had offered. They did not. She saw it all going wrong, but hadn't been insightful enough to know that her immaturity and sense of entitlement, not Ben's emotional withdrawal and subsequent indiscretion, would be the end of them. As she sat there, eyes closed, feeling the sun's warmth and the soft wind on her face, the reality struck her like the sting of a bee. Unbidden tears trickled down her cheeks. She accepted having driven Ben to act. For the first time in her life Valerie admitted that in spite of having tolerant and doting parents, she was not and never had been the perfect princess they had imagined.

* * *

The windows of Dr. Kate Loxley's office provided a broad view of the Thames. It was a rare cloudless day, the low-slung morning fog having dispersed. She could see clearly across the water to the row of gray industrial-looking apartment buildings perched on the rise above the riverbank. A generous amount of landscaping softened the cold look of the architecture, and a few docks, intended for mooring boats owned by some of the residents, had been built straight down from the buildings. All in all, she had to admit she approved of the development, however glad she was not to be a resident.

It was fortunate that she had a thirty-minute break before the next patient. Without doubt she needed some time to process what had occurred during the session with Valerie McKinnon. Dr. Kate, as she urged her patients to call her, had broken her very strict rule of treatment whereby she avoided giving opinions or advice. The stalemate in Valerie's treatment had been going on for an unacceptable amount of time, her patient's lapses in keeping appointments being a consideration. Kate intended to suggest at their next meeting that she find another therapist, due to the general lack of progress. The doctor had reached her breaking point during the appointment that had just ended, a result of being mired in an interminable silence with her patient. Silent, that is, until the moment Valerie's willfulness finally caused the doctor to break her golden rule. Dr. Kate finally spoke first, and everything she had been thinking came spilling out, not only in the form of advice, but in her feelings about Valerie's self-centered and delusional view of her life.

After telling her she was behaving like a willful adolescent in her obsession with Ben, her ex-husband, and that she wasn't trying in the least to move on or take responsibility for her life, her patient just sat still, mouth agape. For what Kate thought could be the first time, Valerie was listening. At least Kate thought she was listening. The roles were reversed, and the doctor was doing all the talking. First, she told Valerie she didn't really want to improve, that she was comfortable in the security of her old behaviors, primarily in her obsession with the man whom she had driven away with her unreasonable demands. Kate was aware of what Valerie had demanded from the marriage because she had revealed a litany of her unmet needs early in treatment, and assumed they would bear repeating ad infinitum.

Then Kate started on the advice. She urged Valerie to change her environment, to remove herself from the reminders of her life with Ben in London. She suggested that Valerie return to America, to the bosom of her family. Once there she could start a new chapter in her life, perhaps meet someone new or even finish her degree. Kate told her to face facts. Because she didn't make it a priority, her business was always on the edge of a financial abyss, and the situation was draining her father's bank account as well as his patience. The frustrated man had contacted Kate the week prior, hoping for the slightest hint of a positive outcome to his investment. She also remembered Valerie's most recent lament about her floundering business. The outburst ended with Kate's advice that first and foremost, Valerie must resume her maiden name, and that the finality of the act would help her to move on, to reinvent herself. Kate had said it all, everything she'd thought since the beginning, and it was cleansing to put words to her frustration.

The doctor could see that her verbal outpouring had left Valerie at a loss. She sat stone-faced for several minutes then drew forward in her chair and got up to leave. Her only retort was to tell Kate that she was considering a short vacation, a change of scene, and would probably be in touch upon her return. Kate just nodded. Her patient turned slowly and without another word left the office.

* * *

Valerie spent a few minutes regaining control of her emotions before rising from the park bench and continuing on to the boutique. As she rounded the corner into the street where her business was located, she saw several potential customers standing outside talking amongst themselves. Valerie hurried up the street to her shop, and spouting apologies for their inconvenience, she unlocked the door. It seemed evident that Chloe, the shop girl who was supposed to be in attendance, had closed for lunch and not returned. The women entered the shop and moved about, inspecting the merchandise, while Valerie fussed at things behind the counter, taking a careful accounting of the cash drawer.

She had become increasingly aware that Chloe was a bit of a flake, but she had a fantastic sense of style and seemed to zero in on what would please a customer. This was her most inexcusable stunt so far. But Valerie knew how difficult it was to find someone truly qualified to work for what she could pay. Chloe was young and hip, and still lived with her parents. Valerie surmised that Chloe's main reason for keeping the job was to take advantage of the small employee discount. Regardless, she planned to give her a good dressing down for her irresponsibility.

The women filed out, one by one, without making a purchase. Valerie sighed, having become used to the fact that most shoppers only want to look and have little intention to buy. She decided to call Chloe, to make sure it was only negligence on her part, not illness. Just as she picked up her mobile phone to dial, the business phone rang. "Hello, Boutique Le Bijou, Valerie McKinnon here," she said in her most business-like manner.

In a hesitant and subdued voice Chloe Lambert began to speak. "This is Chloe. I know you must be beyond annoyed with me for not opening the shop after lunch, but I had a good reason."

"What could be a good reason for me to lose business?"

"I'm sorry if you lost any business, but I couldn't get back to the shop. I'm in the hospital."

"My God, what happened to you?" Valerie said with genuine concern. She began to pace back and forth behind the counter, obviously very disturbed by the news.

"I stepped off the curb and got hit by a car! I was lucky because it had begun to slow to make a turn. It was more of a glancing blow."

"That's terrible. How injured are you? At least you're conscious and coherent."

"Broken ankle, slight concussion and a torn ligament in my knee."

"You poor thing. What can I do to help?"

"Well, they're keeping me here overnight, because of the concussion."

Valerie paused before asking the question that pertained to her own inconvenience. In a concerned tone she asked, "Chloe, how long will it be before you can return to work? Any idea?" She waited, realizing that the young woman probably had no idea.

"I'm in a cast for six weeks, then they say I'll need therapy for at least another month. But I think the doctor said I could be switched to something called a 'boot' in a few weeks. But I still wouldn't be able to stand for long periods."

"Well, well… Seems I'm up a stream without a paddle—we both are."

"What?" Chloe asked. "I've never heard that saying before."

"It's American. Just means that I've got a problem with no probable solution. Your problem will solve itself, in six weeks."

Chloe sighed and said, "I'm so sorry, but I couldn't help it. Are you going to replace me? I really like working in your shop, and I always do my best."

"Don't worry. I have no intention of letting you go. I just have to figure out what to do. I can't be there all the time."

"My sister was here. I told her I might get the sack, and she said she would help out at the shop, if it would help me keep my job. But I have to be honest … she really doesn't know much about clothes. She's only sixteen and still a total tomboy."

"Please thank her for me, but that doesn't sound like the best idea. I think the best thing is for me to close the shop for a few weeks while I sort it out. My ex-sister-in-law has been after me to take a trip with her. If it wouldn't be longer than that, I just might take her up on it." As the thought of closing the shop entered Valerie's mind, the thought of how her father would react to that decision came directly after. She sensed that his tolerance was wearing thin. Daughter or not, his investment had brought little return, if any. Perhaps it would be best not to tell him until after the fact.

Chloe interrupted Valerie's short reverie. "If that's all, the nurse has come in to give me something for pain. I'll probably be incoherent in a few minutes."

"Oh yes, that's all for now. But can I bring you anything? I doubt you really want or need visitors since you'll be going home tomorrow. I'm sure your parents will baby you, so enjoy it while you can."

Chloe laughed a little then there was nothing. Valerie wondered if she had hung up, or if the nurse was administering the drug. Maybe it had taken hold already. Just as she was ready to disconnect the call, Chloe spoke. "I just remembered. A man called several times this morning, looking for you. He wouldn't give his name."

"Are you sure it wasn't Mr. Langdon? He's been after me to go out to dinner with him, but I've declined because there's just something about him that makes me feel a creepy discomfort. Not nice to say." Valerie wondered why she was drawing the injured Chloe into the situation, but continued. "He came into the store asking if he could come back with the portfolio of his company's hats. We exchanged business cards, but I told him that with current fashion trends, the call for hats was virtually non-existent. Then the calls about dinner started—like clockwork."

In a quiet and slurry voice, words disjointed, Chloe said, "Not him… different voice… wanted a number…Olivia…" Then there was silence.

Valerie ended the call. Confusion set in as she wondered why someone would call her shop in search of Olivia. Chloe would be asleep by now. She couldn't know if the girl had found Olivia's number and shared it. *Who in their right mind would give out a friend's number to a male caller, and a stranger,* she thought, and then set about tidying up the shop and removing cash from the drawer. The morning's receipts totaled two, both paid by credit card. Happy to avoid a trip to the bank, she stuffed the cash in an envelope and put it into her bag. After checking locks at the back entrance, she gathered her belongings, switched the sign from open to closed, locked the doors and headed up the street to hail a taxi.

* * *

The last patient of the day had required a little extra time, and Dr. Kate had accommodated his need. But now she was more than ready to end what had been an unusually long and demanding day. The sunlight that seeped through the partially opened drapes had died, telling her that day was now night. She disliked taking the Tube after dark. No Tube after dark was just one of the mandates given to her years before by her late husband. She could still hear his voice reciting the various rules of safety, insisted upon throughout their marriage. Previously a mild annoyance to her on occasion, she now missed the consistent reminders given most mornings as they prepared to leave the house for their workday. It had been four years and she could still hear his voice. Would she forget it as the years passed? The thought disturbed her. She put her computer to sleep, informed her service she was leaving, turned off the lights and headed out to the elevator.

Once on the street, Kate was able to hail a cab very quickly. She was soon on her way home to Boris, her decrepit old Yorkie, and a welcome glass of wine followed by some sort of easy meal. She laid her head back against the seat and reviewed the day. She had had trouble focusing on the patients who came after Valerie. The confrontational experience of that session was weighing on her. Without bidding the memories, she was taken back to the first time she had seen Ben and Valerie, now more than seven years ago. She had consented to treat their marriage, not realizing what she was in for. It became clear early on that Valerie's purpose was to engage an advocate for her point of view and to validate her role of victim.

Ben had been contrite, cooperative and unusually quiet. Kate expected that he had found talking made little difference when it came to Valerie's complaints. It soon became clear that therapy was her idea, a last attempt to keep Ben in her life. In their first session Kate had learned that Ben was guilty of an indiscretion. Though unsubstantiated, Valerie maintained there had been more than one. After a few sessions with both of them together, it became more and more obvious what it must have been like to be married to the woman. She decided to see each separately, and when Ben had the opportunity to speak unimpeded, he was forthcoming about what was the real truth of their life together. Her experience and training made obvious which partner saw things realistically and spoke truthfully.

The more time Dr. Kate spent with Valerie, the easier it was to understand Ben's actions, if not to approve of them. Yet she found the wife to be a very interesting case—a challenge— perhaps even a case study to be written about at some point. She had required complete allegiance, which meant that Ben was expected to bow to her whims and provide the amount of attention she expected. Ben concluded that no one could please her and thus responded to her demands by withdrawing further and further. The more attention she either asked for or demanded through tantrums and attempted manipulation, the less he was inclined to give.

Eventually he had withdrawn from her to the point where his need for physical companionship urged him to cheat. When Valerie became aware of his infidelity, she tried, very poorly, to dispatch herself with pills. It was clear to Kate that the act was Valerie's deluded effort to bring him back to her. Kate's intention in therapy was to guide her to that realization. She confided to Ben that if Valerie had wanted to succeed, she would have taken more pills. Nor would she have scheduled lunch with his sister, whom she knew would come looking for her when she didn't show up at the restaurant. It had been an act of egocentric desperation. It was Ben's sense of guilt that made him agree to take part in therapy. He had quickly established his position and repeated to Kate what he had told Valerie many times: He would not treat her like royalty.

Kate was roused from deep thought by the driver's voice telling her they had reached her address. Checking her watch before paying, she realized that her review of the Ben and Valerie saga had occupied her mind for over half an hour. She scolded herself for failing to leave work at the office. Once out of the taxi she could hear Boris barking his usual greeting from the partially opened window of her third floor flat. He was perched atop the pillow she kept for him on the window seat. She realized that he had spent most of his life waiting for their return, now just hers. A small set of doggie stairs now helped accommodate the old legs that would no longer jump that high. She headed up the steps to the entrance, preparing to shut out the rest of the world and its problems.

CHAPTER SEVEN

A large café macchiato sat cooling beside her iPad, opened to the first page of the London Times. Ignoring both, Olivia Grace McKinnon relaxed at a small table in her favorite coffee bar, fully engrossed in daydreaming. Regardless of her momentary disinterest in the news, and in spite of her relative youth, she regularly made herself aware of national and world events. She was certainly not politically motivated in the regular sense, believing that all politicians were talking heads who could not inherently speak truth on any subject. Asked by her parents about her interest in the news, she explained that the interest was primarily an effort to stay current with how badly those in charge were messing things up. In spite of reaching age twenty-seven, she had not quite advanced beyond the age of youthful idealism. Yet her parents took comfort in the fact that her opinions had not as yet translated into activism. Olivia's most serious concerns usually involved wardrobe. She wondered on a daily basis whether or not she had attained the right look for whatever was in store.

She occupied a tiny flat in Soho, much to her parents' regret. They worried that the neighborhood might not be safe enough for a young woman who had been raised in the protected environment of the countryside. Her rebellions were subtle, but effective. Long after any parental thoughts of childbearing had been abandoned, they had been blessed with Olivia. She became somewhat an object of worship, both to them and to her big brother. Ben had been her protector, the hero of her fairytale games, the one person whom she could not disappoint. Or at least she had tried to make him proud. She suspected it hadn't happened yet, but she was trying—would try harder perhaps. Olivia looked away from the news and gazed out of the floor to ceiling windows at the neighborhood residents busying themselves with daily life. Her thoughts drifted to the memory of years spent daydreaming under the giant English oak that graced the lawn and garden of her parents' home—her home.

Having come down with a slight case of summer lethargy, Olivia had left her job early and made the urge for coffee her first priority. She had taken a shortcut through the neighborhood park and noticed that summer was in full bloom. Bursts of color delighted the eyes of those who chose that route toward their destinations, and she was glad to have done the same. Her leisurely walk had prompted a few ideas regarding the color pallet she would recommend to the new client. The dream of having her own design business seemed as far away as ever, but she did enjoy her job. Paris McKinnon, a doting yet practical mother, had told her that in order to be taken seriously, she would need to soften her look, stop going for the outlandish, and find her self-expression in a less unconventional way. *Not yet. Maybe when I turn thirty,* she thought, straightening the assorted bangles on her wrists.

Olivia stopped her daydreaming and took the last swig of coffee. She closed out the newspaper and brought up her personal notebook page, where she kept the ideas related to her job. She quickly made notes on possible color schemes and then turned off her tablet. The belongings were ready to go, but she was not. Her mind wandered from thoughts of home and family to the last time she had seen Ben, now almost six months ago. They had met for dinner at a trendy Soho eatery. She had intended to treat, but had found herself a little cash-poor then mortified when informed by the waiter of her maxed out credit card. Ben had laughed and shaken his head, like he wasn't surprised, and was only too glad to cover the bill. She had felt small, inadequate, and although her reaction wasn't his fault, she had shut down and ruined the rest of the evening with her petulance. Off and on during the last six months she had thought of getting in touch, but ego had stopped any action. Olivia had wondered from time to time—more often recently—why he hadn't just contacted her. But finally the realization came that it was up to her to smooth the way.

She tucked the tablet into her large bag and headed out into the afternoon. After a few stops to purchase essentials such as cheese, bread, wine and chocolate, she found herself reluctant to go home. There were days when the walls seemed to close in, when the emptiness of her flat accentuated the perceived emptiness in her life. Olivia had always been told that she was a beautiful woman, and on some level she knew it. Her mother didn't understand why with such beauty she chose to distract from her gift with tri-colored hair, unnecessary piercings, strange outfits, and enough jewelry to weigh down even a robust pair of arms. She had insisted to her mother that the colors weren't meant to be permanent, and she had currently opted to leave her hair as nature intended—a glossy dark copper, prone to rogue waves. Her eyes were green as a cat's, her body lithe. She was tall, like Ben, and contrary to family opinion, she could carry off a variety of styles, from Boho to high fashion. A trip through the second-hand and vintage clothing stores was a favorite way to spend a Sunday, depending on weather. There was no doubt she had a flair for fashion; however, she had chosen to work for an interior designer, where she could exercise her love of color and fabric.

Olivia paused outside her building and sighed, trying one more time to think of somewhere else she could go, something else she could do to pass the evening. As she started up the stairs, her mobile rang. The sound was barely audible, considering the street noise and the phone's location in the depths of her bag. She answered and was surprised to hear the name of the client to whom she had been introduced a few days prior. She wondered how Mr. Warren had obtained her number, but then realized he must have picked up one of her cards from the receptionist's desk. *Surely this is about business,* she thought, and said, "Yes, this is Olivia

McKinnon. Hello, Mr. Warren. May I help you with something?" She continued to speak before he could answer. "We do have some fabrics set aside for you to see at your earliest convenience, but I can't really make an appointment now. I'm not in the office."

"Oh, I'm not calling about the decorating." There was a short pause on the other end before he continued, his tone slightly apologetic. "I hope you'll forgive me for being opportunistic, but I couldn't resist taking a chance on inviting you to share a meal with me. I'd like to continue the conversation we started at the shop."

"Mr. Warren, I'm not sure that would be appropriate, given that I'm basically your employee until your office is decorated. And I'm not sure what conversation you're referring to." Worried that she might be dressed-down by her boss if she offended a client, she said, "Does the additional conversation you require have to do with your re-decorating project?"

Not to be discouraged, 'Clive Warren' proposed an alternative arrangement. "No, it isn't about the job. I'd just like to continue the perfunctory getting acquainted conversation we were having. As you may recall, it was interrupted."

Olivia didn't remember much about the conversation, only that he didn't have a long wait before she accompanied him into her boss' office to discuss the project. Once again not wishing to be impolite, she said, "Yes, I remember there was only a short wait before Mr. Saunders called us into his office." Extemporaneous responses to the man's suggestion were becoming more difficult.

"After you had introduced me and left your employer's office, he had nothing but glowing things to say about your taste. But after all, this project is just for a place of business, not a castle, so I would be more than satisfied to work with one of the other associates." He waited for Olivia to respond, but met with her silence, he said, "That would be a more than acceptable tradeoff for the privilege of spending an evening with you."

A few more moments of silence ensued while Olivia pondered the issue. If she had observed correctly, he seemed just a little older than she was, attractive, but more in the way of a rugby player who hadn't shied away from the occasional broken or bloody nose. That, along with the strong jaw and close-cropped hair, had been at odds with the fashionable business attire he sported when they first met in the office. He was definitely rugged looking, well built, and when speaking he revealed, only slightly, his comprehensive school education. She deduced that he couldn't be dull, or a lay-about. After all, if he did actually play rugby, he might be quite intelligent. She had heard it called 'a thinking man's game'—an upper class game that originated in private schools. She reminded herself not to be elitist and focused on the fact that he was employed, with his own office, and he could afford to redecorate it.

Picturing an evening alone in her quiet flat, Olivia spoke. "As it happens, I am free this evening. Perhaps we could meet for a drink and then see if it turns into dinner."

"Great. But I don't want you to have to get a taxi or, heaven forbid, use the Tube at night. So where in your neighborhood might we get a decent meal? And which is your neighborhood, by the way?"

"I live in Soho," she said, adding, "Let me think for a minute." Olivia decided on one of her favorite places, visited infrequently due to the prices." Are you okay with Italian?"

"Sure," 'Clive' answered, "You can't go wrong with Italian."

"Then I suggest Princi. It's just around the corner on Wardour Street, and Wardour intersects with Broadwick. But I must warn you, it's a bit pricey. If you'd like to go elsewhere, that's fine."

"Not a problem. I didn't intend to take you to your local 'chipper.'"

His attempt at humor made Olivia relax a little, and she responded amicably, "Of course I knew that. But there could be a happy medium."

"No, it's Princi. No changes. Why don't I meet you there at eight? I'll call for a reservation. I'll probably use my GPS so I won't be late. You won't have far to go, will you? I could pick you up, if you like. I'd prefer that." He gave her no chance to answer before asking, "Where exactly is your flat?"

Without a moment's hesitation Olivia told him quite specifically where she lived, but still chose to meet him at the restaurant— a must for a first date, if this was truly a date. They ended the call, and she ran up the stairs, already thinking about what to wear.

Olivia reached the door of her flat and began to fumble with her purse, reaching deep inside for the key. Her fingers soon found it, and as she put it into the lock, the house phone began to ring. Once inside, she dropped everything on the entry floor and rushed to catch the call. Just as it went to voicemail she picked up the receiver and said, "Hello, Olivia here."

"Oh, you're there. Good. I wasn't going to leave a message. It would have been too long. Well, I guess I could have just said to call me."

"Is that you, Valerie? It's been so long I can't quite recognize your voice." She was glad to hear from her ex-sister-in-law, but didn't want to gush. "Why didn't you just call me on my cell?"

"I don't know. I just figured the call might be more pleasant if you weren't out somewhere and trying to hear over the din of cars and whatever else." Valerie sounded on edge, anxious.

"To what do I owe the honor of this call?" Olivia asked, making a meal of the whole 'out of touch' thing.

"Are you trying to be clever or just being snarky?" Valerie said, sounding impatient.

"Maybe a little snarky," Olivia replied. "But I am glad to hear from you, finally. I'd wondered if you'd 'crossed the pond' for an extended stay with your parents. Is everything all right?"

"Well, if I visited my parents right now, we'd be at each other's throats. There's no chance I'll 'cross the pond' to see them until I've made some changes." Valerie voiced an audible sigh before continuing. "For the most part, things are all right. At least I'm all right." Her tone had been meek, but when she continued, it became almost arrogant. "And about our lapse in contact? The phone works two ways!" Valerie waited for a response from Olivia, but none came. Suddenly concerned that she might antagonize her further and ruin the plan, she said, "My shop girl, Chloe, is somewhat less than all right."

Sounding concerned, Olivia asked, "What happened to her. Is it bad?"

"I'd never known anyone who was hit by a car, but now I do." Valerie's voice was becoming more agitated as she got into telling the story. "Chloe had just stepped off the curb and was hit by an SUV rounding the corner too fast. It's hard to understand how anyone could miss seeing her. And even worse, the person took off, making it a hit and run. She's in the hospital—concussion, broken ankle, torn ligament in her knee. Of course it could have been worse. A car that size could easily have killed her."

"Poor Chloe. She's so young to have such a close call. Well, actually, age has nothing to do with close calls, but it sounds as if she will be okay…eventually."

At this point Valerie paused while she prepared just the right words. She wanted to ask or, if necessary, manipulate Olivia into taking time off from her job in order to accommodate the temporary closing of Boutique Le Bijou.

Before she had a chance to broach the subject, Olivia spoke, breaking Valerie's concentration. "I would really like to talk longer—catch up— but I have a last minute date and not much time to get ready. We should have lunch soon, or I could call you tomorrow."

Valerie could tell that she was unlikely to get a positive response from someone in a hurry to prepare for a date, so she feigned interest and asked one more question. "Is this someone new? Last time we spoke you weren't seeing anyone—said you were off dating for a while—fed up with their '*modus operandi*' and general annoying nature."

"You caught me at a low point when I said that. You remember that lay-about who tried to move in with me at Christmas time last year?"

"Phillip, or something like that?"

"Yes. When I said those things he was bringing out the worst in me. It was no small thing, getting rid of him. I was attractive to him because I had a job. I pity the next poor cow to fall for that charm. But really, I have to go. Talk soon." Without waiting for Valerie to say goodbye, she rung off and hurried into her room.

Once freed from her conversation with Valerie, Olivia quickly tended to the ablutions involved in preparing for a date. She pulled several outfits from the closet, settling on an Indian gauze skirt, printed in a palette of blues and greens, and a white silk camisole. She slipped into ballet flats and then pulled her copper colored hair back into a small chignon before adorning herself further with long turquoise and silver chandelier earrings and the usual assortment of bangles. Olivia was very individual in her tastes, or bizarre, as her mother referred to them. She owned the obligatory leather jacket, but hers was a vivid cyan blue and cropped to the waist.

Olivia pulled the jacket from the closet, scooped her bag off the hall table, and headed out to meet Mr. Clive Warren. She was running late due to Valerie's call and decided to hail a cab for the short ride to Ristorante Princi. In order to avoid glaring looks from the driver she doubled the fare. 'Clive' was waiting for her in the restaurant foyer and smiled with seeming delight as she entered. He had procured a table at the edge of the patio that would afford a pleasant view of the potted palms and flower boxes. Just as he declared that she looked 'smashing' the *maître di'* approached, menus in hand, ready to lead them outside, where overhead electric heaters kept the coolness at bay.

Once they were seated, a waiter appeared immediately and stood at attention, looking back and forth at the two. "May I take your drink order?" he asked, readying his pad and pen.

In a tone that both questioned and suggested, Gareth asked, "A glass of champagne to launch our evening?"

"I don't mean to be a spoil sport, and I do like champagne, but it invariably gives me a hateful headache, and I have work tomorrow."

"That's unfortunate," he said, "Then is there something you would enjoy, maybe a glass of wine?"

She looked up at the waiter and said, "I'll stick to my usual glass of chardonnay, and since I'm sure you feature more than one, I'll depend on you to choose." The waiter nodded and then looked toward her companion, who ordered a gin and tonic. With a short bow he turned and walked away.

The drinks arrived, and before ordering they settled into a comfortable exchange that touched on current events, the weather, and other general subjects that require no declared opinions or revelations. Eventually they attended to ordering the meal and found it outstanding. There was more talk over coffee and biscotti before Olivia suggested that it was late, considering that she had work the next day. He had been a perfect gentleman all evening and continued by pulling out her chair and helping her on with the leather jacket. As they stood outside the restaurant, breathing in the temperate night air of mid-summer, Olivia began to feel self-conscious, wondering as always how to navigate that awkward moment of parting. She began by thanking him for such an enjoyable meal, and that he had been an interesting dinner companion. He seemed to be tongue-tied by her compliment and looked down at the sidewalk. Rather than respond to what she had said, he hailed her a cab and she climbed aboard. After the exchange of a few words he closed the door, she waved and was gone.

Ten minutes hadn't passed before she was at the door of her flat. The comfort and familiarity of her surroundings seemed unusually welcome. The leather jacket ended up on the edge of a chair, the skirt and shoes were puddled on the floor where they were shed. She removed her jewelry, loosened her hair and splashed water on her face before turning off the light. The bed was as she had left it that morning and she all but dove into the middle, grabbing a pillow to stuff behind her neck. She lay on her back, staring back and forth from shadows on the ceiling to pale light from streetlamps beyond her window.

Regardless of emotional fatigue, sleep was evasive. An evaluation of the evening seemed unavoidable. Comprehensive education or no, Olivia had found her dinner companion to be quite charming, given his rather rough appearance. It seemed almost incongruous that his clothing was perfectly tailored and seemingly of designer quality. She had also found that rough appearance to be in some way attractive. She asked herself why. Perhaps his obvious willingness to butt heads, jump into the fray, tackle the biggest rugby player on the field—if he had played rugby—was a sign that he would also be a protector of those close to him. Although she made the assumption about his playing rugby, not football, she couldn't see him standing still for a mugging. Upon further contemplation of the man's slightly crooked nose, muscular build, and square jaw with just a hint of beard, Olivia realized conversely, and with a little guilt, that all of these same characteristics could also indicate that he was dodgy. *The answer is in the eyes,* she thought.

As often happens on a first date, she had avoided looking into his eyes. And in spite of curiosity about his age, she didn't ask, and was glad that he hadn't asked her to take a guess. That guess would have been mid to late thirties. In fact, she had not questioned her date about anything personal—his place of birth, his schooling, interests, or his business. However, he had been full of questions, asked with interest and enthusiasm. Olivia had been urged to tell much of her life story, as well as what was taking place in her current life. He asked about her friends, whether they lived close by, where her parents lived, if she had siblings. She felt a wave of attraction hit her when he leaned across the table and asked about aspirations for her future life. It all seemed innocent enough— his questions—a way to pass the time, keep the conversation going. Before the tables were turned and she had an opportunity to give as good as she got, question-wise, they had finished their meal and there was no longer a reason to linger.

It had been a comfortable evening, surprisingly, and Olivia was glad she had given in to her boredom and agreed to meet him. 'Clive' had put her in a cab, holding the door open until he could ask if she would see him again. He also slipped the driver some money—she couldn't see how much. She didn't have to think about it. Her answer was yes. On the ride back to her flat Olivia had considered her questionable judgment in dating a client. She knew it was inadvisable, but this was the first evening she had experienced in a long time where she was made to feel special, interesting. It would be just a bit of fun—nothing serious—and she would make it clear to him that it didn't include favors when it came to pricing out his office redecoration—or any other favors he might have in mind—at least not yet. Her next thought was about how much she would enjoy bringing him to meet her parents. She could just see their faces. Olivia could be a slightly evil child.

* * *

Valerie knew that Olivia would not have the funds to flit away with her on a last-minute vacation. In fact, Valerie had no idea where she wanted to go. It just had to be as far away as possible from London and the responsibilities that now seemed to be made up of insurmountable problems. She had been saving for a trip back to the states, but seeing her parents with things in their present predicament had become less and less desirable. They always made her feel like a child, yet with the recent revelations foist upon her by Dr. Kate, she realized that being treated that way may have been of her own doing. For the time being her father had committed to paying rent on the shop, and her credit card still had a decent amount available. She figured that if they shared a room, were careful and kept to a daily budget, they could probably squeeze out a couple of weeks away. Perhaps Olivia could contribute a little, but Valerie expected to take care of the bulk of expenses. She knew that Olivia took no substantial financial help from her parents, a quality that she admired but seemed unable to emulate. Olivia's job as a decorating assistant didn't pay a lot, and from what Olivia had shared, Valerie thought they took advantage of her enthusiasm by working her too hard.

She curled up in the corner of her sofa, picked up her phone from the side table, and although it was too early for her date to be over, dialed Olivia. It went to voicemail, so Valerie left a message requesting that she get back to her, regardless of what time she came in. Before fixing a light supper, she showered and turned on her radio to a classical station, always her preference. She insisted that listening to the flow of music by the masters was like a Zen experience for her—always relaxing. Hours passed with no call from Olivia. Eventually she gave up and went to bed to continue with what she had hoped would be a good book. Less than a few pages into chapter two she nodded off, lights still on, music still playing softly in the background. When the phone startled her awake she had no idea of the time.

She said hello and heard Olivia's voice. "Well, you said to call no matter how late I got home." The silence on the other end made her pause before asking, "Were you asleep?"

"Yes, I had dozed off with my book. I know I told you to call, even late. It's fine." As Valerie spoke, she was already thinking of how to broach the subject of a getaway.

"So what was so important that it couldn't wait until morning?" Olivia waited for her friend's reply.

Valerie hesitated a moment then jumped in. "You remember about the possibility of having to close the shop?" Olivia answered that she did remember, and Valerie continued. "I've definitely decided to close it … temporarily. In a couple of weeks I'll see how Chloe is doing, and then advertise for a temporary replacement, although I think that will be a problem. I'll probably have to resort to hiring a schoolgirl."

"I guess you don't have too many choices right now, but what does this have to do with me?"

Valerie had thought too much about how to present her idea to Olivia, so rather than the rehearsed version of her plan, she began to ad lib. "I need very badly for you to take a trip with me. Don't worry about money. This is something I've been considering for a while, and I can't think of anyone else I'd rather share it with. Chloe's accident could never be called fortuitous—it's awful—but I can't deny that the timing is in my favor. What do you think? Do you have any vacation time coming?"

"I have a week, but if I took longer, it would be without pay. I'm not sure I could weather the storm of a week without pay." The banter stopped as both women thought about what to say next.

Valerie spoke first. "We'll work it out. I'll find the money for you. I'm sure there's some way to get it from my mother. She doesn't really pay attention to how the boutique is doing."

"That doesn't seem right, Valerie. I won't consider it unless you tell her the truth about the trip."

The wheels were turning as Valerie responded to Olivia's sense of right and wrong. She thought it best to appear contrite, and to acquiesce to the demand. "All right, we'll do it your way. Now, since you've all but agreed to go, let's meet for lunch tomorrow and decide on our destination."

CHAPTER EIGHT

Ana had never seen such darkness. There was no moon, and it seemed the only light in the world came from the small lantern that served as a guide to the front door. Ben turned toward her and smiled, then without a word got out of the car. His steps crunched the gravel as he came around to escort her from the car to the house. She emerged rather stiffly, the drive having been long and confining. As they approached the portico, the door opened and Paris walked forward with arms outstretched, her expression both loving and excited. Directly behind her was Ben's father, Hugh, hands in his pockets and a broad smile on his face.

Paris immediately threw her arms around Ben, planting a motherly kiss on his cheek. She then turned to Ana and extended both of her arms, taking her lovely guest's hands into her own. Not only her words, but also the warmth in Paris' expression assured Ana that she was truly welcome. Paris had retained her beauty well into middle age, and Ana could see that Ben had his mother's eyes, both in shape and color—an ocean blue that at first sight of Ben had drawn her to get lost in them. His mother was very feminine in a flowing maxi skirt of gray silk and a gauzy white shirt, tied at the waist. Ana admired the carved silver pendant that hung from her neck on a delicate chain.

They all went inside, and Ben's father took the opportunity to welcome Ana as well, taking her hand in his and planting a quick soft kiss on each cheek. Hugh McKinnon was tall, like his son, and looked the perfect specimen of a robust sixty-something. His face was handsome, with the cragginess and healthy color of an outdoorsman. The gentleman's hairline had receded slightly, a fact well disguised by a very close-cropped cut. Ana found him very dapper in his khakis and navy v-neck sweater, and she could see a resemblance between father and son. Their coloring was the same, and Ben had inherited that smile—the one that could make you think that either man could be enjoying a private joke. But when it was Ben smiling, she found it extremely provocative.

Paris ushered them into the sitting room. Ana found the décor surprisingly chic for the country, yet it was well worn enough to be inviting and comfortable. Hugh offered aperitifs and busied himself at the antique sideboard that had been converted into a bar. Paris approached Ben, reaching up to touch his injured shoulder, and the two spoke quietly while Ana walked around the room, taking in every detail.

The walls held a diverse collection of paintings: a large nineteenth century English landscape, several small portraits, probably family, and a pair of highly colored modern abstracts. Ana was impressed to find that such an eclectic mix could be so complementary. A tasteful touch of bric-a-brac, as well as a few small sculptures, graced both the low table in front of the sofa and those beside several overstuffed chairs. In a corner, near the room's largest window, a baby grand piano stood proudly displaying a large cloisonné vase filled to overflowing with pale pink cabbage roses. A large Persian rug of muted colors, all soft tones of green and rose-tinted terracotta, anchored the furnishings. The fireplace face was constructed of a dark, richly grained mahogany, and the mantle was edged with intricate carvings of flowers and vines.

Hanging above the mantle was a gilt-edged Venetian glass mirror in the shape of a hexagon. An Italian politician had taught Ana how to recognize Venetian glass, and seeing it always took her back to the day of the lesson. She had met the man when she accompanied a male colleague to Italy several years before. The journalist had been assigned to interview the official about the 'Save Venice Inc.' restoration project. The Italian had been charming and very willing to tutor Ana in the history and fine art of glassmaking. He had generously provided her journalist friend with enough information for a long day of writing then insisted they go to *Murano*, where Ana could see the process first hand. She was told that the length of the field trip would require lunch at his favorite *trattoria* on the island. The tour had been interesting, and the *Prosecco* with lunch had been refreshing.

On the return to Venice, standing with her tutor at the deck railing, watching Venice come into closer view, she had suddenly felt a hand slide around her waist, and then down to her buttocks. He squeezed—hard. He leaned toward her and in heavily accented English whispered a very explicit request to be carried out at *Hotel Boscolo Veneti*, the closest venue after docking. Much to his disappointment, especially after having paid for lunch, the pillar of the community was to be humiliated by a hard slap from a woman much too young for his attentions. The next day her colleague questioned the man's sudden uncooperative attitude. The experience had served to chip away at Ana's naïveté, and since then, on the rare occasion when she has seen Venetian glass, it has caused her to smile.

The fleeting memory gone, she was attracted to a collection of framed photos displayed on the mantle; however, as a first-time guest she didn't feel it would be appropriate to linger and stare. She sat down beside Ben on the gray suede sofa. Hugh brought a beer to Ben and a glass of wine to Ana. He gently handed Paris her favorite martini before turning back to fetch his tumbler of Scotch. He then sat down beside her in the matching chair. There was a quiet moment before conversation began, during which Paris uttered a very audible sigh. It seemed as though she had been holding her breath until her son and his friend had arrived and were safely ensconced in her nest.

Ben was sure that his mother had not kept the preceding events from his father, and he was waiting to see how they would segue into the subject. But each parent was playing the charming host, asking questions of Ana about her career, her family, and her hopes for the future. Ben noticed a little discomfort in Ana's body language and was concerned that she was being put on the spot. He hoped she thought they were genuinely interested rather than intrusive.

Finally, Ben interrupted and said, "Let's talk about the elephant in the room." Everyone made some gesture of discomfort during the pause. Ana rearranged herself on the sofa cushion, Paris fussed with smoothing her skirt, and Hugh brushed something imaginary from his sweater.

Hugh ended the awkward moment and said, "Go on, Ben. Give me your version of events. Your mother was quite upset when she told me and may have left something out."

"Mum, I know you've talked to Dad about what you saw and what I told you when you came to the flat." His mother looked down, guilty as charged, and then turned to Hugh and gave another expressive sigh. Knowing there was no escape from their concern, he continued, "Dad, I hope that at least you haven't implemented an investigation. I know that your buddies at Interpol owe you favors."

"No, son," Hugh said, "I don't have enough facts to make it worthwhile."

Paris interjected, "I still don't know what they want." She shook her head and folded her arms across her chest, obviously frustrated.

"We're taking a good part of the weekend to enjoy you being here," said Hugh. "But tomorrow I'm going to escort your mother to the museum and hang around to see if she's contacted again. People work in those offices seven days a week. From now on I don't intend to let her out of my sight." He reached over and squeezed her hand affectionately. "You two will remain here, on the property—preferably in the house."

Ben put his beer bottle on the side table and stood. He walked over to the fireplace and leaned on the mantle, his back to everyone, and said, "I can't stand that I've involved all of you in this mess."

Paris rose from her chair and went to stand beside him, taking his arm and then clutching his hand. "It's not your doing, son. You're the unwilling bystander. They want something from me and were trying to use you as a bargaining chip. We still don't know what that is."

She took Ben by the hand and led him back to the sofa, where he flopped down, rubbed his face with his hands, and ran his fingers through his hair—a sure sign of stress and frustration that his mother had come to know very well. Ana had been taking it all in. Ben had still not admitted to her the reason for his ruse to get her there. But she was analytical, intelligent, and it became clear that all three were worried about her safety as well. She decided to leave the subject of his deception for another time. It was, after all, for her benefit. But he could have told her how he felt, what he feared. She wouldn't have argued. It seems he had somehow become used to women who were contrary and unreasonable. That certainly did not describe Paris. There were so many questions.

A light knock on one of the open sitting room doors drew Ana away from her musings. The woman who stood in the doorway was wiping her hands on a printed apron whose strap hung askew from one shoulder. Her hair was streaked with gray, and assuming she was the cook, Ana thought that she appeared to have enjoyed many of her own creations. The woman smiled and said that the meal was ready to serve. After a short pause she added that timing was important because she had prepared a chocolate soufflé for dessert, and would everyone please not linger before coming to the dining room.

Paris laughed and said, "Edith does her best to run things around here, and we're all better off if we do it her way, especially at mealtimes."

Hugh shrugged his shoulders and reached for his wife's hand, pulling her up from the chair. She put her arm through his and they headed toward the dining room. He motioned to Ben and Ana to follow, and they fell in behind. Leaves had been removed from the table in order to make the meal more intimate and less formal. Ana observed that Ben's parents were not the countrified class-conscious English types she had read about. They seemed very down to earth, and although they revealed that Edith was housekeeper as well as cook, it was obvious they were not taskmasters and considered her a friend, not a servant.

Ben and Ana had made no stops on the trip from London, so the hearty meal was welcome, as was the perfect chocolate soufflé that followed. Coffee was served in the comfort of the sitting room, and soon both Ben and Ana became distracted by fatigue. Paris noticed the tiredness in Ben's eyes and how he unconsciously began to rub his shoulder. As a guest in their home, Ana was making every effort to take part in the conversation, although being a mother, Paris knew that the young woman needed sleep as well.

"I think it's time you young people were in bed." She stood and walked over to Ana, holding out her hand to urge Ana up from the sofa. "Come dear, let me show you your room," she said gently. Ana stood and held her hand out to Paris, who took it in hers and led Ana toward the doorway. "I had planned to put you in Olivia's room, since it's more feminine, but then I remembered the cluttered way she left it last time she visited. The guest room will be much better." She paused and looked over at Ben. "We don't clean up after our children, we just close the door—always have."

Ben chimed in, "That's the truth. Squalor is the only word I can use for the state of my room from the time we came back to England until I went off to university. I guess at some point Mum set Edith loose on it. I came home for the holidays that first year and found it actually habitable."

Ben's mother was quick to add, "It was Edith who insisted. I was against it."

"No more stories tonight," Hugh said. "We've all had a long day, and tomorrow you're to stay put and wait until we come back from London. Then we attack this problem by whatever means necessary—and hopefully with more information."

Ben smiled at his Dad and said, "It seems strange after all these years to have you telling me what I can and can't do again—a bit of déjà vu."

Chin in the air, his expression serious, Hugh cautioned his son. "It was for your own good then, and it's for your own good now."

"I know, Dad. Thanks. I was just teasing. But I do realize the whole thing is no joke." He walked over and put his good arm around his father's shoulder, gave it a squeeze and said good night.

The two tired travelers were herded out of the room and up the stairs. They reached Ben's room first, and he gave Ana one of those captivating smiles as he bid her goodnight and then closed his door. She thought back to the night they had spent on the same bed and how she had watched him sleep, how she had tuned herself in to every nuance of expression on his face. She nurtured him, cared about him, almost felt his pain, and the feelings were all new, unfamiliar. She wondered in an instant if she would ever again watch him sleep.

Paris accompanied Ana to the guest room, turned on two lamps then showed her where she could find fresh linens and sundries. She thanked Paris, who closed the door leaving Ana alone. The room was pleasant, with its chintz curtains and Victorian armoire. The four-poster bed looked like an antique and was covered with a velvet comforter in a muted shade of viridian green. Hand embroidered pillows were strewn across the top, and the bedside table held a small vase of fragrant flowers Ana could not identify. Her suitcase stood beside the door, and she reasoned that at some point Edith must have brought it upstairs. She freshened up as quickly as possible and pulled on a satin slip, kept for the times when her preference for sleeping *au naturel* would be inappropriate. After turning off the bedside lamp she slid contentedly under the soft comforter, and with no more than two thoughts about the day, she was asleep.

Ben had not been as fortunate, finally admitting to himself that the drive had been too much for his shoulder. He wondered if that was his penance for having deceived Ana. He lay awake in the darkness, the dull pain robbing him of relaxation, his brain trying to formulate some sort of plan to help his mother. However, there was very little information, and until she was contacted again, neither he, nor his father, could make any decisions or enlist help from Interpol. Ben could not reconcile the failure to kidnap him with any plan villains might have to go forward with a crime, whatever it was to be. Eventually he got out of bed and rummaged through his luggage for the bottle of ibuprofen. While he swallowed several tablets with a swig of water, he wondered if they had actually abandoned the plan. He hoped that his father would learn something from tomorrow's trip to the museum. He climbed back into bed and lay staring at the ceiling of his room, where so many years ago stars had been painted for a boy who had become fascinated by thoughts of space and time. The first silvery light of dawn had begun to filter through the shutters before Ben finally dozed off into a deep but fitful sleep.

* * *

Ana sat in the sunny breakfast room nursing a coffee with cream and too much sugar. It was the second cup, her need for caffeine being stronger than usual. She had slept hard, with vivid dreams seeming too real to be discounted. She had slept eight hours, but it felt like four. Ben's parents had left very early, long before she came downstairs. Ben's mother had left oatmeal in a double boiler on the stove, a full carafe of coffee, and on the counter next to it, a plate of scones with a crock each of butter and jam. Ana settled onto the cushioned window seat adjacent to the table, coffee in hand, a scone split and buttered on the plate in her lap. The view from the window was lovely. A wide expanse of lawn gave way to a stand of mature trees, spaced far apart—she thought they could be Chestnuts— and directly under the window was a bed of pale pink cabbage roses, no doubt the source of the generous bouquet in the sitting room. Spiky purple flowers she couldn't identify flanked the rose bed on three sides. Ana's thoughts strayed from the visual pleasures beyond the window to the matter at hand. Their instructions—orders really—had been to stay put, but even her short acquaintance with Ben suggested that he was unlikely to acquiesce.

She stood, then walked over to put her breakfast things in the sink before starting upstairs to dress. As she passed the door to Ben's room, he opened it slowly and stepped out into the hall. He was dressed in gray sweat pants and a long sleeve tee whose logo advertised some long-forgotten rock group whose name she had heard, but whose music she had managed to avoid. His hair was tousled and a new growth of beard gave him a casual and sexy air, even though the tiredness in his eyes remained. He saw her and brandished the weapon of his smile, stopping the woman in her tracks and putting her at a loss for words.

"Is it still 'good morning' or have I slept into the afternoon?" Ben closed his door and then leaned against it, waiting for Ana's response.

"You barely made it with ten minutes to spare. It's almost twelve. But I've only been down for about half an hour."

"I just couldn't get to sleep. This whole thing was spinning around in my head until the wee hours, and I know you'll say I told you so, but my shoulder was giving me fits on top of it."

"I'm not one to jump on an opportunity to be right," she said, smiling. "But I would have driven, if you'd asked— even if I had reservations… fear, actually."

"That brings me to the confession I mentioned last night." Ben took a deep breath and waited for Ana to respond.

"Go ahead. But I think I know what you're going to say. I wasn't born yesterday."

"I could have just trusted that you'd do what I advised, but I don't know you well enough to have depended on that. It was clear there was a chance you were in danger too, because of having been seen with me. I just couldn't leave you in London to fend for yourself." Ben paused, again waiting for Ana's reaction. She remained quiet, so he continued. "Whatever this is about, whatever risk is ahead of me, I couldn't worry about what could be happening to you. I figured the best place for you was with me, and with my father. He has years of experience with criminals and has a lot of contacts at Interpol."

"How did that come about?" Ana was suddenly curious about what

Ben's father had done for a living. "Was your father with Scotland Yard or something?"

"No. He spent his career as an investigator with Lloyd's of London. He advanced to running the department that deals with thefts of high-end jewelry, art, cars—whatever wealthy people see as 'priceless' and are willing to insure at exorbitant rates. He was working in their office in San Francisco when I was born. But then he was just an investigator. When he was promoted to department head we moved back to England."

"So that's why he's trying to get on top of this, and why he went to the city with your mother. He obviously knows how to take care of her. Is he in possession of a firearm? I know that sounds formal. It just sounded so crass to say 'gun.'" She stopped herself and took a deep breath. "Sorry to rattle on, but this is a lot of new information to take in."

"In San Francisco he carried a weapon. I stood at attention for many lectures about not touching it. And when I was about ten, he took me out to a shooting range and taught me how to be safe around that weapon—firearms in general. I never liked even holding it, but he said a man never knows when he might have to defend himself or someone else."

"I didn't know that insurance investigators needed to carry weapons."

"Depends on how valuable the stolen or destroyed items are, or how involved the agents are in tracking them down. There's always the possibility of a confrontation. And it's not always an individual. For lack of a better word, 'gangs' of crooks plan some pretty complicated heists—and some are real bad guys."

"Now you're using proper crime lingo." She laughed softly and shook her head.

Ben crossed his arms and continued to lean on the door, his eyes fixed on hers. He thought she might have been wearing what she slept in and noticed the pleasure he felt while examining her tousled hair, lack of makeup, and baggy pants. He shot her a rather seductive smile, and feeling slightly embarrassed, she was compelled to end the conversation and escape his gaze. She quickly told him about the coffee waiting for him, along with the scones and oatmeal. Before he could say anything else she made a hasty retreat down the hall and into her room.

* * *

Once behind the closed door, Ana shed the baggy pants she had found in the closet, perhaps a garment left behind by a previous guest. Next came the satin slip and the cardigan she had pulled over it before going downstairs. She lingered in the shower, wondering what the day would bring. Freshly washed and combed, Ana pulled out jeans and the gem-encrusted tee shirt from her suitcase and quickly dressed. Her one pair of comfortable shoes seemed appropriate for the kind of day she expected, so she slid into them, tied the laces and stopped before the mirror. *I've already been exposed bare-faced, so why bother with it,* she thought, but then settled for a wee bit of mascara and swipe of rose pink lipstick.

Curious about what Ben was up to, she returned to the kitchen, where she found him reading a newspaper, his spoon suspended over a bowl. Steam rose from the mug beside it, and a few crumbs on the table were all that remained of a scone.

Sensing her presence, he looked up, put down his spoon and said, "You always seem to clean up well. Was it a shower that took the tiredness off your face?"

"Must have been," she answered. "But I feel a bit too 'casual' for your parents. I'll need to change before they come back." She wandered to the window, and speaking toward the glass panes, she added, "At least you didn't comment on my shirt again."

Ben laughed, yet said nothing. Ana turned back and came to join him. A note lay open on the table, and she could easily read what was written. Edith had wanted everyone to know that she had gone to the shops and would be back in time to prepare their 'tea'—an English reference that Ana had learned meant dinner. She looked over at Ben and saw that he had almost finished what seemed to have been a very large serving of oatmeal.

This surprised her and she couldn't help but comment. "I haven't had oatmeal since I left home. I'm a bit surprised to see you eating it, evidently with gusto."

"It's best to indulge Mum's need to 'mother' me. You don't want to see her reaction if she comes back from London and sees it sitting there on the stove, all congealed and cold." He waited for her to respond, but her answer was only a smile. Not quite through with the subject, he continued, "When I was a kid, this was breakfast—every day. Even if it was Christmas, or Pancake Day, we had oatmeal first."

"What in the world is Pancake Day?"

"It's part of Lent. Before Ash Wednesday there's Shrove Tuesday, and in the UK it came to be called Pancake Day. It's a day of feasting before the penitential requirements of Lent that start the next day, Ash Wednesday. *Comprende?*" Ana nodded, and then motioned with her hand for him to continue. "Shrove comes from the old English word 'shrive,' which means to confess. People are supposed to evaluate what in their life needs changing. You're probably more familiar with the French version—Mardi Gras. And I'm sure you know that's French for Fat Tuesday—again with the food."

Ben stood, finished his coffee in one gulp, and took his dishes to the sink, where he rinsed them along with Ana's and put them in the dishwasher. Then he contemplated the pan of oatmeal still sitting over simmering water on the big Aga range. "Are you sure you don't have room for just a little?" he asked.

"No thanks. Maybe tomorrow," she answered politely, and he carried the pan to the sink, dumping the remainder down the drain before turning on the disposal. "Mum will think we ate it all. Just as well. It will save a lecture."

Ana shook her head in mock disapproval, all the while continuing to enjoy everything he did and everything he said. She realized the moment had arrived for planning the day and wondered if they would lounge about, sit in the sun perhaps, read books, surf the net—or even sneak out for a walk. Or if one wanted to be practical, might this be a perfect time to return to the interview— the task that had put everything in motion? After all that had happened, it would be difficult to return to the intended basic format: a hint about his next book, his hobbies— his women. She hesitated to ask him about the latter, but her curiosity grew with every hour they spent together. It seemed valid to her that she learn whether or not there was someone in his life. Just because he flirted with her a little didn't mean there was no one else. She knew how men could be—knew too well. Those questions had to be worked into the conversation, but she was truthful enough with herself to realize that the answers weren't necessary to the interview. However, they were necessary to her, considering the feelings of attraction that continued to flourish in his presence.

Ben broke her concentration by announcing his intention to shower, shave, and dress. He assured her that while performing those rituals he would try to think of a way to keep them both from a day of boredom. Leaving her to her own devices he headed upstairs. She wandered around the kitchen, cleaning up a few crumbs, emptying grounds from the coffee maker. She paused at the window above the sink and looked out at the all-encompassing green of the back garden. Ana remembered being cautioned to stay in the house, but the grounds beckoned to her. When they arrived she had seen only the black of night, dark shadows and lighted windows. She wanted to see the house from the outside and thought about sneaking out to take just a short look while Ben was upstairs. With quick steps she left the kitchen and found her way to the foyer. Just as she opened the front door, Ben appeared on the stairs and called to her.

"Hey! Hang on there, Ms. Doherty!" He hurried down and all but dashed to the one open door, pushing it closed before leaning against it. "I don't really think you've forgotten what my father told us, have you?"

"No, I haven't, but I was just going to stand in front of the house for a minute to take a look. Last night I saw nothing but darkness."

She looked down, and Ben was put in mind of a small child caught with a hand in the cookie jar. He hadn't meant to sound angry, or to admonish her as a parent might, but she was his responsibility. Still leaning against the door, he relaxed his stance and crossed his arms. Ana turned away, but he went to her then held her at arm's length. "I'm sorry," he said. "I didn't mean to sound angry, but you gave me a scare. I brought you here to protect you, and that means you go nowhere without me. You really need to take this seriously."

"I can see that the McKinnon men know how to take the bull by the horns. I'm glad you're on my side—both of you."

"Very funny," he said, locking eyes with her. She returned his gaze and for a moment it seemed to be a standoff. The tick-tock of the grandfather clock in the hall was the only sound for at least a minute before Ben spoke. "Okay. We go out together—just for a minute. You will hold my hand and do as I tell you."

Ana found his authoritative tone rather arousing and assured him she would acquiesce to his instructions. Ben opened the door, took her hand, and they crossed the portico, stepping down onto the gravel driveway and continuing to the round planted area with its stone fountain. She turned to face the house, shading her eyes with her hand. It was built of rich honey-colored stone, aged enough to have a few chips and holes well hidden either by lichen or moss. With the gabled roof and chimneys it reminded Ana of the houses in the storybooks of her childhood, and those she had admired in English films. The windows were made of leaded glass panes, and on either side of the portico, trellises of climbing roses displayed blooms of deep scarlet. To the left of the house was a wall of the same stone, covered here and there with Virginia creeper, its five-pointed leaves sprouting from a maze of clinging tendrils.

In the other direction, a gravel pathway led through a carefully trimmed boxwood arch and around the other side of the house to a destination Ana could not see. The path was lined with white daisies and assorted colors of iris, and to the right, some yards away, was the entrance to what appeared to be a typical kitchen garden. The space was defined by a short wooden fence bordered with fragrant lavender bushes in the full flush of summer. A once-white gate stood ajar, and wild morning glory was making a valiant attempt to engulf the fence, its electric violet blooms more of a visual delight than a weed to be challenged. Ana took it all in, and she was charmed beyond all expectation. The early afternoon sun had somewhat diffused all the color that surrounded her, and she looked forward to seeing everything at its most vibrant—perhaps in the morning, or later when Ben's parents returned.

It had likely been only ten minutes, maybe less, when Ben said they should go inside. Now that she had seen what had been lost in darkness the night before, the outdoors drew her even more. She longed to wander the grounds, make discoveries, and encounter nature at the apex of the season. Practicality told her that this would be an unlikely endeavor, given the situation. Yet if Hugh had gained more information, learned something that would relieve all their concerns, she could be free to embrace the English countryside, which she had never expected to fall in love with so easily.

Ben suggested that she get comfortable in the sitting room while he put a call in to his sister, Olivia, to ask if she would like to come up from London for the rest of the weekend. Olivia had evidently not answered because she heard him leave a message. He returned to the sitting room and flopped down in one of the overstuffed chairs.

"I'm not surprised that she didn't answer. She must be at work and can't take a personal call. I'll try again later if she doesn't call me back. Can't believe I haven't talked to her for months." He paused, deciding how much to reveal to Ana. "The fact is, last time I saw her there was a bit of a 'situation,' and she ended the evening abruptly." His expression revealed that he found his sister to be a challenge. "I've waited for her to get in touch with me. I didn't want to push. She can be a bit petulant sometimes, but it's probably our fault. We doted on her, and I always knew I'd end up being her protector. But at this point she'll have none of that."

Ana made an effort to put him at ease. She was surprised he would speak so freely about his family, and she liked that he felt comfortable with her. But of course they were still off the record. "I'm an only child, but I was in my friends' houses often enough times to know that there's nothing simple about sibling relationships." Ben nodded his head in agreement, but said nothing else. "When you see each other I'll bet it will be like nothing happened." She didn't want to pry further about the specifics of the falling out between them.

"I told you I'd find us a way to avoid boredom, but I've failed so far. I hate to think we'll have to resort to surfing the net."

"Well… I did have an idea, but I don't know if you'll go along with it."

"Ah, that sounds interesting—or should I say a little mysterious."

"Neither, really. I just thought that while we have the time, we might get started with the interview that seems to have been the catalyst for this 'snowball rolling down a hill' situation we're all involved in."

"I don't see it that way. The interview was a completely separate thing. You see it that way because I had come to meet you, and it was part of the night I got attacked. You bear no responsibility for what happened, and your involvement was just coincidence. You must know that I would have preferred you not be a part of anything that happened."

"Yes, but as it turned out, it was a good thing I was there. I know, I know—they saw me. But if they know so much about you, or your family, they'd have to know that we weren't a couple. Some woman you may have dated only once—that night—wouldn't make much of a hostage. Unless you do have a girlfriend, and they mistook me for her."

Silence ensued. Ben looked at her—through her, really. At least that's how it felt to Ana. As soon as the words left her mouth, she was afraid she had put her foot in it. Clearly the question would not be a part of the interview, when and if it happened. Her subconscious had betrayed her. However, it had been the perfect segue. Now she wondered if she was in trouble, either as a journalist or as a woman who couldn't seem to escape her attraction to the subject of her assignment. Ana looked around the room, trying to be nonchalant, but her eyes continued to return to Ben and his expression. Very slowly a smile began to cross his face. It was 'that' smile. This time she was sure there was a private joke causing it. She could think of nothing to say and just waited for the smile to subside and for the emergence of either information or admonition for having broached the subject.

"Very smooth," he said, and then waited for her to speak.

"I… I didn't mean to pry. It was just conjecture."

"I'm just pulling your chain. Relax." Ben turned in the chair, dangled one leg over its arm and put his hands behind his head. "For the record, I do not have a girlfriend at this time." His tone was so formal that Ana had to stifle a laugh. But it seemed that was the response he was trying for. Their eyes met and they both began to laugh; the awkward moment having passed.

"Well, since we've settled that, do you want to do some work on the interview? I can run upstairs and fish the tape recorder out of my bag. I can't put off my editor forever. I've avoided checking my phone."

"Sure. I'd actually like to get it over with." Ben sprung from the chair and said, "But first I want something to eat. I'll check what Edith may have left lying around for us, and you run up and get your machine."

Ana nodded, got up, and headed for the stairs. The errand had taken only a few minutes and as she returned to the kitchen, she heard a scratching noise that seemed to be coming from the pantry. Ben turned from his sandwich making and said, "I know that scratch." He wiped his hands on a towel and walked through to the small door that provided pantry access from the outside of the house. When the door was barely ajar, a husky black Labrador retriever pushed his way through and into the kitchen. He panted and danced around Ben excitedly, making small whimpering sounds. Ben squatted and took the dog's head in his hands, looking him in the eye. This seemed to calm him, as did Ben's voice when he spoke. "Sir Frederic, how have you been?" The dog sat down, and then with the speed of a lizard catching a fly in midair, he gave Ben an affectionate lick on the nose. Ben stood, used his sleeve to wipe away the wetness, and returned to Ana, who was standing at attention beside the table, not knowing what to expect when the dog saw a stranger in the house.

"This is Sir Frederic—Freddie to his pals. We rescued him about five years ago, but it seems more like he adopted us. He got his name from acting like he was lord of the manor—still does." Freddie approached Ana slowly and sniffed at her shoes before nudging her with his head. "He approves of you. That's what he does after he makes a decision about someone."

Ana smiled down at the dog and gave him a scratch behind the ears. "He's a big fellow. Formidable. I'm very glad he approves of me." She slid into a chair at the table. Freddie sat rather near and stared at her. "I wonder what he's thinking now," she said.

"When he stares like that he's sending the message that he'd like you to give him a treat. But he's out of luck because I don't know where they are, or what he's allowed to have these days. Mum mentioned she was trying to take some weight off him."

"He looks the picture of health to me."

"We didn't see him last night because he sleeps in the garden shed, or sometimes in the pantry when it's cold, but I don't know where he was when we were outside just now. His usual habit would be to pounce on a newcomer with welcoming licks."

Just then Freddie got up and walked back toward the pantry door. He began to bark repeatedly and pawed at the door. Ben went to him and opened the door. The dog raced outside and about halfway down the stone walkway that led to the gardening shed. He then turned into the bushes, seeming to know where he was going. In a moment he emerged, carrying something in his mouth. He trotted back up the path and dropped his treasure on the stone stoop. A limp and bloody rabbit lay there, legs splayed, it's fur wet with saliva. Ben was more than surprised and told Ana that Freddie was not a hunter, that he would sit and watch a squirrel or a bird with seeming interest, not as a matter of stalking.

"I'm sure this is very distasteful to you. I'm sorry you had to see it."

"I just have to remember that I'm in the wilds of England, where nature rules and it's survival of the fittest."

"That's a bit of an exaggeration. In this case, the rabbit doesn't even look mauled. If a dog had done it, it would be more disfigured." Ben squatted to take a closer look at the unlucky rabbit. He carefully turned it over, moved the fur behind the neck and said, "Well, this wasn't done by any four-legged animal—more like the two-legged version."

"What do you mean," Ana asked, coming closer to see what Ben had found.

"It's been shot—right here behind the neck. See?" He pushed the fur aside to expose the bullet hole. "This rabbit wasn't killed by a hunter. They use shotguns. We'd see numerous small entry wounds from the pellets if a hunter had done this. And if it were a hunter, he would have collected the animal, probably taken it home for tonight's stew."

"I'm not sure I'll ever eat rabbit again... and the French do it so well." Ana's attempt to lighten the moment fell flat.

She turned and walked back to the table while Ben went to the shed for a shovel to remove the furry carcass. Freddie had been quietly observing the scene, and although he would have liked the credit for having provided his family with the evening's meal, he eventually lumbered off into the outer reaches of the back garden. When Ben returned from burying the creature, he had a serious look on his face. Ana questioned this and he told her that the bullet wound looked to have been from a medium caliber handgun, and that it would have had to be shot from quite a distance or it would have nearly blown off the rabbit's head.

They didn't talk for a few moments, and then Ben said, "Who passes the time shooting at rabbits with a handgun?" He paused then shook his head, his expression one of disgust. "And why didn't we hear it?"

"Unless it happened yesterday when no one was home."

"We don't have any neighbors who would do that. It must have been done on our property, or from the woods, because Freddie doesn't venture beyond the field at the edge of the woods.

"Are you sure he doesn't sneak away?

"As sure as I can be. And if he feels like chasing a rabbit, we have them on the property —too many some years. He may like to chase them once in a while but wouldn't know what to do if he caught one. They have their way with the vegetable garden, among other things."

"He seems like a smart fellow, but dogs will be dogs. How can you be so sure?"

"My father trained him to stay on the lawns and in the garden. He was concerned that some nearsighted old geezer who should have had his gun taken away might mistake Freddie for a fox. I can't help but think it could have been Freddie who was shot today."

"I don't know how far it is to the edge of the woods, but if the shot came from there, it might not have been heard at the house." She looked at Ben, who was leaning against the counter with his arms crossed, deep in thought. He didn't speak, so after a minute or so she continued. "So you're saying that the rabbit was probably shot on your property, which means there was a trespasser here at least long enough to deliberately shoot a rabbit—thankfully not a dog. And then Freddie found it and brought it to the garden, left it in the bushes—how long ago we don't know. Then at some point he came to get someone's attention before he retrieved it and dropped it on the stoop—some kind of offering?"

Ben sat down across the table from her and leaned on the table, his hands clasped together tightly. Ana could tell he was mulling over what had happened, but not in terms of animal behavior. "If that were the case, it would be the first time. I don't think that was it."

I don't know a lot about dogs, but I know that cats will bring their night kill to the door to show they're doing their part for the family."

"I'll talk to Dad about it when they come back from London. I don't want to read too much into it. He might even know who it could have been. I'm not acquainted with the neighbors anymore—lots of changes since I left home—but very few people keep handguns."

Ben was relieved that Ana didn't seem too disturbed by the whole thing, and she commented that Freddie had been the one to provide the day's break from boredom. Yet he felt an underlying discomfort about the whole thing and decided to call Freddie in from whatever sunny spot he had found for an afternoon nap. Ben stepped outside the pantry door and called to the dog. It was several minutes before he appeared, trotting around the corner of the house and coming to a stop at Ben's feet. He was very wet. He shook hard, giving Ben a good dousing before charging into the house.

"He's been in the fountain again." Ben found a kitchen towel and began to dry himself off. Then he addressed the dog while trying to dry him off a bit as well. "Must have thought it was warm enough for a swim— huh, pal?"

Ana laughed and ruffled Freddie's damp fur before he flopped under the kitchen table, ready for that nap. Ben finished making the sandwiches and they ate in relative silence. When she could see that Ben had finished, she said, "Shall we retire to the sitting room and get our project underway?" He nodded yes, and they left the kitchen, Freddie tagging along, never letting them far from his sight.

CHAPTER NINE

The McKinnons maintained a brisk pace as they walked the short block from the car park to the museum. It was early, and a carpet of gray mist still clung lightly to the manicured lawns of the museum grounds. The entrance to the suite of offices where Paris worked was still locked, so she opened her bag and fumbled for the key. Hugh was always amazed that a woman could find anything in the dark recesses of this requisite female accessory. They entered to find all completely quiet. When they reached the door to her office, Paris turned and walked across to the office adjacent, that of Lyle Brett. Through the door's opaque glass inset she could see only darkness. Lyle was not yet in attendance. She tossed her office key to Hugh, and he opened the door, waiting for her to precede him into the room. She turned on the lights and found the long pole that she used to open the high window, the only one in the room. Hugh took it from her and pulled the glass pane open, letting in the fresh morning air.

"That's better," she said. "The stuffiness in here could put one to sleep, given the boring nature of so much of my work."

"Well, evidently there's something coming up that isn't boring, or we wouldn't be in the middle of a mysterious situation. Let's go through all this paperwork and see if there's anything new, something that might give us a hint about what possible power you might have that could facilitate a crime—and also be manipulated by a kidnapping."

"I got through less than half the stack last time I was here. There was quite a pile-up after my being gone."

"Do you have any phone messages?"

Paris glanced at her phone and saw the light flashing. There were two messages. She pressed the button and they began to listen. The first message was from her superior, head of the antiquities division, who expressed an urgent need to speak with her about a special situation. He revealed nothing further. She made a note to call his secretary for an appointment as soon as they organized the work ahead of them. Then she pressed the button to hear the second message.

Several seconds passed before they heard a voice, muffled through some kind of device to make it unrecognizable. "We're still watching you and your family. If you don't cooperate, we have a bargaining chip that just might tip the scales in our favor."

Paris paused the message and looked at Hugh. "What could he mean—a bargaining chip? He's speaking in riddles. We know they don't have Ben—he's safely at home with Ana. He is safe, isn't he?"

"Yes. Perfectly. I didn't tell him, but I have a man watching the house— very discreetly of course. If it will make you feel better, we can call them now, or a little later, after we get some work done here."

"No, it's fine. I trust you know what you're doing. But I would like to call later. For now let's see what else this man has to say."

Paris started the message from where it had been paused. Hugh reached for her hand and held it while they listened once again to the muffled voice. "You'd better be in your office tomorrow. A package will arrive, and inside you'll find a tape. Everything you need to know will be there. You'd better take good care of it. Failure to comply will bring you more trouble than you can imagine." The call ended, and Ben's parents just stood still, looking at each other with disbelief.

"I don't even know what day this message was left. Let me check the call log."

Paris scrolled through the call log and saw that the message from her department head had come in the previous afternoon. She then saw that the threatening message had come very early that morning, probably before dawn. There would be another day to wait before they would know what had to be done. From the hallway they heard a door squeak open and then close hard. They both assumed it was Lyle Brett arriving at work. Paris decided to take a minute to poke her head in and force a greeting from him, but more so to ask if there was anything extremely important—imminent—that they should attend to together.

A quick knock triggered a rather harsh sounding permission to enter, and she did just that, forcing a smile and a few kind words. As usual, he was less than receptive. She asked her question and was met with a questioning look.

"I've been waiting for you to tell *me* what's *imminent,*" he said. "I was informed that the relevant packet was in *your* office, waiting to be sorted." His tone betrayed the fact that he resented being out of the loop or passed over in any way. "I've speculated that it must be a very valuable antiquity, or some sort of priceless display." He looked down dismissively, beginning to sort through papers as if she weren't there.

A light clicked on in Paris' head. The words 'valuable' and 'priceless' kindled several ideas about what was to come. "I won't keep you any longer. I'll let you know as soon as I can find whatever seems so important."

Lyle Brett made a sound that resembled a 'harrumph,' and Paris left his office, closing the door hard behind her. She returned to Hugh, shaking her head as she came through the doorway, her expression one of exasperation.

"That man pushes all my buttons—even more so with what's going on. Have you found anything with your sorting?"

Hugh was seated at her desk with a pile of folders to his left. He looked up and said, "Actually, I was just about to come and fetch you away from your nemesis. I think I may have found something."

"Leave it to you, my hero. I really hope you're right."

"This manila envelope contains a file folder, which I've yet to open. I was waiting for you. The rest of the files and your mail were just piled haphazardly on the desk—like someone had been collecting everything intended for you, knew you were coming back yesterday, gained access, and just tossed all of it carelessly on your desk."

"That sounds like our Mr. Brett's style. He has no concern for endearing himself to anyone. I know he resents any action taken that might indicate I'm preferred over him, or, heaven forbid, superior to him when assignments are given out."

"He'd probably like nothing better than for you to retire and leave him a clear path to promotion."

"I do know that he's been passed over more than once, and there's a supervisory position that has opened up, due to a retirement. I believe it's in the department that supervises transport of acquisitions between museums." Paris paused, evidently trying to recall something and then said, "Last year I helped out in that department while one of the regulars was out on maternity leave. I didn't mind it—enjoyed it, really. And the department head, the man who just retired, told me I was a natural."

Hugh smiled at her in that special way. It was a smile of pride, but it always made her look down with embarrassment. He knew he had lived his life with a very intelligent woman, and that intelligence had always attracted him just as much as her beauty. "I've always believed you can do just about anything you set your mind to, my love."

She came around behind him, wrapped her arms around his shoulders, and leaned down to give him a soft kiss on his neck. With her face buried there she muttered, "Thank you for the vote of confidence, but the first thing I learned on that job was that there can be a lot of logistical nightmares." He turned his head sideways and returned the kiss. Paris took a deep breath and said, "Enough nuzzling. Let's see what that file tells us."

Before they could pull it out of the envelope, the office phone rang. Paris answered, her hand shaking slightly due to the thought that it might be whoever was threatening her family. She said hello softly, and upon hearing the voice on the other end, relaxed her demeanor. Her end of the conversation consisted mainly of one-word answers. The conversation ended with her promise to 'think it over quickly and get back to them.' She put down the receiver without saying a word and turned to look at Hugh.

"That was the museum director. They haven't been able to fill the position I told you about. That's why he had left me a message. He asked me to take it on—function as department head until they can fill the position. He also suggested that I apply for the permanent position. It seems the man who retired—Mr. Langley— spoke highly of me. I had no idea."

Her voice trailed off, and Hugh could tell that her mind was now even more overcrowded. But she was preoccupied with her family's safety and was in no position to make such a decision on the spot. Hoping to help her sort through it all, he asked, "How soon do you have to let him know?"

"Tomorrow. How can I decide by then? I'll have to at least ask for an extension." She shook her head in frustration and returned to stand by Hugh, who was still sitting at her desk with the envelope in his hands. "I can't help but think of the 'never rains but it pours' thing," she said, sliding up onto the desk in order to sit and face him. "Never mind that for now. Open it. Open it!"

Hugh slid the file folder out of the envelope, opened it and turned it toward Paris. It was a manifest for a new exhibit. She gestured he should turn it back around then motioned him to get on with it. He began to read aloud. "It says here that the museum is to receive a very valuable group of items." Hugh whistled, then continued, "Wow– they aren't kidding!" Paris motioned him to continue. "Right now it's in the Museum of Subaquatic Archaeology in Cartagena, Spain."

"Well, what is it?" Paris asked, leaning over the folder in an effort to read upside down. "May I have it, please? I can't wait for you to read anymore of it out loud."

Hugh extended the folder to her, and then leaned back in the chair, crossing his arms while watching her peruse the information. The silence seemed charged while he waited for her to finish. It must have been at least five minutes before she looked up and placed the file on the desk. Her expression was blank, but Hugh could see intensity in her eyes.

"It's a sunken treasure worth millions—over 50,000 gold and silver coins … and artifacts. They were recovered from a Spanish warship that sunk off the south coast of Portugal—over two centuries ago—in 1804." She looked down at what was written and continued, paraphrasing. "The coins had been minted in Peru and were en route as cargo on a Spanish warship, the *Nuestra Senora de las Mercedes*. The whole fleet was attacked by the British just a day's sail from Spain and they sunk the ship carrying the treasure."

Hugh interrupted, anxious to add what he had to say. "Now I remember. Quite a while back I read a newspaper article about the ongoing legal battle for ownership between the Spanish government and the owners of the company who discovered and salvaged the ship."

"Seems that Spain was victorious. I wonder if the company got anything at all for their trouble. The expenses must have been monumental. Think of how much the coins alone weigh."

"So…what's the upshot? How's the museum involved?"

"Well…portions of the treasure are going to be traveling exhibits—I guess there will be more than one—and this museum is next in line. Surely it's not just one exhibit. I may have thought logistics were a nightmare, but the security involved in hosting this exhibit will be horrendously complicated. From what it says here, it won't be our responsibility until it lands on English soil. If it comes by air, the transport from Heathrow will be all on us." She paused for a moment then continued. "Surely they won't send it by ship. That didn't work out so well last time."

"Can you imagine any company being willing to insure something like that?" Hugh got up and began to pace around the room, his arms still crossed over his chest. "As far as I know, Lloyd's has always been at the top of that list. I think I'll make a couple of calls, just out of curiosity, and see if one of my colleagues knows about it."

"In my opinion, it's uninsurable—and that's because it's completely irreplaceable."

"Possibly insurable, but not replaceable," Hugh added. Paris returned to the documents, scanning the sections visually and with her fingers until she removed her hand abruptly and looked up at Hugh. "I finally came to the part where it tells which department will be responsible for making transit arrangements for the exhibit." Hugh's body language asked the question for him, and the room was silent for a moment before she answered, "Acquisitions and Transport."

"That's you, sweetheart—if you decide to take the position. You'll be working full time for a while. I admit I'm selfish about our time together, but if this is something you want, I'll support you. I can pick up the slack in other areas—not as well as you, but I'll do it."

"If I work the job for over a year, given I'm chosen as a permanent replacement, I could either go back to part time, or retire at a higher level. I've accumulated at least ten full time years—before you retired and I cut my time in half." They looked at each other, obviously having their own private thoughts on the matter. Finally Paris said, "A little extra money would be nice, right? Who knows—there may be grandchildren in our future, and we don't want to skimp on spoiling them."

Hugh laughed, approached her, and drew her in close, kissing the top of her head. She leaned back, looked up at him and said, "But how could I with this other issue hanging over our heads?" Hugh cocked his head and looked at her, eyebrows raised. She received the tacit message in his expression. "Then shall I call now, instead of in the morning?"

"As you wish, dear girl," Hugh said, handing her the receiver.

She placed the call, but had to leave a voicemail message accepting the temporary position. She rang off and sat down in her office chair. Hugh sat down in the chair opposite her. A smile crossed Paris' face and she said, "It may be that the best part of this change will be that I don't have to start every day with Lyle Brett." They shared a laugh and decided to end the workday a bit early. There were treats to pick up before fighting the traffic back to their idyllic country life. There would be a quick stop at the cheese shop, and then *Patisserie Luc* for a *tarte tatin* to compliment the pork loin roast and *gratin Dauphinois* promised by Edith as they had dashed out the door that morning.

An hour later they were headed for the country. Traffic moved in spurts and stops, but as was their habit, a 'book on tape'—now a book on disk—filled the car with the mellifluous voice of a man reading from Thoreau. They enjoyed sharing the words, and would often discuss what they'd heard over a cocktail. But on this evening Paris reached forward and turned the unit off. With all that had crowded her mind during the day, she was now focused on Ben and his guest, Ana. Of course she had concern for their safety, first and foremost, but she sensed something else going on. She had observed them for only a few hours, but either she was intuitive, or just a mother who was well tuned in to her children. There was a certain presence when the two were in the same room. She could only describe it as some kind of energy—a charged environment—a sense that they were on the brink of something, and that something needed to happen between them. Ana was genial, this much she knew immediately, but she was also beautiful—different—sultry—and those dark eyes? If Ben wasn't drawn into them, he was blind to what was right in front of him. She longed to see her son settled in a good partnership, and if she had her way, there would be little people to love. She wondered if they would have Ana's eyes.

She turned to Hugh and asked, "Do you think those two have something going?"

"What do you mean by 'going?' Do you mean are they involved? Sleeping together?"

"No, from the little I've seen I don't think it's gone that far yet. I just wondered if you sensed the same electricity between them. It's not what they say—it's their body language. Have you noticed that they actually *try* not to touch, at least not in front of us?"

"From the story they told, they were thrown into the deep water, relationship-wise. Their first meeting ended in an all night vigil in a hotel room, with her taking responsibility for his wellbeing. That says a lot about her. And they've stuck together through what's happened so far. I'd say they seem well on their way to 'something.' We'll just have to wait it out. But I do agree with you. There's a connection between them, yet I think at this point it's all in their heads—neither one has taken the first step as yet. It should be Ben."

"But sometimes men are blind to these things, or they wait too long. I don't want to let that happen. He deserves some happiness after what Valerie put him through. He stayed too long, put up with too much. Guess I have to admit I was proud of him though. We raised him to take marriage seriously. A lot of good it did him."

"Now Paris, let us not go back there. Let's look ahead. We'll get this whole mess sorted out and then sit back and let nature take its course— and hope for the best. I like her too, so far."

"I just realized—with everything that happened today I forgot to call Ben. Now I'm nervous."

"If you can't wait, call him on your mobile. Then you can try to enjoy the rest of the ride," he said, his voice slightly impatient, but tempered with affection.

Paris reached for the phone in her briefcase. Her hand brushed against the file she had decided to bring with her at the last minute. She wanted to read it all again. There was something stirring in the back of her mind, but she couldn't put a finger on it. There was a coincidence brewing, but she couldn't quite identify it. If she stared at the words long enough, whatever it was might become clear. But now Ben was the priority.

She dialed their home and after five rings Edith answered, sounding harried and more than a little bit annoyed. "McKinnon residence, Edith speaking," she said and then waited for the caller to speak.

"It's me, Edith—Paris. We're on the road—should be there in less than half an hour. I'm calling to check on Ben. Is he there?"

"They must be around here somewhere. Last time I saw them they were playing with Sir Freddie. When I got back from shopping he was following everywhere at Ben's heels. He told me the furry rascal had been in the fountain again. Said they dried him off, and he took a nap in the sun for a while. Let me look outside and see where they've gotten to. Do you want to talk to Ben?"

"I don't need to talk to him. Just see if they're right outside. I want to put my mind at ease. I'll wait while you check." Paris sat quietly looking out the car window, watching the countryside whiz by while she waited to hear that her son had respected his father's request that they both stay put. Within several minutes Edith returned, picked up the receiver and spoke to Paris. "They're in the kitchen garden, fooling with the pea shoots. Sir Freddie is sitting outside the gate looking forlorn at having been left out."

Paris laughed and sighed with relief. "See you soon. How's dinner coming? Don't answer that—it's always coming on well. You're a fabulous cook. You spoil us. And I have dessert, as promised." With that, she rang off and put her phone back in the briefcase. "All's well for tonight, but we have tomorrow ahead of us. Looks like we may finally find out what those dregs of society want from me. I know I'll be pressured in some way. Can't imagine what we'll do then."

Hugh knew that she was frightened and had no intention of leaving her side until the whole mess was sorted. In the meantime, he wanted to keep his concerns from her, as well as from Ben and Ana. He asked her if she was satisfied, at least for the moment, and she answered him by reaching over and patting his leg affectionately. They rode on in silence. Thoreau would have to wait for another day.

CHAPTER TEN

Valerie entered the bustling café, a popular spot for employees working in office buildings nearby. She was shown to a table for two in a shady corner of the outdoor seating area. Olivia had never been a consistently punctual person, and Valerie hoped this would not be one of her late arrivals. A waiter approached but she declined ordering, saying she would wait for her friend. Earlier in the day her part of London had been immersed in a sultry rain-like fog, but it had dispersed almost as quickly as it had descended. Puddles remained on the tile flooring where the tables stood protected by large umbrellas. Drops of moisture still balanced on the leaves of the few potted plants, and she noticed how they sparkled in the sunlight. A manicured boxwood hedge defined the space, and a few of its inhabitants hopped around, in and out of puddles, chirping and foraging for crumbs. Valerie made these observations while sorting out how she would present Olivia with the idea of a trip. It was cool in the shade, so Valerie pulled on her cashmere cardigan and settled back in the chair, continuing to watch the entrance for her friend's arrival.

Pinning Olivia down to a lunch commitment had been difficult. Evidently she had a new client that was requiring much of her time. She had to admit that Olivia's explanation had in some way fallen short. There was an edge to her voice that revealed there was more to it than being busy with work. Just as she checked her watch for the third time, Olivia swept into the restaurant foyer, a departing gentleman having held the door open as his eyes followed her movements. She looked both chic and Boho in her tall boots, short leopard print skirt, and black silk blouse tied loosely at the waist. A dark indigo jean jacket was draped casually over one shoulder. As usual, her large earrings swung freely, framed by a copper shock of hair hanging in loose waves. Valerie was used to Olivia's 'entrances.' She had been little more than a child when Valerie first met her, but by the time she had reached eighteen, heads always turned when she entered a room.

Olivia looked around and spotted her lunch companion. She waved, walked quickly to the table, and before taking a seat gave Valerie a light kiss on each cheek. The waiter stood at the edge of the outdoor area, staring at Olivia, failing to approach their table or any other. Olivia usually seemed oblivious to the attention she would garner— a trait her mother insisted was a sign that she lacked both guile and conceit. She placed her leather bag on the unused chair and settled back, crossing her arms in front of her.

She cocked her head and looked squarely at Valerie. "Well, what was so urgent that we had to have lunch today?"

"I don't know if urgent is the right word, but my reason is important— to me at least." Valerie leaned forward and put her forearms on the table before continuing. "You remember that I've had to close the shop, right?" Olivia nodded yes. Valerie took a deep breath and said, "I want to take a little trip while it's closed. In fact, I'd be surprised if my father doesn't close it down for good when he takes his quarterly look at the numbers."

"I didn't know it was that bad. But then I haven't really talked to you for quite a while. Why is that, I wonder?"

"I think we can share that responsibility— and for my part, I'm sorry." Valerie leaned back again, still leaving her menu on the table. The same waiter, a tall and lanky young man with a ponytail, had kept his eyes on them— either because they were both attractive women, or because he was anxious for them to order. There was a pause while the two women stared at each other, each waiting for the other to say something.

Olivia broke the stalemate and asked, "What does your decision to take a trip have to do with me?"

"I'd rather not go alone. We always used to have fun together, didn't we— before Ben and I divorced— and even after?" She waited for a response, her expression expectant, perhaps even needy.

"Yes, I looked up to you when I was an adolescent— thought you were beautiful and that I was ugly— typical teenage angst." She smiled remembering what she now knew was silliness. "I never had a sister, so you were conscripted into that role. I was truly devastated when you and Ben split up."

"So was I…" Valerie seemed to stop mid-sentence and for a moment looked off into space, obviously visiting some memory of Ben. Whether that thought was good or bad, Olivia couldn't tell. "So, what do you think? Are you up for a little adventure?"

"What makes you think I can just walk off the job? And even if I could get some time off, it wouldn't be paid vacation. I haven't worked there long enough. I can't pay my expenses without a full month's salary."

"I've already thought about that. Of course I wouldn't expect you get yourself into a fix. I've worked it all out."

"How, pray tell?" Olivia now leaned forward and gazed quizzically at Valerie. At that moment a tiny bird landed at the edge of their table and chirped a request that they drop a morsel of bread onto the tile floor. They both looked away from each other and at the bird, which prompted laughter and a return to their old companionability.

Valerie suggested that they order lunch, and while waiting to be served she would explain the plan. She motioned to the waiter, who with an eye to his tips for the day seemed relieved they would no longer just sit there, keeping the table out of circulation. He took the order and disappeared from sight. As promised, Valerie began her explanation of how they would finance the excursion: the credit card, her small savings account, and the successful plea to her mother, who agreed to keep it between them. She estimated the total amount available and asked if Olivia had any money she could throw into the pot.

"Valerie, you're getting ahead of yourself. I don't even know if I can get a week or ten days off work. And where do you want to go? Have you thought about that? How far the money will go depends on where you go."

"I haven't got my heart set on any place in particular. I just know one thing: I want to get out of England for a while, and I don't want to set foot on American soil."

At that point the waiter arrived with their food, and although they ate for a while without conversing, it was clear that both were thinking about the trip, but for different reasons. Valerie was anxious to avoid the stress of her failing business and her father's wrath, while Olivia had very different considerations— her job being second to her developing interest in Clive Warren. She expected him to call her for another date, but she hadn't heard from him. Much to her surprise, that was all she could seem to think about.

Yet Valerie was not only her ex-sister-in-law, but also her friend. She had helped Olivia navigate her teen years and had always provided a sympathetic ear when she was at odds with her mother, or there was some boy causing her angst, or she needed help with her wardrobe. Her tendency to embrace a more bizarre and edgy fashion sense had not come until her early twenties when Valerie had all but disappeared from her life. During her now infrequent visits to the country, Olivia often heard the whispers between her parents about Valerie's obsession with getting Ben to come back, about her selfish and demanding ways, about the attempted suicide, the depression— all of it— and although she had been sorry, she hadn't reached out to her. Olivia had never been able to understand or accept their criticisms of Valerie because she had never been that way with her. Yet Olivia was involved in her education and trying much too hard to separate herself from family issues, believing at that time that cutting herself off from involvement was the way to show she had reached adulthood. What her actions had shown was that her maturity was still out of reach. What she remembered most was that in Valerie she found what seemed to be a kindred spirit.

She had still been a child when they first met, and for that fact alone she easily attached herself to Valerie. When they were all at the country house Olivia would capture her new sister with requests to come and see this or that—a new rabbit hole in the garden, a chrysalis on the thick stem of a hollyhock, a fashion show of her new dresses for the approaching school year. At meals she would insist on sitting beside Valerie, and if Valerie ate her Brussels sprouts, so would Olivia. She looked forward with great enthusiasm to holidays when she could be with Ben as well as Valerie, whose gifts to her were always perfect. Olivia thought to herself that perhaps it was time to do something for Valerie, just for the sake of how it used to be.

During the time when Olivia had felt so attached to her, Valerie had become more and more sure that Ben's parents didn't approve of her—of them as a couple— especially Ben's mother. It wasn't true, at least at the beginning, but a basic insecurity clouded her interpretation of their interaction. Just the fact that she was an American had made her feel like an outsider, regardless of how Hugh and Paris had tried to make her feel welcome. Any problems between Ben and Valerie remained well hidden from his parents for a long time, and all seemed well at the holiday table. Olivia's presence had always softened the discomfort Valerie felt when being at the McKinnon home. She had served as a buffer—in Valerie's mind anyway. Olivia's blind worship of her had soothed her ego. And it was true that she and Ben were less likely to show animosity toward each other in the child's presence. Since the divorce, Valerie had failed to make any close friends. Whatever friends she had were casual—not the kind in whom one could confide. The truth was that Olivia was the only one she considered 'close.' She had been a child, but now she was a woman, and to Valerie, Olivia still felt like a kindred spirit and the perfect person with whom to escape reality.

The waiter removed their plates and brought coffee. Olivia had been deep in thought, but finally spoke. "I'm not saying I *can* get away, but let's just say I can." Valerie perked up and listened. "I don't know if you remember, or were even told any stories about my grandparents." Valerie shook her head no, and Olivia continued. "They met and fell in love in Spain—Pamplona, actually. If you're interested, I'll tell you the story, but not now."

"I'd like to hear it—I may have just forgotten—but why did you bring that up?"

"Because it's an idea, and we need one. Let's go to Spain—if I can get away without losing my job. If you stay away from the cities and the Costa del Sol, it's not as expensive as France or Italy. I don't know when high season starts in Spain, at least that far north. Pamplona is in Navarra. If you don't object to two-star hotels, it should be manageable for the length of time you mentioned."

"Hmmm ... that's one of the last places I'd have thought of going. In fact, I wouldn't have thought of it at all. I saw us on the Cote d'Azur, or maybe in northern Italy—maybe Florence again. But Spain has two things going for it—I've never been there, and you say it's less expensive."

"I've been to Florence too, and the Cote d'Azur is probably beyond our—I mean *your*— means. I always wanted to go to Pamplona because of my grandparents. It's quite a story, their romance. I've always thought it would make a good book—even a film."

"You've piqued my interest. I don't know what there is to do in Pamplona for a week or more, but maybe there are some side trips to see something interesting. I just know it's probably hot and that there's something that happens there every year—but I can't remember what it is right now." She told Olivia that lunch was her treat and then motioned to the waiter for the bill. He was more than happy to bring it immediately and they were soon out on the sidewalk and ready to part ways. An expectant smile crossed Valerie's face and she gave Olivia a hug. Her expression then became serious, and she said, "I feel like running straight to a travel agent—or my computer, but no point in that until you talk to your boss. When can you do that? Will he be in the office this afternoon? Can you tell I'm anxious?"

Olivia shook her head and smiled at Valerie's enthusiasm then answered, "Yes, I can see that you're anxious. It does sound like it could be fun, if it works out. I promise that if he comes in this afternoon, I'll broach the subject with him. I'm not looking forward to that, but he might surprise me. I'll guarantee him that if he's swamped when I get back, I'll work overtime and make up some of the time, even if he won't pay me for it."

"That sounds like a good enough deal for him. I'd give you the time off!"

"I know him well enough by now to know that if something's free, he's all for it."

"Call me the minute you know."

Olivia assured her that she would be in touch, and they parted in different directions. It had turned into a long visit, and she half hoped her boss wasn't in yet, because to ask a favor on the heels of a longer than permitted lunch might not be the best choice. She took long strides walking the two blocks back to her workplace, glad that they had agreed to meet at a café that was fairly close by. The office door was still locked. Her boss and the other assistant were evidently still at lunch or out seeing a client. Olivia unlocked the door with her own key and then busied herself unwrapping and cataloging the fabrics that had been in the morning deliveries. Soon she heard voices in reception and went to see who had come in. The owner of the design firm, Mr. Cole Saunders, was talking to a man delivering another parcel. Their brief conversation ended, the man left, and Olivia asked Mr. Saunders if she could have a word. He ushered her into his office and sat down at his desk. She declined to take a seat and then began to speak, first having taken in a deep breath.

"I have a request— a big one, actually— and I know you have every right to refuse, given that I've only worked her for a bit more than a year."

"Let's have it— nothing ventured, nothing gained." He motioned her to get on with it and looked down, shuffling papers on his desk and opening the folder directly in front of him. Then he stopped abruptly and looked up at Olivia as he said, "Well then?"

"I was waiting for you to finish what you're doing." He settled back in his chair, indicating that he was now listening, so she continued. "Let me preface this by reminding you that I haven't taken any time off during this year, other than those three days when I had some kind of flu."

"Yes, I remember, and I'm aware you've been diligent— and, may I say, popular with the clients you've assisted."

"Thank you, Mr. Saunders. I enjoy my work. But here's the thing: My sister-in-law— ex-sister-in-law actually— has asked me to take a trip with her... to Spain. She's been going through a rather stressful time, and we've remained friends, even after she and my brother divorced."

"I don't need to hear your family history. The reason for your request is less important than getting a few things straight about what your absence would mean. How long would you be gone?" Before she had a chance to answer he chimed in again. "I hope you know that I wouldn't consider paying you for that time, if I even agree to let you go. You haven't yet earned even a week's paid vacation."

Olivia informed him that she hadn't expected to receive paid vacation, and that she had worked out her finances in a way that would make the trip possible. He didn't need to know that Valerie was treating her to most of it. She had only enough for some meals and maybe a few small gifts for her family—maybe Mr. Saunders as well. She sat down in the chair opposite his desk and waited while he tapped a pencil on the desk and pursed his lips in thought. Several minutes passed before he sat up straight, put down the pencil and leaned forward, his elbows on the desk.

"Go. We'll manage. Ten days is the longest I can let you be gone." He wagged his finger at Olivia and spoke like a Dutch uncle. "Don't call me then and try to weasel more time out of me."

Olivia thanked him profusely until he told her to please leave his office so he could get some work done. On her way out he added that if she didn't get all the new fabrics catalogued by closing, she would have to stay. She hurried out of the office and into the back room, where she worked diligently until the last bolt was correctly placed in its cubby. She glanced at the clock on her desk and saw that it was after five-thirty. Her workday was at a close.

On the way out she peeked into Cole Saunders' office and waved goodbye, mouthing "thank you" to him before closing the door. He was tied to a call with a supplier in China, which was immediately obvious to her because he was speaking Mandarin, only one of the five languages in which he could converse. Once on the sidewalk, she realized that the usual three-block walk to the Tube seemed too far in the humidity that had risen during the afternoon, even if she cut through the little park. She decided to wait at the corner for the next bus that would take her close enough to her flat. The wait was short, and soon she climbed aboard, deciding to take the stairs up to the open-air level. The bus moved in stops and starts, block after block, while Olivia enjoyed the brief periods of cooling wind in her face. As the bus approached her destination she walked carefully down the stairs, ready to hop off quickly.

Within another ten minutes Olivia was unlocking the door to her flat. She pulled open the drapes in the small sitting room and unlatched the window to let in some fresh air. She took in a deep breath and glanced at the blue-purple sky that signaled dusk was approaching. The sun was gone, and another long evening was ahead of her. She kicked off her shoes and threw her purse on the coffee table, the mobile phone slipping out onto the glass top. Deciding that a cool glass of wine might perk her up, she headed for the kitchen. While pouring the chilled Pinot Gris, her mobile began to ring. A flush of anticipation ran through her as she hurried to answer the call. She tripped over the shoes, barely righting herself, and dived for the phone just as it went to voicemail.

* * *

It was after five o'clock, and the pub was becoming more crowded by the minute. Gareth Logan took the last swig of his beer and blamed the din for his headache. The culprit was more likely the beer, his third. He dropped a few coins into the wooden tip box, slid off the stool and headed out the door. He had been avoiding the return to his dingy flat but knew that he had to be there to take a call at six. He crossed in the middle of the block, causing several drivers to honk, and then walked the mere hundred yards to his building entrance. Gareth entered his small flat and flopped down on the lumpy sofa. He blew out a long breath, a sure sign that all was not well in his world. His nerves wouldn't allow him to sit still, so he got up and removed his jacket, throwing it onto the small table in the corner that served for meals and everything else. He grabbed at a magazine and sat down again, this time settling in the ratty lounge chair by the window, where he often used the sunlight for reading. There was only one old ceiling fixture to light the whole dismal room. He flipped through the pages, not really seeing what was there. He swiveled and twitched, rested his head on his hand, flung one leg over the chair arm, and finally got up again. He paced around the room, checking his phone at approximately two-minute intervals.

Gareth was standing at the window when it rang. It was the same voice as last time—the same voice that threatened to have his brother killed if he didn't help them—whoever *them* was. Days had passed since the first call, the one ordering him to meet at that pub in King's Cross, and he had done as he was told—as well as he was able. His efforts to figure out how anyone had made the connection between his brother and himself had been unsuccessful. James had been in prison for over a year, but to Gareth it seemed longer. He still believed his brother wouldn't be there if he'd had a decent solicitor, one who would have advised him to be tried separately from the other two men.

There were two appeals still pending, but in the meantime his younger brother was trapped inside with hardened criminals. It was ruining their mother's health, and he had made her an impulsive promise to see it through to the end, the end being either his release, or a transfer to a less hardcore facility. James had been guilty only by association. The wrong choice of friends, slightly older young men who had turned out to be hoodlums, had led him to be present at a robbery he knew nothing about. His so-called friends had told him to wait outside the local off-license, that he wasn't old enough to buy anything anyway. No one had been armed, the manager nor the young men, but they had brandished all too real-looking toy guns that James had not noticed in their pockets. It was an old story, really… what had happened to him. Gareth might never know how the men with whom he was now forced to be involved had found his brother among all those real criminals, but they had. And now he had to sort it out by any means possible. He had promised his Mum.

"Have you got a second date with her yet," the voice said, its tone brusque, almost surly. "I told you—time is of the essence. We lost time trying to deal with the brother."

"I haven't called yet—I'll do it now—after this. I was waiting for her to get home from work."

"You'd better hope she doesn't stop off somewhere. Make the invitation sound too good to pass up. You know what happens if you drop the ball."

"I know. You don't have to keep threatening me. I get it. But if she didn't like me, I can't *make* her go out with me again."

"Then you'd better turn whatever charm you have up to high. And don't forget to use the alias. You're Clive Warren. By the end of the evening I expect you to have information on everything she's doing and where she'll be for all of this next week. Is that clear?"

"It's clear. But only so much is within my power. And you haven't told me why I'm insinuating myself into her life. When are you going to tell me where this is going? You won't expect me to hurt her, will you?"

"Not at this time. I have others for that purpose, if it comes to that. Just do as you're told and your brother will be fine. She may even be fine. Screw it up and they both pay the price. You will too." The voice paused, obviously letting the threats sink in. Gareth said nothing, just waited to see if there was more. Then the words began again. "Just to confirm that

I'm not bluffing, I think you should have your brother's solicitor contact him—or if he's allowed family calls, you might want to check in on him. Have them transfer you straight to the infirmary. That's where he is."

The voice had become increasingly sullen, and the last sentence carried a downright sinister edge. His last statement hit Gareth hard. Fear crackled through his body as he heard the man's words and immediately began to imagine what may have happened to his brother. He decided to put off his call to Olivia for a little while. First he would call James' solicitor. As an officer of the court a solicitor would be able to get information more quickly. He fumbled through the top drawer of his dresser and found the worn business card, and then dialed the number. The call went to voicemail, but he left the information and with all the control he could muster, calmly asked the solicitor to check in on James—that his mother had been more upset than usual and needed confirmation that her son was doing all right. He rung off and sat down, head in his hands, his mind racing with the demands being made on him, and his growing worries about the advisability of seeing Olivia again. He had to choose. It was either his brother's safety or Olivia's. The choice was impossible from a moral standpoint, but he knew without any doubt that family would have to come first.

After drawing a few deep breaths he dialed Olivia's number. Just as it started to click into voicemail she answered. "Hello, Olivia here."

"Umm, this is Clive Warren. I had said I'd call—remember—when I put you in the taxi?"

He had identified himself and now waited to pick up on her attitude about hearing him on the other end of the line. Much to his surprise, she sounded delighted to hear his voice—or maybe he needed to think that. Yet he went blindly forward and proposed that they see each other again—the next evening. Olivia accepted, but told him she couldn't make it a late night because she was planning a short trip, her boss having surprised her by agreeing to the short absence. Gareth heaved a sigh of relief when she accepted his invitation and asked if there was something special she might like to do. Olivia told him that she knew of a club not too far from her flat that was featuring a small jazz group from the U.S., and since her parents were always 'talking it up,' she thought it might be fun to see what all the fuss was about. He easily agreed and said they could eat first—maybe walk from her flat to a café close by, then go on to the club.

"That sounds like a practical plan," Olivia said. "I'll do my best to be home by five-thirty, but I'll need to spruce up a bit, so why don't you call for me at about seven o'clock. We can grab a bite and then catch the first set. I have to be home by eleven o'clock, latest."

"I'm anxious to see you again, Olivia. I stopped by your office just after noon today—I guess you were at lunch. Mr. Saunders was just on his way out. I told him that I'd be very satisfied to work with another associate. He asked why—had you been unsatisfactory in some way— and I told him the truth. I said that it was more important to me to see you socially than to have you decorate my office. He seemed to understand—gave me a sly smile, actually."

"You don't let any grass grow under your feet, do you, Mr. Warren?"

Her tone was light. She sounded as if what he had done pleased her, which pleased him as well. Yet part of what he felt was relief that she would see him again. He asked for the address of her flat, which in spite of her original hesitation, she now gave willingly. He told her that tomorrow seemed too far away, and she laughed it off, thinking he was now showing her his 'line.' What she didn't realize was that as soon as the words left his mouth, he realized he meant them. He liked her, and that scared him.

* * *

After ending her call with the suitor she knew as Clive, Olivia placed her mobile back on the coffee table. She picked up her shoes from the floor and went into the bedroom to change. In a few minutes she came out wearing leggings and a sweatshirt. She walked into the kitchen and began to gather ingredients for a light meal. Her frig was devoid of choices other than three kinds of cheese, a few bottles of white wine, a bag of greens and a questionable looking yellow pepper. She curled up on the couch, a glass of wine to her left, the meager salad in her lap, and switched the television to the BBC evening news. Before she had eaten a second bite, her mobile rang. She put down the bowl and reached out for the phone in front of her. Valerie was on the line, calling to find out if Olivia had managed to get time off work.

"So, what did he say?" she asked abruptly,

"No one is more surprised than I am. He said yes—but for a maximum of ten days. He warned me not to call him and try begging for more."

"That's wonderful news," Valerie said, sounding relieved. "Tomorrow morning I'll get something booked—the soonest possible flight. I'd go online, but it would take too much time to sift through all the travel websites. I know the airfare will cost more—booking at the last minute. I'll go to that travel agent down the street from my shop and have him find the best fare. He can do the actual tickets and find us a hotel."

"You seem to have taken it all well in hand. I wouldn't know where to start, planning at the last minute like this."

"The agent will actually do the hard part—but still not as hard as the *paying* part!"

"I'll stop at my bank tomorrow on the way to work and get my meager donation to the trip. Also, don't forget to tell whoever books the hotel that we only want two or three stars—three being preferable—if it's not too much. When you get right down to it, making travel arrangements is just another form of shopping."

"Leave it to you to bring shopping into it. Are you still queen of the vintage stores?"

"Never mind that—but yes, and proud of it." Olivia paused, then added, "Oh-oh, I remember what I wanted to tell you. I have a date tomorrow night, so be sure to call me between five and six. I'll be leaving at seven. If I don't answer, try again—I might be in the shower.

Or if you get things settled before then, call me at work. The sooner the better."

"Well, I hope you can organize yourself in time—along with going out for the evening. What if I get us a flight for day after tomorrow?"

"I'll make it an early night—just tell him I have to be at work early. I'll start sorting out some things tonight and if I need to, get up early tomorrow to start packing. It will be fine. Don't worry."

"Don't forget the hat and sunscreen. You reddish-haired types burn easily. I don't want you putting a damper on things by getting a sunburn."

They both laughed and rang off. Olivia felt a surge of excitement, brought on by the fact that the trip was now a reality. She spent the remainder of the evening pulling out clothes and touring northern Spain courtesy of Google. When she discovered that within the week the Festival of *San Fermín* and the running of the bulls would begin, she became even more enthusiastic. It had been during the festival that her grandparents had met. She wondered if there could be a bit of romance waiting for her as well. That would add another element to the trip, and as she lay in bed, waiting for sleep, she hoped against hope that Valerie would manage to make reservations that would place them at the center of the festivities.

* * *

The next day Olivia felt at loose ends and found it hard to concentrate on the decorating assignment she had been given the week before. Mr. Saunders had made a point of needing to have it finished before she left on vacation. But the trip wasn't her only distraction. She was contemplating her second evening with Clive Warren, and found herself becoming more nervous by the hour. Only a short time was needed to complete the project, so she decided to put it away and head home to prepare for her date. She treated herself to a taxi and was soon inside her flat trying to decide what to do first.

Fresh from the shower she began to pull garments out of the closet, tossing them on the bed one at a time, until eventually something struck her fancy. She chose a very dark pair of jeans and a white rayon top, its wide neckline meant to drop off one shoulder. Her earrings were large oval hoops, silver, with several tiny moonstones hanging from each. She chose a velvet wrap in a silvery shade of dove gray and took one last look in the mirror. Something wasn't right, and she paused. She reached for a silver filigree clip and swept up the mass of hair, twisting it casually and securing it high on her head. Several tendrils had escaped, but only served to bring attention to her green eyes and fair complexion.

There were twenty minutes or so before her date would arrive. She set about tidying her small sitting room, fluffing pillows, folding the plush coverlet and placing it on the back of the sofa. Her phone rang as she picked it up to put it in her purse. She answered and heard a very excited Valerie on the other end.

"It's done. We're set! We leave day after tomorrow from Heathrow at ten—not too early for you, is it?" Valerie laughed and waited for Olivia's response.

"No, it's fine—but what airline? And where are we landing? And how do we get to our hotel— are we renting a car?" the questions were flying out of her mouth faster than Valerie could answer them.

"Slow down! Now just listen… Iberia airlines to Madrid; layover is less than an hour; next stop, San Sebastián. Total trip is less than five hours. We'll find transportation at the airport to take us to our hotel in Pamplona. It's about a half hour from the airport, so the agent said. Well, where we're staying is actually a guesthouse—not sure I can remember the whole name, or pronounce it. Something-something-*Alojamientos*. The agent said it had good reviews and there may be a kitchenette. That will save some money. The room only has to be clean and have a private bathroom. We won't be there much."

"True. It's probably 'guesthouse' *Alojamientos*. Wow, you really did a good job. Now if the festival was happening, it would all be too perfect."

"Surprise! It starts the day after we arrive. That's why the hotels were a little more than I expected. They bump up the price during the festival."

"Now I'm as excited as you are. Oh lord, what will I take—I have to think fast—no time for shopping."

"Pack for heat. Remember the hat and sunscreen. Now I have to run. Have fun tonight."

"Wait! How are we getting to the airport?"

"I'm booking a taxi to pick us up—first me, then you—they have a rate to the airport."

"Valerie, I didn't realize you could be so organized... just kidding. Bye."

Olivia set her phone on 'silent' and put it in her purse. The chimes from a nearby church began to strike seven. Clive, as Olivia knew him, was punctual, ringing the buzzer and knocking before the seventh strike. When Olivia answered the door he didn't have to fake his admiring gaze. Once in the hallway she noticed that the elevator was in use, and she didn't want to wait. Neither spoke while they took the two flights of stairs to the street, but as they began to walk in the direction of the jazz club, conversation became brisk and congenial. They stopped at a small café for a light meal, during which Gareth seemed more quiet than he had been on their first evening together. He seemed preoccupied, his expression anything but attentive.

Sensing that his thoughts were elsewhere, Olivia said, "Is there something wrong? You seem to be miles away."

He took an obvious deep breath and answered, "I was, but it has nothing to do with you. I wouldn't want to be anywhere but here—right now—with you."

"Can I help? Is it something about your office that has you stressed?"

"No. No. It's not that—just some business stuff. But I'll do better. My eyes and thoughts will be on you for the rest of the evening. That's how I like it."

"Hmmm—I don't think you should stare at me during the set at the club. The musicians might be insulted. You should stop when you cross the street too. You might get hit."

He chuckled and smiled at her. Noticing the time, he signaled for the bill and they were soon on their way to the jazz club. About two hours later, having enjoyed the music and the stroll back to her flat, he asked to see her the following week. As they climbed the stairs to her flat, she told him about her plans and that she would be out of the country for about ten days. His disappointment was evident, either because he couldn't see her, or because the plan he was ordered to carry out could be impossible and could put his brother in more danger. At that moment he couldn't think of himself as Clive. He was Gareth Logan, an innocent weekend rugby player and employee of a technology services company who had been coerced into taking part in a crime about which he was being kept in the dark.

He told himself to suck it up and do what he had to do, so he thought quickly and asked if he could take her to the airport. She declined, saying that she and her friend had booked a car service to pick them up. In an effort to glean more information he offered again, saying that if the taxi didn't show up, she should call and he would hurry over. But he would need to know the time of her flight, and the airline—just to make it easier in a pinch. She didn't quite understand his request, but saw no reason not to share the information, including the layover and arrival time at San Sebastián. Then he asked about their accommodations. Olivia was happy to talk about all of it— about her connection to Pamplona through her grandparents, about the guesthouse, its name, and that it was inexpensive. He suggested that due to his selective memory, he should write down the information—just in case of any problem they might encounter where he might be of help. Then he held up his phone and took her picture. He said it would help him not to miss her too much. She found his concern unnecessary, but found it all flattering. Reaching into his jacket pocket, he pulled out a notepad and pen.

They were still standing outside Olivia's door when she told him she should go inside. The two stood face to face in the deserted hallway, each feeling self-conscious for a different reason. Gareth wanted desperately to kiss her, but the situation he was in made him doubt the wisdom of that choice. Olivia wondered in that moment what his kiss would be like—whether it would be tentative or passionate. Her preference was a kiss that began as tentative, its sweetness promising an explosion of passion to follow. She looked up and their eyes met. Neither said a word. He realized that this could be his only chance to kiss her. What was to come was still an unknown. What he wanted to do was to tell her everything, to appoint himself her protector, and for them to run far and fast. Instead, he leaned down and took the kiss. Standing on her tiptoes she met his lips halfway. The first kiss did begin tentatively, and he resisted putting his arms around her. Each backed off and looked into the other's eyes again. Before either could take a second breath, he reached for her, his arms pulling her close to his chest. His open mouth devoured hers, and she returned the pressure. She felt his tongue slide into her willing mouth, and for as long as the exploration lasted she was lost in the idea of a romance with this rugged looking yet gentle man. They bid each other good night, each a little shaken by the unexpected intensity of their first kiss. Olivia went inside and just stood in her dark flat, reluctant to turn on the lights that would bring her back to reality.

Kissing Olivia had left him too distracted to remember there was a lift. He took the two flights of stairs to the street very slowly, and once outside he began to wrestle with what was required of him. He stood on the sidewalk, leaning against a streetlight, wondering what to do next. He took out his phone and then hesitated. But there was no escaping his involvement, so he took a folded piece of paper out of his pocket and dialed the number written there. The person who answered Gareth's call had the same altered voice as the man that had recruited and threatened him, issued instructions, given him an alias, and was now generally in control of his life. With much reluctance he relayed the information regarding Olivia's plans and whereabouts for the next week or so. The voice then ordered him to book any airline in whatever class available for a red eye flight to Madrid and on to San Sebastián. If a red eye flight wasn't possible, he was to fly out early the next morning in order to arrive at least a day before Olivia and her companion. The ticket was to be paid for in cash. He had to be in Pamplona before they arrived, but he didn't know why. Before leaving the airport he was to call the same number and tell whoever answered his flight number and arrival time. If no one showed up to get him at the airport, he was to hire a taxi to drive him from San Sebastián to Pamplona, where he was to book a cheap hotel, call the same number to report his whereabouts, and then stay put until he was contacted.

Gareth sat before his computer, an assortment of flights showing on the screen. He made a decision on which to book and held it with a credit card, intending to pay cash at check-in. However, the flight would leave before dawn, before he could make a stop at the bank. The cashpoint wouldn't give him enough for the ticket, and he had to have sufficient cash to pay for a taxi to Heathrow and Euros to get to San Sebastián. He rifled through the pockets of his jacket and pants, hoping to find something to put toward his expenses. His wallet held less than a hundred pounds. The evening with Olivia had taken the rest. Then he remembered the small envelope of cash that had been pushed under his door the week before. The note inside had said "for unexpected outlay in pursuit of your assignment."

At that time he had expected he would find a way out of the mess and wanted no part of owing these people anything. But following the daily threats made to his brother, he knew he was in it to whatever conclusion was in store. A short time passed before he remembered where he had hidden the envelope. His fear and disgust had kept him from opening it or counting the contents, but now there was no choice. A rush of adrenaline shot through him as he finished the tally. It held over two thousand pounds. He pulled his duffle bag from under the bed and stuffed it with enough clothes for a week or so, almost forgetting his razor and toothbrush. He rifled through several drawers for his passport, finally finding it when he dumped contents of the third out onto the bed. He put it on the table beside his bed, along with his watch and the roll of cash. Although he was plagued by anxiety and doubt, he laid down on his bed, hoping for a little rest before the taxi he had scheduled arrived to take him to Gatwick for his dawn flight to Madrid and on to San Sebastián. Emotional fatigue overwhelmed all thought and anxiety, and he fell into a restless sleep.

It seemed the middle of the night when the alarm on Gareth's watch startled him away from the meager three hours of sleep he had been able to manage. He sat on the edge of the bed, for a moment disoriented, and then, wishing it had all been a bad dream, got up and walked to the bathroom. At the sight of himself in the mirror—face drawn, eyes bloodshot— he knew it wasn't a dream. Once resigned to the reality of the task at hand, he splashed cold water on his face and decided not to shave. He pulled on some clothes and then his old brown suede jacket. As he scanned the room he remembered the things on the nightstand and stuffed them into his pockets. He slung the duffle bag over his shoulder and headed for the door, stopping for an instant to look back at his cluttered apartment. He wondered if whatever lay in store would keep him from ever seeing it again.

CHAPTER ELEVEN

The McKinnons returned from London in the early evening. They entered the house and immediately began to look for Ben and Ana. The two were discovered relaxing in the small room that held the only television set in the house. Hugh asked them to come into the sitting room so he could explain what had happened at the museum. Paris asked Hugh for a drink, the day having taken its toll on her. Ben jumped up, offering to get it for her, and asked if anyone else would like something. Ana had no idea what news there was, but the seriousness of Hugh's tone made her nervous with anticipation. Her day had seemed long, with only a few minutes respite playing with Sir Freddie on the kitchen step. Ben was preoccupied, picking up a book and putting it down again within minutes. She felt best if she stayed physically close to him, not letting him out of her sight. The need was illogical. They were safe, or relatively so, seemingly hidden away in the country. But she didn't trust anything anymore. Watching Ben being beaten on the sidewalk had forever changed her.

Ben returned to the sofa, sat down beside Ana, and gave her hand a squeeze. His touch sent warmth flooding through her body, and when he turned toward her, his deep blue eyes focusing on hers, the urges she felt seemed very inappropriate in a setting where his parents sat directly across from them. He had come up behind her while she was at the sink tidying up after lunch. He leaned in close, bringing his head over her shoulder to see what she was doing. She caught the scent of his cologne mixed with clean sweat. In her imagination he had turned her around and planted a decisively lusty kiss on her enthusiastic lips. Ana sensed his interest, sensed the pleasant tension in the room whenever they were together. She wondered what he was waiting for… the right moment perhaps? She had been lost in thought while the three others were talking, and soon she heard Ben saying her name once, then again.

"Ana … Ana … Mum asked you a question."

Flustered by her poor manners, Ana said, "Oh, please forgive me. I was distracted—lost in thought. Please… what had you asked me?"

"With all of us talking at once I'm not surprised you were distracted. What I asked was whether you have everything you need. I know that you weren't planning on an extended stay. I thought you might need some clean clothes, or to have Edith do some laundry for you. You're welcome to anything I might have as well."

"You're very kind. Perhaps I can organize that in the morning." She quickly changed the subject, turned toward Ben, and said, "Do you think we should tell your parents the whole thing about the dead rabbit?"

Ben looked at his parents and began to give more of an explanation. "Sir Freddie brought us an offering this afternoon. He was scuffling in the bushes and came out with a rabbit—shot clean through with a handgun. It definitely wasn't a shotgun. The whole thing was very disturbing to Ana.

Ana chimed in, her face as sad as if she had been related to the creature, "How could anyone just use the little thing for target practice."

Paris chose to answer her question and spoke very gently. "Dear, here in the country we find rabbits to be pests, cute as they are. They are prone to destroy gardens, help themselves to the vegetables, and they proliferate at an alarming rate. Someone may have thought they were doing us a favor."

Ben tried to lighten the conversation, as well as bring it to an end. "True, it was an unpleasant sight, but it sure made Sir Freddie's afternoon."

Everyone chuckled at the thought of the dog prancing proudly to the kitchen door, an offering held softly in his mouth. Hugh got up, walked to the fireplace and put his drink on the mantle. "There are much more important things to talk about. Let's get back to the matter at hand. It requires some organization. Paris now has instructions that she must be in the office tomorrow—that all will be revealed. She will stay in her office while I go into Lloyd's for a meeting. That's a better choice because I can't be seen walking into the building where Interpol has its offices. I've arranged for two agents to meet with me at Lloyd's." Then he was quiet, for a moment deep in thought and tapping his fingers on the mantle. He turned to them and continued. "Hopefully, by the time of the meeting at Lloyd's, Paris will have received the information about what is required of her." He shook his head in disgust. "How did this family ever manage to get tied up in what looks like a ridiculous caper?" He picked up his drink and downed it in one gulp, placing the empty glass on the mantle rather loudly. He then returned to his chair and let himself all but fall into it, the fatigue of day suddenly hitting him.

"Hugh, I think you should tell them about your 'arrangement.' Otherwise they're likely to call the police and report an intruder on the property."

"I suppose you're right," he said, the fatigue showing in his voice. He turned toward Ben and Ana then sat forward, his hands folded, elbows resting on his knees. "I called in a favor. There's someone watching the house and property— just as a precaution."

Ana shared that when she sneaked a walk to the gate, she had seen a car parked across the road and a man leaning against a tree, talking on a mobile phone. For a moment she had been frightened and returned quickly to the house. When she went outside about an hour later the car was gone. She hadn't mentioned it to Ben because she knew he'd be annoyed, and she feared that he might go out into the road and confront the man. She wasn't taking any more chances with his safety. When she stopped talking, Paris gave her a tender and appreciative look, then glanced at her son to see his reaction. A different kind of smile crossed his face, one that she couldn't remember seeing before. He rarely smiled while he was married to Valerie. There seemed to be a special brightness in his eyes and his cheeks were slightly flushed. She recognized the signs and was delighted.

Hugh asked for everyone's attention, and when all eyes were on him, he said, "Tomorrow is the day we get answers. I think you, Ben, and of course Ana, should come with us to London. I can keep an eye on you, and we'll all be together when we find out what's coming."

Paris chimed in immediately. "Yes, your father's right. And I'll feel more relaxed if we're together."

"I'll have to leave for a while, to meet with the agents. Ben—listen to me. You and Ana absolutely must stay at your mother's office, both for your own safety and for hers. I don't like having her out of my sight, but plans have to be put in motion."

Ben nodded his head in agreement, adding, "Good plan, Dad. But I have to say again how much I hate that you're now involved in this. Besides, I want to have my eye on Ana too. We all need to stay together as much as possible."

Paris interrupted. "I'm the one who's gotten everyone involved. I'm the one who's getting the calls— the threats— and I'm the one who's being manipulated— undoubtedly to break the law. At least that's what I'm expecting."

The room was quiet for several minutes before Ben suggested that they try Olivia again. She was bad about answering her phone, or responding to texts and voicemail, but they needed to talk to her. He checked his pocket for his mobile, stood and pulled it out, and then went out into the hall. Not three minutes later he was back. "No joy… again."

"In the morning we'll call her boss." Hugh paused, an expression of annoyance rather than concern on his face. "He should know what she's up to. I'm sure he can cajole her into getting in touch."

"I haven't talked to her since that dinner we had weeks ago. She ended the evening abruptly. I must have done something wrong— who knows with Olivia. She can change moods in a heartbeat. I've left a few voice messages, but no response. I figured she'd get in touch when she was ready." Ben got up and walked to the window and gazed out into the approaching darkness. He turned back, put his hands in his pants pockets, shrugged, and looked squarely at his parents. "Do you suppose you're being punished too—by association?"

Ben's parents looked at each other and shrugged as well. Hugh said, "Stranger things have happened. We are talking about Olivia, bless her heart. We'll find out eventually. It won't be the first time. All three of us share the responsibility for spoiling her."

Paris countered with a defense for her daughter. "Olivia's not a self-centered girl— she's just rather mercurial. She cares about world situations, children and poverty. I know from what she's said— that she has favorite charities and contributes what she can."

"We're not putting her down, Mum. We men just have a hard time figuring her out. She's a unique soul. I knew that by the time she was ten— even before. Maybe it's the creativity that sets the marching tune for her particular drummer." His comment lightened the mood and the three shared the humor, not at Olivia's expense but because they realized how much they loved her. Edith had left them a light supper, and following that, all agreed that it should be an early night.

Ben followed Ana upstairs, while his parents let Sir Freddie into the pantry to sleep and then secured the house. Ben walked Ana to the door of her room, where they stood talking a bit, Ben standing close to her as she leaned against the door. She impulsively looked up at him and found his remarkably blue eyes looking straight into hers. Without touching her Ben leaned down, lightly brushing his lips across hers before kissing her cheek. His lips lingered there, and again Ana was overcome by the now familiar flush coursing through her body. Her impulse was to take his face in her hands and kiss him, not on the cheek but on the lips, and in a way that would carry no doubt of intention. Ana was filled with passion in need of expression; however, she just smiled and touched his cheek with her palm. When he returned the smile, she looked down self-consciously. Something about the whole thing felt adolescent, but the sweetness of the moment made it remarkable. Without another word he turned and walked toward his room. When he reached the door she was still standing in front of hers. He looked back and said goodnight. The reasons for their reticence were clear: He didn't want to seem too eager; she didn't want to seem too easy.

Alone in their beds, imaginations ran rampant. Ben had resisted time and again, wondering if it were the right moment but then deciding there would be a better one. The waiting had become torture. The more time he spent in her company, the more he wanted her. Ana felt a sexual energy between them, but previous experience kept her from being overt in her signals to Ben. Both were aware that danger could be an aphrodisiac, and that when removed from that danger the attraction could diffuse, showing its lack of substance. Being burned by past relationships had made them cautious. Yet Ana realized that too much caution could be like missing the train to an idyllic destination. She truly hoped that Ben would at least buy a ticket.

* * *

Lyle Brett's face revealed a dire need for sleep. He was pale, drawn, and licked his lips nervously as he scanned the flat's sitting room to ensure it was tidy. Satisfied that all was as it should be, he zipped the jacket of his black velour athletic suit and prepared to leave. This casual look was a grand departure from the business suits that always seemed slightly too small. Also absent was the stiff demeanor he was known to present at his place of employment. Lyle was sliding into middle age and was no doubt the least athletic person ever to don such attire. But it did do him the favor of adding a few pounds to his spindly frame.

He collected the mobile phone and keys from the hall table, checked his appearance in the mirror mounted above, and made a hasty exit. Once on the street he decided against using public transport and stepped toward the curb to wave down a taxi that had most conveniently happened along. He slid into the back seat, not noticing the driver glance in his rear-view mirror and then stifle a snigger. Lyle gave the address of his destination and the man maneuvered into traffic. The afternoon rush was underway and caused him to check his watch constantly then mutter to himself. When they arrived at the building, he discourteously tossed the fare over the seat and got out as fast as he could.

As he slammed the door the driver leaned across and shouted, "Wanker!"

He ignored the affront and entered the building, briskly taking the stairs to the second floor. Number 2C was at the end of the hall and he knocked in rapid succession. A large man opened the door—at least he seemed large to Lyle, who was of much smaller stature. The man scowled at him and pointed out his tardiness.

"Traffic and a stupid driver," he said by way of excuse. He puffed himself up then added, "You do know that I'm the one who's heading up this project? A little respect if you please."

The man grunted and turned away, stepping back into the flat as he said under his breath, "Royal prat."

Lyle had never been good at making friends or a good impression—just the opposite. How he had obtained his position of responsibility was a mystery to his co-workers. His presence could clear a room, change a mood, or put people off him for a variety of reasons. It was unlikely he could ever inspire loyalty, or more so, love. One or another of those with whom he made contact on a daily basis wondered how a man could end up isolating himself so efficiently.

He followed the other man through a short entryway into a small sitting room that seemed to be all there was to the flat. The room was stark and contained only a table, four chairs, and an electric heater. The wood floor held a shabby rug, and an L-shaped counter in one corner of the room served as a kitchen. A closed door on the opposite wall must have led to a bedroom. Without a single lamp in the room any illumination required would have to come from the glass dome light in the ceiling. Waiting at the table were two other men, one of whom he had never met. Although the fellow was seated, he could tell he was short and stocky. He sported a shabby plaid Tam O'Shanter, cocked to one side. The choice of cap and his kinky red beard advertised a Scottish heritage.

Lyle had never before seen the man who opened the door, nor did he make an effort to introduce himself. Linus had arranged the meeting place, and whether he had involved this man in their business was a question he intended to ask immediately. The man definitely had a sour temperament, but the most important thing Lyle had to learn was whether or not he could be trusted. He made an effort to be subtle while glancing sideways to visually scrutinize him. He was bulky, head to toe, and stood with his arms crossed, legs slightly apart, staring across the room at nothing. The coarse black hair on his face was less a beard than it was a sign of his laziness with regard to shaving. He wore a brown vest, baggy jeans, and ratty slippers. Considering his footwear, Lyle figured the flat must be his. He would have a private word with his associate as soon as they were finished—find out what he was up to with this Neanderthal.

In the other chair was his associate, Linus Finch, the unkempt man with the smelly jacket who had been a part of both efforts to kidnap Ben. He sat drumming his fingers on the table and looking from face to face. Finally he said, "Any beer around here? A pint would go down easy about now."

Lyle was quick to respond. "This isn't a pub. We're here to get things organized, and I mean organized down to the last minute—no contingency unprepared for." One empty chair remained, but he didn't sit and instead began to pace around the table as he spoke. "The paperwork has been submitted. We have the woman right where we want her. She had no choice but to be quiet and acquiesce." He stopped pacing and finally sat down at the table. "Time is not on our side. Let's hear what you have lined up for the transfer."

Linus Finch turned to his companion and asked, "Well, Fergus, did you find some lads you can trust?"

* * *

It had been less than a week since Fergus MacDonald made Linus Finch's acquaintance. He had done nothing more than start an ordinary pub conversation with Linus while they stood at the bar enjoying a pint. One thing led to another, and with the help of alcohol he had revealed his history of skating just over the line where the law was concerned. He had been 'inside' a couple of times—nothing violent, just one break-in and a con that involved a high stakes card game. Although he treated it as a joke, he confided that he was lucky to be alive after the latter. Linus had suggested they order another pint, but Fergus declined, saying he had to meet a friend. He dug into his pants pocket several times for enough change to pay for his drink, but when tossing it on the counter he came up short.

Linus pulled a fiver out of his pocket and handed it to the barman. "No worries, mate, this one's on me."

Fergus' objections fell on deaf ears, and he decided just to say thank you and let it go. Further conversation told Linus that this likeable man was in sore need of a break. In a hushed voice Linus bragged in general terms about his current involvement in a very 'profitable job.' He then asked Fergus if he would be interested in taking part—but only peripherally. There was no way Linus would give up any part of his share in the expected value. After all, he'd just paid a whopping £4 for the bloke's pint.

Fergus tipped his cap to Linus in appreciation and said, "You're a Godsend, mate. I'm in." He paused before adding, "But I don't do violence. Never have. But I can be a quite acceptable 'dogsbody.'" They shook hands quickly before Linus scribbled his mobile number on a napkin, giving it to Fergus, who did the same.

* * *

Since that night, both men had been engaged separately in preparations and had only spoken by phone, this meeting being the first time they had seen each other since their encounter in the pub. Having been called upon to give his report, Fergus pulled a folded sheet of paper from his coat pocket. He carefully smoothed it out on the table without saying anything.

Lyle said, "Sometime this year, if you don't mind." Fergus looked him in the eye and held his tongue while the dressing-down continued. "Did you or did you not find some strong lads who don't ask questions?"

"Aye—yes. No worries on that front. There be plenty of young chaps out of work and resorting to a bit of shady this or that."

"Remember, they are to know nothing except where to report and what to do. If any one of them asks questions, get rid of him."

"What do you mean—get rid of him? If you mean what I think you mean, I'd want no part of that."

"Don't be a fool. I meant pay him something and run him off." He paused then added, "A threat of some kind might be a good idea. We don't want some young lad going goodie-goodie at our expense."

"Ah… umm… that reminds me. I'm going to need some sort of advance for expenses. I'm a bit strapped at the moment. Those lads want something up front if they're to be on standby."

"All right, all right," Lyle said, obviously annoyed. "But you should have thought to ask Lenny. He handles the purse for such things. Or did I forget to give you his number? He couldn't make it today. Other business."

They all settled back in their seats and said nothing. The buzzing of a fly drew their eyes to the ceiling, where it flew quickly into the light fixture and fell instantly, joining the accumulation of dead insects already there.

Linus was the first to speak. "Well, if that's it then. I'm off to the pub for that pint. Care to join me Fergus?"

Before Fergus could answer, Lyle got up quickly and said, "You had better not let your love of a pint interfere with what I require of you. I want to see the trucks tomorrow—early. Keep your phone on you while you're gone. You'd better hope they look professional… and official."

"I told you, my mate is just out of the nick. Did four years for his trouble. One of the best at performing *cosmetic surgery* on the occasional high-end 'motor.' Fearing the boss wasn't convinced he embellished further. "He could paint the royal seal on a plumber's lorry, and the queen would climb right in."

"Don't be ridiculous. I'll see them tomorrow and then be the judge."

* * *

Lenny Jordan reached into his pocket and fumbled with the Euros he had exchanged at the airport. He paid the driver then got out and grabbed his large bag from the back seat. The cab left him standing on the narrow sidewalk checking his phone for messages and scanning house numbers. Just to his left, set back from the noisy street, a small derelict house sat in the middle of an oversized lot. It was surrounded by dead grass and lay some distance from the adjacent houses. Patches of dingy white stucco had peeled away, exposing the underlying brick and mortar. A roof of chipped and missing tiles completed the sad picture. At the front were a few scraggly shrubs with plastic grocery bags tangled in the brown foliage. The cracked cement walkway to the front door nurtured a proliferation of weeds, and a lone beer can had been dropped in the dirt beside the tiny porch.

He picked up the bulky duffle and approached the entrance. Once on the porch he tried to open the paint-chipped door with the key he had been given. It wouldn't give, so he applied the heft of a shoulder. It broke loose, flew open and banged the wall. Only having arrived in Pamplona early that morning, he had been in a time crunch and was forced to rent the tiny house sight unseen, based on the description given by the agent he had found, courtesy of the rental car clerk. He now intended to look it over and get things ready for its use. The main room was dank and somber, with trash having been swept into one corner.

The combined odors of mustiness and spoiled food hung in the air. The room was devoid of any furniture other than a few folding chairs, a futon frame with dingy-looking pad, a table and small refrigerator—its white color obscured by dark smudges and dried food. Cockroaches scurried across the dirty counter that held only a hotplate and open microwave. Mildew rimmed the edges of the chipped porcelain sink, and rust had accumulated where the faucet was slowly dripping brown-tinged water.

As he looked into the few cupboards on the wall, he wondered how long he might have to stay in the awful place and made up his mind he wouldn't be the one to clean it up. He wandered through an archway into what looked to be the bedroom and found nothing but two old mattresses on the floor and a cot folded up in one corner. The only window was covered from the outside with wrought iron grill work, as were the windows at the front of the house. He noted that as a lucky coincidence. A thin and tattered curtain partially covered the window. Trash had been swept to one corner in this room as well.

Lenny peered into the small bathroom, which was as dirty as the rest of the place, except that he could see rat droppings on the tile floor and in the small sink. The toilet was badly stained, and he pushed down the handle, glad to find it in working order. The window had been nailed shut, and in one corner there was a drain in the floor. A lime-encrusted showerhead dripped rust colored water into a puddle surrounded by a trail of ants. But regardless of how cheaply he had rented the place, the presence of rats was the last straw. Lenny decided that regardless of the house's purpose, it had to be cleaned before his guests arrived and he was forced to stay there. Any concern was for his comfort alone, and time was short.

Anxious to get out of there, he quickly stuffed the duffle into the back of the only closet. He locked the front door and strode a couple of blocks to the nearest bar, all the while wondering who could have lived in those conditions. The establishment's interior was cool and rather dark, its general appearance worn and faded. A thin haze of cigarette smoke obscured the patrons and gave the whole scene a shadowy feel. He ordered a beer and settled himself at a corner table near the restroom. From that spot he could observe everything and everyone.

Before long, a middle-aged woman came out of the restroom carrying a bucket and mop. Her long black hair was tied back with a scarf and she had the weary expression of one for whom life has been a disappointment. The shabby dress and shoes seemed to confirm that luck had passed her by. She put down the bucket and mop then wiped her hands on the brightly printed apron she was wearing. She noticed Lenny staring at her and proceeded to utter several expletives of disapproval. Since he didn't speak Spanish, the effect was minimal. Undeterred, he slid out of his chair and approached her. It soon became obvious that she didn't speak English, although her wide-eyed stare at his tattooed head could have accounted for her lack of response. A patron sitting at the bar saw that the conversation was at an impasse and offered to translate.

Lenny made a monetary offer to the woman, via the translator—one so generous that she was unlikely to refuse. Her first reaction was shock and disgust. Before the patron could clarify what he wanted, the woman had misinterpreted his offer as a proposal for sexual favors. The patron, who was evidently not accomplished at Spanish, tried again and began to do better. Continuing the translation process, he was honest with her about the severe condition of the house, but she assured him she was used to dirty work, hard work. She accepted the job, was given the address, and then she held up four fingers—her way of saying she could be there by four o'clock that afternoon. Lenny handed her the key, and through the patron-interpreter told her to do just as she was told. Then he asked her name.

She nodded her head toward Lenny and said, *"Annunciata—Annunciata Domingo. Encantada de conocerte."*

He told Lenny that she was pleased to meet him, but Lenny failed to return a similar polite response, simply grunting before returning to his beer. As she picked up her cleaning tools he called after her and told her to buy rattraps. The interpreter at the bar turned his head and repeated the request in Spanish. She nodded her head and walked through to the back of the bar and out of sight. He wondered if he had offered her too much money for the job, then realized that considering the state of the place, it was probably not enough. Lenny gulped down the rest of his beer and got up to leave. He emerged from the dark smoky room into blinding sunlight and had a sudden thought that she might just keep his money and not show up to clean the house. He laughed to himself, realizing that was more like something he would do. There were no taxis in sight and he was annoyed that he had not decided to drive himself in the rental car. He walked two blocks to a busier street and was soon able to hail a cab.

Back in his hotel room he flopped on the bed and began to organize his thoughts for the next step to be carried out. Without the success of tomorrow's assignment everything would fall apart. After an hour or so he got up and rummaged through his suitcase, pulling out a few items of clothing that he then stuffed into a small duffle. He tossed in a few toiletries, zipped it up and placed it by the door. He was ready. All he had to do after tomorrow's job was to wait for Linus to fetch Gareth from the airport.

* * *

Annunciata stopped wringing the mop for a moment and slowly straightened her body. She reached behind to dig knuckles into her tight and fatigued back muscles. After the short pause she continued through the list of cleaning duties for her job at the bar. She wondered how things could get so disgusting within the few days that elapsed between her cleaning shifts. Her actions were automatic. She had many years of cleaning behind her and it had put food on the table for her four children. There were many days when she would shake her head, wondering how and why life as a widow had cast her into this menial role. Memories of childhood dreams had become too heavy as the years passed. She took comfort in her robust health and told herself that few women could work at such a pace. However, she could not escape the reality of her age. There would be a day when she would wake up and find that the toll on her body had been too great.

The extra job came to her so unexpectedly that she had worked as fast as possible in order keep her promise to be there by four o'clock. The last chore finished, she found a canvas bag in the bar's storage closet, and after checking to be sure no one was watching she began to fill it with rags, bleach and a scrub brush. Her shift was not quite over, and she didn't want to be seen leaving early. She gathered her personal belongings and with a bag in each hand left quietly through the back door of the bar. She looked up and down the alley for the bar owner's car, but it wasn't there. Although she had already worked three jobs that day and had started at dawn, she was thankful for the opportunity to make a little more money from the rude man in the bar. She hoped it was a legitimate offer and also hoped he would not be there while she was cleaning. Everything about him made her uneasy.

Annunciata stopped at the corner bodega to purchase rattraps and a candy bar. She showed the clerk a paper with the address written on it and was told the house was near the end of the next block. She was relieved not to have to board a bus and possibly change several times. The canvas bags were hard to hold onto and she had to stop twice to rest her arms and renew her grip. When she saw the house all she could do was to shake her head. If the inside was as bad as the outside, she would have a lot of hard work ahead of her. She dropped her belongings on the small porch and fumbled in her purse for the key.

She opened the door with some difficulty, picked up the bags and stepped inside, immediately noticing the unpleasant odors. One at a time she heaved the bags onto the only table then began to walk around the house, making mental note of what to do and how to start. An old broom and mop had been left in the shower stall and would have to do. She had expected having to clean the floors on her hands and knees. First, she swept the trash from all the rooms into one corner near the entrance. She had noticed a cracked plastic waste bin at the side of the house and went out to drag it inside. With the floor cleared she looked around and let out a long sigh. She then began to clean, one room at a time, the odor of bleach becoming almost overwhelming.

By seven o'clock the house was passably clean, and the terrible odors were gone. As Annunciata prepared to leave, the thought crossed her mind that when she cleaned the floors she had neglected to clean inside the closet. Pride in her work would not allow her to leave without completing the task. She retrieved the broom and mop she had returned to the shower stall and approached the closet. Inside she saw a large duffle bag that she would have to remove in order to clean the floor. She tried to lift it, but it was too heavy for her so she merely pulled and pulled until it was clear of the area to be cleaned. She swept the debris from the floor and with the still wet mop she wiped it down, all the while finding her eyes going back to the duffle. It seemed that hard objects were protruding against the canvas. The woman's curiosity grew until she found herself slowly sliding the zipper open. She peered inside then began to rummage around in the contents. The first thing she pulled out was a pair of handcuffs, followed by two rolls of silver tape, another pair of handcuffs and long pieces of chain.

Her heart began to race with the thought of being discovered looking through the man's things. She quickly replaced everything, zipped the duffle and shoved it back in the closet. Using the doorknob to steady her, she pulled herself upright, closed the door and gathered her belongings. A quick departure was all that mattered now. Annunciata put her bags down on the porch, locked the door, and then placed the key on the ground right next to the cement step as instructed. Once she had covered it with a small rock, she made a hasty retreat toward the nearest bus stop.

CHAPTER TWELVE

Valerie awakened just seconds before her alarm sounded. A rush of excitement ran through her as she bolted from bed and headed to the bathroom. The morning's concern was not about primping. She washed her face and brushed her teeth, applied moisturizer and mascara, then decided the minimum would have to do. Just to be safe she dialed Olivia's cell phone, which she knew would be on her night table, the same place she always kept hers. Olivia answered on the fourth ring, sounding half asleep.

"Rise and shine, girlie. It's coming on eight o'clock! We have places to go and things to see!"

"I had my alarm set. It would have gone off in ten minutes. I needed those ten minutes. I had a later night than I'd planned."

"I'm assuming it wasn't an all-nighter, because you sound like you're alone. You can doze on the plane. Go throw some cold water on your face and get yourself organized. The taxi will be here in fifteen minutes and we'll get you within half an hour or so, depending on traffic."

"My late night wasn't for fun. I was finishing up some things from work on my computer so Mr. Saunders won't get into a snit while I'm gone."

Assured that Olivia had not had a bawdy night, Valerie told her to be ready and watching through the window for the taxi to arrive. Olivia intended to travel light, never an easy thing to do, and was sure she could easily manage her suitcase and bag. She did as she was told with regard to her ablutions and then reached for the clothes she had left out the night before. She slid into a pair of leggings, a long sleeve tee, and the requisite black leather jacket. Hopping around the bedroom, she pulled on a pair of socks and ankle boots, threw her toiletries into the suitcase and zipped it closed.

She had just placed everything by the door when a taxi horn blared through her open window. She had almost forgotten to close and lock the window, so with that done, she quickly collected everything, locked her apartment and called the lift. Once she appeared on the street the driver got out to help with her belongings. Soon the women were being whisked toward Heathrow, each imagining the possibilities of such an impulsive adventure.

The flight left about thirty minutes late, most of which was spent idling on the tarmac. The pilot, however, had announced that favorable winds would bring them into Madrid only a few minutes later than estimated. Valerie and Olivia were some of the last to board, and therefore, among the first to disembark, easily reaching the gate to the connecting flight in time for its punctual departure. The view from the plane was clouded by smog until it had progressed well beyond Madrid. The smaller commuter plane flew at a lower altitude, enabling passengers to see the green and gold expanse of the land below. Further on, as the plane reduced altitude on the approach to San Sebastian's airport, the Bay of Biscay glistened in the diffused light of the midday sun.

The runway was on a long spit of land along a river at nearby *Hondarribia*, located on the Spanish-French border—although it was known as the San Sebastian airport. After a smooth landing the women proceeded through customs and collected their bags. There were directions in both English and Spanish to car rental and buses. They debated about how they would get to Pamplona, considered renting a car, and decided against it due to their tight budget. The buses were outside, parked along the curb, and some of them looked quite worse for wear. The conclusion was that a bus was all they could afford, and so they exited the airport and walked the length of sidewalk in front of the building. Taxi drivers motioned to them, but they did their best to ignore the waves, whistles, and the open passenger doors with eager drivers ready to usher them inside. Several of the buses were marked for Pamplona, and Valerie said that without further thought they should just pick one and get on.

At that moment, a dilapidated van maneuvered into a small space between two of the buses the women were considering. The driver honked several times quickly, jumped out of the van, leaving it double-parked. He then presented himself to Valerie and Olivia. He was clean-shaven, and in spite of the rakish straw hat he wore, they could see that his head was shaved. He wore loose-fitting pants that seemed to be covering some kind of heavy boots. Both women stepped back in response to this assault on their attention.

Lenny smiled at them and spoke. "Good afternoon, ladies. I'm from your hotel—the guesthouse—*Gestión Alojamientos,*" he said, the heavy Manchester accent causing him difficulty. "They sent me to bring you."

He had expected to have a rather a long wait watching for the women to exit the airport. Since they had arrived earlier than expected, he would have to 'wing it.' Valerie thought it was rather strange that an Englishman with a definite Manchester droll would be working for a Spanish hotel, especially considering his terrible accent. But she knew the English had been the largest group of expats in the world, probably because of the size of England's kingdom before it began to shrink.

Olivia, always the one to question, asked the man why her friend hadn't been notified that they would be met at the airport. His answer came easily. The van had been in disrepair and had only come back from the mechanic that very morning. It was expected that transportation would not be available, so it couldn't be promised. Both women were satisfied by his explanation, and feeling the fatigue that always accompanies travel, they decided the van would be more comfortable than a bus—but not by much, from the look of it.

As he started to gather the bags and put them in the van, the man called out to say they should call him Joe. Lenny liked the idea of deceiving them—using an alias. His story was that he only worked for the hotel a few hours a week, to collect passengers from the airport, and the rest of the time he was a bartender. He was burly and handled everything as if it were merely a few empty boxes. He ushered them into the back seat and went around to the driver door, hurled himself up into the seat and started the engine.

"There's no air conditioning—it's a luxury in these parts—not too hot today though."

The women looked for seat belts, but there were none. Olivia warned Valerie to be careful not to drop anything in the hole that gaped between them on the seat. Olivia turned to her and whispered, "If this van is any indication of our accommodations, we're in trouble."

"Maybe this is a case of 'can't tell a book by its cover' — if we're lucky. I think we'll have to make the best of it because the town is no doubt booked up for the running of the bulls."

"Just so it's clean—no bugs or creepy crawlies. That's all I care about."

Olivia stopped talking and looked out the window at the green hills and ocean. Within a short while they had turned south and the landscape slowly became more arid. Their driver was quiet. The van bounced along, jarring the women with every bump in the poorly maintained road. They settled back and relaxed as best they could, each daydreaming a bit about what they believed would be a fantastic week of celebration and people watching.

The heat of the day had accumulated in the metal of the old van, and the temperature inside was extremely disagreeable. Clothing stuck to their backs and perspiration glistened on their faces. Finally the scene began to change. Buildings were closer together, with homes and businesses lining the paved streets. Lenny slowed the vehicle as they entered a more congested area of the city. Pamplona was decorated for the running of the bulls. Strips of red flags were strung high across streets here and there, a symbol of the traditional red kerchiefs worn by those who participate in the running of the bulls. Men, mostly young, were strolling in the timeless costume of white pants and shirt with a red kerchief tied either around their waist or neck. Valerie and Olivia settled back and enjoyed the sights, assuming that they were being taken to their accommodation. They soon noticed that their driver had left the town center behind and was driving through what appeared to be a residential neighborhood. It seemed feasible that a guesthouse could be located in such a place, so they just continued to observe. Before long Lenny stopped the van in front of an old house. He proceeded to drive over the curb and across the expanse of dead grass, stopping just feet from the front door.

He turned off the ignition and said, "Here we are. It's time to get out, ladies."

Olivia turned to look at Valerie, her expression one of disbelief. Valerie returned the expression and spoke. "Surely this must be the wrong place. I know the place we booked only had two stars, but this is ridiculous."

"Ladies, I guarantee this is where you'll be staying."

Valerie began to assert herself. "This is no guesthouse. Do you see a sign anywhere?" She quickly pulled her mobile phone out of her bag and then dug for the reservation information so she could dial the hotel's number. She handed the paper to Olivia and told her to read out the number.

"Never mind, you two. You'll be coming with me. You've been provided with alternate accommodations. Now hand me your phones." They looked up at him and saw that he had turned around and was pointing a gun directly at them.

Olivia covered her mouth to stifle a scream, and Valerie simply said, "Oh my God!"

He began to wave the gun in a way that indicated they should get out of the van. Valerie squeezed Olivia's hand and nodded to her in a way that urged her to comply. "Just do as he says for now. We have no other choice."

"But I don't understand. What could he want with us?" Olivia asked.

Lenny's voice turned harsh. "Enough talk. Get out and walk to the door. And keep quiet. If you scream or try to run, I won't think twice about shooting you. And when I shoot someone they don't get up—ever."

The women got out of the van and walked slowly, trembling hand in trembling hand, to the door. He held the gun on them while he unlocked the door and then pushed them inside, closing and locking it behind them. "This is your vacation destination. Whether you ever return from this vacation depends on the actions of someone else. We'll see how important you are to them."

The women were in shock. They were so frightened they didn't notice the condition of their surroundings. Lenny immediately noticed the work that had been done by Annunciata. He detected the odors of bleach and chemicals, probably something used to kill the cockroaches. The counters were still cracked and stained, but they had been cleared of droppings and insects and had been wiped down. The mildew around the sink had been bleached away and the refrigerator was no longer smudged. He hoped she had tended to the inside. It had been plugged in, and he could hear the hum of the motor. Dried food had been scrubbed from the table and the trash had been cleared from the newly swept floor.

The women stood with their arms around each other, not making a sound, but finally Olivia said, "What is this place? It's disgusting. Why did you bring us here?"

Lenny walked over and slapped her hard enough to send her reeling back against the wall. She began to slide down, holding a hand against her cheek. Valerie ran to her, helping to hold her upright as she checked the degree of injury to her face. Her cheek was bright red and she had bitten her lip, which was bleeding slightly. He told the women there was more of the same for each of them if they didn't cooperate. Valerie fought back her tears and asked for the bathroom. He made some sort of guttural sound and pushed one, then the other, into the tiny bedroom. Taking Valerie by the arm, he walked her into the bathroom. There were no longer any rat droppings in the sink or ants around the drain. The smell of bleach permeated the tiny space, and behind the toilet a box of rat bait was open and ready. He came out, closed the door and held the gun on Olivia while Valerie was inside. When she came out, Olivia was urged to avail herself of the opportunity as well. There was no way they could simultaneously attack him as long as he held a gun on them. They seemed to share that fact in the looks they exchanged.

He ordered each of them to sit on one of the two mattresses. One was on the floor beside a radiator and the other was beside a folding bed made of heavy metal. He proceeded to handcuff the wrist of each woman—one to the radiator, one to the metal bed. He closed the only window in the stuffy room, and pulled the tattered curtain closed. They were advised that screaming would do no good, that the nearest building was at a distance, and that with the window closed no one could hear them anyway. He went back into the main room and pulled something out of a leather backpack that lay on the table. From the doorway he tossed a bottle of water onto each of the mattresses and told them that he was going out, but only for a short time, and that they'd do best to avoid shedding tears that would dehydrate them. He turned and left, the door slamming hard before they heard the key turn in the lock.

Neither could believe the reality of what had just happened. In spite of Lenny's advice, they began to sob, their chests heaving to the point of breathlessness, but their eyes dry. Olivia was the first to speak, her voice trembling. "You must realize that no one will ever find us. I don't know anybody who would involve me in something like this, do you?"

"Of course not. And no one knew where we were going other than your boss, right?"

"Well, your travel agent knew. And I told Clive Warren, the man I just started seeing. He asked me when we could see each other gain, so I told him I'd be gone for a while. He asked when I was leaving and offered to take us to the airport. I told him about our plans, but I only met him last week. He's a tech systems guy for God's sake—not a criminal."

"I know your father's been involved in a lot of investigations over the years—all sorts of dodgy goings-on. I'm sure he's made enemies, but he's been retired for quite a while now. Some crook's revenge seems quite a stretch. Listen, Olivia, the only thing that matters right now is that we stay alive— do as we're told. We may be able to glean some information by listening to his phone calls."

"That sounds like a long shot. I wonder if anyone else is coming to help watch us. If so, maybe we'll hear something. A lot of good it will do us to know why. We're still prisoners." Olivia drew her knees up under her chin and buried her face in the crook of her free arm.

Valerie shook her head, realizing she had lost all control over her life. The worries of her London life now seemed the size of an atom. Of one thing she was sure: If it was something in her life that had precipitated their predicament, she couldn't bear having put Olivia in danger. She bunched up her unrestrained fist and began to pound on the mattress in frustration. Clouds of dust rose from the dingy fabric and spread throughout the room, its motes sparkling in the muted sunlight coming through the curtain.

After what seemed like hours, the front door opened and they heard Lenny's heavy footsteps, then the sound of something being dropped on the table, followed by the rustling of plastic bags. The women stayed perfectly quiet and waited for him to check on them. The sound of heavy boots came closer and he appeared in the doorway with a bag in each hand. He reached inside and pulled out a roll of toilet tissue, tossing it onto Olivia's mattress, and then repeated the action for Valerie. From the other bag he pulled out two thin blankets and threw them over as well. In meek voices, they thanked him. He grunted, turned and walked back to the table in the main room. They heard a scraping sound before he appeared again. In each hand he held a lidded bucket. He walked toward the women and placed one beside each mattress. Appalled, they looked at each other, immediately aware of the buckets' purpose: There would be no regular trips to the bathroom.

In spite of their fear, Valerie and Olivia were hungry—physically, if not emotionally. Common sense told them not to ask for food—not yet. The women exchanged only a few words while they sat or reclined on the mattresses—waiting for something, not knowing what. Olivia leaned on her elbow, saying she was reluctant to let her face touch the dirty fabric. Valerie agreed and sat cross-legged, eyes closed, her back against the wall for support. Their watches had not been confiscated along with the phones, so they were aware of the time. Time had seemed to stop, but the day was drawing to a close, and the dusk's fading light no longer brightened or warmed the room as the sunlight had done.

They heard their captor rustling about in the other room, cupboards opening and closing, his heavy boots scuffing along the floor. Suddenly he was standing in the doorway staring at them with the usual gruff expression. "If you two want anything to eat, you have to do as you're told." Lenny walked over to Olivia and pulled a phone out of his pants pocket. She recognized it as her own. "Sit up and look at the phone," he said, holding it in position to take her picture. The phone clicked several times before he put it back in his pocket. He left the room for a moment and came back with a pad of paper and pen. "Now you're going to write a note to your parents and that brother of yours—let them know you're alive … for now."

"I don't know what you want me to write," Olivia said in a soft and shaky voice.

Lenny handed her the pad and pen and told her to write down what he was about to say. "Dear Daddy," he said, stopping momentarily to chuckle. "I'm being held here because Mum has to do something for these people. Please tell her to do it. If she doesn't, they will kill me." He stopped dictating, told Olivia to stop writing, and then looked at Valerie. "Who's this anyway?" He looked back at Olivia. "We only wanted you. Now I'm saddled with this bird."

Olivia complied, answering his question. "She's my friend. She used to be married to my brother."

As the words left her mouth she knew it was the wrong thing to say. Now he would see Valerie as another means of controlling her family. Valerie sighed, realizing that Olivia had now made her more valuable, although she didn't really believe that they were likely to survive anyway. They had both seen their captor's face. That was likely to seal the deal. She had seen enough television shows to know that's how it goes.

Lenny returned to the task at hand and told Olivia to continue writing. The rest of the note confirmed the danger she was in and emphasized that her mother and father were to tell no one, and that her mother must follow instructions to the letter. When she had finished writing he ripped the tablet from her hands and then left the room. Several minutes later he announced he would be gone for a while, then added a warning to be quiet if they wanted to keep breathing. Exhaustion won out over Olivia's reluctance to lie on the mattress. She fell into a restless sleep. Valerie watched her, fighting to stay awake, but finally succumbed to her own fatigue. When they awoke the room was completely dark, the house quiet. They assumed they were still alone. Their hunger pangs were now more severe and they wondered if starvation would be his method of getting rid of them.

The room had become chilly, and Valerie did her best to wrap the blanket around her shoulders. She couldn't seem to accommodate for the arm that was stretched out and handcuffed to the radiator. Olivia had used her blanket as a pillow and continued to lie there staring at a dark ceiling, the handcuffed wrist over her head. Soon Lenny came through the front door, his heavy steps once again accompanied by the rustle of plastic bags. They heard the bags hit the table and waited quietly.

He appeared in the doorway and flipped a wall switch that turned on a glaring ceiling light. "I brought you some food. If you don't like it, eat it anyway. I may not feel so generous tomorrow."

Valerie summoned the courage to speak up and said, "I know you've given us buckets, but could we please use the bathroom. We've done everything you've asked, and now that you're back there's no privacy in here without a door."

Lenny stood still and stared at her. She wondered if the next step was to slap her as he had done Olivia. She maintained his gaze and waited for an answer. Only a few seconds passed, but to her it seemed longer. "You should have used the buckets while I was gone. Remember that next time."

Grumbling under his breath he walked over to her and proceeded to unlock the handcuffs. She quietly said thank you and tried to get up. Her body was very stiff and she let out a groan as she stood. Lenny laughed, obviously enjoying her discomfort, then motioned her toward the bathroom. She took a few steps then asked if Olivia could go as well, when she was back in her handcuffs. He grunted, which she interpreted as a 'yes.' Olivia smiled at her. Once they were both back in restraints, Lenny brought them each a Styrofoam box containing a Spanish tortilla, some tomatoes and a small pile of anchovies. He noticed the two empty bottles of water and fetched two more, tossing them onto the mattresses.

Valerie saw that Olivia was picking at the food. "You have to eat. We have to stay as strong as possible. No matter what he gives us, eat it. And drink your water. We can't survive if we kill ourselves with starvation and dehydration. We don't want to make it easy for him."

Olivia nodded and began to pick at the egg and potato tortilla. Once she started, she began to eat faster, her basic hunger pushing ahead of the fear. Both women finished every morsel and were thankful for it. At least they knew there would be sustenance of some kind. They had water, a blanket and perhaps, just a little hope.

CHAPTER THIRTEEN

Ben and Ana were both awake at dawn, alone in separate rooms. Without the other knowing, each had planned an early walk around the grounds. Ana was sure it would be too early for ne'er-do-wells to be up and about, and that she wouldn't incur Ben's wrath for having sneaked out on her own. Ben came downstairs moments later and found her sitting at the kitchen table, tying her shoes and humming. She looked up, saw him enter the room, and broke into a self-conscious smile, all the while wondering how to explain her actions.

"And just what are you up to this early in the morning?" Ben asked.

"I think the grounds are quite safe at dawn," she answered. "I'm going out for a little walk, and I thought Sir Freddie might come along."

"Oh you did?" He paused and gave her a 'you won't get away with it' look, then continued. "Well, of course he'll take any opportunity to join someone on a walk, but I still don't think it's a good idea."

"Why are you down so early? And with boots on?"

"A walk."

Still fussing with her laces, Ana looked up at him through her dark lashes. Her response was short. "It's not a good idea for you either. Together then?"

"If that's your pleasure," he said, opening the pantry door.

Freddie bounded out, dancing circles around him and panting with excitement, as if he'd heard the plan and heartily approved. All three went out the back door and into the hazy glow of first light. A low fog during the night had left everything as wet as if it had rained. The heavy moisture had dispersed and turned into wispy clouds tinted pale orange by the sunrise. Before they had taken ten steps across the grass Ana's shoes were wet. Ben took her by the hand, leading her back to the kitchen door and into the pantry. Two pairs of Wellies stood along the wall, and he picked up the smaller ones, handing them to her. The fit was adequate and they were on their way in a flash.

Ana followed Ben to the back of the garden and then through a wooden gate set into the vine covered wall. The surrounding property consisted of lawns and venerable trees with wide-spreading branches. Beyond the lawns and across the two-lane road was a field of Rapeseed, its brilliant yellow flowers made even brighter by rays of sun reflecting off the remaining moisture. They walked the lawns, Ana stopping at times to look up through the branches of the English oak and Chestnut trees. Sir Freddie had caught a scent a short distance away and busied himself with an investigation. Ana stopped to look at the trunk of a particularly large Chestnut and then turned around to lean against it.

Ben stopped and faced her; his arms folded across his chest. "You look relaxed, even contented, leaning against that tree." Ben cocked his head and looked squarely into her eyes. "It's hard to believe you're a city girl."

"I think I've made it clear that I like to try new things." Ana smiled sweetly, but Ben found the glint in her eyes very alluring. While he was wondering about the meaning of her comment, she continued. "It seems we've both had *new things* foisted upon us."

Ben took a place beside her, leaning against the massive trunk. They remained there for a few moments without speaking, until Ana said, "I wonder what this tree has seen in its very long life. I can imagine lovers having clandestine meetings under the spreading branches of this very tree. Perhaps a medieval princess was being forced to marry without love, and she would sneak away from the castle to meet her true love for a moonlight assignation under this tree."

"You have quite an imagination."

"I remember something else about Chestnut trees. Of course you've read Orwell's book, '1984?'" Ben nodded yes, and she continued. "Remember the poem? 'Under the spreading Chestnut tree, I sold you and you sold me.'" He nodded again and she went on. "Above the Chestnut Tree Café, a man was suffering from lost love."

"But Orwell's story found romantic love to be a betrayal of love for Big Brother, the only permissible love. That's the point. Lovers saw betrayal as their only choice."

"I know," said Ana. "The connotation is very negative... and a sobering reminder that love is always a risk."

"True. But in spite of your analogy, it seems safe to say that you *are* a romantic."

"I guess I am." She looked down at her feet and added, her tone suddenly somber, "Too many fairy tales as a child—guess I believed the lies."

"I'd never peg you as a cynic." He turned to look at her, but she casually looked away. He could see the subject was uncomfortable, so he said, "I won't ask how you got that way—at least not right now." Ben took her by the hand, pulling her away from the tree and toward the road.

Freddie had abandoned them for his own sort of fun and was headed back toward the house. They crossed the road and Ben stopped at the edge of the field. Ana was amazed that the Rapeseed seemed almost tall enough to hide them. She wanted to be lost in its beauty and asked Ben if they could make their way toward the middle of the field. Her request surprised him, but he hadn't yet learned how to refuse her, so he went ahead, just far enough to push the plants aside for her to pass.

The ground was still damp from dawn's heavy fog, but they trudged on until Ben concluded they were close to the middle. Ana was just tall enough to see 360 degrees of brilliant yellow surrounding her. She laughed with the delight of a child, and Ben tried to remember that kind of innocent joy. All at once she became quiet. There was no sound other than the soft rustling of flower stalks as a breeze began to swell.

She hugged herself and looked at the sky. Ben was confused. He put his hand on her shoulder then turned her to face him. Ana's expression was troubled, her brow wrinkled.

"Ana, what happened? You were so happy a minute ago."

"Too happy—it's a dangerous state."

"Come on, don't get philosophical on me," he said, trying to make her smile.

"That's not what I'm doing. It's just that this is all too lovely, too perfect. I have a feeling of foreboding."

"In what way?"

He waited for Ana to speak, but she hesitated, self-consciously rubbing her forehead. She was standing before him in sweatpants and wearing his mother's muddy boots. Her hair was a tumble of rebellious curls, her nose pink from the morning chill. She was wearing the quilted vest his mother had loaned her, and the hodge-podge of her outfit could easily have made Ben laugh. But he didn't laugh. To him she was beguiling, enigmatic, and although he didn't understand her premonition, he had no doubt she felt it was genuine. How could he make it right, whatever was vexing her?

The breeze continued to swell, and the field rippled like a golden magic carpet. Ana's expression changed. Ben locked his gaze with hers and saw the same need he was feeling. The current of desire between them had grown stronger each day since they met. No longer concerned about the right moment, he reached for Ana and pulled her close. He tipped her chin up to meet his lips. The first kiss was soft and lingering. They backed away from each other, just slightly, each struck by reticence.

Ben leaned forward, took her hands in his, then kissed her forehead and said, "We're completely alone in the middle of this field, and it's going to take all the willpower I have not to take you right here— muddy ground be damned."

Ana was aroused by his remark, and as their eyes met again there was a rush to embrace. Ben devoured her lips— probing, deep, and with the complete freedom granted him by her eager mouth. Their stifled desire was set free—all in one passionate, seemingly unending kiss. Fears born of any previous emotional pain and disappointment continued to dissolve within each kiss that followed.

He held her tightly, his voice low and seductive. "I want you. It would take every word for 'desire' in this writer's arsenal to tell you how much. There's been too much waiting—for me at least." He paused, fearing he might be pressuring her, then said, "But I know this may not be the right moment or the right place for you."

Ana felt the same about him, yet tried to diffuse the intensity of the moment in order to gain control over her own longing. "If you want to fetch your thesaurus, I'd be willing to wait."

Ben loved the way she sparred with him. It had heightened his attraction to her when they first met, and now the effect had become profound. The challenging look in his eyes led Ana to reveal her own need. She spoke softly, her mouth against Ben's neck. "I'd hoped, but I didn't know—even last night when your lips lightly brushed mine on the way to kissing my cheek— I wasn't sure if it was a little accident and the kiss was just a friendly gesture."

She gently put her hands on the sides of his face then kissed him again, aggressively. He broke away from her lips, took hold of her arms, closed his eyes and spoke through clenched teeth. "Why do there have to be complications messing up the natural order of things?"

"There *are* complications… and, so it seems, a mystery to solve. But should we completely put our lives on hold?" Her mind raced with thoughts, each valid reason to wait countered immediately by her lust for Ben. Finally the words tumbled from her mouth, and she said, "You aren't the only one who's anxious."

"Your last kiss confirmed that." Ben slipped his hands inside her vest, sliding them over her ribcage and around to her back.

He found the edge of her shirt and slid his hands underneath, beginning to stroke the smooth skin on her back. Her head fell back as she sighed with pleasure. He leaned forward and kissed her neck like a man yearning for much more than kisses. They dropped to their knees, hidden in the golden Rapeseed, removed from the world around them and oblivious to the damp ground. In an instant they were once again in a tight embrace, exchanging deep kisses accompanied by the soft throaty sounds of arousal.

Ana leaned away from him and said, "Ben, if we go any further, there'll be no stopping—regardless of the mud—and I speak for myself."

Ben looked up at the sky and then at Ana. "You're right. And it's been a very long time since I've been with anyone. Another kiss and I could be like a runaway train."

As he pulled her to her feet Ana looked at him intently and said, "Neither have I, so all aboard… that train's about to leave the station."

Ben realized what she meant, and his eager body responded. He flattened and smashed the stalks where they had been kneeling, using his boot-clad feet. Returning his attention to Ana, he slid the vest from her shoulders and tossed it to the ground. His hands skimmed her torso and waist, ending where the old sweatpants were tied.

"Wait," she said, and then bent to remove the boots. She stepped gingerly onto the crushed stalks without thinking once about her damp socks and cold feet. There was fire in her eyes, but her voice was soft and sensual. "Now, get back to what you were doing."

Both were breathing faster as he slid her sweats and panties down and off. He laid them aside then removed his jacket, dropping it onto the vest as a cushion for their bodies. He quickly unbuttoned his shirt, exposing the torso Ana had admired when nursing his shoulder that first night. She lay down on the padded makeshift bed of leather and flowers then watched him undo his jeans, which he let fall to his ankles. His boxers followed.

Ben dropped to his knees, hovered over her, and met her lustful gaze. He eased the black jewel-encrusted tee shirt above her breasts and did the same with her wispy lace bra. He paused to admire what he saw then kissed each one softly before returning to her lips. He lowered his chest onto hers, and as flesh met flesh Ana gasped, while Ben let out a long sigh of pleasure. His kisses became more demanding, and soon he placed one knee between her legs, edging them open without resistance. Moved by the swirling wind, stalks of yellow danced in concert with the rhythm of their urgent lovemaking. Gusts whooshed and whined through the field, rising in crescendo with the lovers' moans of passion.

Ben collapsed onto Ana. She could feel his heart pounding against her chest. He rolled to the side, pulling her on top of him. They lay in silence, listening to nature's orchestra. Birds circled overhead, riding the wind currents and squawking their delight to the world— to Ben and Ana's private world in the middle of a field, where they were safe and alone.

After a while Ben stirred then said quietly, "We have to go." Yet in his reluctance to return to dealing with the family's predicament, he didn't move from her side.

"Right now I hate those words." Ana said, kissing him just under his chin, then added, "I want to stay here—make time stand still."

"I can't be alone with you anymore or history is going to repeat itself."

Ana would have liked nothing better, but she sighed and rolled away from his arms. After giving Ana's clothes a good shaking, he helped her dress, steadying her as she pulled on the Wellies. As he dressed himself, Ben heard her snicker and asked what was funny. She said she was thankful that Sir Freddie had decided to go home and hadn't come bounding into their private space at the wrong moment.

Ben laughed and said the dog was due for a special treat. Then he turned serious. "We're expected to leave for London before noon. Mum and Dad are bound to wonder where we are. I don't want them to worry."

He slid his hand into her mass of tangled hair, holding it tightly while he kissed her cheek. They made their way back to the road, crossed, and started back across the lawns hand in hand. They stopped for a moment to embrace beside the giant Chestnut tree. When she backed away to look up at him, her face was still flushed with the glow of satisfaction. She took a deep breath and opened her mouth to speak, yet hesitated.

"What is it? If you have something to say, just say it," Ben told her, his tone uneasy.

"Ben, every minute since the night we met you've done nothing but show concern for me—for my safety more than your own." She looked down at her feet before continuing, obviously self-conscious about what she was going to say. "I don't trust easily, but I believe I can trust you—in every way that's important." She then looked directly into his eyes and said, "Just don't break my heart. I don't give it easily."

He leaned in and kissed her neck. Keeping his lips against her skin he whispered, "And don't you break mine."

Ana shook her head no and said, "That's the last thing I'd ever want to do. Now we'd better get a move on before we're both in trouble with your parents. I'm still trying to make a good impression and I don't think my recent behavior would help."

"That's done and dusted, my dear—the good impression I mean." He took her hand and pulled her forward onto the path. "Don't worry. I'll get you in and upstairs before you'll have to explain the 'state' you're in."

They quickly covered the remaining distance to the house. Both were muddy from the knees down and their clothes were damp and dirty. Ben realized his parents would likely be in the kitchen, so he sent Ana inside through the front door, reminding her to remove the Wellies first. She did as he said, then hurried up the stairs and into her room without being seen. Ben stopped outside to remove his muddy boots and brush his pants off one more time. He went inside through the kitchen and encountered his parents finishing their coffee as they cleaned up from a late breakfast. He and Ana would have no time to eat, but he wasn't hungry for food. After his brief tryst with Ana, he could be sated by only one thing.

* * *

Hugh was anxious to get into the city and had put everyone on notice to get a move on. Taking long strides he hurried out the kitchen door to the garage, where he climbed into the Rover and pulled it around to the front of the house. He waited with the engine idling, tapping his fingers on the steering wheel while humming with the radio. But after glancing at his watch and seeing it was almost noon, he began to honk. Paris hurried out the front door and down the steps, followed by Ana and then Ben. Edith stood in the doorway and called to Paris, who turned around before climbing into the back seat. Questioned about whether they would be home for tea, Paris told her not to plan on them, that they would likely grab a bite in the city.

Ben climbed in beside his father, who ordered everyone to buckle up. Somehow he couldn't help adding, "It's going to be a bumpy ride." The tone of their laughter was obligatory and less than hearty. Resigned that his effort to be witty had fallen flat, Hugh smirked congenially and steered the car up the driveway and out onto the road. After about twenty minutes of narrow country road, they reached the main route to London. Hugh's meeting wasn't until two o'clock, and he thought it wise to leave late enough to miss the morning traffic. Once in the city they would have a vehicle at their disposal, rather than be forced to coordinate their activities with the train schedule. His efforts to lighten everyone's mood hadn't worked. Paris was busy on her iPad, trying to retrieve office emails, and both Ben and Ana were quiet. They gazed out the side windows at the passing landscape, both remembering what had happened earlier that morning.

As they approached the outskirts of London the traffic slowed then became congested, so Hugh turned on the radio in search of an update. Paris closed the tablet case, reached forward, and patted his shoulder— a silent message that he shouldn't turn grumpy. Ben sensed Ana's eyes on him and turned around to glance at her in the back seat. The smile she gave him, and the one he returned, told the story of their morning together and confirmed the fact that both had spent the drive to London reliving each moment. His parents would have been delighted, if they knew, but the whole thing was private— their secret and impulsive assignation. He wondered about the duration of their stay in the country, and how he would keep his hands off of Ana when in his parents' company.

After having spent more than an hour on the road, Hugh pulled up near the front of the museum and stopped in a loading zone. "Everybody out… and stay together! Ben, I don't want your mother out of your sight. If she goes to the loo, you all go. Ana goes in with her and you wait in the corridor. Is all that clear?" Hugh's tone was authoritative, but not harsh.

As they all unbuckled their seatbelts Ben answered, "Yes, Dad, I've got it covered."

He opened the rear passenger door and helped his mother out, exchanging glances with Ana, who seemed to enjoy seeing him being told what to do. Hugh had put the driver side window down and Paris leaned in to give him a quick kiss. He assured her he would call her mobile phone as soon as he arrived at Lloyd's and was inside the building. He mouthed I love you and drove away. Paris took both Ben and Ana by the arm and led them around the building to the administrative entrance.

Lyle Brett heard voices in the hall and peered out from behind his office door. He was disappointed to see that she wasn't alone, and shocked to see that she was with Ben. He wondered about the other woman who accompanied them. Something about her seemed familiar. He called out an uncharacteristic greeting and Paris reciprocated. She unlocked the office door and they quickly went inside. Before hanging up her coat she took a moment to scan her desk for anything new that hadn't been there when she left for home the day before. Nothing seemed amiss, so she took her mobile out of her purse and put it on the desk to await Hugh's call. She told Ben to pull the two extra chairs up to her desk. Ana sat down while Ben paced around the office. They were quiet, and the ticking of the clock on the wall seemed to become increasingly louder as the wait continued.

Eventually Ben sat down. He fidgeted in the chair for a while and then leaned forward, elbows on his knees, hands clasped together. He turned to look at Ana and said, "This waiting is killing me."

She nodded in agreement and glanced at Paris, who expressed her own frustration with a loud sigh. Before another word was spoken her mobile rang. It was Hugh, confirming his arrival and that a meeting was going forward, the results of which would depend on what she would find out from whoever contacted her. Paris sat back in her chair, a look of relief on her face. Just then there was a tapping at the door.

"Come in," Paris answered, turning to see who would appear.

Lyle Brett opened it slightly and stuck his head through. Next came his hand, which was holding a rather thick manila envelope. "This came to me by mistake. It's addressed to you." He waved it around a little and continued, "My oh my, it's quite thick."

Paris got up, walked to the door and took it from him. She thanked her colleague and put her hand on the doorknob to close it, but he stood firm in the doorway and said, "There's something else. I want to let you know that I won't be in the office for a few days—maybe a week." He waited for questions, but no one asked why, so he offered the information. "I decided to take a little vacation— not sure where— just need a bit of relaxation."

She thought that his timing was bad and typical of his lack of concern for fellow employees. She dreaded the fact that with the promotion offered, she would be his superior and responsible for his job performance. Considering her increased workload, she asked, "Will there be someone covering your duties while you're gone?"

"The director said he would try to find someone, but at this point I can't confirm that."

Paris hid the annoyance she felt at the realization that she would probably be doing his work as well as her own, but she said nothing—just wished him well and shut the door quickly, causing him to jump out of the way. She returned to the desk, broke the seal on the envelope, and allowed the contents to slide out. The first page looked like a transport manifest. She sat down slowly as she perused what was written. Both Ben and Ana sat forward on the edge of their chairs, waiting for Paris to say something.

She finally looked up and said, "This is the information on an exhibit that's coming in, supposedly within the next few days." She paused, trying to sort her thoughts. "I knew very little about this, but when the director asked me to fill in as head of department, he did say that I'd have my hands full very soon. I didn't make the connection."

"What's the exhibit?" Ben asked.

"Let me read the rest of the document." After a few minutes she looked up again, her expression both concerned and surprised. "I've already received the preliminary information on this exhibit. It's extremely valuable. It's part of a collection of gold doubloons from a Spanish ship sunk by an English warship off the coast of Portugal in the 1800's. It was recently salvaged, and after ongoing litigation with the American treasure hunters who salvaged it, the Spanish government has retained ownership. It had originally been on view in Madrid, but the Spanish government is allowing a portion of the treasure to be a traveling exhibit. The whole of what was salvaged is said to be worth something like 350 million Euros. The value of this portion isn't stated, but it's probably a small portion of the total."

"Still a lot of money. Where is it coming from? Portugal maybe?" Ben asked. Ana had nothing to say, but her mouth hung slightly open at the contemplation of such wealth.

"The previous information I received said the portion coming here is presently in Cartagena, Spain. The fact that it's being moved has been kept quiet—no media coverage. There are instructions not to talk about it until it's in place—here—under lock and key."

Ben shook his head. "Even if a treasure that size could be stolen, there's nothing a thief could do with it. Even a half-million in gold doubloons is rather high profile."

Ana chimed in, "If they found someone who would melt it down, it would soon just be a lot of gold bars. Not sure how or if they could be traced."

"I wonder how pure the gold is. I don't know anything about gold bars, or the karats or how the purity is measured." Ben paused, obviously thinking. "I also wonder if the value is linked to the historical value, or just to the actual weight and purity of the gold."

Paris answered, "I don't have an answer for that, nor do I know where to find out. I imagine someone must have that information." She continued to peruse the document before continuing. "I had thought it would be sent across the channel by ship—off-loaded at Calais and the rest of the way either by truck or train. Let me see what it says about that." She read further, turning over page after page. "Well, it says that transport will be by plane, landing at either Gatwick or Heathrow— to be determined. From that point an unmarked armored truck from a security company will be used. I haven't come across the company name yet." She looked up and said, "Evidently the plans weren't complete when the paperwork was handed over to me."

Ben looked confused, and asked, "So who's in charge of getting it here, then placing it under lock and key?"

Paris looked first at Ben, then at Ana. "Looks like I am. Seems it's up to me to book the transport—unless there's a name somewhere in the ..." She turned the pages quickly, scanning for more information.

A hush fell over the room as each of them imagined what was ahead. Ben was the first to speak and looked at his mother. "I can see now that there's a reason for all this. I just don't know what it is, or how you fit into it."

Paris said, "Well, it must have to do with the control I have over the exhibit—maybe the transport. What else could it be? Whatever they want me to do must be significant or it wouldn't have been worth trying to kidnap you." She began to thumb through the papers again, but stopped and looked at Ben. "Since they didn't succeed at that, what kind of leverage could they have now?"

Ana had nothing to say, feeling that it wasn't her place to offer an opinion. Yet she was very sure they weren't home free. Something bad was coming. She was sure of it. Ben told his mother all that could be done was to wait, that whoever was running things would reveal himself soon enough. Paris felt a rush of anxiety, and her heart began to pound as she wondered what kind of threat was coming.

Ben asked the women if either needed to use the loo. Paris shook her head no, but Ana said yes. Paris suggested that they should get some fresh air in the small garden at the center of the building where there was no outside access. Ben agreed, but said they wouldn't stay away long, that there could be news at any time. As they got up to leave, he told his mother to lock the office door behind them. She did so, and Ben walked Ana down the hall. When they reached the lady's room he took hold of her arm gently and turned her to face him.

"I hope you know how much it means to me—that you've hung in there through what's happened so far."

The intensity of his stare all but buckled Ana's knees. The urge to kiss him, to tell him that she wouldn't want to be anywhere else, required a strong will. She had to make certain things clear first. She leaned back against the wall and took a deep breath. "Ben, you know this all started because of my need for an interview." Ben nodded, his expression showing doubt at what might be coming. Ana reached out to stroke his arm then said, "Since shortly after we arrived at your parents' house, nothing has been about the interview."

Ben took both her hands in his, but looked down rather dejectedly. "Like I said, I've probably done a bang-up job of getting you fired."

"None of that matters." She began to pace in circles, thinking. "I'm going to call my editor and tell him that I can't complete the assignment because something important has come up." He could see she was adamant in her decision. She stopped pacing, faced him, and said, "I'm part of this mess until everything is resolved. You've become many things to me in a short time, Benedict McKinnon. A job is not one of them."

"The first moment I see that I can't keep you safe, you're out of it. Understand that and don't question me."

"You haven't seen my stubborn side yet. I basically won't be letting you out of my sight."

Ben shrugged his shoulders, deciding to let her vent but knowing things would be done his way. He quickly decided to divert the conversation away from a battle of wills and said, "You may come out a winner yet. When all's said and done, this could make quite a story—an exclusive for you. No doubt you'd be back on your editor's good side."

Ana pushed the restroom door partially open then turned around. "Maybe," she said. "As long as the story has a happy ending." She disappeared inside, and Ben leaned against the wall to wait, his face drenched with worry about what that ending would be.

CHAPTER FOURTEEN

Gareth had managed only a meager amount of sleep before leaving for the airport. He was weary and sleep deprived, but spent most of the dawn flight to Madrid worrying about his identity. He would have to go through customs and present a passport that identified him as Gareth Logan. Clive Warren couldn't check in at any hotel because that also required passport ID. Renting a car would present the same problem. Gareth wondered if his alias was now useless to the plan in which he was being forced to take part. He turned the instructions he had been given over and over in his mind, not really believing he could carry through with most of it, but knowing that somehow, he must. His biggest concern was whether he would have to see Olivia, who no doubt had already been taken. Whatever happened from this point on, he hoped it wouldn't include her finding out about his role in her abduction.

After landing in Madrid, Gareth easily made it to the connecting flight to San Sebastian. He was unable to relax, and his fatigue caused him to forget whether someone would meet him, or if he was supposed to take a taxi to Pamplona. Perhaps he had been told that if no one showed up, he was to take a taxi. The uncertainty frightened him. He had come too far to fail now and have his brother pay the price. As the approach to the landing strip was announced and the small plane began to reduce altitude, his heart began to race. He now suspected that courting Olivia had been the easy part, yet he had never intended to connect with her emotionally, let alone so strongly.

The plane landed and Gareth disembarked. He hurried to baggage claim, where he waited for his duffle. A rush of adrenaline accompanied the realization that he hadn't even called a friend, let alone his boss, to say he'd be gone for a week. He knew that merely sending someone a text might cause suspicion. Such an irresponsible move was out of character for him, but his friends knew him too well, and he just couldn't talk to any of them while under such duress. So he sent one text, to his immediate superior, reasoning that if he did manage to get back to London, maybe he'd still have a job. Within ten minutes he had received a favorable response and was walking out of the terminal. He stopped outside and looked around for any sign of a person who might have been sent to pick him up. People walked around him every which way, and he began to think he was on his own and transport would have to be by taxi.

Just then a man inched up to him and asked, "Well, Logan, glad you made it." Gareth said nothing. The man spoke again. "Cat got your tongue, mate? Surely you remember me."

Of course Gareth recognized him, but he looked down at the ground, obviously disturbed to see the man again. "You never gave a name. I didn't expect to see you here. Once you were through threatening me that night in the pub, I hoped I wouldn't have to see you again."

The man let out a derisive laugh and said, "The name's Linus. I'm your transport to Pamplona and the guy who's gonna keep an eye on you 'til your keeper takes charge later. Then I'm off— back to London."

At that point Gareth had little choice but to acquiesce. He followed the man to a nondescript car, threw his duffle into the back seat, and they both climbed in. Once enclosed without ventilation, he instantly became aware of the man's musty odor. He hadn't noticed it in the pub that night. His bald head looked greasy, as did his stringy brown hair. Gareth wondered why a man would be wearing a coat made for the London damp on such a warm day in Spain. He wondered if Linus was an alias, not that it mattered. As they left the parking lot he rolled down his window to let in fresh air. He wondered if he would have to search for a room on foot, or if plans had been made for him. They rode in silence for a while before the man told Gareth where he would be staying. He felt a bit of relief at not having the search for accommodations added to his state of anxiety. Linus named *Gestión Alojamientos* and said he knew there would be a room available. Gareth was also told that right after he checked in, there would be a meeting at the bar next door.

The clerk said a room was available only because the guests who had booked it didn't show up. He went up to the room, threw his belongings on the floor and sprawled on the bed. His head was throbbing from lack of sleep and the ongoing stress of not knowing what to expect. After a while he got up, threw cold water on his face, went downstairs and outside to find the bar. Two doors down from the guesthouse a sign extended from the wall flashing 'Bar' in red neon. Gareth went inside and stopped to scan the room, not knowing whom to look for other than Linus. He was spotted sitting at a table by the wall along with another burly-looking man who had his back to Gareth. He walked over to them and they motioned him to sit. They introduced themselves as Linus and Lenny. No last names were offered, although they knew all about him.

Lenny said that he had only five minutes and that he had to get back to his guests. He told Gareth that part of his job would be to relieve him as caretaker. Adrenaline shot through Gareth's body as he realized that the guests had to be Olivia and her ex-sister-in-law, and that his worst-case scenario seemed inevitable. He was given an address and told to report there no later than six o'clock in the morning, bringing his own food and water.

As he began to get up, Linus reached over and grabbed his arm. "You're not going anywhere yet. What makes you think we're finished with you?"

Gareth sat down again and said, "Sorry. I thought we were finished." His demeanor was submissive, but inside, he was seething.

This time Lenny spoke. "You haven't heard about the most important part of your duties. It's time for you to apply some of your tech-savvy to move things along."

Gareth answered, "I don't understand."

"Your baby brother has a big mouth. He seems to like talking about you—bragging about you—to anybody that will listen. He should be more careful. He told my cousin all about you. Turns out you two made the perfect pair for our purposes."

Linus let loose with a belly laugh that Gareth found disgusting. He was fed up with being strung along and asserted himself by asking straight out what they wanted. Lenny explained that he was to send an untraceable email to an address he would be given. It was to be done from an Internet café in Pamplona. He was told to send it around the world if he must, but it had to be done within the next two hours. They asked him for his email address and told him that the item to be sent would be sent to him first. He was to access his account then copy and paste it onto a new email and send it on as directed. There was to be a blind copy sent to another address, that of their boss. Linus handed him a piece of paper on which was written the ghost account address, the boss' address, and that of the main recipient.

Gareth was still somewhat confused, and questioned the men further. "But even if it can't be traced, I need an address for the sender."

Lenny leaned forward, elbows on the table and shoulders hunched. He spoke in a low and impatient voice. "I've set up an account under an alias with a small provider—known for their discretion. It's paid for through an account under the same alias. So use that and stop asking questions."

"Your plan isn't foolproof. There are people who can follow the course of an email and trace it to the source. It just takes a while—maybe a couple of days. It could be less if the recipient involves their security administration—or Interpol. I can do this, but I can't work miracles or guarantee how long you've got before someone finds the source."

Linus just sat back in his chair with a smirk on his face and said, "Well, you'd better hope you're good at miracles because you know what happens if you fuck it up."

Gareth had run out of reasons to stall and told them he knew how to proceed. There was no choice but to guarantee he would do his best. In his profession, tracing communications that skip around the globe in anonymity was an important part of his job. He was given the address of an Internet café and also given another unnecessary warning. Both men got up at the same time and plodded out of the bar. Gareth stayed there, staring at nothing, until the barkeep told him either to order or leave. He had no appetite for food or drink and returned to his room where he fell face down on the bed, planning just a few minutes rest before dealing with his task. Exhaustion and the need for escape quickly brought sleep.

Within an hour he startled awake and remembered what he had to do. Gareth scooped up his wallet and room key then rushed down to the hotel desk, where he inquired about the address he had been given. It was only a five-minute walk, and soon he was seated at a corner table with a cup of black coffee and a computer screen ready to take him online. He accessed his Internet account and then his email. There it was: the fake account, the email text, and the attachment he was meant to send by a circuitous route to the woman whose daughter was at great risk in a foreign country.

* * *

Hugh McKinnon concluded the meeting with his two old acquaintances from Interpol and headed back to the museum. He had telephoned Paris to see if anything had happened, but was told no, that they were still waiting. It was slow going in the afternoon traffic and he was short on patience. He then decided that the slow crawl of traffic would give him the opportunity to mull over in his mind all that had been discussed. They had come up with several scenarios for making the criminals believe that Paris would do as they asked. Yet he had to ask himself why she would cooperate if there were no danger to anyone—no good reason to acquiesce. Everything depended on the call, if it would be a call and not another tape. He stopped at another traffic light and fidgeted in the seat, his hands gripping the steering wheel too tightly.

The office was quiet. Ben was playing games on his phone. Ana was perusing the shelf of art books in Paris' office, while Paris sat at her desk with eyes glued to the exhibit paperwork. She was anxious for Hugh to return, anxious to find out what their options would be. When they heard the sound, all three looked up from what had been occupying their attention. It was the familiar sound alert from Paris' computer, informing of a new email. Her first instinct was to ignore it, but Ben urged her to view its content. In spite of the attachment being from an unknown sender, it had not gone to the Spam folder. In a job such as hers, emails often came from senders relevant to her work, senders whom she did not know. Therefore, her spam filter could not be set to a high level.

Paris stared at the screen, hesitating to open the email, until Ben said, "No one needs more suspense. Open it, Mum. It could be nothing—just work related."

She did as he said, and after a moment of perusing the content she moaned, "No, no, no … this can't be true."

Ben walked around the desk, put his hand on her shoulder, and looked at the screen. "Did you see that there's an attachment?"

He didn't wait for her reply, just reached forward toward the keyboard, opened it and waited for the download. In a few seconds a photo appeared. His sister was sitting on an old mattress in handcuffs with her hair in tangles and her clothing rumpled. Her face was filled with terror. Beside her in partial view was Valerie, his ex-wife. They could see that she was also handcuffed and filled with fear. Paris continued to utter words of denial—that it was a trick. Ana hurried to their side and all three stared at the frightened and disheveled women in the photo.

Ben began to read the text aloud. "We have your daughter and the woman who was with her. This is the surprise we had for you—a surprise that should make you cooperate. You know how it works. If you want her back still breathing, you'll do what we tell you."

Paris interrupted, "But I still don't know what that is. Oh my God, what will Hugh do when he sees this?"

"Dad will know what to do. He should be here soon. But let me finish reading. Maybe what they want is in this email." Paris stopped talking. Ana squatted beside Paris' chair and gently rubbed her arm in an effort to calm her. Ben continued to read. "Within an hour you'll get a call at your office with specific instructions. And don't bother trying to trace the call. You know about burner phones."

The three looked from one to the other, trying to take in what was happening. Ana went to Ben and wrapped her arms around him, saying softly how sorry she was and that she would do anything to help bring Olivia home safely—Valerie as well. Ben stiffened. Ana stood back and waited for him to speak.

"It's all clear now. I was the one. They originally wanted to abduct me to be the bargaining chip." He looked at Ana and continued. "We wondered why the attacks happened. It's just too fucking easy these days for people to learn all about you—sorry for the language, Mum. All this technology is a mixed blessing—like doing research on our family from top to bottom. Mum, you must be very necessary to whatever they're up to."

Paris spoke in a near whisper. "I'll do whatever they ask—anything. My poor baby girl… I can't stand the thought of her being so frightened."

Ana turned to Ben, a confused expression on her face. "You said attacks—plural. Why didn't you tell me there'd been another one? What happened and where and how did you get free?"

"You'd had enough of my problems. I would have told you eventually, but I just wanted to get you out of town—get us both out of town. It wasn't a lie, just a sin of omission."

Ana shook her head and walked back around the desk to sit down. She knew that this wasn't the time to face off about details or not being told.

* * *

Gareth left the café and headed in the direction of his hotel. He was greatly troubled by his actions and questioned if he should have been stronger, called their bluff about the risk to his brother. He pulled out his mobile phone and called the number he had been given. He now knew that the threatening voice giving him orders over the phone had been Lenny all along. Once he confirmed the email had been sent, his time was his own until the morning. A block or so from the *Gestión* he detoured down the street to his left and began to look for somewhere to eat. He entered the first café he came upon and took a small table by the window. A diminutive old woman with a craggy face shuffled over to take his order. He knew nothing about Spanish food, so pointed to a couple of dishes listed on the menu.

She nodded then pointed to a wall covered in wine bottles and beers before asking, *"¿Lo que para beber?"* He asked for a beer, and she walked away as she had come.

While waiting for the food he became more and more consumed by the events and imagining their possible conclusions. He looked up at the old woman as she set his meal on the table, and in that instant Gareth realized what he must do. After washing down the last of his tortilla and roasted tomatoes with the last swallow of beer, he went to the counter to pay for his meal. Pausing on the sidewalk he contemplated his next move. He needed an Internet café, but not the same one he had used. His long legs quickly carried him the two blocks to a main street, where he hailed a taxi and asked for another Internet café in another neighborhood. The driver understood the key words in his request and nodded as he pulled away from the curb. They must have gone a mile before the taxi stopped opposite just the right kind of place. He thanked the driver for his help by way of a generous tip. The plan was still formulating in his mind, and he hesitated for a few moments before entering.

As he pushed through the swinging door he noticed that most of the computers were occupied. He scanned the room, saw one free station along the left wall, and hurried to claim it. Once seated, he accessed the

Internet and went to Google, where he established an additional email account using his alias. Maybe Olivia had mentioned him to her family. Probably not, but maybe they would recognize the name. He still had the recipient's email address—the one used for his previous task—and this email would go to the same address, directly, and without fear of it being traced. It would be short—just a few words— and he hoped they would quickly figure out Olivia's location and find a way to help her.

He began to type: Olivia and friend—Pamplona Spain—captives— much danger. He didn't sign it. They would see who sent it. His greatest fear was that no one would take it seriously. Yet the right people could trace it quickly—he was counting on that. As he clicked 'send,' a shot of adrenaline coursed through him, followed by the brief feeling of contentment that comes from doing the right thing. He got up, paid for his time on the computer, and decided to walk off some of his anxiety. After being lost briefly, he arrived at his lodgings and welcomed the chance to lie down again. Scenarios ran through his head as he imagined the varied and unpredictable reactions his second email could be causing at that exact moment.

* * *

Paris McKinnon folded her arms on the desk, put her head down and closed her eyes. She was exhausted from the waiting and the eventual bad news they had received. Now there was more waiting—for the phone call that would define what was required of her. Ben and Ana had gone out to wait in the hallway, hoping to give her a rest from talking and a chance to calm down. The news of her daughter's plight had sucked away her strength. She felt like a rag doll unable to sit upright. Her body wanted to fold in on itself in an effort to escape the stress. She made the effort to take deep measured breaths and control the horrid thoughts that continued to pop into her mind. That minor ritual for survival was interrupted by the computer's familiar sound, informing of another message. She sat up abruptly and accessed the inbox. She didn't recognize the sender's name, but considering the situation, she opened it without further thought.

The words jumped out at her, and she was instantly gripped by fear. She didn't get up to go to the door, just yelled to Ben. The door opened immediately, and in a trembling voice she said, "There's another email—just a few words. It's about Olivia—from someone named Clive Warren. Come and read it!"

Ben went to the computer, Ana close behind. They both leaned over Paris' shoulder and read the words aloud. "Olivia and friend—Pamplona Spain—captives—much danger…" He stopped talking, put his hand on his mother's shoulder and squeezed gently. Ana did the same. Paris was still as a statue. All three were silent, thoughts racing. "Mum, this could be the break we need to start looking for her."

Paris spoke, her voice almost a whisper. "Maybe it's just to give us false hope. Maybe they're playing with us—just being cruel."

Ana had been quiet, not wanting to interfere, but it was time to share her thoughts. Very gently she said, "Or it could be a Good Samaritan—or someone who no longer wants to be a part of whatever is going on or is meant to happen."

Ben began to pace around the room. "There are any number of possible reasons for this. It could be a ruse, or a cruelty, but just in case it isn't, I have to do something. I'm going to Pamplona—as fast as I can get there."

Ana could see a fury building in Ben. He would be a loose cannon in Pamplona, and if by some chance he encountered her abductors, his emotions would likely get him killed. There had to be some sort of order to the undertaking. She knew it was imperative that it appear as if Paris was doing just exactly as she had been ordered. The telephone call with instructions had not come yet, but it could at any minute. Nothing should be done until then. Ben was Olivia's protector and it would be beyond difficult to keep him at bay until the right time. She had made one decision that was irrevocable: He would not go to Spain without her.

Ben was still pacing when the phone rang. Paris startled, sat up straight, and reached for the phone. She hesitated and let it ring three times before answering. Ana saw her lick her lips and breathe deeply before speaking.

"Hello. Paris McKinnon here." She waited for the voice on the other end to respond.

The caller spoke through a device that disguises the voice, although she could tell that it was a man. "Did you get the email?" he said.

Paris thought quickly about the fact that she had received two emails, but assumed correctly that this call was about the threat, her task, and nothing else. "Yes, I have it. Is my daughter all right? Could I speak to her?"

"Not a chance. Do as you're told and we'll see about it."

Even with the strange sound of the disguised voice she could hear the underlying tone that suggested he was enjoying her distress. "Tell me what I have to do. Tell me that if I do as you say you'll return my daughter to me unharmed."

"You'll get no assurances until we see that the instructions have been carried out. And don't put me on speaker. I'll be able to tell. That wouldn't be a wise move."

Paris looked worried, saying nothing while she listened to what followed. Ben and Ana hovered over the desk, both trying to hear what they could of the man on the other end. Several minutes passed before she said she understood and hung up the phone.

"I only have two days—*two days*—to set this up. It could be impossible. And how can your father put an Interpol team in place that soon. Whoever these people are, they could be watching any or all of us."

"Two days to do what?" Ben asked excitedly. Ana looked at him, shook her head and walked around behind Paris to place supportive hands on her shoulders.

"It's about the security company who will transport the exhibit. The man I'm replacing left without locking in a contract with anyone. It's up to me to hire it out, and the whole key to this terrible situation is that I'm ordered to hire a fake company and provide all the appropriate paperwork to them for their purpose. Their truck will meet the exhibit at the airport, supposedly to bring it here to the museum. But of course that won't happen. It's to be a well thought out robbery."

Ben sat on the edge of her desk and folded his arms across his chest. His expression was one of tension and anger. He spent a few moments in deep thought before he said, "Someone with a lot of knowledge about how this all works has to be at the bottom of it. A bunch of thugs couldn't plan something like this. They just do as they're told." The women nodded their heads in agreement and Ben continued. "We have no way of knowing whether the person who sent the second email is involved or not. He could have overheard something. But whatever the case, I'm going to Pamplona."

Paris' worried expression deepened as she contemplated Ben's impulsive reaction. "Wait for your father. He and his friends must have some ideas about how to handle this."

"While they're deciding what to do, I'm going to be on a plane—actually *doing* something. I want to be in place when the authorities get there to look for her."

Ana broke the uncomfortable silence that followed his words. "I know you feel you should go. I understand. But when you get there, you'll have no idea what to do or where to look. Two pairs of eyes will be better than one pair. I'm coming with you—no arguments."

Before Ben could counter Ana's declaration, he heard the office door open behind him. He turned to see his father walk briskly into the room. Paris rose quickly from her desk chair and hurried to him, throwing her arms around his waist and placing her face against his chest. With a wavering voice she said, "Hugh, it's terrible—what's happened." She then broke into tears.

"What's all this then?" Hugh asked as he took hold of her shoulders, putting her at arm's length. He could see the terror on her face and felt himself begin to fill with fear.

She seemed unable to speak, and Ben took over. "Dad, we got some bad news. It's Olivia. She's been abducted and is being held in Spain—Pamplona—until, if they can be believed, Mum does as she's told."

"How have you learned all this?" Hugh asked, his worried glance moving back and forth between Paris, Ben and Ana.

Ben explained all of what had transpired since the receipt of the first threatening email with the photo of Olivia and Valerie, and the subsequent anonymous email about their whereabouts. His mother knew what was expected, and they had been waiting for Hugh before taking the next step—making the transport arrangement with the bogus security company. She would have to fill out the necessary forms and make them part of the museum's records.

Hugh sat down on the edge of the desk, deep in thought. Everyone waited for him to speak. "Pulling this off is going to take a lot of coordination between Scotland Yard and Interpol. Since the exhibit comes into the UK from another country, Interpol will want to play lead."

Paris began to rub her arms, as if a chill had suddenly descended on the room. Her only real concern was for her daughter. She would do anything asked of her by the men who took them. Becoming involved with the authorities could jeopardize Olivia's survival, as well as Valerie's, and she agonized over that risk. In a trembling voice she said, "I'm going to make the arrangements as they instructed and notify them that I've complied. We have to buy time—give them a reason to keep their hostages alive."

Hugh shook his head, having known exactly how she would react. Ben stepped forward and embraced his mother. She melted into his arms and began to sob. "Mum, you know it's not as simple as that. I don't want to frighten you further, but you must realize that they may have no intention of releasing either of them."

She broke away from Ben, turned to Hugh, and shouted, "Do something!"

"I'm trying," he said, "But you have to find a way to control yourself while we figure out what gives them their best chance." Paris walked to her chair, wondering how Hugh could sound so calm, and once again folded her body into it like a rag doll. He kept talking, but she had trouble paying attention. "You *are* right about one thing," he added. "You need to appear as if you're complying. That requires you to fill out the appropriate forms, inserting the security company name you were given. Were you told how provide them with proof that the arrangements have been made?"

She perked up and said, "Yes. I'm to overnight them to a post office box at some private mail shop—somewhere in London. All I have is a box number and postcode."

Ben jumped in and said, "If we could locate the shop, it could be watched—maybe catch the guy picking it up."

Hugh nixed the idea quickly, explaining that when the person failed to contact his associate in Spain, confirming receipt of the forms, it could be fatal for the women. Ben realized his mistake and decided it was time to tell his parents about his intention to go to Pamplona. He knew he would be met with logical reasons why it was a bad idea, but he didn't care. Logic wasn't going to save his sister, or Valerie. If there was even one chance that he could find them, he had to take it.

"You may as well know now. I'm going to Pamplona. Whatever authorities are in play at this end, fine. But I'm going to be on the spot, looking for Olivia and Valerie. I'll enlist the help of the police there. If necessary, they can confirm with Scotland Yard. Surely you know there isn't a minute to lose."

Ana had been silent throughout the whole conversation between Ben and his parents, but since he had revealed his personal plan, she felt it was time to speak up. "He's not going alone. I'm going with him. If he argues, I'll just get my own ticket."

Ben response was quick and rather loud. "Then I can have three women to worry about instead of two!" Ana's body language told him that he was about to hurt her feelings, so he regained control. "I appreciate that you care enough to take part in this, but I can't see what you could possibly do to help."

She walked forward to face him, her arms folded across her chest, her stance and demeanor oozing stubbornness. Slowly, she said, *"Yo… hablo… Español."*

The office was quiet. Paris looked sideways at Hugh, who was staring at the floor, hands in his pockets. Ben slung his jacket over his shoulder and said, "Well then, let's go. No time to lose." Ana removed her jacket from the coat rack and quickly slipped it on. The two approached the door then stopped, turning to look back at his parents. "We both have mobiles and will keep you in the loop. You do the same." He paused, taking in the look of fear in their eyes. "I love you both. I'll do my best to bring our girl back safely."

Ana dashed back and embraced each of them. While embracing Paris she whispered, "I'll do *my* best to take care of *him*." She turned and followed Ben out the door."

Paris sat down on the edge of her desk and looked up at Hugh. "Well, one thing's in our favor."

"What's that?" he asked.

"I've never revealed anything about the nature of your work, or your connections to Interpol, to anyone—other than our closest friends. But you were aware of that. There's a glitch in their research. Any bunch of criminals worth their salt wouldn't have chosen this family."

Hugh nodded his head in agreement and said, "That will work in our favor—plus the fact that they're either inexperienced, or just stupid." He walked to the desk and folded his arms around his wife. She gave a small sigh of relief as he pulled her close to him. They stood there a while, quietly comforting each other without need of words.

CHAPTER FIFTEEN

It was just after dawn, and moisture still clung to the tall weeds and surviving patches of grass that surrounded the derelict house. Gareth was on time. For several minutes he stood on the sidewalk and faced the path to the front door, gathering his nerve for the inevitable confrontation he was about to have with Olivia. He cautiously moved forward then stepped onto the small porch and knocked. He could hear heavy footsteps approaching the door, and with a loud scrape and squeaking of hinges it opened just far enough for Lenny to see who was there. When he saw it was Gareth he opened it completely and pulled him inside, slamming the door behind him.

"It's a good thing you're on time. I'm going stir crazy in this dump. I have to get out to the café down the street and get something to feed those whining women. So… you want something?"

"Where are they?" Gareth asked.

"Through the archway—in the only other room there is besides the loo."

"Then I don't really need to see them. They can't come in here anyway, right?"

"You will if one of them needs the bathroom. They each have a bucket, but once a day— if they're quiet— I let them go in one at a time. I'm sure not cleaning those buckets." He waited for a response, but receiving none he continued. "In case the free one does something stupid I hold my gun on the other one." Lenny laughed to himself then broke into a wicked grin.

Gareth felt his stomach churn. His hands were clammy and his head was still throbbing from stress and lack of sleep. He was an unwilling player in a very dangerous game, dangerous for his brother as well as the women and himself. He wondered if Lenny could smell fear. If so, the scent would be overpowering in those two rooms, and mixed with the dank staleness he was forced to inhale, a feeling of nausea began to rise in his belly.

Gareth answered Lenny, his voice indistinct. "No, I don't want anything."

Lenny looked him in the eye and said, "You look a bit green around the gills, mate. Best get used to the situation and do what you're told." He paused and checked his wallet for money before continuing. "Then maybe you'll come out of this okay— still breathing at least."

Gareth sat down at the rickety table and tried to breathe deeply. Lenny stuck his gun in the waist of his pants then threw his jacket over one shoulder. He headed for the door, turned, and told Gareth he would be back within an hour. Lenny locked eyes with him in an icy stare before yanking the door open, walking out and slamming it behind him.

There wasn't a sound from the room beyond the arched opening. In spite of hoping it would stay that way, Gareth was curious. Rising from the rickety chair he walked softly to where he could see into the room without being seen himself. What he saw made his heart sink. Both women were asleep on mattresses that lay on the floor, each woman with one arm extended uncomfortably to accommodate the chains binding them to the radiator and bed frame. Olivia was pale, much more pale than normal for her fair skin. Strands of the dark red hair that had so attracted him seemed pasted across her face, the remainder tangled and dull. Her body was partially covered by a thin blanket. He could see that her clothing was spotted and rumpled.

In the other corner of the room Olivia's friend was hanging partially off the top end of her mattress in order to let her arm bend. She was handcuffed to the radiator, head resting on her wadded-up blanket. She was also pale. Her mouth hung open and her breaths were slow and deep. Her clothing and short hair were both disheveled.

From the look of them Gareth was sure both women had to be in some sort of physical distress, perhaps dehydration. Lack of fluids could make them lethargic, weak and pale. Perhaps sleep was their only escape from the helplessness they felt. In a wakeful state they were part of a real nightmare. He was sure they had no expectation of escaping their bonds, or of living to tell the story. They had seen Lenny's face, and soon they would see his. Gareth was torn between the love for his brother and a woman he cared about. He hoped that the email he had sent regarding the women's location had reached the right person, and that some action was being taken. But he couldn't tell Olivia what he'd done, couldn't give them both hope that could easily be false. The information had to be sent, even if it put him in danger from both sides. If something good came from his actions, at least Lenny and his pals weren't smart enough to figure out that the clue had come from him. His situation was impossible, and either way, he couldn't see how he would live with the outcome of either choice.

Olivia began to stir. Once awake she reached for her bucket and pulled it close to her. Gareth stepped back out of the doorway before she could see him. She stood with knees bent and began to work her leggings down as best she could with one hand. He stood quietly, waiting for her to finish the awkward process. Valerie continued to sleep until Olivia called out in an effort to rouse her. She sat up bleary eyed and looked around until she found the bottle of water she had stashed under the edge of the mattress. She gulped about half of it and tossed it to Olivia, telling her she must drink all of what was left. Olivia did as she was told and they both settled back, each leaning against a moldy wall.

Gareth decided that it would be safer for them if he showed himself while Lenny was gone. Their reaction, especially Olivia's, would be vehement, and he didn't want Lenny to react by hurting either of them to keep them quiet. He took a deep breath and stepped from his place against the outer wall into the arched opening. The women looked up, both with different expressions. Valerie looked confused by the new face. Olivia gasped and stood, backing up against the wall.

After a few seconds she broke into a grin, looked at Valerie, and said, "Oh my God! It's Clive—the man I told you about." She then looked squarely at him and asked, "How did you find us? I can't believe you're here." Turning back to Valerie she exclaimed, "We'll be all right now. Clive will get us out of here." She became very animated and shouted, "Oh my God. We're going to be okay." Still in a panic, she turned to him and said, "You have to hurry. That awful man will be back. I don't know where he's gone, or how long he's been gone. He won't hesitate to kill you—or all of us."

Gareth's body flushed with adrenaline. He had to tell them how it was. How could he tell them that he was now one of their jailers? He would do as he was told but had to figure a way to keep the women safe, as well as his brother. Yet he had no confidence in regard to either challenge. While they waited for him to speak, the dank air in the room seemed charged with electricity.

"Olivia, it's not like that. I hate what's happened, but I'm not here to save you. I'm part of this—but not by choice."

"What do you mean?" Valerie said. She turned to Olivia and asked, "What does he mean?" Her eyes darted back and forth between the two.

Olivia spoke in a monotone. "He isn't here to save us. He's here to watch us. This is what it was about all along." She slid down the wall into a heap then buried her head in the crook of her arm and began to sob.

Gareth had never felt as helpless as he did at that moment. Every fiber of his being wanted to go to her, to comfort her, to free them both and to run. But a thought flashed through his mind. He imagined his brother cornered in a prison hallway, arms held behind him by one prisoner, another driving a makeshift knife into his belly. There was so much blood. His brother sank to the floor, his eyes open in alarm as life drained away. Gareth shook the scenario from his mind and once again focused on the women. As much as he hated the predicament, he had to save his brother. At least the women had a small chance. His brother would have none. Several minutes passed before Olivia had calmed down and Valerie had settled back against the wall, a disgusted look on her face.

Gareth decided to tell them why he was involved. He leaned against the wall and slid down, knees bent, until he was resting on his heels. When he began to speak the women turned their faces away from him. He lowered his eyes and spoke softly. "My younger brother is in jail for a crime that was guilt by association. As bad luck would have it, Lenny, the man who took you, has a cousin at the same prison. Both are in the general population. He heard my brother talking about me, that I was a tech guy ready to start my own company, and for some reason the cousin told Lenny." He paused, waiting for the women to assimilate what he had told them so far.

Olivia turned to look at him and said, "We don't care what your reason is. You lied to me … lied in so many ways. You disgust me." She turned away from him and folded herself into fetal position. Valerie said nothing, just glanced back and forth at them both.

"Please, Olivia. It wasn't all lies. What I had started to feel wasn't a lie. You don't know how much I hated what I had to do. Can't you see that I had no choice?"

With her face still turned away from him she mumbled, "We always have a choice."

At that point Valerie rang in with her take on things. "It doesn't matter how it all came about, or why. Take your egos out of it—especially you, Olivia. The only thing that matters now is what we can do about the situation."

Olivia maneuvered herself into a sitting position and asked Valerie if she had any idea how much time they had before Lenny's return, then answered her own question. "Of course you don't." She turned to Gareth and said, "Clive—or whoever you are—how is this going to play out? Are you going to help us or not?"

"If you'd let me finish telling you how I got involved in this insanity, you'd know why I couldn't help you." He looked from one to the other before continuing. Whatever hope had been present in their demeanor was gone, and both women sunk back against their respective walls like forlorn puppets whose strings had been let go. Valerie covered her eyes and shook her head back and forth in disbelief, while Olivia just stared at him quizzically, unable to accept the new reality.

Gareth decided to make his explanation quick and simple. "One call from Lenny to his cousin and my brother is dead. I have to do what he says. I've had to do other things besides watch you. I'm now deeply involved in the reason for all of this, and no one has told me what that is." Neither woman responded to his plea for understanding. He left the room but remained within earshot.

Olivia said, "We're so screwed," and then there was silence.

* * *

Ben's Jaguar was still at the country house, so once they left the museum, he flagged down a taxi and instructed the driver to take them to Ana's hotel. The afternoon was almost gone, and catching a flight to Madrid with a connection to Pamplona was out of the question. Ana suggested that they enlist the help of the hotel concierge to arrange their travel. They arrived at the hotel and took the concierge aside, quickly explaining what was needed. She agreed to assist them and pointed out that booking an immediate flight would not only inflate the price of the tickets, but could force them to fly first class. Ben confirmed that they would take anything they could get at the earliest possible time. They sat tensely in front of the concierge's desk and watched as she went online to access flights to Madrid, connecting to nearby San Sebastian rather than Pamplona, due to availability. After a few minutes she looked up and told them what she had found, and what the ticket price would be. Ana sucked air in through pursed lips when she heard the amount. Ben agreed and handed her his American Express card. Considering the extensive security protocols, the flight time required them to be at the airport well before dawn.

They thanked the woman and went into the hotel bar to sort out the particulars. Ana suggested that Ben stay with her for the night, but he declined, reasoning that he would need to pack a few things for the trip. She hoped his real reason for leaving had nothing to do with what had happened between them. Surely he wouldn't think she had any expectations, given the situation. But his decision was really about going back to his flat to sleep. He would order a taxi for three-thirty a.m. and pick her up at four. That would easily get them to Heathrow by five. With a take-off time of six-thirty they would be cutting it close. Ana knew that he wouldn't sleep. She felt the same about her own chances.

With everything settled they dashed across the street to a pub and had a hot meal. By around eight o'clock Ben had kissed her good night and was on his way home. Ana had gone to her room and hastily repacked her suitcase. A warm bath was next, followed by a bit of television. She dozed off at around ten, after having requested a wake-up call for three-thirty. Back at his flat Ben called to set up the morning taxi service and then followed a similar routine, stress and fatigue drawing him heavily toward sleep. At around two-thirty he awoke to darkness. He felt only slightly rested but got up quickly and prepared to leave. The taxi arrived as requested and soon he was in front of Ana's hotel. She was waiting just inside the glass doors and rushed out when she saw Ben open the door for her to climb inside.

The security protocol at the airport along with the waiting had seemed interminable, and Ben was visibly nervous while the plane waited its turn on the tarmac. He had a window seat and stared out at nothing in particular. After he had tapped his fingers on the armrest for a while, he spoke.

"The first thing we should do when we get to Pamplona is book a room. I heard two student types talking as we boarded. They're headed to Pamplona—think they're going to run with the bulls." He shook his head and said, "Doubt their parents have any idea about that foolishness. They're worried about finding a room since the festival is already in full swing." Again he began the finger tapping. "When we land I want to find out where I can rent a car. I'm worried. This festival is bound to make everything more difficult."

"One thing at a time. I've heard that in Spain money talks more loudly than in some other places."

"Then I guess the first thing we do is find a cashpoint. That's something I didn't think of. There's a limit on how much I can withdraw in 24 hours."

"Remember, with your Amex you can get cash—if we can find their office. And I have my bankcard. I can withdraw that daily limit."

The plane began to taxi down the runway, picked up speed and lifted, climbing quickly to cruising altitude.

He reached over and squeezed her hand. "I guess it has to be like you said: one thing at a time."

Both were quiet, but the wheels were turning loudly in their heads. Ben admitted to himself that he actually had run off 'half-cocked,' which his father had warned against, but he could do nothing else. He was in dire need of a plan—two plans, actually. There had to be one that involved keeping Ana out of unexpected danger. The look on his parents' face when he announced his intentions weighed heavily on his mind. In spite of his having no doubt about his actions, he regretted causing them further worry. He was filled with determination to return their daughter to them, safe and uninjured.

Ana reclined her seat, leaned back and began turning her mobile phone over and over in her hands. She knew calls were not permitted during the flight, and yet there was no escaping the need to call her editor. She had more than tested the boundaries of his patience. If she could tell him about the course her interview had taken, he would be enthusiastic and give her *carte blanche*. He would want to turn the interview into a sensationalist piece, with no regard for the people involved. She wouldn't do that. Becoming involved with Ben had caused her to question the course of her life in general. She would sooner end her career than use him for personal gain.

Both were startled from their deep thoughts by the pilot's voice announcing the descent into Madrid—first in Spanish then English. They brought their seats upright and looked at each other, both letting out prolonged sighs. Disembarkation went quickly and without checked luggage to collect they were soon queued up for boarding the plane to San Sebastian. With less than five minutes to spare they were led across the tarmac and onto the commuter flight. Another delay before takeoff fueled Ben's anxiety, although it was less than fifteen minutes before they were airborne once again. Flying at a lower altitude gave passengers clear views of the landscape: arid hills tumbling gently into irrigated pastureland; pockets of gray-green forest; roads resembling narrow ribbons strewn across the expanse; and small towns of pale stone and red tile where church spires reached toward the heavens.

Ana turned her gaze away from the window and toward Ben. "Considering the circumstances, I feel a little guilty being touched by all this beauty I'm seeing. If only the reason for this trip, this adventure, were happy—even romantic."

Ben leaned his head back against the seat and closed his eyes. "Me too. Spain has a reputation for being romantic. But the closer we get, the more muddled I feel about what to do first. I was just trying to apply logic when I said the first thing should be getting a place to stay."

"I knew that. Try not to worry. I think that when the time comes, you'll know exactly what to do, and if per chance you don't, you'll have me as backup."

"I already told you! You will not get in the middle of any confrontations that might be ahead of us." Ana's expression told him to change his tone. He leaned toward her and in a near whisper continued. "You're just going to function as a sort of 'mission control'… a liaison between my father and his Interpol cronies—and my Mum. She will be a full time job. I just hope that she'll be too busy with the other end of this debacle to involve herself in what's going on here."

Sounding serious, Ana replied, "I wouldn't bet on it."

It wasn't long before they felt the plane begin its descent. Soon it banked, and came around to approach the landing strip. Neither had expected to see the Bay of Biscayne, and the view distracted them from the slightly rough landing. They stepped out of the plane onto the portable stairs and instantly felt the heat of northern Spain's July sun. Its intense brightness was a startling contrast to the cool mists and soft colors of England.

The terminal was small, with only one baggage carousel. Ben collected their belongings then asked at the information kiosk for directions to the car rental desk. He was in a terrible hurry, and Ana had to scurry to keep up with him. The selection was meager, due to the time of day, and they had to settle on a small blue coup that would surely cramp Ben's legs. They were given a map of the route to Pamplona and told it was a trip of about one hour. They hadn't expected San Sebastian's airport to be so near the French border.

As they exited to the parking area that housed the cars, Ben's mobile rang. He answered right away, seeing the call was from his father. "Dad. What's up? We just arrived. We're headed to our rental car."

Hugh could tell that Ben was walking and told him to stop and listen. "You need to write this down," he instructed. "We've made reservations for you—two rooms at *Gran Hotel la Perla*. It's close to a cathedral. It should be quite central—near the middle of things. I'm sure any taxi driver will know the property."

"I'll be driving, so I need an address."

There was a momentary pause before Hugh continued. "*Plaza del Castillo*... Have you got that?"

Ben answered that he did, and his father made him promise to check in at least once a day for an update on their end of things. He explained that Interpol intended to have several men placed in Pamplona within 36 hours. He was insistent that Ben wait until they made contact with him at the hotel. Ben gave his father no reassurance, just said he understood what had been put in motion. The call ended, Ben shoved his phone back in his pocket and stood in the middle of the passageway without moving. Curious, Ana approached him and asked about the call.

"Everything is in motion," he said. "They've booked two rooms at a hotel named *Gran Hotel la Perla*... It's somewhere near a cathedral. I have the address."

"See? I told you things would begin to fall into place once we arrived. Bless your father for thinking about a hotel. He and his contacts must have pulled some strings to get us two rooms when the town is so crowded with tourists."

"Right. Let's get going."

His mind was elsewhere. He had no intention of waiting thirty-six hours to begin the search for his sister and Valerie. Ana spotted their assigned vehicle, and they gave it a quick once-over to spot any damage for which they could be held liable. The engine coughed a bit before warming up, and after two trips circling the roundabout, they found the route to Pamplona.

CHAPTER SIXTEEN

Earlier that morning an agricultural lorry filled with sheep had broken down, coming to a stop directly on the local railway tracks. The crossing involved was on the route between Swindon station and Paddington in London. It had been necessary to off-load the sheep in order to tow the lorry away. The sheep, however, saw the event as fortuitous and scattered every which way, some escaping into the nearby woods and some deciding to munch grass and weeds between the rails.

The McKinnons were running late and were concerned about missing their train. Hugh pulled the Rover into the Swindon station car park, found a slot, and told Paris to hurry gathering up her belongings. They had rushed to the ticket window before learning that service to London would be delayed for most of the morning, or until the sheep could be gathered and removed.

Hugh didn't look forward to the drive to London, closed in the car with a fretting wife while being plagued by his own concerns. Paris was showing the strain of the whole affair, and Hugh was doing his best to soothe and reassure her, but in fact he was deeply concerned as well and just better at hiding it. He was not only worried about the physical and emotional strain on his wife, but even more so the danger his daughter was facing—and the risk Ben would soon face if he managed to find her. There was no time to wait for the tracks to be cleared, so there was no choice but get back to the Rover and head for London. He had begun to keep Paris with him at all times, and they were due to meet with his Interpol contacts by mid-morning.

Once on the highway, Paris broke her short silence. "Is there a definite plan of action at this point? When I know how this is intended to play out I think I'll be able to cope."

"It's important that we look as if we're keeping to the same daily routine—me dropping you at the museum, or coming in with you." Paris nodded her head in agreement, and Hugh continued. "We'll finalize everything today. The last piece of the puzzle can't be placed until you're contacted again and given the name of the armored car company that's been invented by our crooked friends."

"Friends? How can you even joke with that word? Evil bastards. That's who they are."

Time and miles ticked away before Paris spoke again. "Where are they going to get an armored vehicle, let alone the two it will take to transport the treasure? Only one would have contained what's valuable. The other would be a decoy. Under normal circumstances, any robbery attempt would involve a decision by officers about which truck to pursue."

Hugh accelerated to pass a dawdling old Mercedes and then said, "Remember, just because a truck is *labeled* armored doesn't mean that it actually *is* armored."

"Hmmm ... this is an 'elaborate' plot, for lack of a better word. It's almost too intricate—too easy for something to go wrong ... for them I hope."

"The value of what they want seems to warrant the effort," Hugh said. "Let's listen to some music and try to relax a bit before we hit London."

"All right, but I'm still not sure I can be convincing enough to ensure they believe I've gone along with things just as instructed. You're with me all the time now, and I was told not to involve you in any way or Olivia would suffer. What cruelty!" she said, her voice cracking with emotion. Paris turned to stare out the window, and after a few minutes she had another question. "How can we be sure we haven't been watched? If they don't contact me today with the final instructions, it's bound to indicate that we've *been made*... Isn't that what they say on American TV?"

"My darling, you've always made me laugh, but in this case it's not funny. We have to assume that we've been watched, at least at times. That's why it's important to stick to routine." He studied his wife's worried expression then added, "All I can say is 'fingers crossed' and do your best. I think your mother lion instinct will work in our favor."

Paris shifted in her seat and turned slightly to look at her husband. "I'd like to be a foot taller, a hundred pounds heavier and be shut in a room with this gaggle of idiots. Then I could take them on one at a time."

Hugh checked the side mirror and looked over his shoulder before pulling out to pass a grocery truck. Once the maneuver was completed he said, "That's some pretty tough talk for a delicate beauty such as you." He reached over and patted her knee.

Paris touched his hand for a moment, obviously comforted by his touch. She then reached forward to turn on the radio, dialing to the quiet music Hugh had suggested. In a serious voice she said, "They say that under the right circumstances everyone is capable of violence." Hugh didn't respond. He knew she was right.

Traffic became heavier as they entered the outskirts of London. It was another half hour before they had reached the museum, parked, and settled in Paris' office to wait for the necessary instructions. Hugh passed the time thumbing through an old magazine, while Paris set about clearing the clutter from her desk.

She stopped what she was doing and said, "I must say, I'm very glad Lyle picked this particular week to be gone. I'd hate to have his nose poking into my office and my business while we're dealing with all of this."

Hugh looked up and smiled. "I see you've given up on making a friend of him?"

"Gave up long ago. He's the least congenial little man I've ever met… and punctilious to a fault." She sighed and continued moving folders around in an effort to stay busy. "I'm hoping that with the new job there will be much less need to interact with him."

Hugh looked up again and said, "I had rather hoped I'd be seeing more of you, not less. I'm concerned that the increased workload may be hard on you. Remember? We had talked about you cutting back on your trips into the city."

"Any permanent decisions about my job can wait until the children are home, safe, and settled. Until then I can't think straight. At the start I was just going to fill the position in the interim while they looked for someone. I told the director I didn't want to move into the other office right away. After I use my position to launch this crazy scheme that threatens our children, I'm not sure the position will hold any fascination for me."

As Hugh opened his mouth to comment the phone rang. Paris rushed to answer and her expression told Hugh that it was the call they needed. She said little, except for one-word responses as she wrote something on the tablet in front of her. The call ended and she let out a sigh before tearing off the page and handing it to Hugh.

"So this is the name they've chosen for their armored transport? *Security First?* Not very original. Are you required to have the director sign off on the requisition? He's bound to ask about a company he hasn't heard of."

"No, he's chosen to leave it all to me, which is surprising. But last week I heard that he has some sort of family issue or crisis going on. I suspect it may have to do with a certain woman I've seen dropping him off in the morning. I've also seen her coming out of his office a few times. She isn't his secretary, and I've met his wife."

"Good timing for us then, but not for the Missus."

Hugh pulled a chair over to the desk and sat down to face his wife. "There's something else I've wanted to tell you, but with the call on your mind it wasn't the right time."

"Well? Go on then. What is it?" She settled back into her chair and crossed her arms in a defensive pose. It was a subconscious action, prompted by the series of events she had experienced of late.

"The lads at Interpol asked me about Ana—what I knew about her. I didn't know why, but as it turned out they had decided to 'vet' her. I think that was prompted by the coincidence of Ben first meeting Ana on the same night as the first abduction attempt. They cover their bases."

Paris sat forward in her chair and without a word wrinkled her brow and pursed her lips. Hugh knew that expression, and it meant she didn't agree with their actions. A few moments passed before she spoke. "She definitely had proper identification showing that she's a journalist. The assignment to interview Ben could easily be verified by the magazine that hired her."

"Do we know the name of that magazine?"

"No, I don't. I'm not sure about Ben. I doubt he cares much. He's never been one to 'put himself forward.'"

"She's a charming girl, and the last thing I'd want is to find out is that she's somehow involved. It's easy to see how taken with her Ben has become."

"I suspect he's moved beyond *taken.*" Paris stood and began to pace around her office, obviously turning over in her head every detail she could remember about Ana's demeanor and the conversations they had. She realized there were few, and she hadn't paid close attention— but why would she? Finally she stopped beside Hugh's chair and asked, "What, if anything, did they find out?"

"Remember. What I tell you may be completely unrelated to current events. It would be a colossal blunder to judge her by her family." Paris cocked her head in a way that questioned his statement, and he continued to relate what he had been told by phone that morning. "What Interpol can find out in a short time has always amazed me. I don't think Scotland Yard would have been much help in this undertaking."

"Stop dawdling about! Let's hear it." Paris was becoming impatient. She felt herself incapable of absorbing any more bad news. "Surely that sweet girl is being mistreated by the very fact that unknown to her, she's being investigated."

"I can't give you the conversation verbatim, but here's what I jotted down." He pulled a notebook from his breast pocket, along with his glasses, and began to read. "Her father's name is Ion Cormac Doherty—both parents Irish. He's married to Isabella Cristina, maiden name DeFalla. She was born in Málaga, Andalusia, Spain. They're still compiling 'intel' on the rest of the family in Spain. His parents were Fiona Claire Branagan and Seamus Patrick Doherty. Both came from Galway to the states and operated a small neighborhood market in Belle Harbor, Queens. That's in New York."

"What can these particulars possibly have to do with Ben and Olivia—and most of all, Ana?"

"Well, it seems Ana's father is a *supposedly* reformed criminal. He was sent down for the first five years of Ana's life. She was born while he was inside.

"Ana's father? Was it a violent crime?"

"No, a robbery involving antiquities. You can see why Interpol could question her motives. The depth of his involvement is still unknown. But there was enough evidence to convict him by association."

"Oh my! I wonder how Ana's mother managed to care for a child during that time."

"She was hired to manage a curio shop—a lucky break, considering. I think they said Cambridge, Massachusetts. The owner was often absent, and being a family man, he allowed Isabella to bring Ana to work with her. When Ion was released they ran the shop together and were eventually able to buy it."

"Digging into Ana's life seems to have served no purpose other than to be intrusive."

"Their logic was that if anyone in her family had been involved in the stealing of artifacts, there is no reason why a treasure like the gold wouldn't tempt them to get involved. It's true that Ana's profession is journalism, but that doesn't mean that she's incapable of pursuing other more lucrative work—like playing the part of a facilitator."

"I maintain that it's utter nonsense."

"I could have kept this from you, so don't kill the messenger. It wasn't my decision. Once we involved Interpol it was basically their show. Olivia's safety is worth any price."

"I'm so glad you're out of that whole thing—or *were* out. My God! All those years of worrying about you when you went out with them on this or that hunt for insured valuables and the crooks that stole them. When you have a husband who carries a gun, you never relax."

Hugh knew it was time to cut it short. He got up from his chair and put his arms around his wife. "Well, my dear, all that worry seems to have had absolutely no effect on your beauty."

Paris tried to stifle a smile, but Hugh knew her every expression and that for the moment he had appeased her. He felt it was safe to return to the subject at hand and said, "When will the necessary forms be completed and faxed to the airline so they will release the exhibit to the 'armored cars' we're providing?"

She knew he was referring to the need for Interpol and Scotland Yard to have the information immediately. Flawless coordination between the two would be necessary in order to intercept the transfer of the exhibit and arrest those involved. Hugh had been told that as a fail-safe measure crates identical to those used by the Spanish museum would be used. They would have approximately the same weight and would be given over to the criminals for loading onto the truck. One of the crates would contain enough gold to support a solid robbery indictment, not just attempted robbery. An additional indictment for conspiracy could be possible.

"Now that I know what name will be on the trucks, I just have to fill it in on the forms. It would be best to email a copy to the appropriate person now and tell them that I will be faxing a copy as well. I need to fax a copy to either Interpol or the Yard, right?"

"I'd send it to both. I have their fax numbers in my phone." He took it out of his pocket and began scrolling for the information then reading out the numbers while Paris jotted them down.

She stopped writing and looked up at Hugh. "Once we send this information it's out of our hands. Olivia and Valerie's safety will be in these men's hands. If the whole group isn't involved in the actual robbery, whoever is waiting—the leader maybe— will know something's wrong when he can't reach them. Who knows what he'll do then. Worst-case scenario he'll make a call to wherever they're being kept in Spain. I can't bear to think of what could happen then."

"I know what you're thinking because I've been worried about that too," Hugh said. They looked at each other and Paris' eyes misted over. "Let's not borrow trouble. Remember, Ben and Ana are in Pamplona by now. Our son is resourceful, and regardless of the information on Ana, I think she's on Ben's side. In my profession you learn to read people pretty well. I've been exposed to plenty of tricky people. They have certain mannerisms in common."

"With me it's a gut feeling. I hope it can be trusted."

Hugh stood up and leaned over, putting his hands on her desk and looking squarely into her eyes. "Send the emails then send the faxes. Let's get this show on the road."

Within ten minutes it was done. Paris had done her part as instructed by the kidnapper and also as required by law enforcement. Hugh was sure he would hear from his contacts within an hour. They would confirm that everything was in place. Within thirty-six hours it would be over. Then there was the matter of rescuing their daughter and Ben's ex-wife.

Neither would be content to sit back and wait for news. Hugh pulled Paris up from her chair and held her firmly by the shoulders. She was somewhat startled but said nothing. Their eyes met and he said, "We're going to Spain." Paris recognized that resolute expression. She had seen it many times.

* * *

In spite of the stressful situation in which Ben and Ana found themselves, the landscape between San Sebastian and Pamplona served to provide at least a bit of distraction. The motorway eased through the northern boundary of the Pyrenees, where craggy peaks began to soften into rolling green hills and more pastureland. The sun was no longer overhead and had begun its descent into the western sky, yet the heat of the day remained constant. Without air conditioning the only thing to do was to keep the windows down and allow the warm wind to circulate inside the car. Ben had turned on the radio to help pass the time, but after a while Ana suggested they turn it off, that the lively music was making her more nervous.

"Sure, turn it off, but I can't talk about what we could be dealing with. It would distract me too much from my driving."

"Let's not do that. We need to arrive in one piece. I don't want to talk about it either. It's on our minds, regardless." Ben glanced aside and could see that Ana was pondering something. She broke into a smile and said, "You're a writer. Tell me a story. Can you do that and drive too?" She waited for him to answer, but he just smiled and shook his head no. "Well then, tell me more about your family—off the record. Everything is off the record for now. Amazing how a little interview can escalate into a life-changing situation.

"You've got that right. I suppose we'll have to start over with all that, once this whole situation is resolved—if it's still relevant. The whole idea has lost its shine for me. Of course I was never really keen." He paused then added, "But I do like one life-changing thing that happened."

He quickly glanced at Ana, grinned and winked. She knew what he was referring to and felt a slight flush of embarrassment. Then she quickly returned to the subject of the interview. "It would sure take a different turn at this point. I can see it becoming more of a news story than an interview. Whatever it wants to be, it's the least of our concerns." Ana tossed her hair and continued in a self-mocking tone. "And who knows if I'll even have a job after this. I'm not sure I even care."

"Whoa ... I've told you enough times. I don't want to be responsible for losing you a job."

"You didn't hold a gun to my head!" Ben glanced toward her and furrowed his brow. She quickly added, "Sorry. Bad analogy, considering." Fearing that she might put her foot in her mouth again, Ana changed the subject. "For now let's just try to pass the time as pleasantly as possible." She looked down at the map on her phone and added, "We have about another half hour travel time to Pamplona."

Ana's anxiety had not benefited from the absence of noise, so she fidgeted with the radio, trying without success to locate an English station. Finally Ben told her to either pick a station or turn it off. She apologized and did the latter. The traffic had become congested and the city was in full view. He suggested she get out her phone and enter the hotel address into Google maps. Ana navigated their route into and through the city with only a couple of minor errors. It had taken another half hour before they pulled up in front of the hotel on the *Plaza del Castillo*. Two young men in hotel uniforms quickly approached the car, opening the doors on each side and asking in accented English how they could be of service. Ben asked one to park and lock the car, while Ana asked the other to remove the luggage and take it to the registration desk.

The lobby and main salon were tastefully designed, with an eclectic assortment of art on the walls, comfortably appointed seating areas and an upright piano in one corner. When Ben gave his name to the reception clerk it was obvious by the woman's demeanor and solicitous tone that she had been privy to the special nature of the arrangements. Using his connection with Interpol, Hugh had been able to book two adjoining rooms during the city's busiest two weeks of the year. Ana wondered if someone had been displaced as a result. Formalities concluded, they followed the bellman to their respective rooms.

Ana stood just inside and studied her new surroundings. Sunlight flooded the room, softened by sheer drapes on the windows along the opposite wall. The large bed was covered with comforter and shams of creamy white *Matelassé*. In one corner a small sofa and two chairs were arranged around a glass table that held a color explosion of fresh flowers. She had been in the room less than two minutes when Ben knocked on the common door. She unlocked it and told him to come through.

He looked around the room and said, "I think your room's bigger than mine... but I think my bed is bigger than yours. I'll have to try them both out." He then gave her one of those smiles that she could feel wash through her like a wave.

Ana was a bit confused by his remark, no doubt an effort to lighten the mood, but decided to ignore it. There were other priorities, confirmed by his expression, which had quickly turned serious. The fact that he had undertaken to rescue his sister was once again weighing on him. A moment's suggestive teasing—if that's what it was— couldn't allay his concerns. They were extremely tired from the pressure and hurried nature of the trip. She reasoned that since the afternoon was half gone, there was no point in doing anything but having a meal and getting some rest. When she presented the idea to Ben he resisted, feeling that there wasn't a moment to lose.

"Ben, your father will contact you when the time is set for the fake delivery and interception by the police. Until then these criminals will still think they're in charge. If Olivia and Valerie are all right at this moment, don't you think they'll be all right at least until morning?"

"I don't trust any assumptions we might make. There are so many things that can go wrong with the timing of this thing." He walked to the window, pulled aside the curtain, and stared out at the plaza below. "Who knows how terrible the conditions are for them." He paused for a moment then turned back to face her. "I think I should call my father— tell him that we've arrived and are at the hotel."

"That's a good idea. Maybe he can update you on the timing—whether the plan is in place." Ben went to his room and retrieved his phone. While he was dialing, Ana said, "Please give your parents my best. Tell them I'm going to keep a close eye on you. I know your mother is worried about you being here."

Hugh answered immediately and the two spoke for several minutes, although Hugh did most of the talking. Ben promised to check in often and ended the call by sending Ana's reassurances to his mother. He told Ana that everything seemed to be in place and that the time of the robbery attempt would coincide with the manifest sent to the airlines and the arrival of the plane. Ben seemed less agitated after speaking with his father. He flopped down on Ana's bed and blew out a long breath.

Ana approached the bed and looked down at him. "So what did you learn? You seem relieved—or more likely, exhausted."

"I am tired, but there's definitely no feeling of relief. I'm just glad to know the arrangements are made." He sat up, swung around to a sitting position and began to rub his tired eyes. In a disgusted tone he added, "What a bunch of 'tossers'... those crooks. Did they really think my Mum would sit back and do nothing?"

"I'd be worried they'd get wind of the fact that she's involved your Dad and the law."

"They've been extremely careful, and it's helped that whoever these men are, they seem to be pretty stupid."

"Well then, what are you going to do? Most of the afternoon is gone. What could you possibly do before morning?"

She waited for a response, but Ben hesitated before he answered, "Something. Anything. I can't just lie here and watch Spanish television." His tone was rather harsh, but she knew it wasn't directed at her. He leaned backward, propping himself on his elbows, fixing his eyes on Ana. "I'll tell you what I can do before morning. I'm going to the nearest police station—now!"

Ana heaved an exaggerated sigh and began to shake her head. "I understand what you feel you have to do, but I don't think you'll get the response you want from some desk sergeant. What do we know about how law enforcement works in Pamplona?" She realized immediately that it was a question with no answer.

Ben got up from the bed and hurried toward the door that adjoined their rooms. He turned and said, "One way to find out."

In a moment he returned with wallet and sunglasses in hand. Ana knew she couldn't change his mind, so she quickly looked around for her bag, hoping more than assuming he would want her to come along.

Ben gently took hold of her arm and shook his head no. "A police station is no place for you. I can't predict how they'll react to my request—or should I say *demand*— for help. A woman tagging along could damage my credibility. I don't think the average Spanish male is quite as forward thinking about the fairer sex as the English or Americans."

"First of all, don't *demand*. You've heard the 'trap more flies with honey' saying, haven't you?"

Ben smirked, but he knew she was right. A foreigner doesn't stomp into a police station and make demands. He vowed to control his temper. Yet he needed a way to keep Ana from taking part. The fact was that he had a valid reason for her to stay at the hotel: his parents. If neither of them could be reached by phone, his mother would be especially undone. Ben explained that his father would likely be calling to check on them, and since he had all but ordered his son to do nothing yet, someone had to answer and reassure him.

"So, you want me to lie to your parents?" She crossed her arms and assumed the stubborn stance that had become familiar to him.

His response was simple and immediate. "Yes," he said, then stared at her stone face, waiting for the next expression of outrage. But she surprised him.

"Okay, but it's on you to smooth things over when all is resolved. I don't think they've totally made up their minds about me yet. This could tip the scales in the wrong direction."

"Promise. I'll say I twisted your arm—not physically, but verbally."

Ana sounded very emphatic as she replied, "I suppose that if you promise only to talk to them and definitely not go out on your own—for *any* reason—I'll stay here and do your bidding. And don't forget to get your passport from the concierge."

Ben shrugged his shoulders and held out his hands in supplication. "What could I possibly do? On my own I'd have no idea where to start."

The expression on Ana's face told Ben he had asked the right question. Yet if given the slightest opportunity to take action, he wouldn't hesitate to ignore his promise. Hopefully that decision would be something else he could smooth over. Even though he was unsure as to how it would be received, he needed a kiss from Ana to send him on his way. He was apprehensive about what was going on back in the UK and about how the outcome could affect the women. The obstacles before him seemed insurmountable, but he had to do something. If the police balked at getting involved, he would just have to think of another way. These thoughts flashed through his mind as he approached Ana and put his arms around her.

"A kiss for luck?" he asked.

"Two kisses," she said. "One for luck and one for using good sense."

Leaving Ana's presence had become more and more difficult as their days together passed. He would take comfort in the fact that she wouldn't be directly involved in anything to come. Ben smiled as she stood on tiptoes to reach his lips. Two sweet kisses later they embraced, and then he was out the door. Riding down in the elevator he decided to ask the concierge about the location of the nearest municipal police station. Coming out of the elevator he looked around the lobby for a staff member. He spotted the concierge seated behind an ornate desk, talking on the phone. The young woman ended the call when she saw Ben approaching and flashed an alluring smile as she rose to extend her hand.

"How can I be of service?" she asked in a lilting Spanish accent, taking Ben's hand for what seemed to him a little longer than necessary.

"I need to find out where the closest police station is located."

"Have you had a problem? Has something happened?" she asked, her expression changing from coy to apprehensive.

"No, no." Ben had to think fast—give her a reason why he would be headed to a police station. He said the first thing that came to mind. "I'm a writer. Part of the reason I'm here in Pamplona is to do some research for my current book. It's a crime story and centers in northern Spain."

The young woman became excitable and asked what books he had written, were they available translated to Spanish, and what was his name again? He politely told her that he didn't have time to talk, but that if she would leave her name at the desk he would try to remember to send her a copy of his latest book when he returned home. This more than satisfied her, enabling him to steer the conversation back to the question at hand. Fortunately there was a station, a *Comisaria,* right in the plaza where the hotel was located. She walked outside with him and pointed across to its location. He thanked her and began walking briskly toward the building.

CHAPTER SEVENTEEN

In a few hours the sun would set on another day of Annunciata Domingo's rigid and exhausting life. She left the tall building through the employee entrance and started down the sidewalk to her bus stop. People seemed to race past her, her own pace being much slower than it had been early that morning. This was the only job that brought her to an affluent part of town. Two bus transfers were necessary to bring her close to the building where she cleaned a fancy apartment every week. She had never seen the people who lived there, but referred to them as *los ricos*, the rich ones. The man at the security desk would give her the key, and it usually seemed as though no one had set foot inside from week to week. There was little to do and she had finished in time to have part of the afternoon to herself. The agency had found her that job, but she found others on her own—as many as possible—regardless of how distasteful by comparison.

She reached the bus bench and sat down to wait. Usually she enjoyed the waiting. It was her small break before arriving home to different yet still tiring demands. But for at least two weeks every year the bustle of the city center teemed with crowds and extra noise. The constant movement of vehicles, citizens and tourists blurred her vision. She closed her eyes and tried to quiet the thoughts that had plagued her since she cleaned the derelict house and found the bag. The hard-faced man had given her a bad feeling from the first time she laid eyes on him. But who was she to turn down work? Annunciata was still frightened by what she had seen. Yet she was more frightened about what might have happened if she had been discovered nosing through his things. Suspicious things.

The screeching tires and blaring horns of a near miss between two cars startled her. She opened her eyes and focused ahead on the Plaza del Castillo across the street from where she was sitting. Suddenly, and for the first time in years, she decided not to go straight home. She got up, held her purse tightly and walked to the corner. She waited for the green light, crossed quickly then slowed her steps as she entered the beautiful plaza. The street noise seemed to fade as she walked toward the long benches, colorful flowers and patches of green grass. A breeze, not more than a whisper, rustled the leaves of a nearby tree that cast a bit of shade on the bench she had chosen for her task. She realized that she must pray. Faith would bring the answer to her dilemma of conscience.

She folded her hands in supplication and sat quietly, again with eyes closed, her face turned skyward. What had been a soft breeze grew into gusts of warm wind that gently interrupted her meditative state. Calmness washed over her as she stood to leave. There was a newly found confidence to do what she knew was right. She called her children from the public phone at the edge of the plaza, telling them she would be late and not to worry. Annunciata was now free to take action.

Noticing the *Comisaria* just across the plaza from where she stood, she took it as a sign and managed to muster enough energy for a fast walk to the entrance. She approached the reception desk rather meekly and waited for the young officer on duty to finish speaking with a woman who was wiping away tears. In a few moments the woman turned, pulled her sweater tightly around her, and walked to the waiting area.

Annunciata was flushed with adrenaline when it was her turn to speak. The officer was respectful and patient, listening to her search for the right words. Giving more information than was necessary—from the man's offer of a job to the terrible condition of the house—she finally came around to the subject of the closet and what she had seen in the duffle bag. After scolding her for having snooped into the man's belongings, the officer told her that having such things did not break any laws and there was nothing the police could do. Refusing to be placated she pointed out the presence of the two old mattresses, the window that was nailed shut, and her strong 'feeling' that something sinister was going to happen or had already happened in that house. Annunciata admitted to him she felt guilty for having waited so long to come forward, but that she had been frightened of the man. The officer wanted to know why the man frightened her. Had she been threatened? She told him she had not been threatened, but his demeanor was threatening. She described him: the shaved tattooed head, the bulkiness of his frame, the mean eyes. And as she finished, her body shuddered at the memory of her encounter with him.

The officer turned away from her to answer the phone, but she remained standing at the counter with a dejected look on her face. She was not satisfied with how the information she had offered was being handled and was quite sure it was because she was a woman. She believed some men still felt that women were prone to flights of fancy, being overly emotional, and seeing boogie men where there were none. Yet she was a sensible woman, independent, and remained adamant about the danger she perceived.

As he hung up the phone the officer saw that Annunciata was still standing at the counter. He could see that she would not be easily dissuaded. Perhaps if he would let her sit down and talk to one of the other officers at his desk, she could be appeased. When he began to walk toward where she was standing, she was staring at him. He proposed the offer for her to talk to another officer, but when he looked through the glass partition into the squad room he could see that all the men were busy either with other people or paperwork. Just as he was asking her if she would be willing to wait, a man came bursting through the main doors and all but flew toward the desk. The man stopped there, leaned forward with both hands on the wooden edge and began to speak.

"*Por favor… ¿Alguien hable inglés?*" Ben asked, sounding breathless.

"Si, yo hablo un poco— pero no muy bien," the officer answered.

"I don't care. A little is better than nothing."

"¿Cuál es el problema, señor?" He paused before trying his English. "The problem?"

"My sister and a friend have been kidnapped. We have every reason to believe that they're being held here in Pamplona." He paused, waiting for a response that didn't come then continued. "We know they boarded the flight from London, but after they landed at the *Hondarribia* airport, there was no trace of them."

"Que?No entiendo," the officer said, shaking his head in frustration.

"Oh great," Ben said under his breath. "Okay… let me try to make you understand." He paused while summoning a few words from memory that he hoped would get his message across simply. *"Mi hermana y un amiga …"* The officer nodded that he understood, and then with his brain spinning, Ben fumbled for the most important word. Suddenly he spit it out. *"Secuestrados!"*

Ben stared at the officer and waited for a response. The young man's expression was blank and vacant. Clearly he had no idea what to do with a tourist making far-fetched accusations of kidnapping. Ben broke the uncomfortable silence. "Let me speak to your superior … *el Jefe … pronto por favor!"*

Annunciata had backed away from the counter, but easily heard the exchange. Under her breath she repeated, *"¿Secuestrados?"*

The officer became flustered and self-consciously ran the fingers of one hand through his thick dark hair. He inhaled and exhaled deeply, turning slightly to pick up an intercom handset. Ben assumed he was calling for backup—someone better than he was at placating tourists— and he maintained his stance, leaning on the counter, seeming ready to spring into action, yet having no idea as to what kind of action to take. Annunciata inched closer to Ben. She had understood enough of what he had said in Spanish to know why he needed help, and she could see—almost feel—his desperation. The English language was foreign to her but she knew that somehow, she must communicate with him. She believed that her prayers had brought her to this place, at this particular time, and she found herself drawn to the distressed man beside her.

Through the glass partition separating the squad room from the public area, both she and Ben could see the animated conversation between the young man and an officer of higher rank who had come out of a separate office. Eventually the officer, dressed in plain clothes, went back into the office, took his jacket from the back of the desk chair and put it on. He walked toward the door of the squad room, the young man following close behind. Ben backed away from the counter and stood straight, his body stiffened by how badly he needed to be taken seriously and get his message across.

The superior officer came through to the public area and approached Ben. The man was tall and slender, with a classic Spanish profile and abundant wavy hair streaked with gray. In heavily accented English he said, "*Señor,* I am Gonzalo Macias, *Inspektorea* Macias. I understand that you have some concerns about relatives who are visiting Pamplona?"

Ben thanked the Inspector for his assistance and proceeded to explain what little he knew about the situation with his sister and ex-wife. He tried to explain the significance of the email they had received about the women's location and insisted that law enforcement should become involved. Ben knew very little about the specifics of the collaboration between Scotland Yard and Interpol with regard to apprehending the thieves 'in the act.' And besides, he wasn't free to speak about any of it. All he could safely reveal was that they were kidnapped as a way to facilitate someone's help with a robbery in England, and that an attempt had also been made to abduct him in London.

Annunciata listened carefully, although she didn't understand what was being said and was limited to observing body language. She recognized the hand gestures made by Inspector Macias in an effort to make Ben to speak more slowly, although he continued to use adamant hand gestures of his own in trying to make himself understood. Finally the words stopped, and both men were quiet. The Inspector was the first to speak.

"*Señor,* I see that you are much distressed." He paused and looked squarely at Ben, who heaved a sigh then waited for what he hoped would be a positive result to his plea. The Inspector continued, his tone apologetic. "These ideas you have are vague. Pamplona is not a small town. How could we possibly search for two women who are ... *oculto* ... how do you say?" He thought for a moment then said, "They are *hidden*—hidden in a city that is overrun with tourists, pickpockets and other opportunists."

"Your English is very good, but my Spanish is not," Ben replied, "And I understand that this is law enforcement's busiest time of year, but the safety of guests in your city must be a priority. The women arrived here as tourists, excited at the prospect of taking part in the festival. They disappeared from the airport—never checked in at their hotel. Surely this is cause for you to be concerned as well."

Inspector Macias answered in a tone both polite and somewhat brusque. "Our concern doesn't mean that we can be of help to you." Ben looked at the floor and shook his head in frustration. The Inspector continued, "There is nothing to go on—not a clue. You would have to bring me *something* ... somewhere to start."

"Your detectives – sorry, I mean your deputy inspectors—could start at the airport, see if anyone remembers them, or saw them get into a vehicle. Maybe someone in the terminal saw the women being met by someone. They are both beautiful women. People notice beautiful women."

"That is true, but every *Comisaria* in the city is stretched to the limit due to the festival. Every year we are forced to enlist the help of the *Guardia Civil.* I'm sorry, *Señor,* I can't spare the manpower. Perhaps you could enlist the help of the *policía* in *San Sebastián.* They are closer to the airport. Perhaps an officer could accompany you to make inquiries there."

Ben shook his head no and said, "There isn't time for that. Their lives are in danger right now!" He waited, hoping the Inspector would reconsider, but the man just stood before him with his arms folded across his chest. Ben was just as impatient as the Inspector, but wouldn't give up. "I can't tell you how, but I know they're in the city. Remember the email confirming that?"

"Do you have a copy of this email?" Ben's shook his head no. He stepped sideways to lean against the counter, no doubt finding that the whole exchange was going nowhere. "You have no way of knowing if it was legitimate information. I have had experience with investigations where very creative efforts were made to … how do you say? … 'Throw us off the scent.'"

Ben continued to be unflappable. "But it's all I have, and something has to be done—now!"

"I would urge you to be careful. You are in a strange city, which is, unfortunately, overrun with people of all types. You could easily get yourself into trouble." Ben shifted from one foot to the other, impatient to take some kind of action yet reluctant to offend Inspector Macias by cutting short what he was trying to say. The Inspector sensed this and brought his comments to a close. "As I said, there's nothing I can do for you at this time, with what little information you have to offer. If you learn more, if you get specific information, return to the *Comisaria* and have me paged. If that happens, I will do my best to sort this out." He paused then added, "And if you come upon some immediate information about the women—something dangerous—you can always dial our emergency number—zero nine two."

Ben realized that there was no point in continuing to pursue police assistance. He thanked the Inspector, who excused himself and returned to the area behind the glass partition. Ben watched him go into his office and shut the door. Feeling tired and discouraged, he sat down in one of the chairs that lined one wall. Elbows on knees, he put his head in his hands and was still. After a minute or so he raised his head, rubbed his eyes, ran his fingers through his hair, then slumped down in the seat. With his eyes covered he hadn't seen Annunciata walk over and sit down beside him. He glanced sideways and saw her, wondering why she was looking at him. The first thing he noticed was that the woman's eyes were kind, but also that her face showed fatigue.

She inched forward in the chair, put her belongings on the floor between her feet, then folded her hands in her lap and began to speak. *"Señor, no hablo Ingles, pero he oído que hablan español. ¿Sé que el miedo a dos mujeres?*

Ben understood that she had overheard him speaking Spanish to the young officer and also knew what he had said. He couldn't imagine why she was questioning him. After all, what could she know? He decided to indulge her. There was something in her expression—the haunted look in her eyes. It moved him. Knowing the limitations of his ability to speak the language, he figured he wouldn't understand much.

"No hablo bien, Señora, pero voy a tratar de entender," he said, hesitating between words, and hoping she understood that he would try to understand what she would say. It had been a long time since he tried to use what he learned in school.

The duty officer had been watching them and came out from behind the desk to ask if the woman was bothering the Englishman. Ben told him no, that they were trying to communicate, although it was said with hand gestures. Doing the best he could, Ben recalled enough words to ask if there was an officer who could translate for them. The young man looked into the squad room and saw the required person. He went to the doorway and called to the uniformed man, who acknowledged him then came out to see what was going on. An explanation was made regarding what was needed. The officer buttoned his uniform, adjusted his tie and approached Ben. Like the Inspector, he spoke with an accent that gave his use of English a pleasing cadence.

"I understand that you require a translator—that you wish to speak with this woman?" He gestured toward Annunciata, who looked self-conscious. This kind of attention was foreign and made her uncomfortable.

"Yes, thank you," Ben said. "I speak a little Spanish, but not enough for a conversation."

The officer turned to Annunciata and asked what it was she needed to tell the man. She repeated the story as she had told it to the young desk officer, pausing now and then to wait for the translation to be made. Ben listened with intense concentration and a wrinkled brow. Soon he was aware of everything she had experienced and seen in the house. She described the man who had hired her—the bald tattooed head, the evil she saw in his eyes, his brusque manner—then all but pleaded with the officer to take her seriously. When Ben heard the translation describing the man, he knew immediately that it was likely the same man who had attacked him twice in London. He told the officer about his encounters with the man, and at last feeling he was getting somewhere, he asked to have the Inspector paged. While they waited he asked the officer to tell Annunciata why he needed the help of the police, about his sister, Olivia, and about Valerie.

When he finished, she shook her head in disbelief and said, *"Aye … las mujeres pobres."*

"Si," Ben said, agreeing that the two were indeed 'poor women.' He took Annunciata's hand, looked at her squarely and said, *"Muchas gracias, señora. ¿Por favor, cuál es su nombre?"*

"Annunciata. Annunciata Domingo, señor. ¿Hice lo que me dijo?"

He told her that yes, what she had said helped more than she could know, and that perhaps now, with this new information, the Inspector would help him. She smiled and nodded, knowing that she had done the right thing. Gonzalo Macias came striding out of his office, his expression one of impatience. Clearly he wished the pair would be on their way, but he was mandated to treat tourists with respect and cooperation. He faced them and explained that the officer who translated had told him all of what had been said. He reasoned that even though the man described seemed to be the same one each had encountered, there was, alas, no proof and still nothing to go on. He took the time to explain the same in Spanish.

Annunciata stood and faced him, asserting herself and pointing out the coincidence regarding the house. Macias explained again that it wasn't against the law either to rent a house or hire someone to clean it. And within that house a person could keep whatever he wished, within the law. He pointed out that rope, tape and handcuffs were legal possessions. He found no significance in the presence of old mattresses. She sighed, slumped her shoulders then turned to Ben, who had understood much of what she had been told. The Inspector repeated his admonitions and his offer to help if something definite developed. He then returned quickly to his office and shut the door.

It had been over an hour since Ben had arrived at the *Comisaria,* and the woman had been there longer. They sat together for a short time, Ben mulling over in his mind what his next step would be. He was on his own. This he knew. Ana would be wondering where he was and what he was doing. She would worry if she didn't hear from him. Yet he knew she would balk at what he planned to do next. Actually talking to her face to face would be his undoing. He couldn't mislead her and wracked his brain for a way to handle it. Annunciata sat beside him, tapping her foot impatiently and glancing in his direction every few minutes. She finally spoke up.

"*¿Señor, qué va a hacer usted?*

She had asked Ben what he intended to do, and he wasn't sure how to accomplish telling her. In his halting version of Spanish he managed to ask her to come with him to the hotel lobby. He knew that once there, the concierge would translate for them. While there he would ask the woman to give Ana a message—to say he was in a great hurry, not to worry, and he would call her soon. Annunciata nodded that yes, she would accompany him, but she looked confused. He reached down and took her belongings then helped her up. She willingly followed him out of the *Comisaria,* the duty officer tracking them with his eyes all the way to the exit.

They crossed the plaza and entered the hotel. Ben waved to the young concierge, who eagerly left her desk to attend to the handsome guest. She also hoped to satisfy her curiosity about the shabby woman beside him. He explained that he needed help communicating and would she translate. She agreed, and Ben explained to Annunciata that he would like her to come with him in his car and show him the location of the derelict house. She answered that she would help in any way possible, but that she would have to see a map of the city to find the street and work out the best route. She had lived in Pamplona all her life, but the nicer residential neighborhoods remained foreign to her.

Outside the hotel's main entrance, the attendants waited beside the lock box that held keys to the guests' cars. Ben asked for his rental car and within five minutes an attendant pulled the car up in front of them. He left the engine running and came around to open the door for Annunciata. Ben motioned her to get in. This type of attention was also foreign to her, but she did as she was asked. Ben slid into the driver's seat and gestured that she should buckle up. He turned toward her and smiled, all the while thinking it was going to be very difficult to understand her directions. He asked her for the address then entered it into the car's GPS. He had expected a long drive in traffic across the city to some remote neighborhood, but he was wrong. The address seemed to be less than two miles from the hotel.

After several wrong turns in spite of the GPS, he found the street. She became agitated, but confirmed the location of the house, a little more than half way down. Ben slowed the car and proceeded down the street. The houses were large, and most were partially hidden behind stucco walls with tall iron gates that discouraged entry. The neighborhood had seen better days. Cracked stucco and fading paint told the story, as did the wild overgrowth of gardens, barely visible through the ironwork.

Suddenly Annunciata pointed ahead and to the left. *"Ahí está la casa! A la izquierda!"*

"¿Esa pequeña casa?" Ben asked. She nodded confirming that to the left was the little house. He pulled to the curb, just shy of the property line. It sat back from the sidewalk, square in the middle of a rather large and neglected lot. It seemed very out of place on what had surely been an affluent street. He wondered if at one time it had housed servants, or maybe a groundskeeper. But that wasn't important. Only what he might find was of any concern.

They sat in the car, saying little. Ben kept his eyes on the house, looking for any sign of life. After about thirty minutes Annunciata managed to explain that she had to get home to her children. He apologized for taking so much of her time and reluctantly started the engine. Once back at the hotel he had a taxi summoned for her. She balked at the idea, knowing she couldn't afford the fare. He told her not to worry and handed the driver more than enough for the fare and a generous tip.

She saw what he had done and said, *"Usted es muy amable, señor Ben."*

Ben smiled and said, *"Es a ustedes... muy amables,"* that she was the kind one, and the only one who had been interested in helping him. Her expression told him that his Spanish needed work. He asked the driver to wait a moment, and while ushering Annunciata into the back seat, he asked for her contact information. He was surprised to see that she had a business card. She hesitated then pulled a pen out of her bag and wrote something on the back. She asked the driver to translate and said that in case he forgot, she had written the address of the house on the card and would he please let her know what happened. He nodded yes and she got into the taxi. Her last words were that she would pray for his sister and her friend. He thanked her, shut the door and waved as they pulled away.

It seemed as though it had been half a day since he first entered the *Comisaria,* but in truth it had only been about three hours. He missed Ana and knew that he had probably caused her worry of some kind. There was nothing for it but to deal with the situation. He hoped that there would be an update from his father. In the elevator he decided to return to the little house early the next morning. He would sit in his car and wait again, hoping to see someone coming in or out that would look either suspicious or clearly innocent. He had no time to waste on useless leads. Yet in his gut he felt the cleaning woman was onto something.

Ana heard his key in the lock and jumped up from the chair where she had been reading something on her tablet. When Ben came through the doorway she threw her arms around his neck and looked at him, trying to read his mood. As her relief subsided she backed away a few steps, folded her arms and glared at him.

"You *do* know how long I've been waiting, don't you?" She waited for a response, but there was nothing from Ben, who seemed not to know where to start. "Where have you been?" Her tone was more questioning than accusatory.

Ben reached for her hand and led her to the small sofa, where he sat down before beginning to speak. "First, I went to the police station across the plaza. No one was of much help until a woman who was listening to me spoke up about why she was there. She heard me trying to get things across to the officers." He waited a moment for Ana to take in what he had said, then continued. "She had seen something very suspicious at one of her jobs—a filthy old house she was hired to clean. She doesn't speak a word of English, so it wasn't easy. I got one of the officers to translate. She described the man who had hired her—said his demeanor was threatening—that to her he looked 'evil.' He sounds just like the guy who attacked me twice in London—has to be—the shaved tattooed head, brawny build." Clearly agitated, Ben got up and began to pace.

"That's a coincidence worthy of consideration—too much of a coincidence!" Ana said, motioning him to go on.

"It's what she found while cleaning the place that was the 'capper.' There was a duffle in the closet that contained handcuffs, chains, and some sort of tape." Ana's jaw dropped. "She offered to show me where the house is located. She had the address, but didn't really know how to get there from here. I came back to the hotel to get the rental car. I didn't have time to come up and tell you what was going on. Sorry about that, but I didn't want to lose her help, and she had a family to get home to."

Ana said that she understood, but her emotional side was at odds with what she knew was logical. She had to fight the hurt feelings that resulted from being excluded and spending the day waiting by the phone. But he was here now, and she was relieved. Ben told her the rest of the story—how he went to the address and watched the house for a while, but intended to go back early the next day. She told him adamantly that she was going with him. He knew there was no point in arguing with her after the day she'd had. He also knew there would be fallout when she came through to his room in the morning and found him gone. He intended to be up and out before dawn and parked near the little house, watching.

The feeling of Ana's body against his back interrupted his train of thought. She wrapped her arms around his waist and held him close. This small intimacy rekindled the feeling of deprivation he had been fighting since their encounter in the field. He gently moved her arms away from his body and turned to face her. She didn't say a word, just looked up, stood on her tiptoes and planted a soft kiss on each bristly cheek. With a weary sigh he pulled her closer, wrapped her in his arms and kissed her, once softly then again with an open hungry mouth. They seemed to suspend breathing while one kiss flowed into the next. Ben was unaware that he was backing Ana toward the bed. When her legs touched the edge, she dropped to a sitting position and fell back, her heart beginning to pound in her chest as she focused on Ben standing over her.

He looked down with eyes that seemed to ask if this was the moment, if more was going to happen between them again—right now—finally. Ana read his expression, and although she wanted nothing more than to make love to him, she said, almost pleading, "Oh Ben, not like this." Most likely it wasn't Ben's desire she was trying to control. It was her own.

He backed away and ran his fingers through his hair self-consciously. She wanted to reassure him. "I want what you want, but it feels selfish and won't make the right kind of memory."

Ben shook his head in frustration and said, "I know. I know. This is like being in a special kind of jail—convicted for lust."

She smiled and made a face that put down his sense of humor on the subject. She reached out her arms and he pulled her up into another embrace. With her face against his chest she said, "We're both tired. But in spite of that, after what just started I know we need to be in separate beds tonight—with a door between us."

"God, I don't know what I was thinking. Olivia and Valerie are in trouble, and here I am fighting a strong urge to take you to bed."

"We're both looking for an escape—a distraction from the anxiety." She paused then drew him to her gaze. "And we both have tension to release."

The desire in Ben's expression burned through her as he said, "You have no idea."

He held her tightly, pressing his face against her neck, inhaling her scent before slowly tracing his lips upward to her eager mouth. When the kiss ended they abruptly pulled away from each other, struggling to let the moment go. Ben held her at arm's length and locked eyes with her. A palpable energy surrounded them as they fought for control. It was Ana who finally broke the spell. She gently kissed his cheek and said good night, but not before reminding him to wake her when he got up in the morning. She turned away and went through to her room, closing the adjoining door. He listened for the lock to be turned, but heard nothing. At this point he was more tired than hungry for sex, and the fatigue helped sublimate his desire. He shed his clothes, took a fast shower and slid into bed. After setting the alarm on his phone, he turned off the light and gave in to the stress of the day, the exhaustion that would shelter him from worry about what was to come.

The same scenario played out on the other side of the door. Ana fell into a deep sleep, visited by dreams of being in Ben's arms, sharing passion seemingly too real to be a dream. Yet an unseen force soon pulls him away from her. She senses danger but cannot move to help him, as he is drawn further and further out of reach. In the wee hours she lay awake, disturbed and fearful of sleep that could take her back to what could even be a premonition.

Ana knew that given a choice Ben would leave her behind when morning came. He didn't need the responsibility of her safety along with what he could be facing. She knew that without a gun he had no weapon other than his wits, strong emotions and adrenaline. Those intangibles wouldn't go far if faced down by a gun. Maybe she could help—somehow—and she had seen the address scribbled on the card given him by the cleaning woman. Hopefully it would still be on Ben's night table in the morning. She promised herself not to get in the way, just to hang back, wait, observe, and have the police number ready on her mobile phone. Once the decision was made to be a part of whatever lay ahead, Ana dosed, not realizing how soon dawn would come.

*　*　*

Ben was awake before the alarm on his watch had a chance to rouse him. He went to the window and looked out onto the plaza, his apprehension giving way to resolve. The sky at first light changed slowly from gray to a muted coral and promised a scorching day ahead. In the distance, toward the hills, a ridge of clouds roiled like tumbling balls of cotton, gathering strength in promise of a cooling afternoon rain. He turned back from the window and walked quietly to the bathroom. After quickly brushing his teeth he splashed water on his face, ignoring the stubble of two days without a shave. His clothes from the previous day lay strewn on the floor, so he just picked them up, eased into the jeans and rumpled shirt then plucked his jacket from the chair. He couldn't bring himself to leave without laying eyes on Ana one more time, so he approached the adjoining door, the memory of their kisses washing over him. With every swell of desire that had moved them, since that first time, they had stopped, reminding each other to look ahead to the time everything would be resolved, everyone safe. Why had they waited, he wondered? It had come to this: he was unsure it would ever happen again, unsure he would still be alive when the sun set on this day that could bring danger, sorrow or more frustration.

He carefully put his hand on the door handle and opened it without a sound. Fearful of waking her he didn't step through, only took a moment to study her. He remembered that first night in the hotel room, how he had watched her sleep— the soft and steady breath from her open mouth, the lusciousness of her lips, the tangles of dark hair falling across her face. It was time to leave, and his chest ached at the thought. The reality washed over him. He had fallen in love.

CHAPTER EIGHTEEN

Paris stared down at the two folded sweaters lying on the bed next to her open suitcase. She was distracted from packing by Hugh's voice in the background, carrying on a serious conversation with his contact at Interpol. At this point she didn't care about the success or failure of the robbery, only about the safety of her daughter, Ben and his ex-wife. Although she still resented Valerie for the hell she put Ben through when they were married, she would never wish the woman ill. Paris had no qualms about going to prison, if it should come to that. No sacrifice was too great for her children. She had to admit that continuing to ruminate on unknown outcomes was overdramatic. Hugh would surely chastise her for taking on the role of sacrificial lamb. It was common sense— he wouldn't put her at risk. Besides, Interpol and Scotland Yard knew everything already. Yet that fact worried her as well.

Hugh put down the receiver and approached her. "Everything is in place. The cargo plane lands in about two hours."

"When it lands we'll probably be in the air—headed for Spain. How will we know what's going on?" There was desperation in her tone. The waiting, worry and anxiety were becoming too much for her. Hugh was better at hiding it. Paris knew that about her husband, and it caused her even more worry.

"I'll check in right before we board. Then until we change planes in Madrid we won't know anything." Hugh could see her body tense and then go slack as she sighed in frustration. He made a last effort to put her at ease. "I'll check in while we're on our way to make the connecting flight, then again when we land at San Sebastián airport." He slipped his arms around her and said, "That's the best I can do."

Hugh's gentleness caused an emotional wave to wash over her, and her voice trembled. "Olivia's life was in my hands every day when she was small. Then little by little I had to let go—but never like this." Paris turned away from him and walked to the window. With tears welling in her eyes, she stared down at the garden that had given her such pleasure in every season. But at the moment, summer's bloom seemed gray and lifeless. "I don't know how to turn her life over to a team of strangers."

"We have no choice, darling girl." His voice remained tender, and that tenderness fully unleashed the tears Paris had been holding onto for days." She walked into his arms and began to sob, her body heaving with each tearful gasp.

He held her there, in the middle of the room, until she quieted down. He hoped that she had released enough anxiety to get her through the next few days. She took a few tissues from a box on the night table and said, "Let's get out of here. The trains are running again and if we get busy, we can make the six o'clock. That will get us to the airport in sufficient time."

"That's my girl," he said, giving her an affectionate squeeze.

They finished packing, zipped the small cases and headed for the car. Hugh drove faster than usual, screeching tires several times as he rounded curves on the country road that led to the station. Paris asked for several reassurances that he had indeed arranged with the hotel to have their room held no matter when they managed to arrive. Once on the train Hugh made a call that confirmed everything was organized and in motion. He leaned back and closed his eyes, hoping to quell some of his own anxiety. Relaxation wasn't in the cards. Every few minutes his wife would reach for his hand the hold it tightly for a minute or so. The train arrived at Paddington a bit early. They detrained and hurried to the center of the station to consider the options for Gatwick. After a short discussion Hugh concluded that in order to access the Gatwick express train at Victoria Station, a taxi would be better than taking the Tube. The commuter traffic would be building, but considering their weariness, stress level, and luggage to manage, a taxi was definitely the best choice. Within a few minutes they were on their way to the station.

* * *

Linus Finch zipped up his one-piece uniform that boasted the *Security First* company logo on the breast pocket. He had deigned to get a haircut and a shave and had reluctantly tossed aside the old wool jacket that was his trademark. He came out of the bedroom to find Fergus MacDonald struggling with his uniform's zipper, which refused to close over his ample belly.

"Suck it in, you bloody 'git,'" Linus growled. "We're in a time crunch. Where are your boys… with the trucks?"

"They'll be here, don't you worry." Fergus did as he was told and pulled in a deep breath, tugging the reluctant zipper up and over his girth. "There. Bob's your uncle!" he said, adjusting himself and smoothing back his wiry red hair.

Linus went to the window and checked the street. Dawn was at least an hour away and they hadn't slept—hadn't even tried. The instructions from their boss were to be ready and waiting to leave when they received confirmation of the plane's arrival time. The trucks and drivers had to be ready as well. Perfect timing was the key, so he was told. He looked at the charcoal pre-dawn sky and wondered how things were going in Spain with Lenny and his charges. He knew Lenny wouldn't hesitate to kill them all, if those were his orders. And should anything go wrong at the airport he had one imperative. He had to let the boss know—somehow. Then with one call from the boss to Lenny in Spain, the two women and Gareth Logan would be dead. He suspected that's how it was meant to be from the beginning.

Fergus was on the couch, head back, eyes closed, the fabric of his uniform straining across his body. He jumped when the buzzer sounded.

Someone downstairs wanted to be let in. Linus went to the intercom and found it was the drivers, who had parked the two trucks around the corner. They came noisily up the stairs and once inside were admonished for taking a chance on waking the other tenants. The first question out of his mouth was to ask which of the trucks was the decoy.

The two drivers looked at each other, and one answered, "Whichever one you want. You do know that neither of them is really armored, right?"

"Of course. I'm no idiot. Now shut up and sit down. We don't move until we get the call."

* * *

Lyle Brett sat at the kitchen table nervously tapping one foot and staring at his open laptop. He proceeded to hack into his work account, and from there, found links to the acquisition department and information on the events of that particular day. He clicked on 'new acquisitions' and found a file on the Spanish gold that was in transit from Spain to London for display at the museum. He had checked and rechecked the information. The departure time from Madrid and estimated arrival time at Heathrow's cargo terminal were part of the file, as was the hangar number where it would be offloaded.

"Well, Paris McKinnon, you've done a good job, " he said aloud, and then added a caveat. "But sorry madam, the plan has changed." He leaned back and smiled, his expression both devious and full of greed.

He picked up a pencil and looked at the lined tablet that sat beside his laptop. He had prepared a timetable and was checking it over one last time. The timetable accounted for traffic at that specific time of day, unknown holdups like roadwork—even school buses or the odd ambulance slowing things down. There would be the usual slow moving traffic after entering the airport proper, and other trucks would also be collecting cargo—perhaps from the same hangar. It was his nature to be precise and he liked being that way. One day in the employee lounge he had overheard a colleague refer to him as punctilious, yet he had taken it as a compliment. Now satisfied that he had chosen the appropriate time for the trucks to head for the airport, he got up and went to the kitchen. After starting the coffee maker he went through to the bedroom and got himself ready for the day—the first day of the rest of his life, so he imagined.

Lyle emerged in the black velour tracksuit—his idea of a disguise—then began to gather up any and all tangible information that could tie him to the coming event. He stuffed everything in a trash bag and set it by the door. He would dispose of the whole lot somewhere along the way, a good distance from his flat. All he kept back was the timetable, and a check of his watch showed that it was time to make the call.

He dialed Linus' mobile phone and he answered after the first ring. "Yeah, is this who I think it is?"

"Don't be a smart-ass. Just get things underway—now!"

"Where will you be? I thought you'd want to be there—make sure we don't fuck up."

"Don't you worry, I'll be around," Lyle said. "And you won't fuck up because you know the consequences. If you do, the police will be the least of your problems. The last thing you want is Lenny on your tail. He's devoid of loyalties." He paused slightly then chuckled. "But sometimes a sociopath can come in handy."

Linus failed to see the humor in that observation and said he had to get each driver into his truck. His last instructions were that he and Fergus each were to ride with one of the drivers. The conversation with Linus had triggered a flush of anxiety in Lyle. No longer in the mood for coffee, he switched off the pot then stuffed his phone in one pocket, his wallet in the other, and grabbed the trash bag as he left the flat. It was a short taxi ride to the parking garage where the unobtrusive little Prius he had rented was waiting. Before getting into the car he disposed of the trash bag in a nearby dumpster. Soon he was pulling out into the damp gray of a London dawn. Within a few minutes he received a call confirming that the trucks were underway.

* * *

The McKinnon's had boarded the plane for the first leg of the trip to Pamplona and were settling into their seats in first class when Hugh's mobile phone began to buzz. Paris sat forward in her seat and waited to hear at least one side of the conversation. He said little, mostly listened, and soon ended the call. He turned to her and said, "I'm glad they called before take off, since I have to put the phone in airplane mode."

"Well, why did he call?" she asked, moving to the edge of her seat and turning to face him. She seemed to be holding her breath.

"It was my contact at Interpol. He wanted to tell me that everything is in place—also that the plane is on time. They posted information on the museum website about the number and location of the hangar where the plane will be unloaded. Confirmation came that the crates have been prepared and will be the first things to offload."

Paris sat back, sighed and said, "So it's *show time*."

"They really do have this sort of thing down to a science. As long as the crooks don't get suspicious before they start to load the crates, we should be okay."

"Worst case scenario, they get spooked and someone calls Spain—or whomever." She covered her face with her hands and said, "Oh God!"

"Don't borrow trouble. We've done all we can. Did the best with what we had."

"I know, but the stakes are monumental. I still keep hoping I'll wake up and find I've only been having a nightmare."

"It is a nightmare, but we're not in it alone. Remember, Ben's already there. And as I said, he's intelligent and resourceful."

"He also may be putting himself at risk, depending on what he's found out. We haven't heard from him since yesterday. Last time I spoke with Ana she was still waiting for him to return." She began to shake her head back and forth in disbelief. "It's too much—it's just too much."

The pilot announced they would soon begin taxiing to the runway and were cleared for takeoff within ten minutes. The pair settled back and fastened their seatbelts. Hugh reached for Paris' hand and she leaned to the side, resting her head against his shoulder. Soon they felt the pull of the plane gaining speed, and then the moment of smoothness as the wheels retracted, confirming the plane was airborne.

* * *

It was barely light when Lenny's alarm sounded, and he rolled out of bed grumbling. Young revelers making the most of the festival atmosphere had robbed him of a decent rest. He had been forced to trust Gareth with controlling the women while he returned to his shabby room for the sleep he had needed but didn't get. Shaving was too much trouble. He splashed cold water on his face then rummaged through the few clothes he had packed. Soon he was ready to go, wearing his uniform of ratty jeans, faded tee shirt sporting some sort of biker logo, and the battered old motorcycle jacket that was his armor. Last but not least he pulled on the heavy Dingo harness boots that he viewed as a weapon second only to his revolver. His waist felt naked without cold metal pressed between his back and the waistband of his jeans. Gareth had his revolver. He had left it with him—just in case. Lenny would have liked nothing better than to use it on the young smart ass. The only way he could be controlled was with frequent reminders of the threat to his younger brother. *Whatever works*, he thought as he felt around in the bottom of the duffle for his spare weapon. He soon found the small pistol that slipped easily into an ankle holster hidden inside the top of his boot.

Lenny's accommodations were sparse, but the small hotel was within walking distance of the house. He pulled his phone from the charger, pocketed his wallet and left. Stepping out onto the sidewalk he felt the cool morning already giving way to another hot July day. The cafés wouldn't be open for a while and he badly needed coffee. His sour mood grew with each step, although the distance to his destination was short. He rounded the last corner and was relieved to see the house just up the block. Picking up the pace he was soon at the door, key in hand. He went inside, re-engaged the lock then called to Gareth, who would be told only what was necessary regarding the events taking place in London. He had spoken with Lyle the night before but wanted an update on the morning's progress and his final orders. Whatever Gareth might hear wouldn't really matter once he had no further use for the man.

* * *

In another part of the city, Ben was also up at first light and ready to go. He came out of the elevator and headed for the doors leading outside. The car and baggage attendants were not yet on duty, so he collected the rental car keys from the concierge, who was doing his best not to nod off as he leaned on the long wooden counter. The night before, Ben had asked the attendant where his car would be parked and requested the closest spot possible. Its location was only a short walk from the hotel entrance, and within a few minutes Ben was on his way to the neighborhood where the small house was located. The traffic heading in the opposite direction seemed unduly heavy for such an early hour, yet thankfully sparse on his route. He easily remembered the directions from the previous day, and soon he was turning into the street, proceeding at a snail's pace toward the house.

On his first trip to the house Ben had stopped the car some distance away. This time he took a chance and parked directly across the street. He slightly lowered one window then inched down in the seat far enough not to be noticed but still able to see across to the front of the house. It was quiet—no people or movement for what seemed like a quarter of an hour. He heard a gate clang then sat up and checked the street. A young woman was hurrying along, heels clicking on the sidewalk—heading to her job, Ben assumed. He settled back to watch the house, and as the minutes passed there was still no sign of life. Doubt inevitably began to creep into his thoughts. He questioned the decision to focus on this house, to depend so completely on the description of a man given to him by that woman, a stranger.

* * *

Ana had neglected to close the drapes completely before falling into bed the previous night, thus allowing an intrusive beam of sunlight to cut a path across the carpet, onto the bed and across her face. She sensed the light and woke with a start. Her first thought was of Ben—whether he was up and had left without her. She suspected all along that he had stopped talking because arguing wouldn't change what he intended to do, and she wasn't to be part of it. Up in less than two seconds she went to the adjoining door and carefully opened it to peak through. Ben was gone and had probably been gone for some time. Her first thought was to retrieve the card scribbled with the address of the house he had described. Part of her wished it would be a wild goose chase, but on the other hand she hoped he was really onto something. The card was still there. She snatched it and quickly returned to her room. Ana's next thought was of Ben's parents. Convincing them to stay in London had been unsuccessful. Neither she nor Ben would be there waiting when they arrived, but this was no time to be concerned with propriety or manners. She was needed elsewhere, even if Ben didn't agree.

She grabbed her large hobo bag, a sweater, tee, jeans and sneakers, placing everything on the bed. Removing her phone from the charger, she slid it into the bag, along with a visor and pair of sunglasses. After a splash of water and a quick turn with the toothbrush she was pulling on the jeans and tee. She tied the sweater around her waist, picked up the bag and headed down to the lobby. The concierge was too busy to order her a taxi so she went outside and asked the attendant for the closest taxi stand. He insisted on walking her to the corner where he flagged one down. Ana thanked him and climbed in, handing the driver the card on which the address had been written. After a quick U-turn the taxi sped away from the plaza and into the bustling morning traffic. Speakers behind the seat assaulted her with music much too bright for that particular day. She asked the driver to turn it down, and he obliged, glancing at her in the rear-view mirror.

Ana didn't care about the unfriendly glance and just continued to imagine what she might find when they reached the address. The distance seemed to pass quickly, and her fear was growing, as was her intense longing for Ben. All she really wanted from life at that moment was to be in his arms, to be alone with him and away from all the trouble that had kept their relationship from evolving normally. Yet she wondered if without what had happened, they would ever have moved beyond that one rainy night in the pub. Danger can bring clarity, and for Ana it meant the nagging ache of need. She needed Ben and now believed she always would. Her thoughts raced, each unrelated to the next. Fear fed doubt and doubt urged regret. On that chilly morning they had been safe from the adversity that was about to overtake their lives. After all, the birds had cried out to them, their wings outspread as they rode the currents overhead. She thought that, just perhaps, their cries were a warning: that moment was all they had, or worse yet, all they would ever have.

* * *

Inside the dingy little house the tension had become volatile. Gareth came through the bedroom doorway and stopped short, not making a sound. He tried to read Lenny's mood from the expression on his face as he listened to whoever was speaking on the other end of the phone. Gareth tried to appear disinterested and turned back to the bedroom. He stood flat against the wall and listened carefully, signaling the women to be quiet. Although Lenny kept his voice low Gareth gleaned one disturbing fact: Lenny's boss had decided that getting rid of the women was the best choice whether or not the robbery was a success.

"Yeah, him too," Lenny said, his voice intentionally muffled. He ended the call and placed the phone on the table.

Gareth had still managed to hear what was said. Once he heard Lenny's conversation, he knew immediately that he was to be disposed of as well. His thoughts raced. He feared that his brother would be another victim and never know why. He would have to confront Lenny, and it would be an uneven fight. Besides having a violent nature, Lenny was stronger than Gareth, and his additional height would be no compensation for Lenny's brawn. Yet a faceoff would be his only chance for survival.

Lenny stood by the table, his back to Gareth, who rushed through the doorway and jumped on him. Surprised by the attack, Lenny spun around, trying to disengage Gareth's arms, tightly clasped around his neck. With the weight of Gareth's body on his back, he spun in circles, using the momentum of Gareth's weight to break his hold. After breaking free he remembered putting his gun on the table. Gareth had been flung to the floor but saw the gun as well. They both dove toward the table, trying to reach it first. Lenny expected the gun to be no problem once he attacked and disabled Gareth, but he briefly gained the upper hand by body slamming Lenny, knocking him off balance. He fell, hitting his head on the table and becoming disoriented. Totally unfamiliar with any kind of weapon, Gareth hesitated before picking up the gun. In the meantime Lenny staggered to his feet and lunged toward him.

They continued to struggle for the gun, ending up near the small table. Lenny tried to bang Gareth's hand on the edge, hard enough to release his hold on the gun, but it went off and fell to the floor with enough momentum to slide into the bedroom. Valerie, handcuffed to the radiator, had been shot straight through the bedroom doorway, but neither man had noticed. Lenny seemed unconcerned with the location of the gun and lunged toward Gareth, grabbing him by the shirt and pulling him closer. He delivered a strong right hook squarely to Gareth's face and he stumbled backward, dazed, his body stopped by the wall. In what seemed like an instant Lenny was on him again, this time with his hands around Gareth's throat. His arms flailed as he began to lose breath, his face flushing red from the pressure of blood unable to circulate from his head. The expression in Gareth's eyes was one of both terror and resignation. His knees began to buckle as the two men locked eyes. Lenny's eyes were cold, his expression one of evil intent.

* * *

During the violent confrontation in the house, Ben had remained parked across the street and was becoming more and more impatient. Just as he had decided to give his surveillance only another half hour, he heard the crackling sound of a gunshot. There was no mistaking it, and he looked around, uncertain of the direction from which it had come. The adrenaline rush that came with hearing a gunshot triggered him to take action. He jumped from the car and ran to the house, knowing something had to be done to move things along, to find out whether he was even on the right track. While crossing the street he looked up and down for signs of activity, but there were none. He proceeded slowly up the walkway to the front door then stood still, listening for any signs of life. At first he heard an angry voice, followed by the sound of furniture hitting the floor. Less than a minute passed before he heard screams. Neither man was aware that someone had been watching the house and was now listening at the door.

Ben hoped the woman who screamed was either Olivia or Valerie, but regardless, he made the decision to intercede on her behalf. Finding the door locked he threw his body against it. The degraded wood frame gave way and the door fell forward, providing access to the house. The first thing he saw was a man with his hands around another man's throat. Ben had no way of knowing whether the man being strangled was involved in the abduction, so his first instinct was to help him. He caught a glimpse of the women, but knew he must first disable the man whom he immediately recognized as the one who had attacked him twice in London.

Lenny heard the door fall to the floor and turned away from Gareth, distracted from the pleasure he felt while strangling the man. Ben charged at him, but Lenny just laughed and pushed him aside. His attention was now on Ben, and Gareth had to take advantage of this momentary freedom. He gasped for breath and steadied himself before going to the bedroom door to look at the women. He could see Valerie was bleeding from her abdomen and knew that if Lenny subdued the man, all four of them would not survive. Olivia was sobbing and trying to reach for an unconscious Valerie. Lenny and Ben were circling each other like wrestlers at the start of a match. Gareth took advantage of the moment by rushing back into the room and grabbing the handcuff keys from the cupboard knob.

Things were happening fast, but it seemed that everything was moving forward in slow motion. He proceeded to unlock Valerie from the radiator then Olivia from the cot. Olivia scrambled to where Valerie lay drifting in and out of consciousness.

Gareth went to Olivia and helped her up. "Run! You can't help her! Get out of here while you can."

"How can I leave her?" Olivia cried out. "She'll die!"

"If you don't run—*now*—you'll die too!"

Olivia was weak and unsteady on her feet. She moved through the outer room as fast as she could, momentarily leaning on one chair, then the other, before reaching the open door. Ben continued to spar with Lenny but managed to shout to Olivia, telling her to run outside and find help. Her face full of terror, she obeyed. Ben and Lenny were engaged in a physical struggle that Gareth expected would not end well for Ben. He seemed mesmerized, watching the men wrestling for control. He stood in the doorway, his back to Valerie, who had regained consciousness and was moaning on the floor of the tiny room.

Just as he had done with Gareth, Lenny punched Ben in the gut then the jaw, sending him hurtling backward against the wall. He stomped forward, and before Ben could recover from the punch, Lenny grabbed for his throat with both hands. Ben felt the painful pressure of Lenny's thumbs cutting off his breath, but with residual weakness in his left shoulder he was unable to pull Lenny's right hand away. He struggled with Lenny's left hand, trying to wrench it from his neck and gasping for breath at any slight break in the pressure. In spite of his efforts to break away, Ben's focus began to blur due to the restricted blood flow. For a moment his only awareness was of the pulsing in his neck and the loud ringing in his ears.

A crackling noise suddenly broke through the ringing, and he felt the pressure on his neck release. He focused on Lenny's eyes. They were vacant, his face absent of any expression. Weakness overtook Ben. His knees gave way and he began to slide down the wall. Lenny fell toward him, glanced off the wall, and dropped on his back, hitting the floor hard. The man was lying completely still, his eyes wide open as if staring at Ben. Then Ben noticed blood begin to trickle from the side of Lenny's mouth. There was a hole in his chest, around it a widening circle of blood soaking his shirt. Ben regained his composure and strained to turn the bulky man over. That accomplished, he saw a smaller hole in his back, barely ringed with blood. Since the hole in his chest was obviously an exit wound, Ben wondered how the bullet hadn't injured him as well. He turned to look at the wall, seeing immediately where the bullet had lodged and cracked the plaster, its trajectory just missing his body.

Ben's observations were made in an instant, before he could wonder where the shot had come from, or who had shot Lenny. His eyes tracked along the floor to the doorway, where he saw that Valerie had managed to crawl or drag herself that far before once again losing consciousness. The gun was in her relaxed fingers. He realized that she had also managed to drag herself to wherever the gun had been, but where it had come from he had no idea. In spite of her wound, she had managed to pick it up, take some sort of aim and shoot. Valerie had made a lucky kill shot from the floor and saved his life. He rushed to her side and felt her carotid artery for a pulse. It was weak and her breathing was shallow. The wound was off to the left, about midway below her ribcage.

Valerie's eyes opened slightly and with a trembling voice she whispered, "Cold … cold." Ben saw she was shivering and feared she had gone into shock. He took a blanket from one of the cots and covered her.

Gareth was crouched in a corner, all but holding his breath in order not to be noticed. He imagined every scenario he could be facing, and the reason for his actions wouldn't matter. Coerced or not he was still guilty of taking part in detaining the women. Yet all along his greatest need had been to free them, to take Olivia in his arms and comfort her. That scenario had played over and over in his mind since the moment he had first seen the women suffering. He had chosen his brother over the woman he could easily have loved. He would never forget the look on her face when she learned of his part in the kidnapping. And now he wasn't even sure he had managed to save his brother.

Gareth inched along the wall in the main room, clearly planning to make his break while Ben was distracted. Just as he decided the moment was right, Ana appeared in the doorway and shouted Ben's name. Gareth stood completely still, hoping she wouldn't see him. Ben turned away from Valerie, a look of both surprise and exasperation crossing his face.

"You shouldn't be here!" he shouted back at her.

Ana could tell he was furious. "Are you okay?" she asked, ignoring his reprimand. She immediately noticed the blood on his face and neck—more blood than on that first night when he was attacked. There was more blood on the front of his shirt. Adrenaline flooded her body. Instinct compelled her to make physical contact as reassurance that he was truly all right, but she held back. Distracted by the need to embrace him, she stepped through the doorway without a thought for her own safety. Neither she nor Ben had noticed Gareth cowering in the shadows.

Ben absent-mindedly rubbed his shoulder as he answered. "I'm okay, but Valerie's been shot. It's bad. I sent Olivia to call an ambulance. Did you see her out there?"

"Olivia's sitting in the taxi I came in—shivering and crying. The driver called emergency services. I don't know how long it will take." When Ana started to walk toward Ben she saw the man lying on the floor, a circle of blood on his shirt. "Oh God… it's the man who attacked you in London." She looked back and forth with disbelief at Ben and the man with the vacant stare.

"He's dead—thanks to Valerie." He turned back to his ex-wife and brushed the hair from her pale face. "Another minute and I would have been the dead one." The truth of his close call became more real to him as he verbalized it to Ana.

"But how…" Ana asked, her brow furrowed, her focus shifting to Valerie. She reacted instantly and rushed to her side, instinctively grabbing the other ratty blanket to apply pressure to the wound. She feared that the woman's only chance to survive was to slow the bleeding.

Before he could answer Ana's question, Ben remembered the other man. He glanced around the main room and saw him standing in one corner. He was very still and partially hidden by the refrigerator's shadow. "Stay with Valerie," Ben said as he quickly stood up and started toward Gareth.

Gareth saw Ben coming toward him with a murderous expression on his face. He put up his hands in a defensive posture and spoke with fear in his voice. "Wait man, you don't understand… Let me explain. They were going to kill my brother!"

Ben was so filled with rage he heard little of what the man was saying. He lunged forward and yelled, "Fucking bastard!"

With a hard push Gareth managed to deflect Ben slightly, upsetting his balance. Gareth assumed there would be no reasoning with the man, so before Ben could grab for him again he rushed through the open door and broke into a full speed dash up the street. Without a word to Ana, Ben chased after him. He ran toward his rental car, shouting at the cab driver to stay with the women. Although the call had already been made he repeated the order to keep calling emergency 112. He could still see

Gareth running toward the intersection. He jumped into the car, skidded into a quick U-turn and took off in Gareth's direction. While still a half block away he saw Gareth jump onto a bus. He increased speed, fell in behind the bus, and continued to give chase. In spite of traffic he managed to keep up. When it made regular stops he was close enough to see that Gareth didn't jump off.

After following the bus in a straight line for more than a mile, a detour sign caused the driver to make a sudden change in route. At the next stop Gareth did jump off, stopping to look around, wondering which way to go to make his escape. His short pause enabled Ben to spot him, so he pulled to the curb and abandoned the car. Just as Ben got out he heard what sounded like a rocket, and then the dull roar of a crowd in the distance. Gareth had spotted Ben and made the mistake of waiting to see what he would do. Like a shot, Ben took off after him, both men dodging pedestrians as they ran one block, then two. Ben was keeping pace with the younger man when he dashed into an alley. Gareth stumbled slightly when making the sudden turn, and Ben began to gain on him. The pursuit changed course when Gareth, then about twenty yards away from Ben, tried the gate of a walled property. It was locked, but he scaled the wall with ease and dropped to the other side just as Ben reached the outside of the wall.

The house had two doors that opened onto a patio crowded with chairs and pots of flowers. A long table held preparations for some sort of party. Landing hard, Gareth tried to resume running but tripped on a chair, momentarily losing his footing. Both doors leading into the house were ajar, and Gareth ran through one of them just as Ben managed to get over the wall. He followed Gareth and saw him running toward the end of a dim, tile-lined corridor. Ben entered the house, welcoming the coolness but continuing to pursue the man pace for pace. Gareth reached the end of the long hallway, Ben only a few yards behind. Both men heard loud voices and laughter that seemed to come from above the stairwell to the left. Gareth was trapped against a massive carved door, the main entrance to the house. Just as Ben reached out for him, Gareth pulled the door open. The roaring of a crowd flooded the house as Gareth dashed blindly through the doorway. Confronted with a street barrier, he body-slammed it, forcing it aside. He ran straight into the middle of *Calle Estafata,* nearly colliding with the last few bandana-clad runners. The ground trembled beneath his feet as he heard a faint rumble becoming louder. In that instant the bulls rounded *Mercaderes* corner into *Calle Estafata* and advanced on him at full speed. He was stunned, paralyzed on the spot, and before he could react with evasive action they plowed over him, one pausing to toss him aside with its horns. Ben came through the door and stopped in his tracks, horrified by the scene in front of him.

Even though ambulances were always on standby during the bull runs, the crowds made it difficult to reach an injured runner or bystander with immediacy. Ben ripped off his shirt and knelt beside Gareth, hoping to control the profuse bleeding from his inner thigh. Yet it became obvious that manual pressure would not have helped such a gaping wound. An ambulance reached the location rather quickly, but to Ben the wait had seemed unduly long. As the emergency medical technicians transferred Gareth to a stretcher Ben could see by their expressions that his condition was grave. Ben managed to pass for a friend and was admitted to the ambulance. They left the scene, siren blaring, but Gareth's femoral artery had been damaged. The situation urged Ben to see Gareth only as another human being, one who needed comfort in the face of his possible death. He soon lost consciousness and while the ambulance sped through the crowded streets he stopped breathing twice. Resuscitation was effective only once. He died from blood loss before reaching the hospital.

* * *

At some point during the mid-morning Ben's parents had arrived at the hotel, having no idea what had transpired. They asked the concierge to call

Ben's room then Ana's, but neither answered. While discussing whether they should just go to their room and wait, the concierge received a call. Ana was on the line requesting that Paris and Hugh be given a message immediately when they checked in. The concierge passed the phone to Hugh, telling him it was Ana Doherty.

"We were so sorry not to be on site to meet you, but so much has happened and there was no chance to call."

"What do you mean? Is Ben all right? Has he made any progress in finding Olivia? Is it Valerie who's with her?"

"I'll answer all your questions, but right now you must get to the hospital to see Olivia."

"What? Olivia? Then he found her. Is she all right?" Ana paused, trying to find the right words. Hugh became impatient and all but yelled into the phone. "For God's sake tell us!"

Paris tried to grab the phone away from Hugh, but he held tight, turned to her, and said, "She's alive."

Ana continued, "Yes, she's okay, or at least she will be. The doctors said she's dehydrated and malnourished, and other than a few superficial scrapes and bruises she seems unharmed. I rode in the ambulance with her. She was completely lucid—kept asking for Ben—was Ben okay … over and over."

Ana hesitated, unsure of what to say and how to say it. When Hugh finally spoke, his tone of voice betrayed his impatience. "What? What haven't you told us?"

"It's Valerie. She's been taken into surgery. She was shot during a struggle between the kidnappers. The doctors said it doesn't look good. She lost a lot of blood."

Paris tugged on Hugh's sleeve. "What about Ben? Ask her. Where's Ben?"

Ana had heard Paris ask the question and gave the only answer she could. "I don't know where he is. He took off after one of the kidnappers and I hate to say that I haven't heard from him since."

Hugh sighed, immediately thinking of how he would tell Paris that Ben was presently out of touch, who knows where and doing who knows what. He asked Ana for the name of the hospital where Olivia and Valerie had been taken then assured her they would get a taxi and be there as fast as possible. As he handed the phone back to the concierge, Paris looked hard into his eyes, her expression beseeching him for more information. "I'll tell you everything in the taxi," he said, grabbing her hand and heading out of the hotel. Several taxis were waiting for fares near the entrance. Within moments they were on their way to *Hospital de Navarra*.

CHAPTER NINETEEN

Agent Mosi Azikiwe waved his team forward. Weapons at the ready, the six men followed him into the warehouse where the crates from Spain would be offloaded. He directed them to secure hiding places behind other cargo waiting to be picked up. Once everyone was in place, he pulled out his mobile phone and contacted his superior. He confirmed the team was ready and asked if the plane carrying the fake cargo was on schedule. It was due to arrive within the next half hour.

After just a few years at Scotland Yard, and although he was only thirty-five, Azikiwe had advanced rapidly in Interpol, having received commendations for several major arrests made under his command. His team was loyal and had observed both his bravery and his concern for their safety.

He had been shown the manifest naming the security firm whose supposed armored trucks were scheduled to transport the gold. An identifying mark had been made on two of the crates to be unloaded, specifying to the agents that each contained just enough gold to qualify the heist as a major crime. Once the crooks had touched, moved or opened even one, the arrest could be made.

The agents passed the time without conversing, each with his private thoughts. Agent Azikiwe was no different as he contemplated the possible outcomes of the confrontation to come. It was his habit to create a backup plan for any unknowns he could imagine. Although his agency policed the world, so to speak, he felt his work carried an element of patriotism to England, his adopted country. He was an idealistic man who had not allowed himself to become jaded by his early exposure to the sordid side of life. Having come from Africa with his parents at a very young age, he was by all counts an Englishman. Yet he still remembered the poverty and violence he saw before his family fled to the UK.

Agent Azikiwe checked his watch again and saw that a half hour had passed. He called to the men, telling them to be alert, that it wouldn't be long. Just as he finished speaking he heard the sound of a plane engine approaching. Keeping his eyes on the entrance he carefully stepped backward toward where his men were hiding.

"Showtime, lads! Look smart!" he shouted as he joined a pair of agents behind several pallets stacked high with bags of mortar.

The plane taxied to a stop just inside the hangar, one of several at Heathrow where arriving cargo was warehoused after being processed. Before the passenger-crew door opened, the large cargo-hold door dropped open slowly. Workers jogged into the hangar and pushed over a mobile staircase to rest against the plane. The crew opened the door and disembarked. Agent Azikiwe came out from behind the pallets and told the crew to exit quickly toward the closest terminal for their own safety. Those flying the plane had been told at takeoff there would likely be an attempted crime and to follow whatever instructions they were given. The three men and two women making up the crew obeyed the agent's order immediately and were soon out of sight. The workers left the mobile stairs against the plane and followed the crew outside and toward the terminal.

The Interpol team waited silently for the whole thing to play out. Within a few minutes an airport worker, driving what looked like an electric baggage carrier, approached the warehouse entrance from the vehicle side. Two slow moving trucks followed, both chassis either perfect imitations of armored trucks or reclaimed versions of the real thing. The company name appeared on the sides: An ornate silver logo with black letters stated 'Security First.'

The truck being driven by Linus Finch pulled up to the opening and stopped. He gave the once-over to the whole area, intent on spotting anyone who might be working there and thus able to observe his actions. The second truck paused slightly behind, leaving Linus to take the lead. He turned the vehicle in a way that enabled him to back into the building, all the way through to the plane's cargo door. The other driver positioned his truck in the same way, and within a couple of minutes they were climbing out, ready to take possession of the crates. Linus looked around, expecting someone to appear with a clipboard, demanding signatures—something. And some help would have been nice. He wondered where everyone was, why the cargo door was left open with such a valuable cargo inside. But that was fine with him, and all the easier. Maybe they wouldn't have to shoot anyone.

Linus motioned to Fergus McDonald and the two drivers to get out. Azikiwe's team watched as the four men got out of the trucks and stood in a group to assess the situation. Two of the men were wearing some sort of uniform, but the two younger men were shabbily dressed in jeans and hoodies. Although the team couldn't hear what was being said, the body language was easy to read. One of the uniformed men was clearly in charge. He was giving orders and motioning the three others to get up into the cargo hold and begin to unload the crates marked for the museum. The Interpol team was chomping at the bit and anxious to leave their hiding places to apprehend the motley crew, but their superior signaled them to hang back. He knew that unless they were caught in the act of opening the crates and handling the gold, the charges would be minor—at worst, attempted robbery and trespassing. They were going for the major felony that attempting to steal such a treasure would impart.

Linus stood beside the open cargo door, its lowered ramp a direct invitation for the men to enter and help themselves. Interpol had made arrangements to place the crates containing gold at the front, the decoys just behind. After one more scan of the hangar all four men climbed into the cargo hold. The agents couldn't see clearly what was going on inside the plane, but soon two crates appeared, each being carried by two of the men. One crate was put on the ground, the other set inside the truck. Both were stamped with the name of the museum in Madrid. Linus reached inside and pulled out a crowbar, his avarice taking control of his judgment. He had to see the gold. He motioned the two drivers to get back up into the hold and bring the other two crates down. Once the gang of thieves touched the valuable contents, Agent Azikiwe would motion his men forward and hopefully apprehend all of them without shots fired.

Fergus hovered over the crate as Linus began to pry open the lid. The wood easily snapped loose and they pulled it off, tossing it aside. Raffia packing material had been used, and both men began to dig through it, scattering it on the floor. Linus was the first to touch something solid. Using both hands he slowly lifted the treasure from its resting place then held it aloft, turning it, obviously unsure of what the carved gold box would be used for. Just as he started to open it the agents appeared from their hiding places and advanced on the perpetrators.

* * *

Lyle Brett pulled his rental car onto the shoulder of Heathrow's southern perimeter road. He stopped where there was no hedge growth, giving him a decent view of the cargo hangars, then settled in to wait. At the instant he could see his trucks pull out and away he would make haste to the preset location where once he was there to supervise, the valuable cargo could be fully unpacked and evaluated. So far everything in London had gone as planned, but he was disconcerted by the fact that Lenny hadn't checked in. He knew better. Lenny was supposed to be glued to his phone, to be ready when it was time to eliminate the women.

Considering it was Lyle's first crime, he was in deep and he knew it—was even proud to be taking what he believed was a minor risk. He congratulated himself, deciding he had a real talent for this sort of thing. In all areas of his life he had always preferred to keep things simple when it came to cleaning up loose ends. Loose ends had to be tied up, and Londoners disappearing on a trip to Spain was perfect. He couldn't have planned it better himself. How nice of them to take that vacation. No way to trace anything to him. His uneasiness grew as he peered through binoculars at the entrance where the trucks had backed in. He saw no activity and the moments dragged. If he stayed parked on the shoulder much longer someone was bound to stop and ask if he needed help. Worst case, it would be airport security police.

* * *

Linus and his cohorts had temporarily lost sight of their need to make a quick getaway. They were engrossed with the ancient box, its rich gold color gleaming brightly as it caught the light from a flickering fluorescent tube overhead. The men passed it around, seemingly spellbound by its beauty, their gaze so single-minded that they failed to hear the agents approaching. With guns drawn, the agents moved to surround the four men, who startled and turned away from the crate. Fergus had been taking his turn holding the box and quickly tossed it back into the crate before beseeching Linus with his eyes. It was a what-do-we-do-now expression, for which he received no reply. Linus was paralyzed on the spot with his jaw dropped open and eyes expressing terror.

Agent Azikiwe ordered the four to lie face down and put arms behind them. They complied and were handcuffed. When asked who was in charge, Linus was mute; however, Fergus was quick to offer assistance. Linus was dragged to his feet, all the while denying that he was the group's leader. Regardless of his declaration agent Azikiwe took him aside, out of earshot of the others, and said the window for a reduced charge would close very quickly and was dependent upon what he could offer as means to apprehend his boss. After only a few minutes of questioning, he sang loud and long, naming Lyle Brett as the brains behind the caper. He gave up the location where they were to bring the gold, and suggested that Lyle could be watching from somewhere close to the cargo building. One agent was left with the four handcuffed suspects, who had been secured to the heavy mobile staircase still resting against the plane.

* * *

The waiting had been interminable and the anxiety had caused Lyle Brett to break out in a drenching sweat. He was afraid to get out of his car for a better view of the building, and if he did, he would have to put on the car's emergency blinkers. That would draw attention. His meticulous brain could not accept that something might have gone wrong. He paused to check the map on his tablet screen and wondered if they had been forced to leave by an exit he hadn't considered. He could continue on that road and get a view of the rest of the building, maybe see if they had been forced to exit from the tarmac. But that didn't make sense. Lyle checked his watch again before letting out a string of profanities regarding Lenny's failure to contact him from Spain as planned. He carefully pulled into the light traffic and drove on until he was opposite the short side of the building, where there were several oversized garage-type doors. One was open. There was an exit that would take him to the parking lot on that side, and he gave in to the temptation to pull in and take a closer look.

Agent Azikiwe gave the order for three of his men to return to their vehicle then drive the perimeter road and parking lots to look for whom he referred to as 'Brett.' During the questioning he had also managed to get a description of the man. The other three agents would stay with him to wait for the valid security trucks to come for the gold. Linus and the others were ordered to sit on the floor in a circle, backs to each other. Now there was nothing to do but wait.

After about a quarter of an hour the sound of screeching tires broke the silence. It ended with what was obviously a collision. Azikiwe feared for his men and ran toward the nearest exit to the parking lot. There he saw the agents' car stopped just behind a Prius that had crashed into the cab of a truck being loaded with building supplies. The front end of the Prius looked like an accordion; the driver having hit the truck at high speed. His agents got out of their vehicle and surrounded the crushed Prius, ready to arrest the driver, Lyle Brett. They had spotted him in one of the parking lots and had approached slowly. He had seen them and took off, back onto the perimeter road, where the agents gave chase. They had ended up back where they started. A van had crowded the driver off to the left, forcing him to exit again.

The agent joined his men at the scene of the crash. One of the agents had just finished calling for an ambulance, but clearly there was no hurry. Without a seat belt Brett had been thrown hard against the windshield. The car burst into flames before the body could be removed. There would now be a delay before the forensics team could complete crime scene protocol. A van arrived shortly to take the other men to jail. He called his superior to report that all was secure. He always felt great satisfaction when he could report there were no shots fired.

CHAPTER TWENTY

Ben stood outside the ambulance doors, watching closely as the emergency medical technicians zipped the unidentified dead man into a body bag. He stepped aside as the body was transferred and strapped to a collapsible gurney, lowered from the vehicle and wheeled quickly through the double doors of the *sala de emergencias*. Ben's sense of regret for the part he played in a man's death momentarily overshadowed his anger about the man's role in the kidnapping. Yet he couldn't ignore the fear on the man's face when confronted. There was no doubt in his mind that the man was complicit or he wouldn't have tried to escape, but there was more below the surface. How he was involved could remain a mystery.

The adrenaline that had enabled Ben to give chase was spent. He felt drained and could no longer ignore the now familiar pain in his shoulder, nor the difficulty he had opening his jaw. In fact he ached from head to toe, having just survived a fight for his life with the man who had pursued him in London. He paused by the entrance, deep in thought, realizing that impulsiveness and anger had driven him to chase another man to his death. In order to live with that memory he would have to find out who this man was and why he was there.

Ben's introspection was interrupted by the sound of a police van screeching to a halt beside the ambulance. Two uniformed officers got out and started toward him. A middle-aged man with a nervous demeanor was walking behind them. He had pulled his *boina* low over his forehead in a failed attempt to protect his identity. He scanned the surroundings as if expecting paparazzi to leap out at him. When they reached Ben, one of the officers asked in Spanish if he was the man who had ridden in the ambulance from *Calle Estefata*. Ben asked him to repeat in English, and haltingly he did so. The man pushed forward and pointed at Ben, confirming verbally that he was the one who chased the poor man into the path of the bulls. Ben suddenly realized that he could be in serious trouble. There was no point in denying it, yet there was much to tell about the reason he had given chase and about the man's culpability in the kidnapping of his sister and former wife.

One officer pulled out his handcuffs and circled behind Ben, who asked if he was under arrest. The other officer shook his head no then motioned his partner to put the handcuffs away. He spoke to Ben again in Spanish. Ben understood enough to know he had to go with them to the station, so he gestured toward the vehicle and said, *"Vamonos."*

Ben was desperate to find Ana and his parents, see Olivia, and find out if Valerie was alive. But since there was no way he could communicate effectively with the officers, he thought it best to comply. It was a short ride to the *Comisaría* located closest to *Calle Estafata*. It was there he had met Annunciata and sought help from Inspector Gonzalo Macias. As they walked Ben through the entrance he strained to see whether Macias was in his office behind the glass partition. Relief washed over him when he saw the inspector sitting on the edge of his desk talking on the phone. The officers led Ben to the counter, where the man on duty prepared to take his information and schedule him for questioning. Ben couldn't wait. He spoke as well as he could, asking if the officer spoke English. The officer indicated that he spoke a little—a must, he said, considering the trouble tourists get into.

"Please listen ... *Escucha por favor,*" Ben said, hoping to show his sincerity by attempting to speak the officer's language. "Inspector Macias... I know ... *Conozco* ... I spoke with him yesterday about what has happened. *Por favor,* let me see him."

The officer scrutinized Ben's bloodied face and disheveled appearance suspiciously as he picked up the phone to page the inspector. Ben shifted from one foot to the other and self-consciously rubbed his shoulder. His bruised jaw had become swollen and there was dried blood on his face and clothing. Inspector Macias leaned forward to put his call on hold and answer the page. When Ben heard the officer speak to the inspector he interrupted. "Tell him it's Ben McKinnon, the man who talked to him about his sister's disappearance."

The inspector heard Ben's voice in the background and immediately got up from his desk. He came through the door with his arm extended for a handshake. When he was close enough to get a good look at Ben he asked, "*Dios mio!* Were you mugged?"

"No sir," Ben answered. "I was in a fight for my life … and my sister's."

"Come with me." The inspector's tone had turned serious and he took Ben's arm, leading him into the private area where his desk was located.

Ben sat down carefully and with a slight groan. Inspector Macias asked if he needed medical attention. He declined and said there were more important things to deal with. The story of what had transpired since they last met unfolded quickly as Ben recounted the details of what had occurred up to the time he arrived at the hospital. Macias had to remind Ben that English was his second language and he should slow down. Protocol dictated that he reprimand Ben for conducting his own investigation, pursuing the kidnappers and chasing a man who could have been armed.

Ben countered with the fact that no one at the station would take him seriously and he knew there wasn't a moment to lose. The inspector reluctantly admitted regret for not having been of more help. He was convinced it was fate—*'suerte,'* as he put it—that Ben had overheard the woman reporting what she thought was suspicious activity in the little house. The inspector made it clear that after he read the police report there would be more questions for Ben to answer. After all, a man had died.

Two men died, Ben thought. It was evident that a report on what had happened in the little house had not yet reached the *Comisaria.*

The inspector excused himself and went out to speak to the officers who had brought Ben in for questioning. They turned and left. Ben was once again relieved. When Inspector Macias returned he asked what, if anything, he could do to help. Ben needed to know where his sister and Valerie had been taken. After Macias made a couple of calls Ben was ushered into the back of a police car and on his way to *Hospital de Navarra.*

Heads turned as Ben walked through the hospital lobby to the information desk. Before he could make an inquiry, the nurse on duty told him in heavily accented English that access to the emergency room was down the hallway to the left. He wondered just how bad he looked, but then explained that he was looking for his sister, Olivia McKinnon. He knew it would be useless to inquire about Valerie and hoped that with Ana's help his parents had found their way to the hospital. Time dragged as the nurse checked the computer for Olivia's name.

Finally she looked up and said, "No, *señor,* I do not see her name."

"But I know she's here. The police checked for me."

"If she is still in *emergencia,* we would not yet have her name."

Ben let out a sigh of frustration and asked, "So you said emergency is down the hall to the left?" She gestured in that direction. He turned, walking away as he said, *"Gracias."*

At the end of the hall were double doors stating '*Prohibida la Entrada.*' To the right of the doors was a window and counter with a woman seated on the other side. His inquiry yielded the information he hoped for, and within a few minutes he was led through to a curtained cubicle. He heard his mother's voice. The nurse pulled the curtain aside just slightly and there sat everyone he cared for most.

Paris and Hugh sat on either side of the bed, each holding one of Olivia's hands. Ana stood on the opposite side of the bed from Ben. She looked as if she were carrying the weight of the world. Yet when Ben pushed aside the curtain completely and her eyes locked with his, all the fear drained from her expression. She quickly approached to embrace him. He winced with pain when she tightened her arms around his torso. She backed off quickly and took a closer look at his face, and as she touched it gently her pent up tears began to flow. Ben carefully embraced her as he glanced first at his father then his mother, waiting for them to speak. Foremost in his mind was Olivia's condition. Paris urged him to speak softly because Olivia had been given a sedative and what she needed most was rest.

Following the initial relief and outpouring of tears Ana became aware of Ben's swollen face and the dried blood on his clothing. Back at the little house everything had happened so fast she hadn't had a good look at him. In spite of her insistence, he refused to be seen by a doctor. The next logical question was about Valerie, although he was afraid to ask.

Hugh's voice was subdued, his tone serious. "She's still in surgery. The doctors say her generally weakened condition and blood loss could work against her. I asked for odds, but they were reluctant to say."

Ben shook his head in dismay and said, "She has to live. She saved my life."

Paris gently let go of Olivia's hand, laying her arm on the bed without waking her. She rose from the chair, and as she walked around to stand by Hugh she motioned to Ben.

"Come out in the hall so we can talk, but softly. I want to know everything that happened. What does it all have to do with the gold shipment?"

"I don't know the whole story at the moment," he said. "It's all related, but I don't know how. The inspector I talked to about finding Olivia and Valerie, a man named Macias, is looking into it. He'll need to check at the station nearest the house. All I can tell you right now is what happened there and at the Bull Run." He paused, thinking of the man who died and that he felt somehow responsible. "I chased one of the kidnappers into the path of a bull." He looked directly at his father and said, "I didn't even know the bull-run was going on. And he had tried to explain something at the house, but I was so angry that I wouldn't listen."

Ben seemed saddened as he continued to recount what led to the man's death. "He was younger than me—no more than thirty maybe—athletic type. He looked scared and had to be guilty of something or he wouldn't have run." Ben thought for a moment then murmured, "Or maybe he wasn't involved by choice."

Hugh could see that the outcome greatly troubled his son. "You took quite a risk deciding to give chase. As far as I know you were unarmed, and there was a possibility the man would turn on you rather than run." Ben nodded in agreement but looked down as if guilty of something. His father added, "But that didn't happen, and I assure you I would have done the same. I think we can be quite sure the man was involved somehow. I'm proud and very thankful you're all right— other than some aches and bruises."

"Ben looked up and said, "Seconds before that thug would have squeezed the last breath out of me, Valerie made a lucky shot and killed him. I had started to lose consciousness."

Ana moved closer to him and took hold of his arm. "It was the same man that attacked Ben twice in London. There's no doubt. I saw him lying dead on the floor."

"And Valerie killed him? How did she get a gun?" Hugh asked.

"She had already been shot with the same gun before I arrived. She must have dragged herself to where it had landed on the floor before losing consciousness. I don't know how it got there, and I didn't see her shoot him. I was fighting for my life… and losing."

That information was too much for Paris and although she maintained a stoic expression, tears began to run down her cheeks. Hugh wrapped his arms around her, and the tension drained from her face. Ana told them how she had stayed with Valerie until the ambulance arrived, but that she was unconscious and in shock, unable to say anything about what had happened.

Paris got herself under control and asked, "Surely they can't charge Valerie with anything. Can they, Hugh?"

"Right now our only concern should be whether she survives the injury, but I can't see how she would be held accountable in this type of situation. Once the police have the whole story, she would more likely be made the heroine."

Just then Hugh's phone began to vibrate in his pocket. He excused himself and went out to the hallway. Paris commented that perhaps the call was about the robbery. Ana wondered how the police would be able to tie the gold shipment and the kidnapping together.

Ben said, "We have to wait for the report on how things went down at the airport—whether one of the men arrested gives up the others. The whole thing is clearer to me now, but we have to hope it becomes clear to the Spanish police."

Paris added, "That's Interpol's job."

Hugh ended his call and returned to the ward. He peaked through the curtain to check on Olivia then motioned Ben to come outside with him. Once in the outer hallway, they spoke in hushed voices. "It was my Interpol contact. The intervention at the airport turned into more than just apprehending thieves 'in the act.'" A nurse passed them and put a finger to her lips, shushing them further. Hugh leaned in closer to Ben and continued in a near whisper. "There was a chase that ended with one dead. They think it was the man behind all of it. He ran his car full speed into a large truck being loaded, and the car burst into flames on impact. They're going to need DNA and dental records to confirm identity."

"I hope there's enough left of him to make an ID." Then Ben asked, "Are any of the rest of them in any shape to talk?"

Ben wanted all the facts before being formally interviewed by Inspector Macias. Hugh explained that one of the men offloading the gold had been more than willing to give up his boss and everyone else involved. Interpol's plan had gone off without a hitch. Ben added that he was expected at the *Comisaria* by the next morning at the latest to give a full statement of the events in the little house. But he turned down his father's offer to accompany him. Hugh was anxious to share the news with Paris and Ana so he asked that they be buzzed through again.

Olivia was now awake, and her first words were about Valerie's condition. When she saw Ben she reached out for him. He came closer and she took his hand in both of hers. "Thank you for saving me," she said, and then repeated it several times.

"Anytime," he answered, trying to lighten the moment. "Like I always used to tell you after one of your ill-conceived pranks: Try to stay out of trouble."

It was the first moment of lightness in such a long time, and they were still smiling when the curtain was pulled aside and a doctor entered, still wearing surgical scrubs. His expression was somber, and in Spanish he introduced himself as Doctor Garces, then told them to please wait. As a whole, they expected bad news about Valerie, but remained silent. A long minute later the nurse entered the cubicle and apologized to the doctor for making him wait. In passable English she told them she was there to interpret, that the doctor was concerned his dubious command of English might cause confusion when talking about the patient. They listened closely as each sentence was slowly translated into English. Valerie had survived the surgery—*un milagro* — he emphasized.

The nurse nodded and said, "Yes, a miracle."

Doctor Garces continued and she translated. He cautioned them that although Valerie was stable at the moment, her ability to recover remained to be seen. Their relief was peppered with ongoing worry for the outcome. The doctor excused himself, but before he could leave, Paris asked to speak with him privately, along with the nurse who could translate. They stepped outside the cubicle where she asked him how long Olivia should stay in hospital, considering that taking her home would involve travel to England.

He informed Paris that speaking only of Olivia's physical condition she could be discharged by morning but would be taken to a room if a vacancy opened up. He explained that the hospital was full due to the usual things that happen to tourists at the festival, and that he wasn't referring only to accidents during the bull runs. She understood and said a room for Olivia wasn't important, since she would likely leave the next day. Paris was told that the doctor had been contacted by the police commissioner's office to say Olivia would not be permitted to leave until she had been questioned about her experience and what she may have overheard. She thanked them both and walked back into the cubicle. She told them what had to happen before they could leave. Hugh assured her that Interpol would intercede with the police and arrange for her statement to be taken in her hospital room.

Ana had barely taken her eyes off Ben. She could read the subtle signs that he was in pain. She had seen those same signs after the attack on the first night they met. Finally she spoke up and asked for a vote on how many thought he should be checked into emergency and looked over. He tried to minimize the obvious but was outnumbered. Ana led him away and said she would let them know how he was as soon as she could. A moment after they left, Olivia perked up and looked first at her mother then her father.

"All right, who is Ana? I've only been awake a few minutes, but the chemistry between them is too obvious to miss." Hugh remained stoic, but Paris smiled and nodded her head in agreement. "Why didn't I know about her?" Olivia asked.

"It's all quite new," Paris answered. "It's a very long story, but basically they met for an interview at a pub in London. Ben was attacked outside as they were leaving—the first kidnap attempt. After some passersby drove the men off, she took charge of him and his injuries. The rest is history, as they say."

"There's more to it than that, my darling," Hugh said. "He was attacked again the next day outside his flat." Olivia became wide-eyed as he continued. "Ben brought her to the country for a few days—part of a plan to keep them both safe from whoever was after him." That kidnapping was a failure, but the 'mastermind' had set a plan in motion to use you as backup. It wasn't long until you were abducted and demands were made. Since you and Valerie were together, it was obvious they had to take her as well." He paused, giving Olivia time to absorb the story. "It was an elaborate plan that was supposed to end with the perpetrators stealing a fortune in Spanish gold that was bound for display at the museum where your mother works. The kidnapping was all about manipulating her to cooperate."

Paris sat on the bed beside her daughter and took her hand. "The success of their plan was supposed to be your ticket to freedom, but they didn't succeed. Interpol was there to intercept them as they were caught opening what they thought were crates of antiquities."

Olivia said, "But I heard that awful man who attacked Ben talking to somebody and telling them that they no longer needed us and that he was going to 'tie up loose ends.' I don't think there was ever any intention to let us go."

Hugh leaned in and put his hand gently on her shoulder. "The so-called 'ticket to freedom' didn't exist. I believe he was going to kill you both—that it was the intention all along." He paused while his daughter took in another disturbing fact.

Olivia began to cry softly and Paris reached up to stroke her hair. She seemed to be remembering something important. "What happened to the other man? No one spoke, so she asked again, "The young man? I knew him— in London. Said his name was Clive Warren. I met him through my job and we dated a few times. I really liked him, and he seemed to like me a lot too." She stared at the ceiling and said, "Oh my God … I was really attracted to him, but I guess he was interested in me for another reason." She looked up at her mother and said, "Imagine how I felt when he showed up in Spain and turned out to be one of our captors."

"All part of someone's elaborate plan—apparently that 'someone' was the man who died at the airport while trying to escape Interpol," Hugh said, beginning to pace at the foot of her bed.

"But I don't think he wanted to be there—Clive I mean," Olivia said, looking puzzled. "At one point he tried to explain himself—something about danger to his brother. When push came to shove and he knew we were to be killed, he attacked that ugly hulk of a man who had chained us to the beds and practically starved us of food and water."

Paris looked at Hugh and said, "There is no punishment that will satisfy me." She buried her face in her hands, overwhelmed at learning the details of what they had endured.

"They have been punished, Mum. They're dead. Anyway, Clive temporarily got the best of the big guy, but shortly before that they struggled with a gun and Valerie was shot. They continued to struggle, and I remember the gun sliding into the room where we were." Paris shook her head in disbelief but signaled her daughter to continue. "Clive— or whatever his name is—was— looked very fit. He held his own from what I could hear. He must have knocked the other guy silly for a minute before he got attacked again. Then Ben broke through the door and distracted the man. There was just enough time for Clive to free our wrists from the handcuffs. He told me to run, but I didn't want to leave Valerie. He said if I didn't go, I'd die. By that time the man had attacked Ben. I ran and it's all a blur after that. I'm not really sure I've got it all straight."

Hugh assured her that no one could account correctly for every moment when under such stress. He explained what he knew, that Ben and the man had fought, and that Valerie had managed to get off one fatal shot. Olivia said that Valerie's shot was a miracle and that now she deserved a miracle of her own. Ana entered the cubicle and inadvertently interrupted the conversation. Concerned for her other child as well, Paris stood up and tensed her body.

"Nothing serious with Ben," Ana reassured them. "Just bruises and a little re-injury of the tissue around his shoulder joint. No broken ribs or internal bleeding. They have him icing his jaw and shoulder, and we're waiting now to see if they'll release him soon. He was advised to rest for a day or two." Now that she had relieved their minds she wanted to get back to him. "We're about three cubicles down. I'm going back to make sure he does as he's told."

When she had gone, Olivia became quite verbal about how she wanted Ben to be happy and hoped Ana would be right for him, but even though she had a good feeling about them, she would have to get to know Ana before passing judgment. Her strength was returning and she seemed almost euphoric. Then she started on the Ben-Valerie issue. She was sure that Valerie still loved him but knew it was over. She made a special point of the fact that in spite of great injury, and without thought for her own safety, she had managed to get to the gun, take some sort of aim and fire. Valerie's concern was for Ben, not for herself. She put aside the self-centeredness that had been so damaging to their marriage. Olivia hoped that Ben would have an opportunity to thank her. Perhaps the animosity between them could be put to rest. After her comment that it's always better to have an amicable divorce, she stopped chattering because a nurse came through with a tray of food. She set it before Olivia, kindly ordering her in Spanish to eat every bite in order to regain her strength. She complied.

* * *

The emergency room doctor had insisted that Ben lie down while waiting for the results of his jaw x-ray. Impatient and anxious to leave, Ben studied Ana as she sat beside the bed with her eyes closed. He wondered how she could relax at all considering the din outside their small curtained space. A moment later a nurse stuck her head in and told Ben there was an Inspector Macias waiting outside the emergency room.

Ben said, "If it's allowed, send him in."

"*Sí, pero sólo cinco minutos,*" she answered, turning away to fetch him.

The Inspector cautiously stuck his head through the opening in the curtains and said, "I'm told five minutes is my limit. Do you have any major injuries?" Ben shook his head no, and the inspector came into the cubicle. "*Señor* McKinnon, I have more information now than when we spoke at the *Comisaria. El Superintendente de la Policía de Pamplona* is now working with Interpol to bring this to a close. It is becoming evident how today's events are related." He paused a moment as his expression turned serious. "Yet it seems that you are directly related to another death."

Ben put down the icepack and answered, "You must mean the man at the little house."

"Yes. Can you explain what happened?"

"I was in a fight for my life with him, and my ex-wife managed to get off one shot that killed him." Inspector Macias crossed his arms and looked at Ben quizzically. "I know it sounds unbelievable, but it happened. Surely you can't be thinking that she's culpable in his death."

The inspector was quiet for a minute then asked, "Who was this man? What did he have to do with the events in London?"

It was painful for Ben to talk. Ana put the icepack in his hand and guided it back to his jaw then said she would explain. About twenty minutes later she finished telling the story of the attacks and kidnap attempts in London, the threats and demands received by Paris, and the coincidence of the women's trip to Pamplona. Ana added that Olivia had been seeing someone new in London, and the same man had turned up as one of their captors. She said they still had no details about the ruse used to abduct the women upon their arrival at the airport outside Pamplona.

Inspector Macias shook his head and said, *"Es muy complicado ... "* His voice trailed away as if he were organizing the whole scenario in his head.

"Yes, very complicated— and also quite hard to believe."

Hugh McKinnon pushed aside the curtain and stepped into the cubicle. Having heard Ana's comment he asked, "I heard you say that something's complicated. I guess you were referring to this whole thing— beginning to end."

Ben introduced his father to Inspector Macias, who seemed anxious to get back to his purpose for being there. Macias explained that Pamplona's *Superintendente* was out of sorts because his officers were not made a part of the rescue or informed of what was happening in London. Macias admitted that his superior's attitude didn't make sense. He had no idea why the man thought he should have been part of an action in the UK. The Interpol agent in charge was due in Spain the next day to meet with Macias' superior and explain why information about their actions was late reaching him.

Hugh then posed questions to the Inspector about what would be required of Ben in order to bring the investigation of events at the little house to a close. Macias emphasized that Ben would still have to come to the *Comisaria* to give a formal statement regarding his part in both of the related deaths. Ben's father stood taller and tensed his muscles. Macias quickly assured him that it was likely to be just a formality.

"'Likely' to be a formality?" Hugh said, crossing his arms in a defensive posture.

"A man who was being chased is dead," Macias said, "and you can't expect us not to thoroughly investigate." He was observing Ben's reaction as he continued. "I'm sure that as soon as there's a positive identification of both men, especially the one killed by the bull, we will find that your actions were justified."

At that point Ana jumped in and said, "We know the name he used with Olivia—Clive Warren— but it was probably an alias. Is there any way to trace both men to where they were staying?"

Macias answered, "Well, your sister will have to be questioned before she can leave Pamplona. I'd prefer to do it while I'm here, while certain facts are fresh in her mind. But I must defer to her doctor."

"I think she'll be anxious to tell you what she knows."

"We have the dead men's wallets and perhaps by now the investigators have found something like a key or a receipt that could provide more information. The passport of the man you chased states his name as Gareth Logan. I hope by the time I see you tomorrow we will have confirmed their identities and be able to release you both and close the case—this part at least."

Ben sat forward, suddenly remembering the rental car he had left parked on the side of the road. Macias assured him that it would eventually be towed to the police lot where he could retrieve it. As he shook hands with the men and started to leave, he added that any storage fees would be waived. Hugh strongly suggested that as soon as any further tests were completed, Ben should say goodbye to his mother and Olivia and get a taxi back to the hotel. Hugh returned to his daughter, and a few minutes later the doctor who treated Ben came into the cubicle to announce there were no injuries other than superficial bruising to his face, neck and torso. Ben declined the offer for strong pain medication and then was told he could go.

After doing what his father asked, he and Ana left the hospital and were soon on their way to the hotel. Ben rested his hand on hers but stared out the window, obviously pre-occupied.

Curious as to what was troubling him, she asked, "Are you worried about the statement you have to give tomorrow?"

He answered, "No, that isn't it. It's the woman—the one who's really responsible for Valerie and my sister being alive."

"Annunciata?"

"Yes, Annunciata Domingo. The woman works all the hours God gives and still struggles to raise her children."

"You sure learned a lot in a short time. Of course you want to do something for her, and rightly you should, but rest tonight and in the morning get the business at the *Comisaria* over with. Then we'll figure it out." Ana thought for a minute and added, "I'll bet Olivia and your parents will want to meet her."

"I hope the officer at the desk took down her address yesterday."

"I would think the police could easily track her down."

"I don't remember where she asked to be taken. She might not have gone straight home. You'd think I'd hit my head."

"You could still be a little disoriented. From what you described, your oxygen supply was compromised. Like I said, you need some rest." Ana laid her head back on the seat and a minute or so passed in thought before she continued. "It might be a lot to expect of her— to ask that she meet everyone."

"Maybe, but whatever I have to do I *will* find her." Ben turned to Ana with a broad happy smile, the first since they had arrived in Pamplona. Then he winced and rubbed his jaw.

* * *

Back at the hotel Ben settled on the bed holding another icepack to his jaw—this one just a towel filled with ice from the machine. Ana had a feeling of déjà vu, remembering that first night when she had dealt with his shoulder by making the same kind of makeshift ice pack. She went into the adjoining suite to shower, during which time Ben nodded off, the icepack having fallen aside. Wrapped in a fluffy robe provided by the hotel, Ana came back into his room just as the phone rang, startling him awake. She answered then handed it to Ben, saying it was his father. They spoke for several minutes then ended the call. His parents had left the hospital and were back in their hotel room. Olivia was doing well and the last word on Valerie was that she was stable. The caveat was that she would have to remain stable for several days before her ability to recover could be assured.

Ben settled back against the pillows and Ana went to refresh the ice pack. Once it was back on his jaw she excused herself, saying that she needed to sort through her clothes. In truth she needed time alone, time to think. With all the turmoil around her she had no time to sort through her own feelings about all that had happened. Since they first met, she and Ben had shared truly carefree moments only once. Even as their attraction for each other grew, there was always a mutual presence of worry and threat. Those moments were burned into memory— the powerful flow of passion they had tried to stifle because of the obvious threat to his family. The battle had been lost. They didn't realize, sequestered in the dense growth with birds cawing and circling overhead, that two women Ben cared about were headed for Spain and a horrendous experience.

Ana went to the window and stared out at the last moments of dusk. She was weary, but her mind refused to calm itself. At this point she was sure to have lost the job she was assigned—maybe future ones as well. Her professional reputation was bound to suffer. How would that affect her connection to Ben? The dynamic between them would now change in some way. Ben would no longer have a commitment to make himself available to her for any reason. Was his attraction to her fueled only by the heightened senses of the situation, or did it go deeper? It had been unnatural—the way they had been forced into a premature intimacy by the events of that first night. Although not sexual intimacy, there existed a sexual undercurrent she had sensed from the moment they met. Should she play it cool now, offer him some space? Surely he would want to return to England, spend time with his family. She would be an outsider. She would have no place at the table. And there was Valerie. Could her heroic actions soften him toward her? If she recovered, might they reconcile?

Overwhelmed by all there was to contemplate, she turned away from the approaching darkness, walked to the bed, threw herself down and began to sob quietly. Emotional and physical exhaustion soon brought sleep. An hour passed before she was awakened by Ben's knock on the door adjoining their rooms. Startled, she sat up, and without a thought to her red puffy eyes she told him to come in. He had showered and dressed, but still sported the stubble of several days without a shave. His hair was still damp and combed straight back. Other than the bruising on his jaw, he looked fresh and as vital as ever. Ana was suddenly aware of her own appearance. She brushed the hair away from her face and then looked down at the bed in a vain attempt to hide the fact that she had been crying. Her puffy eyes didn't escape Ben's scrutiny.

Ben frowned as he asked, "Have you been crying?" He answered his own question. "Of course you have—I can see that." She didn't reply. "I can understand that this whole thing has taken a toll on you too. I know we aren't your family, but you've treated us as if we were."

"Oh, it's nothing," she replied. Ben's expression told her he wasn't buying it. "Well… I guess it's not *nothing*. The gravity of the day's events just got to me all of a sudden."

In a tone that reflected doubt he said, "I think there's more to it than that. I know I frightened you today. One thing is sure: If you had been in a similar situation and able to run off, leaving me wondering what would happen, I would be terrified … and more than a little angry… mad as hell, actually."

"Of course I'm not angry. But I was terrified. This was my first experience with feeling helpless—being involved in something really serious. I guess I knew all along, from our experiences in London, that if I stuck around, things would get dicey."

"When I decided to come to Pamplona, I should have insisted you stay in London. I truly didn't think it would lead to this degree of violence. But once I was involved, I had to follow through. She's my sister."

"Of course you did. I admire and respect your decision. But the whole thing had another result—an unexpected one."

"Unexpected?"

"Yes. I guess it would be easier to refer to an old adage that applies—sorta." She took a deep breath and began, stumbling slightly with her words. "They say one never realizes what they have until they lose it, or I might say *thinks* they could lose it."

Ben cocked his head trying to understand, but didn't say anything. After a pause Ana blurted out, "You! You! I was afraid of losing *you!*" Ben backed away slightly, surprised by the intensity of her remark. "The hours after you ran off were excruciating, and as every minute passed I realized how much I didn't want to lose whatever it was that had started between us." She began to pace around the room, arms folded to her chest, waiting for a response and feeling as though her honesty could make a fool of her.

"Nothing between us has changed because of this. Well, I guess it will change, actually, because now a murdering crook isn't chasing me, and I don't have to worry about Olivia. That sounds pretty good to me."

Ana smiled self-consciously and abruptly sat down on the small boudoir chair in the corner of the room. She looked down then combed through her tousled hair with her fingers. Ben stood his ground, waiting for her to say something. Finally, in a voice so soft he could scarcely hear it, she said, "Me too."

Ben walked over and pulled her to her feet. "Hold me gently," he said, carefully placing her arms around his torso.

She obliged and then kissed him softly on the lips, taking care to avoid the small cut, and then on his jaw. They remained standing in each other's arms until the ringing phone in his room interfered. Ben went through and answered the call. His father was on the other end, calling to tell him that Valerie was awake, and although they can't see her until she's out of ICU, she keeps asking for 'Ben.' After he assured his father he would be there soon, he returned to Ana's room to share the news.

"Valerie's awake! I think maybe the worst of *everything* is over—or almost over."

"That *is* good news—the best," Ana said, rising onto her tiptoes and kissing his cheek.

Ben slipped his arms around her waist and in a more serious tone replied, "Well, she's not completely out of the woods, but at least she survived the surgery." He hesitated then said, "I have to go—thank her for saving my life. Dad said she's asking for me."

Ana maintained her happy expression, but although she was relieved for Ben's ex-wife, she was also troubled by what this might mean to her connection with him—in spite of the divorce. She couldn't avoid the thought that he might still feel some sort of obligation to Valerie, both with her recovery and the future status of their previous relationship. Ben had said very little, other than the marriage had been increasingly troubled and difficult. Clearly she could have no control over what happened, but she wanted to be there.

"Let me come with you," she said immediately. "I can visit with Olivia and your parents while you see Valerie."

"Thanks, but I have no idea how long I'll be. Just wait here and I'll stay in touch—promise," Ben said, not realizing he had caused Ana to feel like an outsider yet again. She resigned herself to more hours of doubt ahead and put on a happy face when wishing him luck. She feared he could be walking out the door and back into his old life.

CHAPTER TWENTY-ONE

In less than an hour Ben was standing outside the ICU entrance, waiting for permission to enter. Shortly the head duty nurse opened the door and in halting English asked his name and the name of the patient he wanted to see.

"Por favor esepere aqui." she said, then closed the door and disappeared for several minutes, while Ben waited impatiently.

Upon her return she opened the door wider and motioned for him to follow her. She led him into a room where he was ordered to wash his hands thoroughly and to put sterilized scrubs over his clothing. Due to the language gap these instructions were primarily accomplished with pointing and hand gestures. He was then shown to a small room that seemed more like a cubicle. There were walls but no window, and inside he saw only a small table and the bed where Valerie lay sleeping. The wall facing the corridor was glass, which facilitated keeping an eye on the patient. A Venetian blind afforded privacy but was fully opened. She looked small, pale and defenseless. Cords attached her to several monitors, while IV bags were delivering fluids and transfusing blood. Small tubes in her nostrils supplied oxygen and a sterilized bonnet resembling a shower cap covered her hair. She appeared to be sleeping, but soon responded to the slight noise of the door as he entered.

Her eyes opened slowly and she noticed him standing there. She smiled weakly, but there was a vacancy in her eyes that Ben thought might be a result of the drugs she'd been given for pain. He walked to the side of the bed and took her hand in his. Her lips and mouth were very dry when she tried to speak.

"Ben... you're okay... right?" Her speech was slurred, and when he nodded yes she seemed not to notice the bruising on his face. "I told that ugly man my husband would come for me." She paused, trying to find her words. "I told him you loved me and you would come. *I did, I did...* but he didn't care." Her speech became more fuzzy and trailed off as she closed her eyes.

Ben had tried not to show his shock when she began to speak of them as a couple. A few minutes later Valerie opened her eyes again and spoke. She asked when they could go home to their flat in London, and then asked if her parents could visit. Her expression softened as she said that when she was feeling strong again it would be time they had a baby. Valerie was rambling, obviously under the influence of medication, and Ben looked down at the floor, not knowing how to respond. He could tell she was having trouble staying awake and hoped she would drift off so he could step out and find her doctor. Just as he completed the thought Valerie startled, and with one hand she reached for the other, the one Ben was holding. She suddenly tried to move.

The distress in her voice was obvious as she spoke. "Where's my ring? Someone stole my ring!" She looked at Ben, imploring him for an answer. He was struck speechless. Summoning what strength she had, she demanded, "Ben! I need my ring!"

"Don't get upset. I'll see what I can find out." In order to keep her calm that was the only answer he could give. He excused himself under the guise of making inquiries about the ring.

She called after him in a weak scratchy voice. "Come back soon."

Ben stopped the first nurse he encountered in the corridor and tried to communicate that he needed badly to talk to Valerie McKinnon's doctor. He apologized for forgetting the doctor's name. She seemed to understand and pointed to a chair where he assumed he was meant to wait. After about a quarter of an hour that seemed much longer, he saw a lanky man in a white coat push the ICU door open and stride quickly toward him. It was the doctor who had come to Olivia's room to tell them about Valerie's condition. As Doctor Garces re-introduced himself, Ben recalled his difficulty with English, so he proceeded to speak slowly, describing her strange behavior and seeming departure from reality. However, to be very sure of what he was being told, the doctor asked him to wait while he looked for an English-speaking nurse. He soon returned with the nurse who had assisted him when speaking with the family. He told Ben that memory loss could be a side effect of not only the emotional trauma of her experience, but also as a result of blood loss and short term oxygen loss. He then related the fact that while on the operating table her blood pressure had dropped twice, and although her breathing stopped, they had managed revive her. He said the memory loss could be short term, yet there was a possibility it could be emotional—that she could be taking refuge in a time of life where she felt safe. He asked if she had ever experienced psychological problems.

Ben told him about the ongoing problems for which she was still being treated, and that they had been divorced for several years. He added that there was no going back. The doctor nodded his head in understanding then said that given her previous situation, the lapse could be more complicated and less temporary. Asking about her next of kin he emphasized they should be notified and advised to be present. The doctor extended his hand to Ben, offering to be of help in any way he could. He thanked the nurse then excused himself, citing his need to finish rounds.

Ben's thoughts ran rampant, and he shook his head in frustration. He cared deeply about her recovery, and after all, besides the fact that she had been his wife, she had saved his life. But where did his responsibility end? He wasn't prepared to live a charade for her sake. No one knew how long her break with reality would last. Ben's focus was now on Ana and where their developing relationship might go. Valerie was his past. He decided to put his rumination aside long enough to inform his parents of what they were facing. Valerie's parents needed to be on the next plane for Spain. When Ben peeked into her room he was glad she was asleep. He returned to Olivia's cubicle in the ER, where his parents continued their vigil at her bedside. His Dad was on the phone and his sister was sitting up, her color having returned to normal, her eyes alert to the surroundings. All three turned to look at him as he entered.

"Well, we have more of the unexpected to deal with."

Olivia was quick to question him. "Is it Valerie? She's still okay, right?"

"Physically, yes—for now. Psychologically, no."

Paris joined the conversation. "What in heaven do you mean, psychologically?"

Hugh glanced from one to the other as if waiting for the other shoe to drop, but before Ben could continue, Hugh's phone rang. When he heard the voice on the other end he put his hand up to hush the others. He listened carefully then thanked the caller and rang off.

"That was my colleague at Interpol about the DNA results on the man killed at the airport. They put a rush on it, but they aren't in yet." He turned to Paris and said, "But there is news. You may need to sit down for this one, my darling."

Paris leaned against the small chest of drawers and said, "I don't know why I would care who it is one way or the other. I'm just glad the person is dead, and I don't feel guilty for it." She stiffened and crossed her arms.

"You may not care, but you *will* be shocked. It was Lyle Brett, that little prig in the office across from yours."

She slumped into the closest chair and shook her head in disbelief. "Surely not…"

"The identification will be confirmed by DNA and dental records, but it will take a few days." He quickly added, "The car's VIN number was still readable. It was a rental and easy to trace. From that point it was a short step to identify who rented it. He wasn't smart enough to use an alias."

"If the person who crashed it was actually the one who rented it," Ben said.

"I have no doubt about that. As soon as his cohorts were arrested in the hangar, one of them gave up Brett's name —just minutes before the crash."

Once Paris had recovered her composure the words began to flow easily. "Seems I wasn't just imagining he was jealous of me… and there's no doubt he came across as a narcissist. But this?" Paris stopped talking, but the wheels were still turning. Everyone just waited for her to continue. "It would take a sociopath—a megalomaniac—to believe in the success of such an elaborate plan—ill conceived as it turned out."

"Considering he had an assortment of conspirators and their individual 'schemes' to coordinate in two different countries, he actually came quite close to succeeding. That terrifies me. The girls would have been collateral damage," Hugh said, beginning to pace back and forth in the small enclosure.

Paris looked into the faces of her loved ones, and her voice quavered as she spoke. "I feel so guilty for making you all a part of this, for creating so much risk in your lives. If Valerie should die, I won't be able to live with myself." She broke into tears and Hugh moved to embrace her.

Each in turn made their case about her lack of responsibility for all that had happened. She expressed regret at ever having shared a word about her family or any of the details of their day-to-day lives. She was sure he gleaned the information through eavesdropping on her visits with coworkers. Their families were most often the topic of conversation. When considering all the coincidences that meant nothing at the time, she understood the covert reason for his unexpected leave of absence. He was putting the last details of the plan into action.

"He would have had a very difficult time trying to dispose of the gold, even if they had gotten away Scot-free," Hugh said.

Ben added, "I have a suspicion he would have had it melted down—

shaped into bars. What a waste of valuable artifacts. Or it's possible he already had some foreign buyer ready to take it off his hands."

"He may have hoped to accomplish one of those plans, but it hardly matters now. We'll never know what his next step would have been." Hugh said. "The 'loot' is safe in the hands of the museum. I understand the Spanish have several special guards en route to personally keep an eye on the exhibit."

"Who could blame them," Olivia said. "I wonder how he managed to collect such an assortment of misfits to do his bidding."

Hugh had one more piece of information. It had been confirmed that the young man killed by the bull was not 'Clive Warren,' but a man named Gareth Logan, employee at a computer company in London. He turned to Olivia and said, "I mentioned to Interpol what you told me about his brother in prison. Their inquiry showed that he does indeed have a younger brother in prison."

Ben said, "Well, that's another piece of the puzzle, but do we know how it fits?"

Hugh replied, "I think that as the investigation progresses they'll find some link between one of Brett's goons and some prisoner in the same facility. He was probably manipulated with a threat to his brother's life. The young man is all right at present and will be separated from the general population until the investigation is completed. The Interpol team stopped one of the men apprehended in the storage hangar before he could complete a call to execute any more of Brett's plans."

"There's still the matter of who sent that email hinting at where they were."

"We may never find out," Hugh said, clearly frustrated. "Whoever sent it was good. The agency is still trying to trace it."

Paris, who had been quietly pacing the room, joined the conversation. "It had to be someone who cared about one of them—or both."

Hugh nodded his head in agreement and said, "My best guess is Gareth Logan, aka Clive Warren."

Ben looked down, and in a subdued voice he said, "This became a case of 'let no good deed go unpunished.'"

His father was quick to respond, his tone emphatic. "Ben, your actions were justified. He made a choice. But of course such an outcome is regrettable." Paris was quick to add that Ben's justifiable actions were also foolhardy.

It was a lot to take in, and the group turned quiet, each one lost in thought. Ben broke the silence by returning to the subject of Valerie. He repeated his previous statement that they had something unexpected to deal with. Ben explained Valerie's reaction to him, her seeming refuge in the past, and the upset about her wedding ring, something she hadn't worn for a very long time. He then told them what the doctor had said. Everyone agreed the Amesworths should be informed and arrangements made to get them to Spain right away. Hugh offered to pull some strings to get them on a plane within hours and asked Paris to call them. She left the ER and dialed Valerie's parents. She wondered how best to tell them what had happened, and that they needed to come immediately.

Ben called Ana to tell her what was going on and to explain he was headed back to Valerie's room to keep up the charade until an evaluation was made of her psychological condition. Since it would be touch and go for another twenty-four hours post-surgery, he was concerned that any additional shock could be damaging. Ana tried her best to be sympathetic, but there was a nagging doubt about Valerie's influence on Ben, and whether she could pull him into the past with her. She decided to go to the hospital and see first-hand what would transpire.

* * *

The cab pulled up and stopped at the hospital entrance. The driver turned around and informed Ana of the fare. Anxious and distracted by her situation she paid him too much, the amount of the tip putting a wide smile on his face. She got out, thanked him, and hurriedly followed the walkway to the hospital entrance. She approached the main reception desk and asked for Olivia McKinnon, hoping the woman on duty spoke English. She was directed to the ER, where Olivia still remained, and while en route a variety of scenarios passed through her mind. Would they be glad to see her, or would they feel she was an intruder? Would Ben chastise her for not waiting at the hotel? Would he be keeping vigil at Valerie's bedside and not even notice she was there? Where had her self-confidence gone? Was this the price one paid for caring... for falling in love? Was she in love? She couldn't deny that something profound was changing her, hour by hour, day by day. It was Ben. Her heart had become vulnerable.

Her earlier presence in the ER meant nothing to the nurse on duty. It took some fancy verbal footwork to gain entrance to the area where Olivia was being cared for. Ana walked slowly and quietly to the fourth cubicle on the right. She heard familiar voices and stopped for a moment to regain her composure before carefully pulling aside the curtain. Hugh and Paris turned in tandem as she stuck her head through the curtains and asked if it would be all right to come in. Paris came forward with open arms and embraced her. Hugh then took her hand in both of his and squeezed gently, saying he was glad to see her. Olivia was quiet for the moment but smiled at Ana.

When the greetings were over, Olivia said, "Ana... to say thank you just isn't enough, but it's all I've got for now. You're a big part of the reason Valerie and I are alive."

"Oh no," Ana replied. "It was Ben who risked his life. I came along when the worst was over. But I'm sure glad I ignored his order to stay put and followed him to the house anyway."

"How did you know where to go?" Hugh asked.

"Just lucky. I found a business card on his nightstand with a Spanish address scribbled on it. I didn't know if that was where he'd gone, but why else would he have it? That was the only clue."

In a vain attempt at humor, Olivia said, "Perhaps a second career as a detective?"

A collective smile was all they could muster before her parents expressed their appreciation to Ana and shared the new information just received about those involved. She tactfully tried to change the subject— to find out where Ben was and how Valerie was doing. Paris said that of course she needed to know what was going on with Valerie and suggested they go out into the hallway. She then explained about Valerie's lapse in awareness and the refuge she seemed to be taking in the past. Ana's expression made it clear that she was concerned, not only for Valerie, but for the situation's effect on Ben both now and in the weeks to come.

Paris knew immediately what was bothering Ana. She took Ana's hand, looked her straight in the eye and said, "My dear, you do know that Ben is just doing what the doctor has advised… keeping her calm until she's a bit stronger and can be evaluated by a neurologist or psychiatrist." Ana nodded, and Paris added, "Regardless of what's going on right now, that relationship has been over in every respect for a long time now. Most of their impulsive marriage was a very unhappy time for Ben, but he put forth great effort before admitting it was over and that he no longer loved her."

Ana looked down and said, "With what Valerie went through I was feeling quite guilty for thinking about myself."

"Nonsense! That's just being human. Be patient. Her parents will soon be on their way here to take charge of her care. I'm quite sure that as soon as she's strong enough they will have her airlifted either to London, or if she's up to it, the States." Paris paused for a moment then corrected her statement. "Maybe it will be better to have her in London where she can be seen by the psychiatrist she knows." She led Ana by the hand back into the cubicle then turned to Hugh and said, "What was her name? Valerie's psychiatrist?"

"Dr. Locksley… Kate, I think. If Valerie doesn't snap out of this, Locksley would be their best bet."

Paris agreed and pointed out that her parents could have an extended stay in London ahead of them. She was sure they would prefer to take

Valerie 'home' and realized there was no point in further discussion of the matter. Paris sat down on the bed near Olivia and took her hand. Hugh gestured that Ana should take the chair then he settled on the edge of the nightstand and put his arm around Paris. She felt better for having spoken with Paris, who urged her to tell Hugh more of the details of her experience.

Just as she was preparing to bring up the subject, the curtains were pushed aside and Ben came through. The first thing he saw was Ana, who jumped out of the chair like a startled rabbit. He seemed slightly irritated, yet glad to see her in spite of it. Over a week ago he had realized that she was a woman to whom orders would mean nothing— if she had her own agenda. Better that he weigh his words in the future. Perhaps she would be more amenable to the word 'request.' And yet that rebellious quality had helped save two lives.

"Ben, I couldn't sit in that room any longer, *again*, waiting for the phone to ring," she said, her tone mildly defiant.

"I get it, Ana, but one of these days you could find yourself in a dangerous situation by not paying attention to someone concerned for your safety."

Ben's words made her feel like an errant child, but one who could, when warranted, defend her actions. "Well, this was not one of those cases. I shall, however, take heed of your counsel in the future."

Her formal choice of language caused everyone to chuckle softly, which diffused the moment of tension between the two. Ben sighed and shook his head in mock frustration. Hugh then pointed out that Ana was a journalist, and waiting around wasn't in their handbook. Ana felt that the comment was his way of chastening Ben for being cross. Yet she knew that his short fuse had to be the result of this latest complication. They both thought the worst was over, but now there was Valerie.

She longed for that time, not long passed, when in spite of the escalation of violence it was just the two of them—each protecting the other in different ways. Once again she remembered the flowers, the scent of leather as he drew her close—but most of all, the kisses. If she closed her eyes, she could almost feel them again. And the fact was, she liked what he had just said to her. It showed that he cared. But those brief moments of indulgence in the countryside had been their only real physical connection. From that point on, their energies were completely focused on Olivia and Valerie. Throughout, Ana's main function seemed to have been to nurse Ben's series of injuries. He didn't need her for that anymore, and she wondered if he would still need her in other ways. It would never sort itself out unless they could be alone together again—put distance between themselves and all that had happened. Her reverie was short-lived. She was called back by hearing her name.

Paris had decided that Ben and Ana should leave the hospital for a while to have a meal and some conversation. She pointed out that Olivia was fine and that specialists would no doubt be examining Valerie and conducting whatever diagnostic procedures were required. She had appointed herself as orchestrator of the interaction between her son and his ex-wife, and was determined that he not be drawn back in due to his sympathetic nature. She remembered clearly Valerie's penchant for manipulation. It wouldn't be a surprise to Paris if the woman were feigning the memory loss. Not that she lacked pity for what had been endured by both women, but she remained suspicious that Valerie might try to turn it to her advantage.

Olivia and her parents collectively shooed Ben and Ana out of the room with firm instructions to stay away until morning. Ben would be allowed to check in once by phone. He knew better than to argue, so he took Ana's hand and led her out of the cubicle then out of the hospital. Once on the sidewalk they looked at each other with mutual expressions of self-consciousness. Both said sorry at the same time, dispelling any previous conflict. However, the somber air between them remained, the day's stark truths weighing heavily on both. They walked slowly to a nearby café that advertised *tortilla española* on the sidewalk menu board.

The aching in Ben's body had subdued his appetite and he had declined the custard offered by a nurse. He couldn't remember the last time he'd had any food. When asked if she had eaten, Ana had to admit it had been over twenty-four hours. Something simple and hearty, like potatoes and egg, seemed just the ticket. Fortified by the food and strong coffee they hailed a taxi and returned to the hotel.

* * *

Ben looked exhausted, his face showing the emotional strain of seeing Valerie. Even for Ana it had been almost too much to take in—the facts concerning the robbery along with Valerie's lapse from reality. Ana was struck by the fact that whenever they had found themselves alone— whether in a hotel or house, under a tree or in a field—there had been a developing crisis in the works. First there was the attack, the night together in her hotel dealing with his injury, and then the next attack followed by their fleeing to the Cotswolds. There were an occasional few moments alone in the house, but there was Edith, the housekeeper, who was wont to pop in unexpectedly. They had never been more isolated than in the field, the place where they had finally given in to the lust. She wondered if their passionate moment had been tainted due to what was going on around them— at least for Ben. The uncertainty caused her to question whether the moment would ever come, or if that was their one chance, if everything had peaked among the flowers and was now on a downhill slide. Not for her—of that she was sure. But now, again, the moment was wrong.

"Ben, you look war-weary," Ana said. "With everything that's been going on, I doubt your body has let go of the trauma it experienced. You need to sleep."

He sat down on the edge of the bed, kicked off his shoes, then took a deep breath and blew it out. "Right. But here we are alone again in a hotel and I'm still basically useless."

Ana stepped back toward the adjoining door then stood looking down at her shoes. She emitted a sigh and said, "Yep… seems to be a pattern with us. Or maybe an omen?"

"Not an omen— just consistent bad timing… so far." He swung his legs up onto the bed and leaned back against the pillows. "I know this is a well-worn adage, but it applies here: the best things in life are worth waiting for."

"You've 'set the bar high' with that statement, but from my side I tend to agree with your little adage—in some cases." Ana smiled, clearly teasing, but Ben saw a hint of embarrassment on her face. He found it arousing in spite of his aching fatigue. She added, "It might be dangerous to have such expectations. It could be a formula for disappointment."

"I'm not worried," he said, locking his eyes with hers and grinning provocatively.

Ana felt the familiar flush run through her body. Such a small thing, that grin, but it touched her to the core. It took more than a modicum of control to keep her from dashing to the bed and throwing herself onto her back, arms extended, and begging him to take her post-haste. That instant of reckless imagination gone, she shook herself back from the brink. The sometimes-pragmatic Ana took charge. She walked to the bed, bent over, kissed Ben's forehead and told him to sleep well. He took hold of her arm rather tightly and pulled her down. She fell against his torso—rather clumsily, she thought. He leaned forward and slipped his other arm around her back, and without a moment's pause his lips met hers, his tongue forcing exploration of her mouth in a frustrated attempt to enter her in some way. Then as suddenly as it had started it was over.

Ben backed away, and Ana pulled herself up into a sitting position. When he had regained control he said, "Do you still question whether it's worth waiting for? Still worried about disappointment?"

"I think not," Ana said, still a bit dazed from the suddenness of his actions and their effect on her. She knew the effort had to have caused him some pain.

He reached for her hand and squeezed it gently. "Just so you know, I'm not partial to stopping again, but I really want us to be free of all the drama around us."

She smiled in agreement then said, her voice calculatingly soft and breathy, "And I don't want you exhausted when that time comes." She kissed him lightly, got up and headed toward her adjoining room. As she reached the doorway she looked back and said, "Sleep well." Ben let out a frustrated groan, and without a thought to undressing he reached over to turn off the bedside lamp.

After quietly closing the adjoining door, Ana stood for a moment and looked around the room, empty but for a suitcase and clothing strewn on one of the chairs. She took a deep breath, exhaled and walked to the window, fearing that in spite of her own fatigue, Ben's impetuous actions would be enough to keep her awake with longing. The summer night had settled on Pamplona, and below her window the plaza's street lamps lighted the way for groups of people who moved about, enjoying a reprieve from the heat of the day. There was comfort in knowing that although in a different room, Ben was safe and sleeping. She quickly removed her outer clothing, tossed back the duvet, and fell across the bed. Ben's kiss, the feel of his arms around her, and his words— especially his words— occupied her thoughts until she fell asleep.

CHAPTER TWENTY-TWO

Ana was jarred awake by several quick knocks on one of her room's two doors. She waited, and the next knock definitely came from the door adjoining the rooms. Evidently Ben was awake. It was barely light, and Ana could have easily drifted off again were it not that she was anxious to see him. She was still sprawled crosswise on the bed, but sometime during the night she had pulled the bed cover over her body.

"Wait a sec," she called out, and at the same time reached for clothes from the rumpled pile on the chair.

"Are you decent?" he said, opening the door just a crack.

"Almost," she said, pulling on the last item of clothing before giving a final okay.

Ben seemed surprised when he walked into the room and looked at her. "Aren't those the same clothes you were wearing yesterday?"

"Well, I noticed you went to sleep in yours, but I took mine off last night. When you knocked just now I was still asleep. I had to put on something— the first thing I could grab.

Ben adopted the provocative expression that had affected Ana since they first met. Then he smirked a little and said, "I hope some day soon you won't want to put clothes *on* when I come into a room. I'd rather you'd want to take them *off*." He deliberately stared hard into her eyes and waited for a reaction."

Ana's reaction was strong, but she kept it invisible. The bit of shyness she felt was easily subdued by her desire. With Ben's family crisis at an end she could let her feelings re-emerge. Not to be outdone, she accepted his verbal challenge and said, "Well, that kiss last night might be a deciding factor… but of course I'll probably require some more convincing."

Ben liked her answer. Ana could see that in his smile. And yet acting coy had never been part of her repertoire, nor did it really fit the image she had worked hard to create— at least professionally. She was a journalist and had to be independent, insightful, and once in a while, even pushy. Undeniably this man had turned her upside down and sideways, but it was good— all good.

A few moments passed while they stood facing each other, yet with separate thoughts. Ben wondered if the waiting after their first encounter, plus the burden and seriousness of the distractions, had taken the starch out of the anticipation— at least for Ana. It could do that. Yet for him the desire just continued to intensify, and he knew it was really up to him to free them from their complete immersion in recent events. He wanted to find a way to let her know he was working on it— if, so far, only in his mind. They had to hold on until Valerie's parents arrived in Spain. Then he hoped to feel less responsibility to stay close to the hospital. And it wouldn't be too long until his parents would whisk Olivia back to the Cotswolds, where she would be nurtured and indulged and Sir Freddie would be constantly at her heels. Ben expected she would soon run screaming back to London to resume her independent life. He laughed to himself, knowing just what she was in for.

Switching back to the present, Ben said, "Sorry, but I have to check in at the hospital. And then I want to see if I can find Annunciata Domingo. Maybe there's something I can do for her to show my gratitude. She's probably wondering how it all turned out."

"I'm not waiting around in this room again. I'll come with you to the hospital, say hello to your parents and Olivia, then do some digging."

"Some digging?" He noticed that she seemed exited.

"I'm going to drop in at the police station and see if I can get her information from Inspector… what was his name?"

"Macias. But he might not be on duty. Better call first."

She agreed, and then her expression turned serious. "I'd better hone my journalistic skills with this little assignment because I'm quite sure I no longer have a job with the magazine."

"Wow, sorry— *again*," Ben said, frowning. "I really feel bad about that. Hard to believe that in all this time there wasn't a minute for that interview."

"I find that easy to believe, considering recent events. Besides, I've learned an awful lot about you, just by association… although none of it relates to your writing." Her expression turned sly, and Ben wondered just what she was referring to. After a short pause she turned serious again. "One thing is certain— everything that's happened to you would make quite a story."

"Not sure about that," he said, shaking his head in the negative. "It's mainly about Valerie and Olivia. They were the ones at the center of it, danger-wise."

"I seem to remember some guy trying to either kidnap or kill you. What was it? Three times?"

"True, but still…"

Ana threw her arms up in frustration, convinced that Ben was extremely reluctant to be the hero of the story. She shooed him back to his room and promised to be put together in half an hour. When she had freshened up she was the one who knocked, this time asking if he was decent. He told her to come in, and when she did she found him standing by the bed in only a towel. The bruises on his body were evident, and although she was sympathetic, the sight of his bare torso took her thoughts elsewhere.

"I'll be ready in a few," he said, and then grabbed the clean clothes piled on the bed before disappearing into the bathroom.

* * *

During the cab ride to the hospital Ben commented that the city now looked different to him, that when they first arrived Pamplona seemed like an adversary, a threat to finding his sister and ex-wife. Ana agreed that she saw the city differently as well. She told him it was time for them to enjoy it, but Ben pointed out that he wasn't sure he could wipe everything from his mind well enough for that. He then assured her that if not in Pamplona, they would definitely find enjoyment somewhere.

When they reached Olivia's cubicle, she had just finished dressing in the clothing her mother had purchased in the hotel shop. She said her parents were settling the bill and planned to take her back to the hotel. They agreed that finding hers and Valerie's belongings would be a lost cause, and that they had surely been disposed of in order to erase any trace of the two women being in Pamplona. Olivia whined to Ben that her parents insisted on switching to adjoining rooms, where Paris could keep a motherly eye on her until they returned to London. Then she begged him to intervene with their plans to whisk her off to the country. He told her to stop fussing, that she still needed rest. There was a brief pout, but resigned to her fate she flopped down on the bed to wait.

Ben told Ana she might as well leave for the *Comisaria*—not wait for his parents to return. He predicted everyone would have a meal together after his parents moved rooms and got Olivia settled in. Ana impulsively gave him a kiss on the cheek and then wondered if she should have done so in front of Olivia. She turned to say goodbye and saw Olivia's wide, somewhat teasing smile. Ben winked at her and she left.

While en route to the *Comisaria,* Ana reviewed the methods for investigative reporting she had learned but not put into practice for quite a while. She checked her purse for a pad and pen to use in case the inspector didn't want to be recorded on her phone. She and Ben had forgotten to check whether Macias was on duty and she hoped that even if he wasn't on site, someone could be persuaded to show her the file containing Annunciata's information. Stepping out of the cab she remembered the first rule: walk with authority and adopt a confident stance. An open smile, preferably sincere, was also a plus. Then it was pretty much a matter of 'catching more flies with honey.' Ana didn't consider that to be a sexist ploy because affability was appropriate in all cases. And besides, men did catch a lot of flies with honey— the flies being of the female variety— and for both personal and professional reasons. Then came the realization that she was well on her way to becoming a cynic.

At the entrance a uniformed man on his way out smiled and held the door for her. Quickly scanning the room, she noticed the information counter and the officer sitting behind it. Ana approached with confidence and a smile then asked for Inspector Macias. In order to see into the inspector's office, the man craned his neck to look over the heads of the men sitting at their desks. Macias' chair was empty.

"No es aquí, señorita," he said, looking back down at the open file on the counter.

She persisted, asking, "English?"

"Sólo un poco," he replied, sounding indifferent.

Her shoulders drooped, knowing it would be a miracle to accomplish the goal she had set without a decent command of Spanish for her and more than a little English for him. The officer sensed Ana's frustration and told her to wait. He stepped away for a moment and waved to another officer, motioning him to come over. One problem was solved. The officer spoke English, and she was able to question him about records associated with the recent kidnapping of two women. He said the files did exist, but that not just anyone could come in and expect to see them. Ana made an effort to stand taller, and then related to him, slowly, the facts of her involvement and the need for the information about the woman who had been instrumental in finding the two victims. She stressed that it would be to the woman's benefit if they could find her. He was unimpressed with her plea and shook his head no. So with her determination still intact Ana thanked him, hesitating to walk away without what she came for. Concurrently, a nicely dressed man with a leather satchel under his arm strode hastily through the entrance, pushing open both doors at once.

Another officer, who had just come into the foyer from the office area, saw the man and called, *"Saludos, Macias! ¿Cómo estás?"* Ana spun around and headed straight for him.

* * *

A short while later, Ana came out of the *Comisaria* with a smile on her face and headed across the plaza to the hotel, the desired information safely in her possession. Back at the hotel she sat down in a lobby chair and dug out her phone, deciding to call Ben rather than text him. The call went to voicemail. She left a message, figuring he must be in the ICU checking on Valerie. On her way to the elevator she heard the familiar alert of an arriving text message. Ben told her to stay put, that he was on his way back to the hotel. Her short response said she would be in her room.

It had been a restless night, and after carrying out her assignment at the *Comisaria* Ana felt drained. She flopped down on the bed to wait for Ben, pulled a pillow under her head and decided to close her eyes— just for a minute. The next thing she heard was Ben's voice.

"Ana… Ana… are you feeling okay?"

She snapped awake and saw him leaning over her. "I'm fine. Can't believe I dozed off."

"I can believe it. It'll take some time before we recover from everything." Ben sat down in a chair near the bed and asked, "So, what did you find out?" As she got up to retrieve the information, he added, "And by the way, good job."

"All in a day's work." She pulled a folded piece of paper out of her bag and handed it to him. He opened it and read what was written.

"This is only her address and telephone number… but that's probably all we need. There's no way to tell if that's a mobile or residential phone number."

"Doesn't really matter," Ana said, looking at him and waiting to hear about whatever plan he was hatching.

"Before I call I need to decide what I can do for her that would really mean something. And Dad wants to be involved." Ben threw his head back and stared at the ceiling, rummaging through his thoughts, hoping for inspiration.

"Well, she has kids," Ana said. "And you said you can tell she works long hours to keep her family going."

"And...?"

"I think the only significant thing to do would be financial."

Ben nodded in agreement. "Maybe if she had a little money to keep the kids in school, she wouldn't have to work quite as hard. I don't know how many there are, or their ages."

"You could just ask."

Ben felt a bit silly, not applying his own logic, but didn't say anything. After another short conversation on the subject it was decided that a trust for their education expenses would be of the most help. They would have liked a way to give her everything, but it was doubtful a woman like Annunciata would take it. He expected resistance to any interference. At least he hoped she wouldn't see it that way.

Ana suggested that for the time being he should just telephone to say thank you and let her know how right she was to go to the police. She hoped he could summon enough rusty Spanish to carry it off. During the conversation he could ask about the children, their ages—casual things. Ben decided that he would proceed to make arrangements with his attorney when he was back in England. She would receive a formal notification of the terms, written in Spanish, and a personal letter from him with further thanks. He hoped that would be the most tactful way to handle it. Face to face, she might feel awkward. The last thing he wanted was to make her feel inferior in any way by offering her money. It wasn't intended as a reward, only a gesture of appreciation. He hoped she would see it that way. The letter would make that clear. However, he was intent upon sending her some personal gift—perhaps for Christmas. He was frustrated that there seemed to be no way to give cash to such a proud woman. And that was what she needed most.

Ben's decision energized him and he jumped up from the chair, winced a little from the sore ribs, and then pulled Ana up from where she was sitting. He embraced her, quickly planting a kiss on her unsuspecting lips. The spell was broken by the buzz of his phone. They were to meet at eight for dinner in the hotel restaurant. Ana knew he was anxious to see Olivia outside a hospital setting.

* * *

Hugh tapped his fingers on the table, impatient for Olivia to make a choice from the menu. She admonished her father, saying it was hard to decide, that everything looked good. Paris joined in by telling him in her own way that he could relax now. She surprised everyone by using the word 'chill' when addressing him. Then she reminded Hugh of how hungry their daughter had been while detained. He apologized and instructed everyone to order and let Olivia go last. A half hour later they were tucked into their dinner and the conversation was quite cheerful, considering.

Coffee was served, and a short lapse in their chatter gave Paris the opening she had been waiting for. "Ben, your father and I, Olivia too, feel that you should take some time away before you return to London." She waited to see his initial reaction before continuing. "Spain is a beautiful country. Go and make some *good* memories."

Hugh chimed in and said, "Ana, wasn't your grandmother from Spain, somewhere in the south."

Surprised, Ana said, "Andalusia… But how did you know that? I don't remember mentioning it. Did Ben tell you?"

Ben looked at his father quizzically while Ana tried to remember if she had even told Ben that little detail of her background. She believed she had not. Of course Ben's father knew everything about her roots. Interpol had done a background check on Ana, and Hugh had clearly put his foot in it with that comment. He looked at his wife, who just shook her head and stared at the ceiling, waiting to see how he would get out of it. He didn't want to compound the situation with a lie so decided to come clean. Ana was seated beside him at the table, Ben between his mother and sister. Hugh took a deep breath and began to explain the protocol he had practiced during his career, which had included frequent collaboration with Interpol. While he spoke, Ana maintained a stoic expression but looked down at her empty plate. His tone seemed apologetic here and there, but he related what he felt had been his responsibility to his family.

Hugh gently placed his hand on Ana's arm. She looked up, turned, and their eyes met. "Dear girl, we've all grown to like you very much, but at the beginning, as a result of the attacks on Ben, we had to explore every avenue to figure out what was going on." Ana nodded in understanding and Hugh continued. "You were basically a stranger in our midst. I admit that all my years dealing with theft and violence has made me cynical—and, I'm sorry to say, rather suspicious."

Ben jumped in and said, "Dad, what did you do?"

"I wasn't aware at first, but Interpol had decided it was relevant to have Ana's background investigated. Given the coincidence of your first meeting and the first attack, they had to verify her identity and be certain that she hadn't led you into the dangerous situation you encountered in London. We had to be sure she wasn't a part of some kind of larger scheme. At that time we didn't know that Olivia was about to be kidnapped."

"Dad, it was supposed to be *me*. You know that, don't you?"

Hugh indicated in the affirmative and then returned his focus to Ana, who had been quiet throughout, and said, "With more time to observe you, and given the way you've supported Ben and the family, I would have concluded that no background check was necessary. I can only apologize with the excuse that Ben's safety was our ultimate concern… until the situation escalated."

Ana smiled at Ben's father, leaned over and kissed him on the cheek. "I understand, and it's okay. I get it. And you probably saw my father having gone to prison as a red flag. Right?"

Ben frowned, looked at Ana, and said, "I didn't know that. But why should I? It's your business, not mine. But now I'm curious."

Ana felt she should tell Ben the story of how her father had been framed, but later, in private. His parents already knew, and they could tell Olivia.

Paris soon decided that her daughter had had enough excitement for one day, so she urged her up from the table, excused them both and hurried Olivia to the elevators. She planned to escort her to her room and put her to bed. Hugh then begged off, citing fatigue as his reason. However, he felt that Ben and Ana should have time on their own. They went into the hotel bar and ordered snifters of brandy, which they took to one of the leather couches. Ana held the snifter to her lips, sipping slowly, and Ben was reminded of that first night, the warm brandy glistening on those lips. He imagined then how they would taste, how they would feel if he kissed her. Now he knew and wanted more. Returning to the present he asked if she had the energy to tell him about her father. She said yes, but only enough for a condensed version. Ana began to share the facts about her background, and once she had started, the words flowed freely.

"My father was in prison when I was born. I didn't meet him until I was almost six years old. He had no idea he was working on the periphery of a group smuggling artifacts that had been altered to contain stolen gems. Holes were carefully drilled into the bottoms, the stones were dropped inside, and a master restorer patched the materials. My father was a courier for a legitimate collector and made trips to countries where desirable items were for sale, usually by another collector. It was a small community of interested parties. But nothing being purchased or sold was stolen or pilfered from governments; however, they did end up being defaced."

Ben was quiet, waiting for her to continue. Ana sighed, obviously saddened by the recounting of what had happened, but she went on, explaining the course of events exactly as Hugh had related them to Paris.

"What did your mother do when he went to jail?"

"Well, she delivered me shortly after he went away. I can tell you, it had to have been a terrible time for her. She had no idea how to support me, or if she did find a job, how to arrange care for an infant." Ben reached for her hand and held it while she told the rest of the story. "Mother had learned a lot from my Dad about antiquities and the like, and she was able to find a job in a curio shop. The owner was a family man and allowed her to have me with her in the shop—even when I was a tiny baby. He obviously felt sorry for her and took a chance."

"She must have had a guardian angel—if one believes in such things."

"Seems that way. Maybe it was the owner of the curio shop. I remember his kindness."

"Could be," said Ben, smiling at the thought.

"By way of my heritage, my father's Irish. My mother's Spanish. Her family came from Andalusia. I always loved my grandfather's name: Javier Alonso de Falla. It has a certain 'ring' to it. I always wondered if we were related somehow to Manuel de Falla. Silly I suppose. Anyway, my grandfather was a carpenter, and they moved to Seville to find work before coming to the United States. My grandmother was Sofia Cristina Jurado. I have her middle name."

"Any family left in Spain?"

"Oh yes— my uncle, Juan Carlos de Falla. He spent most of his life as a flamenco guitarist and vocalist. He's getting up there in age but still tours with a dance company whose studio is in Seville. Most of the time he lives in Granada with his wife, Tereza."

"You seem to do a good job of keeping up with everyone. Have you met all of them?"

"All but Carlos, his son. He owns a restaurant in Ronda. I think it's called *Alcazar*— reminiscent of the Alhambra in Granada."

"We could trace your family across a lot of Spain."

Ana chuckled and nodded her head in agreement. My grandmother returned to Spain after my grandfather died and lived out her life in the town where she was born."

"In Andalusia, right?"

"Yes, in Ronda."

"Well, it's clear we don't know very much about each other—me more than you. My side of things has come at you full force."

"That's okay," Ana assured him. "It will all balance out. We just need time to talk."

"That's quite a story about your father. What did he do when he got out?"

"The man who owned the curio shop decided to retire. He sold the shop to my parents and they still operate it."

"Where?" Ben asked, obviously very interested in every fact concerning Ana.

"Cambridge... Massachusetts."

"Wow..." he said, standing up and pulling her to her feet. "This gives me food for thought about a little respite before we go back to London. Let's sleep on it and talk in the morning." Ana was curious and preferred not to wait, but she nodded, stood up, and turned toward the elevators. Ben followed her.

Once they had entered Ben's room, both seemed to deflate. Their fatigue was not yet assuaged and neither had slept well the previous night. Ana asked Ben how he was feeling, whether he needed something for pain in order to get to sleep. He expressed that he was feeling better and didn't need anything. She approached him and reached up to touch his shoulder, then his face, before asking if his ribs could take a gentle hug good night. He reached out, pulled her close and kissed her sweetly. *One more night*, he thought, *then no more 'adjoining' rooms*. His plan for their little respite would not include separate beds.

They hesitated to part for the night, but it was late. In spite of the hour and his discomfort, Ben asked Ana to wait, that he had something to say. She perked up and turned her attention to his expression. She couldn't quite read it and hoped what he had to say wouldn't be upsetting.

Ben sat down on the edge of his bed and said, "Ana, about these separate rooms. I know it has seemed silly to stay separate. My parents may have booked two rooms, but there was nothing keeping us from 'sharing,' if you know what I mean."

"Yes, I know what you mean by 'sharing,'" she said self-consciously. "But there were some rather good reasons to the contrary."

Ben sighed, clearly being unsure how to explain why he hadn't pushed for more togetherness. After a short pause he said, "Well, aside from the fact that I've been dealing with injuries, I was thinking about the 'why' of my parents making a two-room reservation."

"It's pretty clear to me, Ben," she said, seeing that he needed a little help with his explanation. "Your parents didn't know if we were in a relationship, or how far it had gone. But most of all, they didn't know at that time whether or not I was to be trusted."

Ben continued, shaking his head, admonishing himself. " I have to admit, I'm almost forty years old and I still care what my parents think. I wasn't comfortable with having them think we were 'co-habiting' in the midst of this family crisis." He paused then added, "It seemed really inappropriate."

Ana could tell he was struggling with his explanation in order not to have her feel she had been in any way undesirable, or that he was losing interest. That had gone through her mind, unbidden, but she pushed the thought away with logic and the reality of the situation. She decided to lighten the moment with a little humor and hoped he would take it that way.

"Ben, listen. First of all, I think your respect for your parents is lovely." She waited a moment then looked him straight in the eyes and in a mock-serious tone added, "But aside from that, you wouldn't really have been much good to me the last few days anyway!"

He took it the right way and said, "True… but I'm hoping to make up for that."

Then came the smile, the one that made Ana blush and look away like an adolescent in the throws of first love. Ben stood up and walked to the chair where Ana had settled. "Get up, woman," he said. She did as she was told and stood before him. He came close, lifted her chin to meet his gaze and said, "One more night—two at the most."

She repeated his words back to him and he took her in his arms, kissing her in a way that did not say goodnight. They parted and Ana went through to her own room. She left the door ajar. Ben stood there, looking at the slightly open door, summoning his will power in order not to pass through it. He knew that in the morning he would wake feeling more like his old self. After pulling off his clothes he slid into bed, making the silent pronouncement that in the morning his aches would be gone and everything would be on the way to wonderful.

* * *

Ana's eyes opened at dawn. The emotional roller coaster of the last few days had made for another restless night. Fed up with trying to get back to sleep she threw off the covers, got up and walked to the window. Street lamps still lit the plaza and whatever glow was rising in the east was out of her western view. This restlessness was about more than what had happened. The crisis was over, and now the reality of whatever was between them would be tested. *No more adrenaline to fuel desire,* she thought. Yet she scolded herself for doubting their connection. Regardless of how it started, they both had been swept along by circumstances— thrown together, really. Old hurts plied her doubts. She wondered if a broken heart was in her future.

She recalled what Paris had said— that *Ben* should get away and see Spain. Her name wasn't mentioned. Was that an oversight, or was it a subtle message? It didn't really matter in the end. Walking away from Ben wasn't an option. Ana wanted him too badly, and if it were to be only an affair, she would have to take that and make the most of it. She continued to ponder the direction her life could be taking, and as she jumped from thought to thought her heart began to pound. Finally she returned to the bed and tried to quiet her brain. The only conclusion she could draw was that since the future was out of her control, she should live for the moment. This relinquishment brought her peace and she dozed off again.

After an hour or so Ana was awakened by the familiar knock on the adjoining door. She told Ben to come through then sat up in bed, unconcerned with her appearance as she applied the new 'what will be will be' attitude.

"I like you all tousled and with a sleepy-looking face," Ben said, walking toward the bed. He put his hands on his hips and stared down at her.

Ana slid down and pulled the covers up around her neck. "Not too much of a shock I hope," she said, using one hand to push the hair away from her face.

"You're adorable," he said, and proceeded to fling himself onto the bed, grab her and pull her over on top of him.

He held the sides of her face and began to pull her down for a kiss. She resisted and said, "Ben, we can't! Remember… we have a little charade to maintain, and your parents could be at the door any minute."

Ben groaned with frustration and conceded that she was right. He slid out from under her and off the bed. He had left the adjoining door ajar and heard a faint knocking coming from his room. He went through, pulling that door closed then answering the other. It was his father, who walked quickly into the room. Ben realized it was another close call, and he'd had enough of the pretense.

"Do you know when Valerie's parents will get here?" Ben asked.

"They're on the way from the airport as we speak. I imagine they will go straight to the hospital, but I've booked a room for them here."

"That's a relief. I don't see how I could keep up this charade with Valerie for another day." His father nodded in agreement, and Ben added, "Dad,

I've got to get out of this town. So does Ana, but me especially. When do you think we could leave?"

"Well, I'm hoping they can consult with a psychiatrist, maybe a neurologist, shortly after they arrive at the hospital. They will ease her into the present— tell her that the two of you are divorced. Then we'll see how she takes it and what's to come after."

"Should I be there?"

"My opinion is no. Your absence may help her to face reality. And for God's sake, son, you've done enough!"

Ana hadn't come through to Ben's room to see who had knocked, and taking advantage of her absence he had the opportunity to talk with his father about his intentions upon leaving Pamplona. Ben made it clear that Ana had no idea what he was planning, but he hoped she would agree and even be excited at the prospect. He had put out a 'feeler' the night before, hoping to stir her interest. Hugh agreed wholeheartedly that it was a perfect idea and offered to do whatever he could to get things underway. Ben definitely needed some help in order to put things together in such a short time.

Hugh said, "I'd like to tell your mother, but that's up to you, Ben."

"Actually I'd like to wait until I've told Ana."

"That's fine," his father answered. "But I'm sure she will be in favor of the two of you getting off by yourselves. This has been a crazy way for two people to get to know each other."

"We really don't know each other very well. I hope this time I'm planning will take care of that. I have to see what we're like together when there's no crisis and no one is trying to kill me."

"Smart move, son. You know we want you to be happy… and to put it in your mother's words, 'settled.'"

Hugh opened the door to leave, and as he stepped out into the hall, Ben said, "I wonder if she still wants to interview me…" His father laughed as he walked away down the hall.

He was emboldened by his father's offer of help and hurried back to

Ana's room, stopping to knock lightly before slowly opening the door. Wrapped in the robe provided by the hotel, Ana was standing in front of the window. Ben walked over to her and put his arm around her shoulder. She was still tousled and as he turned to kiss her forehead he could detect a sweet and feminine morning scent that was new to him. He led her to a chair and told her to sit, that he wanted to share an idea with her— an idea for their 'respite.'

She folded her hands in her lap, looked up at him and said, "I'm all ears."

"First, I really need you to be sure about the name of your grandmother's town. If you can remember anything specific about the place, maybe I could help."

"I *am* sure. It's Ronda. There's a bridge, a really tall bridge. It's just been too long to remember details from my parents. I remember saying goodbye to her though. I was a kid and didn't realize I wouldn't see her again."

"Aha! The bridge. It must be Ronda. What I'm remembering is from university. We would-be writers take a lot of literature classes. Hemingway… 'For Whom the Bell Tolls.' It's a favorite of mine. But never mind that now.

"It's built on high cliffs and there's a river running through the middle of town. I remember hearing that," Ana said, sounding enthusiastic.

Ben got up and said, "Sounds spectacular. Let's go down to the lobby and use one of the guest computers to get some details."

Ana dressed quickly and they were soon seated at a computer. Ben accessed Wikipedia first, but said he didn't need a history back to the dark ages so switched to a travel site. They confirmed that a river did run through the town and accessed photos showing the extreme topography of the mountains and the precarious-looking location of the town.

"This is it!" She turned and smiled at Ben, then asked, "So what's your end game, sir?"

"My end game is to invite you to come with me to Ronda. It sounds like a perfect get-away to me. What do you think?"

"Seriously— you and me? Trouble free? But what about Valerie?"

"Her parents arrive momentarily—maybe already. I talked to Dad and he thinks it would be better for her to be urged toward reality without me in the vicinity. Doctors will supervise and her parents will be there to support her. The more I'm involved or make myself available, the more she could resist and want to stay dependent on me."

"Wow! This is a lot to take in. But it's good stuff now." She jumped up and threw her arms around Ben. "I would absolutely love to see Andalusia, and finding my *abuela's* little town will be icing on the cake."

"I doubt it's a little town anymore, thanks to tourism. My Dad is going to help get things arranged. Maybe we can take advantage of his connections again. His buddies are good at finding empty seats on planes that are supposedly full."

"Yes, I've seen him at work. Airplane seats are probably the least of it. There's no doubt he's a valuable ally!"

Ben laughed and told her they needed to get busy preparing to leave at a moment's notice. Just then his mobile phone rang, with Olivia on the other end. He spoke with her briefly, learning that Hugh hadn't quite been able to keep from spilling the beans. But Ben didn't care. He had awakened with no throbbing of his injuries, and with a day or so of beard growth any discoloration on his face wouldn't show. He felt strong again and up to the task, whatever it might be. He called his father's room and told him where they would be going. Hugh asked about their preferable form of travel, but Ben was mainly concerned with how long it would take. He was told to have some breakfast and wait for a call. They went into the dining room to wait. Ana said she was probably too excited to eat, but managed to down a large pastry with her coffee.

Hugh called within a half hour. The first option was a flight to Madrid, and then the hour and a half flight to Málaga-Costa del Sol airport. There they could rent a car for the drive to Ronda. Or they could take a train from Madrid to Ronda. But that took over three hours. It was all coming at Ben too fast. He asked Hugh to slow down. The point was that there was no decent direct flight from Pamplona airport to either Málaga or Ronda. Madrid was a must.

Ben said he would discuss it with Ana and get back to him as soon as he could. After trying to keep things straight when he talked to her, he decided to simplify by asking his father which means of transport in which combination would take the least amount of time. They moved to the lobby to wait. It wasn't long before his phone rang and the litany of travel choices began again.

Ben had to stop him. "Dad! How did you get so much information so fast?" Hugh laughed on the other end of the line. "Please, Dad, just tell me the fastest route."

Hugh said he'd get back to him soon. Ben rang off and sat back. He told Ana there were too many choices, and he would like her input. She said she agreed that the best route was the fastest one, but she hoped they would have a chance to see the landscape other than from the sky. Considering modes of travel triggered a memory. She had forgotten to tell Ben something else she had learned from Inspector Macias.

"Ben, I forgot to tell you what became of the rental car you left on the street. I was too focused on the Annunciata issue."

"Oh boy… I probably have some hefty impound fees to pay. And I may have to drive it back to the airport."

"No worries. He had it taken to the local rental office, and there are no fees."

Ben nodded, smiling. "Macias is a good guy."

"Yes, he was very charming and helpful to me when I asked him for that information."

"Of course he was charming." Ben quickly got up from the chair and pulled Ana up from hers. He looked around the room, and seeing that no one was watching, he gently held her face in his hands, kissed her cheek, and said, "A man is automatically charming to a beautiful woman."

"Whatever works," she said, loving his comment, but loving his touch even more.

CHAPTER TWENTY-THREE

After a quick dinner in the hotel dining room and coffee in the lounge, Ben and Ana decided to make it an early night. A short while later Hugh looked for them in the lounge. They weren't there, so he decided to try Ben's room. While in the elevator he considered whether it was wise to appear at the door without calling first. He decided to chance it, regardless of any possible awkwardness. Ben answered his rapid knock and invited him inside. Ana heard them talking and came through from her room. The three sat down and Hugh began to submit the travel information he'd garnered, hoping for their approval. He was quite businesslike in his presentation but gave off an air of excitement, as if he were the one embarking on a small adventure. He advised a combination of air and train travel. They would fly from the small airport closest to Pamplona, landing in Madrid. There they would change planes for Málaga-Costa del Sol, where they could board a train bound for Ronda. Ben nodded his approval and looked to Ana, whose expression was somehow reticent.

"I had really hoped to see the landscape from ground level," she said, wondering if Ben would remember her request from their first conversation about the trip.

Ben jumped right in and said, "You'll definitely see everything you want to see. I can promise you that."

"Maybe you could rent a car and do a little touring," Hugh added. "And I'd imagine there are good views from the train. In any case the trip from Málaga to Ronda isn't very long."

Ben asked, "So, time-wise, how long *is* this trip—counting stopovers?"

"Well, you could actually fly from Madrid directly to Ronda, but it would be a small plane. Takes about three and a half hours. And we don't know how Ana feels about smaller planes."

She made a face that strongly conveyed her opinion. Since that wasn't going to be an option, Ben asked, "How long is the drive from Madrid to Ronda?"

"Too long. At least six hours." Ben's father said. He put up his hand to signal that the scrutiny of routes was at an end. "All right," he continued, "I think this is best: Pamplona to Madrid, about an hour with a thirty-minute stopover; the flight from Madrid to Málaga, an hour and a half. Then the two of you can choose whether to get a car and drive to Ronda, or take a train. It's a little over an hour either way. How does that sound?" He glanced from one to the other then added, "Ana sees some scenery and the whole thing takes around four to five hours tops."

The two looked at each other, nodded and smiled. "Done deal," he said. "Now what do I need to do— probably give someone a credit card number?"

"All taken care of, son. Your mother has been on her tablet researching hotels, and she found one that she thinks is just the ticket. If you would rather make your own arrangements, that's fine and we'll understand. But you both have had so much on your plates. We want to make it easy."

"Dad, what can I say? You're the best. Thank you."

Ben and his father stood up and shared a manly embrace with the requisite pats on the back. Ana found it hopeful that Ben didn't wince from pain. After expressing her own appreciation, she cited her meager travel wardrobe as a reason to hurry down to the hotel shop. Ana didn't really need to explain. Both men understood the workings of the female mind when it came to shopping. Hugh told Ben that he would try to deliver a printed itinerary before morning and emphasized that they would need an early start.

"Thank Mum for me, please, and tell her I'll see her before we leave. I know her taste is impeccable in most things, so it's probably the same with hotels. I'm sure she remembered that I like small places— family run. If you want every amenity, just stay in London."

His father nodded in agreement, told his son goodnight and headed down to the bar for a nightcap. Ben expected his mother would join him to gossip about the whole thing. He leaned against the door, crossed his arms and looked at Ana, smiling but cautious. "Wow, I guess we're really doing this. Are you good with all of it?"

"It doesn't seem real right now, frankly. It's such a departure from everything we've experienced together so far." She paused then said, "Well, *almost* everything."

Ben nodded. "I know what you're referring to, but saying *that* part was the best part doesn't sound like much considering that virtually everything else was just awful."

"Trust me, it was definitely 'much.' Now I need to grab my wallet and get down to the shop! I'm tired of having basically nothing to wear and looking ill-suited to the environment."

Ben shook his head, teasing, and opened the door for her to leave. She promised to use her own door when returning in order to avoid disturbing him. Sleep did seem to be the best idea so he took a quick shower, dried off, threw the towel aside, and slid into bed. But sleep didn't come easily, and he was relieved a while later to hear Ana unlock then close the door to her room. What she might wear didn't matter to him. She was everything he wanted just wearing jeans and that gaudy tourist tee shirt with the jeweled crown. He would never forget easing it above her breasts during their brief escape from reality. Knowing she was there on the other side of the door brought relaxation, and he drifted off.

With the two bags from the shop nestled in the chair, Ana undressed, splashed water on her face and slipped into her one nightie. While closing the drapes she took one last look at the lighted plaza below before climbing into bed. Once quiet, Ana noticed how fast her heart was beating. She was unsure of what this trip with Ben would mean to her life, so she told herself to just breathe and trust that all would be as it should be. Ana had never believed in destiny. Yet at this point it was difficult to deny that some unseen force had conspired to bring her to this pivotal moment. It all could have gone so differently, and she shuddered at the thought. She began a mental list of everything that was good in her life. Like counting sheep, the exercise urged her into the arms of Morpheus.

* * *

It was barely light when the phone rang in Ben's room. It was a wakeup call from the concierge, evidently set up by his father, who had said they would need an early start. He went to the adjoining door and listened for any sound that might indicate Ana was awake. It was quiet. He knocked several times before she answered in a sleepy voice, "Okay… I'm up." She rolled over and emitted a quiet groan. It had been a restless night, courtesy of her uncertainty.

"We need to get packed. Dad will probably be bringing the itinerary any minute."

Ben turned toward the bathroom and saw an envelope that had been pushed under the door while he was sleeping. It contained the itinerary and plane tickets, along with a note saying that at eight a.m. there would be a hired car in front of the hotel ready to take them to the airport. Rather than yell through the door again he telephoned Ana's room. She reached for the phone by the bed and answered, seeming startled to hear Ben's voice on the other end telling her they had to leave soon.

"Yes, I understand… I'll hurry," she said, throwing back the coverlet.

A quick look out the window revealed a cloudy sky, and beyond the city's skyline a ridge of darkness seemed to be moving toward the city. Within fifteen minutes Ana had readied herself, gathered her belongings, and checked the room for anything left behind. She knocked lightly and went through to Ben's room, without waiting for him to answer. He came out of the bathroom half dressed, shirt in hand. He put it on and quickly buttoned it while Ana stood by, quietly admiring him. Ben smiled as he snatched the familiar leather jacket off the chair, but he didn't say a word.

"I'm ready to go," Ana said. "I just need my luggage brought through so you can call the desk to have it picked up."

"I can manage two pieces of luggage. It will save time."

Ana was wary and questioned his choice. "Remember your shoulder… and everything else that hurts."

He countered immediately. "Nothing hurts," he said, his tone adamant, then hoisted the two bags— one in each hand.

"You know best," Ana said, thinking that it was the wrong moment for any type of challenge to his masculinity. She hoped it was true— that his injuries had mended.

They entered the elevator and moments later walked out into the hotel lobby. Ben's parents were seated there and stood to greet them. The previous night Paris had requested a breakfast-to-go for two, to be ready by eight in the morning. Two coffees and a cellophane bag of pastries sat on the table next to where she had been sitting. She picked up the coffees and handed them to Ben, then gave the bag to Ana. Before goodbyes were said a middle-aged man in a suit came through the entrance and went to the desk to have the concierge notify the McKinnons that their car had arrived.

Hugh spotted him, and figuring he must be the driver, waved him over to their group. They conversed for a moment and Hugh showed him the bags. The man picked them up, nodded respectfully to both women, and exited the hotel. They all followed him out and waited while he stowed their belongings. Ben commented that hiring a limo was a bit over the top.

Hugh laughed and said, "Nonsense! Nothing but the best for our hero and heroine."

The driver then opened the rear door, motioned to his passengers, and said, "We really must leave or you may miss the flight."

Ben suspected that the man wasn't a limo driver by profession, but more likely another Interpol friend of a friend reciprocating as a professional courtesy for some previous favor done. There was a bit of drama in Paris' goodbye. She found it difficult to contemplate having Ben out of her sight again after what had happened. Hugh lovingly admonished her for being tearful and they all embraced, Ben assuring her that the purpose of this separation was for pleasure. After one last kiss on his mother's cheek he ushered Ana into the back seat, but then hesitated before getting into the vehicle.

He faced his parents and asked a last one-word question. "Valerie?"

"Doing well," his father said. "Her parents are with her, and as soon as she's a little stronger they plan to return to London and stay on with her for a while. It's been decided that she'll do best under the care of a therapist with whom she's familiar. That's Kate Locksley."

Ben felt a great sense of relief. With a last wave to his parents he climbed into the back seat beside Ana. As the vehicle pulled away he reached for her hand and gave it a gentle squeeze. She was reminded of the first night and the taxi ride to her hotel, Ben holding her hand, gritting his teeth in pain. So much had happened. She wondered if he was remembering as well. As if on cue, each turned to the other, smiled, and took a deep breath, letting it go slowly as if releasing all the fear and danger of the past weeks.

The vehicle was headed south toward the same ridge of dark clouds that had been advancing on the city. Just as they left the environs of Pamplona and turned onto the airport route, the sky opened up. A summer cloudburst reduced visibility so badly that the driver pulled over to wait it out. Though intense, it passed in minutes, allowing the driver to continue. Ana expressed her concern about the delay and the plane's departure time, but the driver assured them the distance was short and they would make it with time to spare. The small airport was nestled between rolling plains, and in the distance a gentle slope of green foothills, washed clean by the rain, caught the morning light. The vehicle slowed and stopped in front of the entrance marked 'Iberia.'

The driver got out quickly and opened Ana's door before retrieving their bags from the trunk. Ben climbed out the other side and waited with Ana. He tried to tip the driver, but when he refused it was clear that he didn't chauffeur for a living. They each thanked him, took their bags and went through the entrance for departures. The check-in line was short and soon they were crossing the tarmac to board the plane.

When they had settled into their seats Ana couldn't help but comment that she was amazed nothing had gone wrong so far. Ben urged her to change the cynical perspective so it would be easier for him to do the same. She knew he was being facetious, yet there was a degree of truth in what he said. Making the shift from a mindset of danger and crisis to one of relaxation and romance didn't come easily. The 'buckle seat belts' light came on and the flight attendant went through her protocol. The plane began to move toward the runway, where the pilot waited for clearance to take off. Soon they felt the plane increase speed, and moments later they were airborne.

The landscape below was familiar, the same golden expanses and gently undulating hills they had seen on the flight to Pamplona. Both were having moments where comprehension of recent events seemed beyond them. Ben settled back in the seat, his expression pensive, a distant look in his eyes. Any residual pain was now emotional. It would be a long time before he came to terms with his part in the death of Gareth Logan. He bore no moral responsibility, yet that was cold comfort. Time passed without conversation, and Ana sensed that quiet was best while he struggled with leaving the whole experience behind him. She wondered if he would ever return to Pamplona of his own accord.

CHAPTER TWENTY-FOUR

The flight from Madrid landed on schedule and they easily made the connecting flight. A short while later the plane made a smooth landing at Málaga Costa del Sol airport. While Ben waited at the luggage carousel, Ana made a quick dash to the cashpoint for Euros. He was surprised when his phone rang, and his first reaction was fear that something was wrong. It was his father calling to say he had decided to re-check the train schedule for Ronda and found that the trip took two and half hours. Previously he hadn't considered all the stops and decided to take it upon himself to make other arrangements. A private car company would provide their transportation to Ronda. The driver would be waiting outside the airport exit with a sign reading 'McKinnon.' Ben expressed his appreciation and confirmed the fact that the last thing he wanted was to spend over two hours on a train.

Their luggage came down the chute just as he ended the call. He explained the change in plans to Ana and minutes later they exited the airport. A well-dressed young man with a closely trimmed beard and chauffeur's cap was standing curbside with the aforementioned sign. Ben waved, and the man quickly came over to help with the bags. They settled into the comfortable back seat and put themselves in the driver's hands. Soon they were leaving Málaga behind and traveling into more rural surroundings. The altitude was changing gradually, as was the terrain. Grasslands with grazing cattle soon gave way to almond orchards, and then rows of grape vines, heavy with ripening fruit. The miles passed with little conversation and a lot of looking out windows until the startling appearance of an extensive outcropping of rocks that seemed to reach for the sky.

They finally came to the mountain road leading to Ronda, where a ridge of low-hanging clouds had obscured the sheer cliffs of the spectacular *El Tajo* gorge. Perched on a plateau above, cathedral spires glistened in the sunlight, and a sea of tile roofed buildings stood silhouetted against a backdrop of vivid blue. Visibility was low as the car made its way, the driver carefully navigating the steep curvy road. As they ascended into the cloud it began to break apart, tufts of white scudding across the sky on the wind. Then the town appeared, bright and beckoning.

The private car made its way through the streets of Ronda's old town then slowed and stopped in front of the entrance to *Hotel Montelirio*. A young valet hurried to open the car door for Ana, while the driver retrieved their bags from the trunk and placed them on the sidewalk. Ben dug out his wallet and prepared to tip the valet, who gestured 'no' and asked politely in Spanish for them to follow him inside. He also intended to tip the driver, but he declined, saying that it had been taken care of. They thanked him and he drove away. They stood there for a moment, taking in the town's skyline, then went inside.

The first thing Ana noticed was an arched portal leading to another part of the hotel. It was framed in shades of blue leaded glass. An eclectic assortment of paintings graced the walls, and she could see comfortable seating areas tucked in corners and bouquets of fresh flowers placed just right. Once they had handed over their passports and signed the register, the concierge gave Ben two key cards and a pamphlet about the seventeenth century palace that now housed the hotel. The valet motioned them to follow him and they proceeded up a curved staircase to the second floor. Ana found the surroundings authentic and charming. The young man led them down a corridor made bright by walls painted a soft yellow ochre. At intervals along the way small wooden tables held object d'art and the occasional vase of roses.

He asked Ben for the key, unlocked the door, and ushered them inside before following with the bags. A generous tip sent him out of the room smiling. As was her habit, Ana focused on each detail as she walked around the room. The old hardwood floors were highly polished, and a massive, intricately carved dark wood armoire dominated the room. On a small round table, a basket filled with cheeses, snacks and a bottle of wine welcomed new guests. The half-vaulted ceiling was trimmed with wooden beams, and at the lowest angle was an attached canopy suspended over the large bed. French doors opened onto a tiny terrace from which could be seen a panoramic view of the rolling green landscape and seemingly bottomless gorge of the *Guadalevín* River.

The room was pristine to the tiniest detail and invited comfort and relaxation. However, relaxation was the last thing on Ben's mind. As soon as the boy had closed the door, Ben locked the deadbolt. His eyes fixed on Ana, who was standing at the French doors looking at the view. He threw his wallet and sunglasses into a chair and softly called her name. She turned to face him, crossed her arms and cocked her head slightly. A sexy yet somehow self-conscious expression washed over her face. Ben's thoughts since having left Pamplona were dominated by the realization that he was finally free to express what he felt. He hoped it was the same for Ana. Now there would be no circumstances or distractions forcing them to subdue that mutual ardor. Nothing could keep them apart.

Ben walked toward her and said, "I think it's time to toss out that 'unrequited lust rulebook' and just let things happen. What do you think?"

"There couldn't be a more perfect place to *let things happen*. I wonder what it will be like to be comfortable, warm and dry, and on an actual bed."

Her comment brought a smile to Ben's face and he opened his arms to her. She approached, and he held her tightly for a moment before letting a kiss convey his intentions. Ana returned his passion as the first kiss blended into another, then another, while he pulled her closer and closer to the bed. Ben turned away for a moment and in one motion yanked back the bedding. He pulled off his shirt, tossed it aside and unsnapped the top of his jeans. At the sight of him, her heart raced, and deep in the pit of her belly the pressure of arousal made its presence known. Ben's arm slid down, his open hand against her lower back, bringing her firmly against him. His desire was evident and aroused her further.

Ben kissed her again and whispered, "Okay if I undress you?"

"Yes, but I could do it faster."

Her seductive tone fed his sense of urgency. He backed away slightly and took her by the shoulders. "You should know that after all this waiting I'm likely to just ravish you."

"Mmm… that sounds fine to me. I'm past waiting too."

"But I can promise you long leisurely afternoons of making love and shutting out the world… at least for as long as you want me."

"Seriously?" Ana said, admonishing him for the remark.

"Well, what I want is time to pleasure and memorize every inch of you."

Ben's words sent a shiver through her body. Ana kicked off her sandals and began to pull off her shirt. He stepped in to help by unfastening her jeans then sliding them down and off. When she was standing before him in only bra and panties, he told her to stop, that he wanted to remove the rest. Still looking directly into her eyes, he reached around and unhooked the bit of lace that clung to her breasts, letting it fall to the floor before quickly stripping off the panties; in his haste tearing them slightly. It was his first look at her nude, and she was everything he had imagined.

Ana climbed onto the bed, but stayed on her knees, legs slightly apart. She looked straight at him from under dark lashes, and with one finger she motioned him to join her. Ana's eagerness and provocative expression grabbed Ben where he could feel it most. He climbed onto the bed, put his arms around her and eased her down onto the mattress. She felt the weight of his body against her chest as he once again began to devour her with demanding kisses. The moment yearned for was now a reality.

She noticed his hand sliding up her inner thigh and opened her legs slightly, inviting him to explore. Ben's touch took her breath away. Ana adopted the rhythm of his movements until she was consumed by the pleasure. Without a word Ben climbed onto her and noticed the flush of pink on her cheeks and chest. This excited him further and he surrendered to his hunger, thrusting forward, entering her more forcefully than he could have predicted. Ana let out a gasp as the sensations washed over her. To Ben her body was inviting, intoxicating, and the sexiness of her sounds as he moved drove him to an explosive release. He collapsed between Ana's legs, satisfied and spent.

Ana wrapped her thighs around his back and held on as tightly as she could. "Stay—don't move. I love having you this close."

He obeyed but said nothing, just continued to wait for his heart rate to slow and breath return to normal. The balcony's French doors had been left slightly ajar, admitting a welcome cooling breeze. It was late afternoon, and muted streaks of sunlight cast a trail across the dark wood floor and onto the rumpled bed. Twilight was hours away, but if they stayed, eventually they would be cloaked in darkness, still listening to the faint sound of guitars coming from somewhere in the hotel. Ana finally had to shift under his weight, and he rolled to one side. With their arms still entwined she straightened the leg closest to him, draping the other over his waist.

Once they had settled on the pillows facing each other, he gazed directly into her eyes and said in a near whisper, "Baby, for me that was worth the wait."

"Perfection," she said, uttering a sigh of satisfaction, followed by a smile.

Lying there quietly, wrapped together, neither interested in moving, a veil of serenity settled over Ana. Ben shifted slightly and rested his head against Ana's chest, his ear touching the spot where he could hear the pulsing beat of her heart. Soon his breathing became slow, deep, and she felt his arm relax into the curve of her hip. Ben had been lulled to sleep by the heart he had promised not to break.

Ana's serenity was short-lived. She remained wakeful, unable to surrender completely to the air of contentment that had settled over the room. The reality of all that had happened flooded her mind. Chance had set her on a path that was beyond her wildest imaginings. It was difficult to realize how one decision, a decision to help a man she'd just met, would lead her on an adventure that made every other experience in her life pale by comparison. Now that man lay sleeping in her arms, his every breath lightly touching the skin just above her beating heart. And she knew how close she had come—they all had come— to losing him, and that his loyalty had almost gotten him killed. Their relationship had evolved out of worry, danger and great risk. Were their intense feelings just a result of the constant adrenaline rush, and would the satisfied lust diminish his interest? Those were questions that couldn't be asked.

After a while she had to shift her body. Ben stirred then opened his eyes. "How long was I asleep?" he asked.

"Not that long," she answered, "but we have only a couple of hours before nightfall."

"'Nightfall'… Well there's a word you don't often hear."

"I may have read it somewhere. But the only books I intend to read in the near future will be yours. At some point I hope you'll tell me what you're planning next."

"Maybe," he said, rolling away from her and stretching.

"Playing hard to get, huh?" Ana shifted then sat up against the pillows. "Anyway, right now all I really care about is food. Are you as hungry as I am?"

Ben answered by getting up and fetching the basket from the table. "A snack will keep us going for that sunset walk. We'll eat something else later."

* * *

In a short while the pair stepped out of the hotel and into the street, deciding which way to go. Ben took the lead, and they walked in the direction of *La Plaza de Toros,* the oldest bullring in Spain. Peaceful wandering was in sharp contrast to anything they had yet experienced in their relationship. They were charmed by the houses, some with terraces crowded by pots of blooming flowers, and others where abundant bougainvillea climbed up and over railings. A profusion of passionate colors swirled in the breeze like the ruffled skirt of a flamenco dancer.

They continued to walk in companionable silence until Ben spoke. "If you can keep it under your hat, I'll give you a verbal peek at that 'next book.' You tried to quiz me about it on the first night we met." Ana nodded yes and made a zipping motion across her mouth. "I'm going to use the story of how my grandparents met as a basis for the book… just a basic plot. I'll fictionalize the rest— invent some mischief for the main characters. The setting? Spain. It was always going to be Spain."

"Those details are just what I needed. Wish there was a way to use them, but as we know, I'm probably unemployed."

"I knew I'd need to visit Spain again. It had been a long time. There are places I'd like to see either for the first time, or again, and some where I'd like to spend time— do the whole 'find your roots' thing. But the last thing I expected was to be here under these circumstances. Rather bizarre. I have to admit that starting another book seems distant right now."

"I can understand that. But you will write it, when you're ready. So tell me the story. What's all this about 'roots?'"

Ben took his arm from around Ana's shoulders and instead, took her hand as they walked. "Well, first let me give you some back-story on my grandparents. My grandfather was a student at Cambridge— reading for the law. Alexander Wallace McKinnon— good old Scottish name."

"So I see your middle name honors him?"

"Right. And I remember him being quite stern— a far cry from his youthful escapades."

"Escapades, huh? Now I'm even more curious. Get on with it!"

"This is the way my father told the story to me: It was summer break from classes. He and his buddies decided on a lark to go to Pamplona and run with the bulls. I doubt his parents knew about that, or even where their twenty-year-old son was really going. They were traveling on a dime and managed to book a one-star hotel not too far from the center of things. Before leaving England they vowed to do the run together, all four, or not at all. On the first full day in Pamplona one of the guys got sick, either from too much drinking the night before, or some bad food. That created a three-day delay for all four of them."

"I'd bet it was drinking," Ana said, "That seems to be a priority while at university."

"Maybe both. But while he was waiting for his friend to get better, my grandfather—let's just call him Alex— wandered around, hung out in plazas, bars, and walked endlessly through the town."

Ana pulled Ben toward a bench in the small plaza they were crossing, using tired feet as an excuse. As they sat there the lights came on around the area's perimeter. Waiters were setting candles on the outdoor tables of a small café, and shopkeepers were turning their signs from *abierto* to *cerrado*.

"Ah, that's better," Ana said, smiling. "Now I want to hear the rest."

"As you wish, but we can't rest here long if we want to find a good place to watch the sunset." She asked for five more minutes, and he went on with the story. "My grandmother's family had lived in Pamplona for generations. Julieta Luz Navarro was a student too— at Universidad de Pamplona. Summer classes were being held, but there had always been a short break during the festival. Girls weren't allowed much freedom in those days, and their honor—we'd call it 'reputation'— was fiercely protected. Granny told me that she and her friends had to wangle opportunities to shed their chaperones and do what youth needs to do.

"One evening during the festival she and her friends made up some story that allowed them to get out for a while to watch all the foreigners and other young people partying in the plazas and bars. That same evening

Alex was also wandering around and stopped to rest on a bench at the edge of the fountain in *Parque de Taconera*. The group of three young women strolled by, and the long black hair and graceful movement of the girl on the right drew his attention. He called out to them and asked where in the neighborhood he could get a good cheap meal. They strolled back to him, and the group struck up a conversation. His eyes continued to drift back to the black-haired girl with the dark penetrating eyes. She spoke just enough English for him to understand what she said. He didn't know Spanish— just learned a few tourist basics I guess."

"I can see this story is headed for romance." Ana reached over and patted Ben's arm. "I do love a romance," she said, "and I feel a little guilty now for not having read anything you've written before I came to interview you. But the piece was to be about *you,* not a book, per se." Ben didn't respond, and for a moment Ana wondered if she had offended him. "Just listening to this first bit of the story tells me that you're an exceptional story teller. The words flow as if you were actually writing, not just conversing."

Ben glanced sideways and grinned. "You're good for my ego. After all these years I might be guilty of embellishing the story a bit— but not the facts." He stopped to visually scrutinize the surrounding area. "You know, it's probably not a good idea to be wandering around after dark in an unfamiliar town. I haven't seen any taxis around here." Ben got up and held out his hand, a signal they should go. "I think the *Puente Nuevo* is the place to be when the sun goes down, plus it's close to the hotel. We'd better get a move on."

"Don't walk too fast to talk. I want the whole story… but you can give me a condensed version," she said, trying to keep up. "But I assume you'll draw it out in your book—however you plan to use it and whenever you write it. It's amazing that you remember details like the name of the fountain where they met."

"If you'd heard the story told as many times as I did growing up, you'd remember too. As they got older they loved to tell it at family gatherings.

We could see it pleased them, so we gladly listened." He paused then added, "I don't think people ever tire of the great love stories— fictional or historical."

"Or current?" Ana said, giving him a provocative look. Ben winked at her then stopped to lean against a building, but she took his hand and pulled him along. "Come on. We're losing light… and I never tire of love stories either, so get on with it."

"Okay! Now try to picture it. As the girls turned to leave, Alex summoned his courage, reached out, and touched her gently on the arm. She turned back with a questioning expression. He spoke slowly and asked if she could meet him later in the *Plaza de Castillo*, because he'd like to talk to her. He complimented her on her knowledge of English. She rolled her eyes as if to say that if he chose to come to Spain, he should be speaking her language. She said her plans were uncertain, but that perhaps she would end up in the plaza. She warned him that it would be very crowded and noisy, that several popular bars bordered the plaza. She added that Ernest Hemingway often attended the festival and that Alex might catch a glimpse of him in one of his favorite haunts, if he knew what the man looked like.

"Alex reluctantly left her and found his way back to the seedy guesthouse. His friend was a bit better, but not well enough to run for his life, and wouldn't be for another couple of days. Excited at the thought that the black-haired girl might actually appear, he cleaned himself up and hurried through the cobblestone streets to the plaza. All types of people, young and old, were engaged in revelry of some sort. It was difficult to believe that the *Festa de San Fermín* had begun as a religious observance.

"He waited first in front of the *Café Bar Torino*, hoping for a glimpse of Hemingway, but concluded it was too early in the evening. He strolled the perimeter of the plaza and looked into two more bars for the same purpose. He didn't find Hemingway or Julieta, so he walked to the center of the plaza, gazing into the groups of people milling around, and finally he saw her standing demurely at the edge of the crowd. He approached, and when she spotted him she smiled. They spent that evening together, and the next, and the next.

"At one point, in a moment of youthful lust, he took her in his arms and kissed her— right there in the crowd of revelers. After that night they became inseparable— wandering the neighborhoods together, watching people, generally getting to know each other. He carried a Spanish dictionary and tried to speak her language when he could. But neither of them thought far enough ahead to realize that if he didn't declare himself, their time together in Pamplona could end right along with the celebration."

Ben stopped talking for a moment and Ana said, "I'm hooked! This would make a good movie. But first you have to write the book."

"You're getting way ahead of yourself. It wasn't all smooth sailing. My grandfather almost blew it. A couple of days later, when the friend had gained back his strength, the group of guys made their plan to join the bull run the next day, which was also the last day of the festival. When he met Julieta that evening he was wearing his 'whites' along with the traditional red waist tie. He had decided to get the 'feel' of the outfit and also get some of the attention he had seen other runners get from the crowd."

"Uh Oh," Ana said, "I can see trouble in paradise."

"Yep, and it was a turning point in his life. Julieta issued him an ultimatum. I think you can guess what it was. She told him that if he ran with the bulls and managed *not* to get killed, she'd never speak to him again and he'd never see her again."

"A strong-minded young woman. I like that. Kind of sets the boundaries for the burgeoning relationship in general."

"He had to decide whether to look like a wimp in front of his friends and break the vow they had taken, or take the chance of losing her forever. He had no way of knowing whether she was bluffing."

"Knowing how important bravado is to young men of that age, I could see him going ahead with the original plan to run. To give that up for a girl would have opened him up to a lot of put-downs and teasing, and maybe his buddies would have given him the complete brush-off."

Of course Ana had pre-determined what the outcome had been, but Ben waited to continue, trying to build a little suspense. "I don't think I have to tell you what happened. Here I am— one result of his choice." He glanced aside and saw she was smiling." He uttered two more words. "The end."

"How lovely," she said. "How many years were they married?"

"When my grandfather passed away they had been married sixty-six years. She followed shortly after, which isn't unusual for people as close as they were."

"You would definitely honor them by including something of their story in one of your books."

"That was my plan, but right now the thoughts I have of Pamplona are anything but pleasant. I hope that changes. I had always planned to go to that plaza— find those bars, have a drink and toast them— but I never expected my return to Spain would be so negative. I was just a kid the only time I was here, and then it was just Madrid."

"Did your grandmother ever try to teach you Spanish? Kids learn languages so easily. I've forgotten most of what I learned at my grandmother's knee."

"No, she didn't. I think she was focused on me becoming a proper English gentleman. That's something I never really understood, with her being Spanish. I would've thought she'd have had me in a little bullfighter's suit."

They both laughed and continued to find their way toward the bridge. A couple of blocks on they rounded a corner, coming upon a small cobblestone plaza dominated by a colorful tile fountain. Seated on the edge was a man, sixtyish perhaps, with his beret— *boina*— tipped just right. He was tuning his guitar, concentrating as he prepared. He began to play, and Ana recognized Francisco Tárrega's *Recuerdos de la Alhambra*.

The melody took her back to childhood and her grandmother's love of Spanish music.

As if being conducted by magic, the water splashed and fell in a rhythm complementary to the music. At a nearby *tienda* a young girl stepped from behind an outdoor rack of brightly colored clothing. She seemed shy, but began to move to the music. The guitarist gestured an invitation for her to dance. The girl approached and they exchanged a few words before she began to sway gently to the music. Ben and Ana stayed to watch the scene unfold. The girl turned toward the *tienda's* entrance, where an old woman had come out to watch her. The girl seemed excited to show the woman the flamenco steps she had learned and began to dance. The old woman began to sing the old gypsy *cantos* and clapped the traditional rhythms to accompany the dance steps and the guitar. The sun was low, and at the *taberna* across the square, fairy lights began to sparkle in the flowering vines surrounding an outdoor seating area.

The musician finished his song with a flourishing run over the strings then tipped his *boina* to the young dancer. She giggled and waved goodbye as she was ushered back into the building. A brightly painted door closed behind them, and soon a sign saying *cerrado* appeared in the window. The man got up, put his guitar in its case, walked over to the *taberna* and disappeared inside. It was suddenly very still but for the sound of the fountain, its own melody carrying into the evening.

They just stood there a moment before Ana said, "I'll have you know I had my own castanets." She looked down, a bit embarrassed by her revelation.

Ben backed away and gave her a quizzical look. "What's the story on that?"

"My grandmother wanted me to learn flamenco, the traditional *baile Gitano*— flamenco Roma— the original gypsy form— to get in touch with my heritage. I did love the music though. She would quiz me on who had composed whatever music was playing. I gave it my best, but I was hopeless... no decent sense of rhythm."

"You'd never know it to look at you," he said, teasing. "I can see there's still a lot to learn about you, Ana Doherty."

"Well, my middle name is Cristina, for my mother and my grandmother. You'll just have to discover my hidden qualities… but let's change the subject. I'm getting hungry."

They left the enchanting little plaza and strolled toward the *Puente Nuevo* Bridge. At some point, Ana had no idea when, Ben had managed to collect some facts about Ronda and was anxious to share them.

"Of course you probably know that Hemingway spent a lot of his time in Spain— even fought in the civil war. Ronda was a favorite of his. He called it the most romantic village in Spain. It's a bit more than a village now, but you can see what he meant."

"You've certainly done your part to help renew his observation," Ana said, putting her arm through his.

"It's also called 'the city of dreams,' but when you consider the atrocities perpetrated here through the centuries it's hard to think of it in only romantic terms. There's a lot of history since it was declared a town in the fourth century— by Julius Caesar."

"I'm not up on the history, and maybe I don't want to know."

"I won't be generous with description, but that 'romantic' bridge— and the gorge— were used for easy executions. One good push— problem solved." Ana didn't react so he continued. "In Hemingway's novel, *For Whom the Bell Tolls,* Fascist sympathizers are thrown from the bridge. Many people believe this fictional story about the Spanish civil war was based on what actually happened."

Ana put an end to the negative turn of the conversation, and said, "I prefer to think of all the special moments lovers have had on the bridge."

"You mean like the one we're about to have?" Ben asked.

"Exactly."

They hurried on, reached the bridge, and strolled out toward the center. Ronda's elevation allowed the summer twilight to linger, and they could just see the river, it's water still reflecting the sunset's last vestiges of color.

Yet parts of the gorge were already in near-blackness. As Ben and Ana leaned out to look at the river, their arms touched. Both were quiet until he slipped his arm around Ana's waist and pulled her close to him. Ben turned his head toward her and she instinctively did the same, looking up to lock with his gaze. A seductive yet self-conscious smile crossed his face and he paused, trying to find his words, remembering his past.

Ben would admit to being somewhat of a lothario in his youth. An idealistic and aspiring writer, he was brimming with love sonnets just waiting to be offered to the parade of desirable girls who frolicked through his college days. Now he found himself tongue-tied and sure it was real— this love— because it had turned his brain to mush. The water was deep and turbulent, but he dove in, refusing to lose Ana to his silence.

"I wanted to tell you before this, but conditions weren't right… I'm in love with you, Ana."

He studied her expression, waiting impatiently for a response. Ana's heart was pounding with an odd mix of joy and fear. She fought hard not to become vulnerable, but there was no denying this man had her heart, probably since that first night, watching him sleep with an icepack on his shoulder. She put her arms around him and her face against his chest, taking in the familiar scent of the leather jacket.

"I love you too," she said softly.

Ben leaned down and kissed her gently. "That's a relief," he said, pretending to wipe his brow. "A guy is never really sure until he hears the words." He stared for a few moments at the great expanse of the gorge, pondering what to say next, and then he faced her again. "So I guess I've got my story. Would you be interested in living a sequel with me?"

For a moment Ana didn't understand. He hurried to add, "I mean live the stories with me— travel, research, have the adventures— be my inspiration."

Then she realized he was going to incorporate all that had happened to them into a novel, and the sequel he referred to would, or could, be a story to last for the rest of their lives. His declarations were the last thing

Ana expected, but she remained composed and answered that yes, she was interested in living a sequel— along with anything else he had in mind. Ben pulled her close, gave her a lingering kiss then smoothed away a lock of hair that had blown across her face.

Ana took his hand in hers and asked, "Now that I've said yes to your sequel, do you think maybe we could do that interview?"

Ben laughed and said, "We could if you still had a job!"

Ana shrugged her shoulders and smiled. After a moment's hesitation, she took Ben's face in her hands and kissed him hard. For that moment there was no one else in the world. They turned back to the view, watching as the sun disappeared and the river turned from blue to gray to black. Ana grew pensive as she took in the beauty around her and considered the direction her life had taken. She leaned closer to Ben and said, "Have you ever watched a leaf drop into a path of rushing water and start its journey— bobbing, tumbling, slowing, spinning, ricocheting off one obstacle after another? Our lives are like that…"

ABOUT THE AUTHOR

In Marcia Morgan's debut novel, *Good Deed Bad Deed*, she expresses her preference for location-inspired storytelling and turns to Mystery, the genre she most enjoys as a reader. Her own travel experiences, and an ongoing curiosity about places yet unseen, all serve to create a backdrop for the characters to make their way through the story. She hopes to attract readers who enjoy an armchair adventure, especially one with a steamy romance in the mix.

The author was born in Santa Barbara, California. In addition to travel, her enduring interests have always included creative writing. She has a strong foundation in vocal music and has enjoyed performing alongside professional musicians. While raising a family, she kept her interests alive with 'stolen moments,' found between 'rides to practice' and answering the question 'what's for dinner.' She is deeply grateful for a lifelong marriage and for the privilege of being a stay-at-home mom. The author has three adult children and lives on California's Central Coast.

Made in the USA
Las Vegas, NV
22 October 2021